AFTER THE FIRE, A STILL SMALL VOICE

Evie Wyld

After the Fire, a Still Small Voice

JONATHAN CAPE
LONDON

Published by Jonathan Cape 2009

4 6 8 10 9 7 5

First published in Great Britain in 2009 by
Jonathan Cape
Random House, 20 Vauxhall Bridge Road,
London SW1V 2SA

www.rbooks.co.uk

Addresses for companies within The Random House Group Limited can be found at:
www.randomhouse.co.uk/offices.htm

The Random House Group Limited Reg. No. 954009

A CIP catalogue record for this book
is available from the British Library

ISBN 9780224088879

The Random House Group Limited supports The Forest Stewardship Council (FSC), the
leading international forest certification organisation. All our titles that are printed on
Greenpeace approved FSC certified paper carry the FSC logo. Our paper procurement
policy can be found at www.rbooks.co.uk/environment

Mixed Sources
Product group from well-managed
forests and other controlled sources
www.fsc.org Cert no. TT-COC-2139
© 1996 Forest Stewardship Council

Typeset in Galliard by Palimpsest Book Production Limited,
Grangemouth, Stirlingshire

Printed in Great Britain by
Clays Ltd, St Ives plc

For the Stranges

1

The sun turned the narrow dirt track to dust. It rose like an orange tide from the wheels of the truck and blew in through the window to settle in Frank Collard's arm hair. He remembered the place feeling more tropical, the soil thicker and wetter. The sugar cane on either side of the track was thin and reedy, wild with a brown husk and sick-looking green tops. The same old cane that hadn't been harvested in twenty years swayed like a green sea. Blue gums and box trees hepped out of it, not bothered with the dieback. Once it would all have been hardwood. In the time his grandparents had lived out here, just the two of them, before the new highway, maybe then this place was a shack in the woods.

The clearing was smaller than he remembered, like the cane had slunk closer to the pale wooden box hut. The banana tree stooped low over a corrugated roof. He turned off the engine and sagged in his seat for a moment taking it in. There was a tweak at the back of his neck and when he slapped it his palm came away bloody.

'Home again home again diggidy dig.'

He could have driven here without thinking. He could have turned the radio up loud and listened to the memorial service at Australia Zoo. They were calling them revenge killings, the stingrays found mutilated up and down Queensland beaches. He could have let his hands steer him to Mulaburry, those same roads he'd hitched along as a kid, sun-scarred and spotty, scrawny as a feral dog without the bulky calves and wide hands he had now. But never mind that, he'd still pulled over on to the slip road and smoothed out the map and read aloud the places, and he still sent his eyes over and over the landmarks, searching for the turn-offs he knew were not written down. The tension in his arms had got so strong he wanted to bust a fist through the windscreen but instead, as a road train roared by and rocked the Ute in its wake, he'd clutched the wheel, crumpling the map as he did it, feeling small tears made by his fingertips. He had gripped the wheel hard so that it burnt, and he pushed like it might relieve the feeling in his arms. But it didn't help and then he was outside, banging his fists on the bonnet for all that he was worth, his nose prickling, his throat closed up, the bloody feel of some bastard terrible thing swimming inside him. And when he was done and spent, he had climbed back into the truck and refolded the buggered map, and when he couldn't make it fit together he'd laughed softly and started the engine.

The air outside was thick with insect noise, heavy with heat, and the old gums groaned. The padlock on the door was gone and the idea that some other bastard might have claimed the place as his own nearly made him turn round and shoo all the way back to Canberra. The whole thing was suddenly hare-brained. Tearing through drawers at home trying to find some sort of clue as to what he was supposed to be doing, he'd found an envelope with a picture of his mum in, taken on one summer holiday at the shack. There she was, hanging up a sheet in the sun, the same wide teeth as him, the same sort of boneless nose. Different hair, though – hers a blonde animal that moved in the wind. He was like his father, wiry, black, not from these parts. By her shoulder was the window and inside you could just make out a jam jar with a flower in it. It was like being smacked on the arse by God. Couldn't have been more than a month after she was hanging up that sheet that they'd been driving in his dad's old brown Holden when a truck hadn't stopped at the intersection. When he woke up there was no more mum and no more old brown Holden.

It wasn't difficult getting out of the rental agreement. He'd been late and short in the last three months since Lucy left. A week from then and he was on the road, two suitcases of clothes, the rest of everything in boxes for the op-shop and the padlock keys burning his thigh through his pocket. He'd taken the first part of the journey that evening, ended up in a motel close to midnight, with a sun-faded poster of a lion eating a zebra above his bed. He hadn't slept, he'd drunk from a three-quarters empty bottle of Old and he'd let himself think about Lucy then. The sick feeling of trying to make it all right. The endless meetings they'd had across the table, to see if there was a way round it. The months afterwards when he'd sweated if he dropped a plate, the look on her face. Careful, or I'm going. Or when the coat hangers tangled themselves and made a jangling as he shook them, her pointed silence. There were other things he thought of in that wide-awake night. Being alone, fixing himself up. Getting done with the drink, sorting through the things in his head as she'd wanted him to.

He stopped the Ute and opened the door. Holding his hat on to his head, he stepped into the sound of cicadas that shrilled like pushbike bells from the cane. He slammed the door louder than he'd meant to and walked towards the shack. The smell of sweet ozone and the clump of his boots in the dust was alien. It was darker and smaller than he remembered. It tilted inwards a little like a sagging tent. He cleared his throat.

'Hey!' he called before reaching for the door. Inside it hadn't changed, and it made his chest tight to see. There should have been broken windows, mess left by kids, dust and leaks, mould on the walls. But there was not. The shack had a feeling about it like it'd been waiting. There were no wildflowers in jars, it wasn't

3

swept, there wasn't the sparkle of sand in the cracks of the floor-boards, but the placement of *things* was just the same. It was like the last person there could have been his grommet self fifteen years ago and it made a warmth at the back of his throat. No one was there. There were no other belongings, just the old things that had lived there for ever. On a high shelf a grey elephant, a kewpie doll and a mother-of-pearl shell. The wedding-cake figurines of his parents and grandparents that had always stood on the telephone table, dustless inside their glass bell jar. There was no tele-phone – he'd forgotten that. Sat on the stack of plastic chairs in the corner, a Father Christmas with a felt body and a rubber face. The wood-burning stove that had been put together a little wrong and now and again used to chug black smoke into the room, which would have his mother up and in the doorway coughing and flapping with a tea towel. He took a step inside and heard the familiar creak of the floor. The place wouldn't recognise him this heavy or hairy. The sink was dry, with a sprinkling of dead flies upside-down in it. The beds were there too, a double and a rickety single all close together so that as a kid he'd lain awake, wide-eyed at the sound of his parents at night, wondering what is that and why are they doing it? A thin blue and white striped blanket covered his old bed, tucked at the feet in the way he hated, where you'd have to kick your way free, so your feet didn't pin you down.

He dragged out the mattresses and afterwards he slung the bed frames in the back of the Ute. The idea of sleeping on either of them filled him with dread. The smell might be there, his mother's hand cream, or the witch hazel his father used for aftershave, in the days before he stopped bothering. Later it was more of a flaying than grooming. There might be particles of their skin there, he might find a long blond hair and know it was not his. They were things that needed to be forgotten about, for starters.

4

He'd bought some kerosene with him, and he found a place out of reach of the fingers of the cane and poured it on to the mattresses, knowing he was pouring too much. He threw on a lit match and felt his eyelashes singe, turned away and didn't watch the beds burning. He moved his suitcases into the shack and tried the taps. Nothing came out, the dead flies skitted around the basin, blown by the breeze of his hand. So he'd need to see to a water tank. There was no fridge, but there'd never been one – they'd kept beer and milk and Cokes cool in a deep rock pool where the water moved gently. They'd caught fish as they needed it, and there were always abalone, oysters and octopus to be had. But things changed. He'd get a cold box in town when he went looking for a camp bed. Chances were the stove was buggered after such a long time, but he gave it a look-over anyway. Something dreadful had happened inside, and nothing he could think of made any sense. A big rat or a bandicoot, something with hair and long yellow teeth, claws and a thick backbone, had been cooked whole and left. The thing looked like it had exploded and then been cooked again, the stuff was black and hard and old. It was long past smelling, which was good. He found a stick and gave it a poke but it was welded on. He straightened up and looked at the stove with his hands on his hips. He rubbed the grit of hair on his face. He wasn't sure how much he'd want to use it anyway even if he could get the stuff off. Like a man slow-dancing with an orang-utan, he walked the stove and cylinder, corner by corner, out of the shack and well away from the burning mattresses. He left it, squat and angry-looking, at the entrance to the clearing.

The week after his mum had drifted in burnt flakes to the seabed a chill Sydney morning woke him, so that his face was wet and his shoulders were stiff. That was when he'd seen the first one. Padding out of his bedroom, a blanket round his shoulders,

5

thoughts of morning hot chocolate and warm bread, his stomach had sunk and growled as he saw her slip from his parents' room. The old woman from the flower shop, but for half a second he would have sworn it was his mother, and in that moment he'd wondered if the past weeks had been imagined. There was no explanation for a woman coming out of his parents' room apart from it being his mother, and he stood with his mouth open, his knees weak and his heart high in his chest. But only the vague shape was hers, only the long hair, the small hands. This woman was old and nearly dead. She met his stare with a look like she'd been caught stealing butter from the fridge, but she was old and so wouldn't have any trouble about that. Her eyelids were shaded blue, her fingernails were red and her yellow dress was something a lady in a picture might wear, but not her. She hesitated and then smiled at him, and he could see that her teeth were not her own, but belonged to a much younger person with much bigger teeth. She made for the stairs, holding her high heels in one hand, her handbag in the crook of her arm. As she passed him she touched him on the head. 'Okay, kiddo,' she had said and tackled the stairs in her stockinged feet, mindful of their slipperiness.

Those women, the ones with the clothes that smelt of piss and smoke, the ham thighs showing through the slits in their skirts, the skin and bone of their chests and the unlikeliness of their make-up, the rouge that seemed to float above the skin of their cheeks, the lipsticked teeth either false or yellow. The smell of his mum was gone from the house a month after she was in the sea, and it was replaced with something wide open and stinking. After his father stopped baking bread there was nothing to mask it apart from the smell of old beer and damp rot, like the house was growing soft and sinking into the ground.

*   *   *

The wood of the dunny shed had turned silver and it snagged the tips of Frank's fingers when he opened the door. Inside, the porcelain bowl was almost hidden beneath fireweed that geysered out of it, some of the plants five feet tall. Through the green he could see a crack running the whole way down the throat of the toilet, something black, like good soil, pushing behind it. It had been a joke his dad had loved – the porcelain drop dunny. The smell was like a garden shed, no shit, but a gentle manure, potato-y, cool. Spiderwebs coddled the corners, white and flossy, and a skink ran across the cistern. The whole thing looked more like a fancy bird bath than a loo, and he closed the door and let it alone. The burning mattresses gave off a smell of rubber. He watched the fingers that peaked on the fire and snatched at the moths gamely flying over the top, disintegrating them in snaps and pops.

He thought of the morning Lucy left. How he'd sat at the kitchen table, listened to the sound of the schoolkids on their way to soccer practice, the shouts and magpie noises of girls laughing. A line of sunlight cast on to the checked tablecloth, and he had counted the squares. He'd walked his finger on to a red square and thought of her marching towards him, sticks that she found interesting under her long arm, her hat throwing a shadow down to her shoulders. White square; pale hot hair that flew in her face, white clay, dust, and thrash caught in it like a gill net. Red square; the first time they'd had sex, all knuckles and knees. White square – the mole under her breast – red square – the clasp of her eyelashes – white square – the smell of her neck – red square – the sound of her sleeping – white square – the sound of her crying when she thought he was asleep – red square – the silhouette of her hand over her mouth in the dark – white square white square white square.

The sun had moved across the table and on to the floor where it disappeared up the wall. He'd listened to the kids returning from soccer practice, had heard the bell sound in the school up the road and the day ending for them in kicked cans and squabbles. He listened for keys in the front door. He drew his fingernail around a red square so that it stood out from the others.

She did not come back that night, and it was dawn before he'd moved to the toilet where he let out a jet of strong greenish piss. He didn't flush but went into the bedroom where he'd checked the wardrobe. Plenty of her things were still there, but her pack was gone, along with her good jeans and her work jeans. They were not in the dirty clothes. He avoided the photographs around the house – the ones that he knew off by heart anyway. Three on the mantelpiece, two on the chest of drawers in their bedroom. One by the window trying to catch his eye with its reflection. Taken soon after they met, she wore some terrible yellow dungarees and her hair had blown into Frank's face. His teeth showed, smiling, through the hair, wide and laughing. You couldn't see the kink in his nose where it had broken. You could see the crows' feet, which made him look older than he was, and happy, and the dark line of his eyebrows tilted upwards like he couldn't believe his luck, not yet thirty and suddenly there was all he'd ever wanted. He looked half a head shorter than her. The picture showed how she couldn't ever leave him because they held hands.

Opening the desk drawer he saw that her passport, usually bulldog-clipped to his own, had gone too. He tried her mobile for the fifth time, and it went straight to answerphone and he hung up. He spent the rest of the morning with the phone in his hand sitting on the edge of the bed, but nobody called him.

She'd come in the night before, a secret look about her, and Frank had thought for a while that she was pregnant. It had taken him so by surprise, but it all added up – she'd told him she was going to see a friend who was upset and she might end up staying over – she was worried about it, that was all. She wanted time to

8

get used to the idea, had booked into a hotel for the night, or maybe she'd stayed with a friend, talking it through. She was scared, worried about how he might react. He felt his palms tingle and realised he was excited. He wanted to pull her down into a chair and make her tell him. He had it ready what he would say, and how happy the next days would be. This all happened within ten minutes of her getting in the door. He poured her a glass of wine to test her, but she drank it. A glass of red now and again was good, he'd read that, that was fine. But she'd have to stop the cigarettes.

She looked at the red and white tablecloth, rubbed a spot of grease away with her index finger and started. 'Look, I've been to Sydney.'

Were the doctors better there? She caught his eye, smiled and looked down again. She was nervous.

He took her hand. 'How come?' He could feel that his eyes were wide open, he didn't want to miss the moment. She looked at him again. He inhaled.

'I've been to see your father.' His hold on her hand grew slack but other than that nothing changed. He kept his gaze steady and she must have taken that as encouragement, because she started talking at ninety miles an hour.

'I had to ask around a bit, but the shop's still there, and once I found it and I went in, I could tell he was the right one, he looked just exactly like you, it was weird, a bit smaller, tired, but it was like you were there. And I talked to him, I actually bought a pie first, just to be sure, and then we got talking and he really was a nice-seeming guy. Charming. Friendly.' She paused, thinking Frank might say something but he didn't, just let his hand hang open on the table. How could she have done that to him? She didn't seem to notice he'd let go of her hand. His old man, who when he looked at you looked up and to the centre of your forehead like he was

9

reading something printed there, whose body was old, mouth slack and full of dark teeth from drink and banana paddle-pops, the wrappers wet in his pocket. Who still somehow managed to bring home, every so often, a young pretty thing, in between the old and the fish-smelling, the fat and moustached women that he found by the bucketload. The daytime drinkers and their terrible loud voices, their piss, dark and strong in the toilet. That was ten years ago. It was a surprise he was still alive, let alone that he still managed a day's work.

'And anyway,' she went on over his thoughts, 'I didn't tell him who I was or anything like that, but I asked for directions back to the train station and he drew me a map.' She scrabbled around in her handbag and brought out a paper napkin, carefully folded, and laid it on the table like it was a child's drawing. 'He knew it just like that.' She took a long gulp of her drink and pushed the map closer to Frank. 'He did look tired, though. Really tired. And alone. I really think now's the time, love. We could just go and say hello, take it from there.'

Where did all this 'we' come from? She looked at Frank like he was a puzzle she'd just fitted the last piece into. He sat back in his chair and drained his glass, and when he'd finished he threw the glass on the floor and it smashed. The colour had gone from her face. He held her gaze a moment and hoped that she understood what he thought about what she had done and the anger that was barely kept inside him. He was going to leave the house then, but it wasn't enough, the smashed glass seemed pathetic, like a tantrum, and she had to know it was not. He found that his hand was holding her face and squeezing it, and he'd been sure he was going to say something, but he just squashed her face with his hand, feeling the teeth through her cheek, feeling her breath hot on his palm and already there were tears, but what did she have to cry about? Then he didn't want to touch her any more and pushed her away, and there came a noise from her and her hands went up to her face. Still there was something he wanted to say, he heard it rumbling inside him but it wouldn't come. He left the house leaving the door open, spent the night in the park and knew that she would not be there when he got back and that that had been it, his chance to prove himself, to show that his old overreacting self had gone for good. But she'd seen his father. Christ, she'd talked to him and he had not.

He took shallow breaths. He picked up a back board from an unframed picture and snapped it in two.

There, he thought. At least that's that taken care of.

He strode into the kitchen, whistling tunelessly, because no songs would come to him. He thought he would take a bath and dragged his clothes off standing at the kitchen sink. He put on some toast and went to the bathroom, but there was a large spider in the bath.

'Get the fuck out of my bath, you shit!' he shouted, turning on the hot tap and leaving the room. He picked his clothes off the kitchen floor and put his shirt back on, but he didn't manage the pants.

The toast pinged up and, crying, he buttered it and daubed it with jam, inhaling deeply and letting out long shaky breaths. He ate it breathlessly between hiccups. His mouth, which at that moment had nothing to do with him, would not stop making the sound 'Aaaaaaaa' like a stiff door opening. He lay on the floor, a smear of jam on his cheek, and mashed the last of the bread into a wet pap with an open bawling mouth. The crusts sat on the floor. He swallowed and breathed in sharply, then cooled his crying to a whimper, then to sniffing and then just to staring. The sun moved across the kitchen floor, regardless.

On his last night in the flat he sprayed air freshener until the insides of his nose were raw, to get rid of the smell of her. But still she flooded in, got behind his eyes, up his nose, at the back of his tongue. Those white days in the city when he would wake to condensation fogging up the bedroom window, and from where he lay it looked like the world had left while he was asleep. She smelt faintly of beeswax polish. On those cold mornings when they lay in bed, and he missed Sydney and the things that were there, she pressed her feet into the backs of his calves and even their coldness was comforting. It was enough to leave the blank window of Canberra outside a little longer.

At the roundabout before Mulaburry Town, on the grass verge, a boy sat cross-legged reading a book that could only have been the Bible. Frank watched him in his rear-view mirror. The kid wore boardies and a big yellow T-shirt, his hair was almost white from sun and sea and his arms, long and brown and smooth. Frank shook his head. Cutting school to read the Bible by the road. Things had changed.

Behind the camping shop was a recycling yard and he moved the old bed frames as quietly as he could, gritting his teeth when they clanked together, hoping no one would come and tell him to dick off. He left them leant up against the bottle bank and hurried round to the front of the shop, trying to look like he'd just arrived.

The old lady in the shop said, 'The council come on a Tuesday and take away the larger refuse.' But she said it with a wide smile, as though he'd asked.

'Right,' he said, smiling back but not knowing what to say, waiting for the feeling of delinquency to run out of him.

'Need any help, darl?'

'I'm after a camp bed.' Move it along, he thought, move it along, make it seem like you don't think you've done anything wrong. It was only dumping a couple of bed frames. Is that bad? How bad is that?

The lady sold him a camp bed, a sleeping bag, a campervan water tank, a two-ring stove with extra gas and a discounted bag full of broken mosquito coils. Packing it into the back of the Ute, he realised he was still wearing the smile he'd gone in with and his face was smacked red around the cheeks. His hands shook and he held the back flap of the Ute, tried to look like he was securing it, but he just gripped and waited to feel still again. 'Calm yourself down, you silly bastard,' he said under his breath. 'Just calm on down.'

He remembered there being lots of shops on the main street, but apart from the camping place, a baker's with a couple of aluminium chairs out the front and a closed greengrocer's there were just empty windows with whitewash or newspaper covering over. He checked his mobile phone, which only seemed to get a signal at certain corners of the town. Of course, there were no messages. Might as well turn the thing off for all the good it'd do him out here. He bought a loaf of bread and thought he would ask the man behind the counter if there was a supermarket nearby, but somehow the words got stuck on their way out, somehow he thought he wouldn't be able to get them out in the right order. He was going to buy a pie, which he remembered being good from there, but when the man smiled and said 'Whadcanigettcha?' he felt shy and his palms sweated as he replied, smiling too widely, 'Just a loaf, thanks.'

He grasped desperately in his pocket for change, horrified that he might have forgotten to bring any cash, and when his finger-tips met with coins he was so grateful that he found himself saying *thank you, thank you* in his head as he counted them out.

The Bible kid was not at the roundabout as he drove back but he saw a sign for the Bi-Lo Superstore, with a painting of a prawn at the helm of a ship, wearing a crown. Captain King Prawn at your service. Sailing the stormy sea of low prices. He smiled and let it occupy him until he drew into the car park. What had been there before he couldn't remember. He must have passed by it a hundred times with Bo, it was on the road to the surfing beach, but he couldn't think what was there before. Hardwood, or cane or maybe a golf course. None of it seemed right. He hadn't thought about Bo Flowers in years.

The place was huge, and every angle of it caught the sun and shone it back at the sky. Inside, it was freezing cold and there were computer games and fried food and places to sit and drink coffee and eat chips. A brown-ankled girl sat on her friend's lap and whispered something into his ear, which made him slide a hand up her leg. Three girls next to the couple shared a packet of Cheesy Os and they all laughed watching the two of them. The floors shone smooth and the grocery department was lime green and housed heaps and piles and stacks of oranges, watermelons and nectarines.

Someone called Jack owned most of the shops inside, sometimes he was Crazy Jack, where there was a bargain to be scratched out, some cheap cut of meat to buy, but equally, when sophistication was called for, Jack could rise to the occasion, as in Frère Jacques, the boutique. A woman, stuffed like a peach, tried on hats, looking at herself in the window. She looked right at Frank and the hairs on his arms stood up. There was a smell of glad-wrapped meat, too many people too close. An A4 black and white poster advertised a missing girl, her face a thumb smudge. The posters appeared on every glass surface, even at the meat counter, stuck on from the inside so the paper looked soft with damp.

Nothing in the aisles suggested eating. He had abandoned a shopping list, thinking he'd be able to pick out a few days' worth of meals by sight, but the foods were oddly arranged, so that bacon was next to cheese, tins of beans next to washing-up liquid,

14

frozen pies next to frozen crinkle-cut carrots. In his basket he had butter, apples and a pack of soap. It was something like the packed lunches his father had made after his mum died, for those first couple of months when he'd still given it a go. Frank would shift nervously on his bottom on the dinner bench, waiting till they'd all said the food prayer before opening the box and seeing what catastrophe was hidden inside. It started as a can of sardines and half a green capsicum. By the end of the next month he was lucky to find anything edible at all in there – a bit of fish batter left over from the chip shop, a sachet of powdered gelatin. Once a balled-up sock and an old tangerine. He walked back to the front of the shop to start again.

Later, he bought calamari and chips and sat on the seafront on the bonnet of the Ute. There was no rush to get back to the shack. A bit of a fix up on the roof was probably in order, but it hadn't rained in months and the sky was white and high. He'd anticipated that the place would need a bit more work, had thought it might be good for him to keep his body occupied for the first week or so. He saw how clean his fingernails looked, holding a calamari ring. The waves were peppered with surfers, even in the small swell. Seagulls picked through rubbish baskets, fat-throated, and eyeballed the passers-by, scratching out deep croaks now and then, and dancing with their red feet. He threw the last few chips to them and watched as they screamed and shook and picked at the food and each other. A surfer took a big wave too short and smashed himself into the sea spectacularly. Frank smiled to see him surface, shaking the salt out of his nose and ears. It looked good in the water. He and Bo used to hitch a ride out sometimes to surf with an old polystyrene board. It gave an instant rash that stayed around for weeks.

It was bad to admit to, but at school Bo Flowers was not the sort of kid you had any choice about hanging out with. He had a smell around him like he'd been licking his fingers, and the minute you caught his eye you knew that was it – you were friends for good. He told lies, not a bad thing in itself, but it was the kind of lie Bo always went for. 'I went to the Goldcoast with my dad once and I surfed a nine footer. And I didn't fall off, and there was a white pointer but it didn't bother me, we just rode the wave in together. And everyone on the beach was cheering because they said I was the youngest kid ever to do that. They said it might go in the record book. For next year, though.' The kind of lie that went on and on so that no one felt all right with picking him up on it, so that gradually everyone just went quiet and waited for someone else to talk.

The kid's old lady beat the shit out of him in a regular way. He was a big lug of a bastard, with soft brown eyes like a calf and a dead dad. Bo had this idea that the two of them were friends because Frank's mum was dead too. But that wasn't really why, Frank knew, it was because he was too soft to smack the boy in the mouth, which was the way everyone else dealt with him. It was the thing he understood. But it was good sometimes. They'd bite school together and it was always better getting in trouble with a mate. Frank knew what to do when Bo turned up with black forearms from shielding his face from when his mum'd got hold of a shoe. Do nothing and act like nothing the hell was up.

And the time they snuck into the pub and sat at the back tables with a beer each and felt so big, and then the landlord came out and he lifted Frank up by the collar and said, 'You tell your old man to keep his filthy grubbing hands off of what isn't his,' before breaking Frank's nose with the ball of his hand and throwing him out of the door with a kick in the arse. June Shannon from the flower shop saw it happen and she gave them a smile that was not meant to be nice. That time, Bo didn't say anything about it other than 'We could go pinching at the bottle mart?' and they both sat on their bums in the gutter outside the pub and laughed hard so that his nose bled to buggery and that only made them laugh harder, and Bo farted loudly from the beer and it set them off again. He was okay, Bo. He couldn't hit his mum back, after all.

Frank drove right off the dirt road to the shack and down to his beach, feeling full and heavy. The small bay was a mix of rock and brick clay, run off from the last floods marbling the sand with mud. No footprints, no tyre tracks on the road down. The smell that prickled the insides of his nostrils was hot salt fish and oranges, and the sound was of a long exhale. He unpeeled himself from his shirt and shorts, and stepped out of his pants, happy to be free of the wet heat of them. He caught them on his foot and flung them up into the air.

He clambered ape-like to a high rock and looked down at his beach. The bream hole, his mother's spot, was full of white salt foam. Standing there cooking the first inch of his own flesh, he squinted at the glare that came off the sea. It was ugly somehow, the sand a bit too deep in colour, the water a fleck too grey and sharky, imperfect. He stood like Peter Pan; hips thrust forward, naked apart from his old hat thumbed to the back of his head, fists on his waist, smiling like a split melon because all of a sudden things felt good.

'Mine,' he said out loud so that his voice bounced off the rocks. This is what it is to have land, he thought, his eyes following the line of the shore. He did a small low jump and ran, his hat flying off and settling somewhere down the beach, feeling the enthusiastic sock of his dick bouncing from side to side as he ran for the water. He dived into the base of the first small wave that came in, thinking only as he hit the water face first that it would have been a good idea to check for rocks. But he came up in one solid lump, making a clean 'boc' sound with his mouth. It was colder

17

than the water he was used to swimming in, there was a tightness in his chest, which was good. He floated on his back, feeling like a fat otter, letting the salt water into his mouth, to clean right inside him, where city dust lay on the tops of his lungs. The currents were strong, and he kept half an eye on the shore while he grabbed up handfuls of sand and scrubbed himself raw. When he was pink and shining, the sky was a low purple and the heat had gone out of it. He took a wave all the way into the sand, the foam bubbling at his chest.

With the sea still streaming from his ears, he found his hat and dragged his shorts on to wet legs while sandflies and mosquitoes bit and blew by him. He ignored them and poked around in a rock pool, squatting by its side. There used to be abalone on the rocks, but not now. Fingernails of crab shell floated among the weed, an empty hairy leg – octopus dinners. His insides garbled with the thought of clean fresh food. Sea animals would fill him up with goodness, push out the jam rolls and meat pies of the city.

'Yars yars yars,' he said into the rock pool, stirring up sand with a stick. The sky rolled in the moon and then it was night time.

He woke in the dark with the feeling that there had been some noise or movement in the shack, like a soundless bird had flown in one window and out the other ruffling the air as it went. He listened for feathers landing on the floor. Past the frogs and insects, the drill of night things, he heard it again. The night sounds dipped and let the noise through – a faraway cry, something prehistoric like the noise of a pterodactyl in an old plasticine movie. His ears became full of the sound of his own blood and he ticked off in his head all the explanations. 'Bird' was what he arrived at. Some kind of bird was what the Creeping Jesus was. Owl. Jabiru. Cockatoo. He listened past his own breathing, past his own blood, then past the outside noise, banana leaves on corrugated iron, past

18

the scrubbing of the gum trees in the little wind, he listened so that his body went stiff, though he didn't dare clench his fists for the noise it might make.

Again, like wind dropping, the nightbirds tucked their heads under their wings and the sound echoed from far away in the bush, a siren, a vowel noise that was long and thin, and when it reached its peak it broke and turned into a low howl, tailing off like a sad question. He kept his eyes open until they wouldn't any more and when he slept there was nothing.

At dawn something scrambled across his feet in the snub end of the sleeping bag and he fell on the floor kicking the air furiously. He didn't find a spider or a mouse, but a pair of balled-up women's toe socks that had been hidden at the bottom of the bag. He held them in both hands, resisting the urge to bring them up to his face. Those shapes, those spaces between her toes. He went outside to the burnt-out fire, holding the socks between his index finger and thumb now, like they might sting. He put them in the ashes of the mattresses, then fossicked around for a piece of wood to put on top of them and hide them from view. He used a few twigs to make a pyramid over the socks and lit them, watching until they were on fire.

The sky was pale and the morning dew had already burnt off. A troop of magpies gurgled in the blue gums and he could smell hot eucalyptus and salt water. From the borders of the cane came a crumping noise as something large sloped off towards the trees. A lost cow, maybe, or a feral sheep down from the hills. He threw more wood on top of the socks and made a billyful of tea to start the morning off.

Before the iron roof turned to a griddle he was up on a ladder, patching up the rust-bitten roof. Even in the first sheets of sun the metal began to expand and shift, creaking and popping in the heat, and he couldn't rest his hand in one place for too long, feeling that he would leave the skin behind. On the roof were all kinds of uglies: leaf insects, their tails up and ready to strike, spiders – redbacks, huntsmen, fat black-bodied ones and hard little yellow jumpers. A whitetail nestled in a rusted pipe, which he gingerly rolled off the roof, then watched as the bugger tottered away after the pipe hit the ground. The banana tree nodded softly, making a sound like rain on the roof. It was a good sound. He filled his lungs with hot air and stood upright to piss in the direction he had thrown the spider. He rolled an orange between his palms, softening it, then bit into it with his front teeth and sucked it hard so that stars came to his eyes. He looked at the cane flowing softly in the breeze that never seemed to reach him, saw the tops of three or four tractor sheds like capsized boats above the level of the cane. He took a strong back swing and hurled the sucked-out orange in the direction of one of the roofs, saw it swallowed up and was surprised for a second that there were no ripples.

When he turned round and saw the face watching him from the edge of the clearing he had to crouch down, his heart fat and loud, to stop from falling over. The person slipped out of the cane and strode forward, and Frank clutched his hammer tightly. The man walked quickly and lightly towards the shack, one hand up in what was possibly a friendly gesture. He let his hammer go and stood up. 'A-roo, a-roo, a-roo!' called the man, jogging a bit now to come and stand at the bottom of the ladder.

'Hello,' said Frank and the man beamed with brilliant white teeth. He had the look of a young boy dropped into a grown man's body. The skin of his face was salt-rubbed, his eyes red and bright from the sun.

He squinted up at Frank 'How is it?' he asked, presenting a bronzed hand so that Frank had to come down the ladder and shake it. 'Bob Haydon – heard a noise someone was moving in around here.'

Frank took the hand which was cool and big. 'Frank Collard,' he said in what he hoped was a friendly tone. Unable to think of what else to say he added, 'I've moved in.'

'Can see that, mate!' Bob talked in a shouty way, like a welcoming dog. 'Sorry for sneaking up on you, was having a bit of a ramble and wondered what was going on – sometimes you get kids around here, you know, up to no good and that sort of thing.'

Frank nodded and smiled, wondering how long Bob would stay for. 'Can I getcha a drink?' he asked, thinking Bob would probably say no, that he couldn't and had to be getting on.

Bob looked at his wrist where there was no watch. 'Why not? Wet the head?'

Rooting through the cold box Frank's stomach moaned, but he found the beers anyway, floating among sliced cheese and wet bread. Beer for breakfast. Not a great start.

Bob perched on the steps and lit up a cigarillo. He flapped out a match and delicately put it back into the match box after testing it was completely out with his fingers. 'Ta,' he said, accepting the bottle, and seeing as his other hand was full, he angled the bottle head on to the skin of his inside elbow removing the screw top with a quick jerk of his forearm. 'It's a good place you've got yourself, mate. Always wondered who it belonged to.'

'Was my grandparents', long time ago – haven't been here since I was a grommet, though. Don't think my old man would've either.'

'Ah – well – I've only been here meself a year or so – me an' the wife are westies, tell the truth. Perth. Other side of the bloody world it feels like some days.'

Frank nodded. ''S a big place.'

A fly landed on the outside corner of Bob's eye and he blinked it away. 'Good-oh. 'S just you, Frank? You're not fixing her up for the family or nothing?'

Frank tightened his bum and swallowed his beer in a lump. 'Just me, I'm afraid . . .' he was going to go on and wing it, say something jovial.

But Bob said, 'Seems like a pretty lonely thing to do.'

Frank looked up at an aeroplane that glinted cleanly.

Bob smiled and shook his head. 'Look, I'm sorry, mate, I'm going on like a lunatic. Thing is we're all a bit jumpy at the minit. A friend's girl's gone missing, been gone a fortnight and we're all pretty pip to it just now. 'S why I was lurking in the cane there.'

'Sorry to hear it,' said Frank. 'You reckon she's just done a bolt? Saw the posters in town, she looks about the age to.'

'Yeah,' said Bob, not agreeing but being polite. 'Yeah, let's hope so.' There was silence and Bob looked into the middle distance.

'So, do you work the cane?' asked Frank, the question coming to him like a lightning bolt.

'Nah, tried it for a bit, but if you don't know what you're up to it's a bugger's muddle. I do a bit of fixing up of cars, but my wife keeps chooks. We get by – less work than proper farming. We live over east.' Bob pointed with his chin. 'You can see our water tower from here – connected by the cane.'

Frank looked, knowing that he wasn't tall enough to see over the cane. He nodded. 'Chook farm, eh? Meat or eggs?'

'Both. You got any need for a couple of hens? Dead or alive?'

'I could definitely think about it.'

'You do that. So,' said Bob, with the look of someone who had finally come to the meat of the conversation, 'are you a fishing man, Frank?'

Frank shrugged.

'Some good shores around here. Get your nice pelagic type, come in close to the bays, you can get out there on the right day on a surf ski with a hand line and come back a happy man. Just last week I was out there, trolling – 40-kilo line – light-weighted squid and pilchard duo – bait got monstered, I take off like a steam train; next thing I'm being pulled through a school of bluefins, two or three pretty big bronze whalers feeding in there. Took two hours to get the thing back, had to hold her head out of the water for twenty minutes before I could haul her up. All the time I'm thinking something's going to come and take the side out of her, or me, or both! Anyway, monster of a thing, 15 kilos. Wife made sashimi the first night and now we're on to a steak a day. It's a good freezer.'

Frank's mouth was dry and he tried to keep up with a look of interest and friendliness.

Bob looked at him. 'You using an eski? I've got a kero fridge you can have if you're after one.'

Frank felt like a heel. 'If it's going spare I could really use it, thanks.'

'No worries. It's a nice place you've got. Got a nice feeling to it.' Bob drained the stubbie, unfolded upwards off the step. 'Righto, Frank – well, you need anything – turn left out the end and we're second track you come to.'

'Thanks. I'll bear it in mind.'

'No wuckin furries,' Bob said, shaking hands again and smiling with a squint that made the sun always in his face. ''Sgood to meet youse anyways. I'll come by some time soon with that fridge.'

It was awkward not knowing how to see the man off, to walk with him all the way to the end of the track seemed a bit much, but he was still talking, so Frank followed.

'Looking for work?'

'Will be. Would you know of anything going?'

'Could be. I work the marina on and off. Usually there's something a bloke can do. You look a strong enough bloke, Frank.'

'I do okay.' He tried not to pink up. 'Done a bit of labouring around the place.'

Bob looked at the horizon. 'There's a fella, Linus, works the marina – he's a bit older than the usual – might remember your grandparents.' Frank stopped, surprised. 'Don't worry, mate, I just parked me car round the corner so's I could sneak up on you – you don't have to walk me home. Aroo,' Bob said with a wave and disappeared round the tallest cane.

2

The day the king of England died it was all over the wireless and Leon was supposed to care, even in the heat with the cream on the cakes turning sour and the flies making it in through the fly strips. The Pancake Day decorations in the shop were taken down to make way for a Union Jack, a picture of the dead king cut from the paper to hide the centre where his mother had fouled up the lines. That long face and the hair combed over like a pill, that Pom look like he'd eaten too much butter. Even when his father unveiled a red, white and blue tiered 'Cake of Mourning' and put it in the window to melt in the sun, and the butcher's wife balled a hanky up to her face when she saw it, even then, what held Leon's attention were the fine rabbit-brown hairs that had started to separate his face into sections. He took his time running his fingers over them, knowing that this was it – this was the thing that would save him from the pet names and public cuddles of his mother. This was manhood in all its creeping stinking glory and it had happened to his face. It was one of the best things, that he was the only boy in his year with a hairy face. It was rumoured that Briony Caldwell had one but she shaved it off, dry, with her dad's cut-throat every morning.

From the downstairs wireless came the sound of the British national anthem and his father singing boldly over the top of it.

> God save our great big king
> Long live the lovely king
> God save our king!

'You can't save what's already dead,' Leon's mother's voice cut over, but it only made his father sing twice as loud and Leon saw out of the bathroom window how the postman shook his head at the foreign voice that rom-pom-pommed out of the bread shop, and slipped his letters under the door like he always did, rather than bringing them into the shop and risk talking to the European type of loonie that lived there.

Work could start on a wedding cake up to a month in advance. Leon was sous chef and he took the job seriously. Even when he'd been younger there had never been a time when it had been okay to lick the bowl.

'That is for inbreeders. If you are happy to eat the batter, why bother cooking it at all?'

His father taught him to prick the cake using the thinnest skewer, to make sure it was properly baked. The ritual was carried out with every cake, even though no cake had ever been too wet. 'It's all mathematic formula – like Albert Einstein,' he would say, weighing up the ratio of flour to egg and the weight to the wetness. 'You make a mistake and it's only down to your own stupidity,' sagely extracting the perfectly clean skewer, steaming hot, and fixing Leon with a look that conveyed that something of grave importance was going on.

The icing was white like light in a copper pan or the sun off the water. It burnt a flash into your eye. It was shaped into a brick and rolled out flat like a pillowcase, then folded back in on itself until it was thin and could be draped over the cake in one piece. Dressing the lady, his father called it, and he thumbed the sheet gently into the creases of the cake, like he was circling a narrow waist. Then he would line up his coloured dyes, each thumb-sized bottle with a handwritten label, every shade of colour separately explained: *Buck-eye Brown – the approximate softness of antler moss;*

Baker's Rose – a warm cheek; Australian Copper – flesh tone; Holiday Red – a fun-time girl's lips.

Glancing at the notes he had made about the couple to be married and talking the process through with Leon, his father would add tiny amounts of dye to the unset marzipan.

'She had a beautiful mouth, that young lady – almost the same colour as her cheeks, but so big, those lips.' A single drop of red dye would spider out, an ink spot on white linen, and find its way into the creases of white sugar. Pounded with a wooden spoon, the pops and cracks of air bubbles bursting against the side of the stoneware bowl would reach the shopfront where his mother served the everyday cakes. From the blanket of white would come the hue of skin. A dot of blue and yellow produced the lawn for the couple to stand on, the earth that cemented them to their wedding day, the memory of wet grass, the touch of each other's hands, damp from attention.

Once the marzipan had rested, his father took pinches of each colour and lined them up on the back of a hard-backed cookery book, which he would hand to Leon. He'd talk him through rolling and kneading, teaching him, not too much, but just enough – don't make the sugar sweat.

Out of Leon's paws came a crumbling mess, a mix of nose and hat, of shoe and skin that ran together from the heat of his palms, blending grey in the middle. Out of his father's hands a tiny sculpture, a person in a pleated dress, with a nose like a blade, grasping her wedding handkerchief, thin as a leaf, perfectly able to stand on her own two feet. Undiluted dye picked out the lips and eyes. The black dye was used only on the man – for his hair and shoes, sometimes a moustache if his father was feeling playful. He never used black on the bride. 'Black is black,' he would say quietly, his face close to the statue he was working on, his eyes fixed, 'but brown is a mixture of everything. Brown is better for a woman.

When painting a woman you must dip your brush in a rainbow.'
He would look at Leon here, stop his work to ask, 'You know
who said that?' When Leon shook his head he would go back to
work, as if he'd decided not to tell him a great secret. 'Well,
whoever it was, he knew his women.'

When he was younger Leon would poke his tongue out of the
side of his mouth and frown as his hand shook with the effort of
stillness, and his paint-brush gave his monster bride a red slash
on the head, a beard instead of eyebrows or a target on her chest
instead of a flower.

His father would sit the pair next to each other, and examine
their work side by side. 'Your bride has a well-rounded bosom,'
he would say, ignoring the fact that she had only one. Looking
at his own work, his father would stand with his hand on his chin,
sucking his tongue and say, 'You know – I think I really need to
do more work on noses.'

Leon would squint at the perfect tiny woman who stood on
the bench top, and his palms would itch to be as large and gentle
as his father's. On his fourteenth birthday he could roll out a
perfectly formed woman, but his hands still shook when he tried
to paint her. The couple his father had made for his own wedding
sat high up on a shelf in a bell jar but Leon knew them by heart.
His mother held, for some reason, a stuffed bear against which
you could see the tiny pinking of her fingernails. Her lips were
bowed and smiling, and she had bitter-chocolate hair that reached
to her pencil waist. The toe of one shoe pointed out underneath
her skirts and it was blue like a duck egg. His father wore a sugar
tuxedo broadly stretched over his chest. On his lapel was a poppy
and you could make out the black seeds in its centre. He wore a
moustache that he didn't wear now, two lines neatly executed in
black.

*   *   *

At school a fat-necked boy called Darren Farrow announced that world war three was happening and pretty soon it would be the end of everything. He said it with his head tilted back on his neck, he said it looking down his nose, pointing out his chin. 'My brother's off fighting 'em an' pretty soon I'm gonna run off and join him. He says we'll show those Japs what the carry-on's about.'

'I thought Japs lived in Japan?' said Amy Blackwell, whose father owned the fruit shop, and everyone looked at her.

Darren Farrow fixed her with an ancient and wise look. 'Those Japs get *everybloodywhere*. All over the place.' And she was silenced.

'It's like your sort,' Darren explained, pointing at Leon. 'All your sort with your dark hair and funny ideas about washing.' Leon said he didn't know what ideas Darren thought he had about washing, but he was happy enough to stuff his fat neck with the cream buns he'd made with his two very own stinking hands.

Leon went home after clearing up the blood in his nose, but his mother still noticed and still caused a fuss. 'With all this going on, and even the babies are at it, trying to kill each other!' she cried, dabbing at the smear of new blood on his cheek with a Dettol-soaked napkin.

He did not like being called a baby and rubbed his nose till it bled again. His mother came downstairs with her coat and hat on, and marched him out of the door. They nearly crashed into Mrs Shannon from over the road, whose face was always swollen and dark from something that happened in her home, but she still smiled at Leon: it looked like she winked behind her dark glasses. After half an hour on the bus they arrived at the Farrows' house in Glebe. The Farrows lived in a sandstone building next to a church and it made him hot inside when he thought about their own small rooms above the cake shop, the crumbly walls dark and the smell of toast in the curtains and the blankets. The Farrows' house had a cream ivory push-button bell, but his mother didn't like to use it, so instead she knocked hard on the door. No one answered so she knocked harder, until Leon was squeezing her hand in embarrassment. A woman appeared, a look on her face like she couldn't believe there was someone at her front door. He bit both his lips at the same time and tried not to blink. He saw the end of his nose, red with where he'd been thumped and he could see the tops of his cheeks as well, and they were also red.

'Mrs Farrow.'

The woman looked Leon's mother up and down, a blink of recognition showing, she let her face set into a small hard smile. 'Mrs Collard.'

'I'd like to talk to you about your son. He's hit my boy on the nose and gave him blood.'

Mrs Farrow's eyes came to rest on Leon, and he looked away, like he was thinking about something else. Her English always got worse when she was nervous or angry. He would have liked to have run off then, left his mother to deal with it herself. 'I think you're trying to tell me your boy had a nosebleed, Mrs Collard.'

'Yes, well, fine, but it was your boy, and we'd like him to sorry.'

'To a-polo-gise,' Mrs Farrow corrected.

His mother clutched his hand and he tried to slip it out from her grasp. The shame, he could taste it.

Mrs Farrow gave them a prim smile and called out behind her, 'Darren! Come down here, please. I need you to assist Mrs Collard with her enquiry.'

Leon's mother shifted feet. He noticed the bluebirds that were painted round the porcelain number 23 that was stuck to the Farrows' front door. There was a lumping down the stairs and Darren appeared, his nose a strawberry like Leon's.

Mrs Farrow put her arm round her son's shoulders. Darren caught Leon's eye and looked at the floor with a small smile. 'Now then, Mrs Collard.' She spoke slowly and loudly. 'As you can see, any brutalisation that my son visited on your boy was returned doubly. I'd have thought you'd have more pressing issues to think about these days.' Darren smiled wider at Leon and Leon looked away, knowing Darren was on the brink of laughing.

'You shouldn't let your son hurt my little boy.' Leon's mother turned to face Darren. 'Say you are sorry.' But her voice was softer, as if she'd just then become very tired. Darren looked lost for a second but, looking up at his mother, he gained strength and his smile returned.

'My boy say sorry to you?' Her voice rang shrilly in the settling air. 'Mrs Collard, are you quite retarded? Do you know there is another war going on? Do you know about the Communists, or do you just keep to your own news? My eldest is out there now, waiting to be shipped off. What are you doing? Sitting in your cake shop taking money from the people who put you up when your own country decided they'd had enough? Well, I think that's rich. It's you who ought to be apologising; it's your son who ought to be thanking my boy for letting him stay in his country.' Leon's mother had lost the pink of anger, and seemed very small and grey on the doorstep. A neighbour watched lazily from under a sun hat on the other side of the fence. Mrs Farrow was still talking when Leon's mother turned them both round and started off down the pathway, firmly holding Leon's hand.

'Yes, yes, off you go. And if you have a change of heart,' Mrs Farrow carried on, 'we'd be more than happy to hear your apology. That's if you can say the word. Flaming clog wog.' The door shut and Leon managed to free his hand from his mother's grip. He reckoned Darren was probably watching from a window, laughing at the sight of him being yanked along. His face boiled. They walked home not talking or touching; even when his nose began to bleed again they both just let it.

31

The next day at school, Darren had been talking. Briony Caldwell piped up at him as he crossed the playing field, 'Youse might be the first kid to get a hairy face, Collard, but yer mummy still holds yer hand to cross the road! Does she wipe yer bum too?' Of all people, Briony Caldwell. Darren smirked from afar.

Amy Blackwell caught Leon's eye and she held a pencil under her nose and crossed her eyes. For a moment he thought she was doing an impression of him, and he was about to turn away scowling, but then she smiled and he realised she was playing up Briony. Briony noticed too and stared hard at Amy. Amy stuck a finger up at her behind a piece of paper. Only Leon saw, it was only meant for him to see, and it made his breath shallow in his chest.

Someone lobbed a toilet roll at him.

'Eye ties don't use toilet paper, they use their hands!' shrilled Darren happily. 'He uses his mum's hand!'

The class erupted and Leon rolled his tongue into his cheek and willed his face not to become red, kept the hidden finger of Amy Blackwell in his mind, the pencil moustache, the crossed blue eyes.

Something was going on with his parents. A few times he'd come home to find a stale silence, his parents avoiding each other, or they might be having a row, which when he entered the room carried on in Dutch. Whatever it was, he could tell that his mother was angry.

'What's happening?' he asked her one night, finding her tucked up on the sofa, a tissue bundled in her fist.

'Nothing, darling. You know your father. He's just being a pig head about something.'

'About what?'

'Your father thinks he's more Australian than anything else, that's all.' She looked up at him as though she hadn't seen him before. 'You're getting pretty tall there, chicken.'

He smiled because finally she seemed to have noticed. 'Please don't call me chicken any more.'

She gave him a blank look that meant she was pretending not to understand.

At the Easter show his father went off alone to talk crumpet with someone, and Leon wandered in and out of stalls. There were kids his age orange-mouthed with fairy floss and wild-eyed with sugar, but somehow it didn't seem to mean much to him and he drifted home early, reddening at the giggling herds of girls and the clowns and mascots that stalked him.

At home he sat at the kitchen table and sorted through his father's photographs of brides to be and lined them up with photographs of their cake-top statues. He tried to see what it was that made each face different, what exactly it was – not just the hair or eye colour but the sugar bones underneath the skin, the weight of a tongue in a closed mouth. Upstairs, floorboards creaked like the deck of an old boat under his mother's feet.

The sky was dark blue before his father returned home, stumbling a little as he came through the door. He was smiling broadly and his cheeks were flushed, and he held a big chocolate egg in the crook of his arm like it was a baby. He set it on the table and Leon could see that there was a fist-sized hole that had been eaten out of it.

'Ta-da,' said his father and stood back so that they could both admire it. 'That's a Darrell Lee egg.'

Leon nodded. 'Looks good, Dad.' It looked dumb, especially the way they were both supposed to look at it and be impressed. His father stepped behind him and all of a sudden put his hands on Leon's shoulders and breathed through his open mouth. Leon looked up and tried to see his father's face behind him, but couldn't quite.

'It's all going to be good, you know?' said his father, his voice a little too loud for the room. 'We're going to keep those buggers away. We're going to look after what's ours.' Leon could smell the sweetness on his breath, and wondered who his father thought was going to try and nick a half-eaten Easter egg, even if it was a Darrell Lee. His father stepped to the side so that Leon could see he had raised a finger to bring his attention to what he was about to say. 'Before you were born, Japanese came into our harbour. Men died to keep us safe.' He looked at Leon hard as if by looking he might be able to press the weight into him. 'Me and your mother adopted Australia because our own land became hostile. And they embraced us with open arms.' He raised his arms and gestured at the ceiling. 'We have built this shop. We have built a life. And it is a good life. This country has given me your mother and it has given me you, and I mean to defend our good life and our good country.' He sat down now, heavily, and put his hand on Leon's arm. For a horrible moment he thought his father might cry. 'I know you would too if you were just a little bit older.'

From the doorway, his mother asked in a voice that cracked in her throat, 'What have you done?'

The next few days in the shop passed in silence. Leon took himself off, spending the steamy autumn hours walking into town and watching cars drift over the harbour bridge. He looked at the brown calves of girls but felt like someone might hit him on the back of the head for doing it.

Over tea the next week – pressure-cooked potatoes, a chop each and carrots – his mother broke her silence. She spoke slowly like his father might not understand. She spoke in English so that Leon would. 'You know what war does. Donald Shannon wasn't like that before he went away. And that's if you're lucky enough to come back.'

His father put down his knife and his fork. From somewhere, a place Leon had never known to exist in his father, a deep rumbling: 'Be quiet, woman.'

Hot potato stuffed up the back of Leon's throat and his feel for his food changed, like it had been turned to bin scrapings.

'I expect support from my wife, Maureen.' After a moment's thought he said, 'These are not Germans.'

His mother flushed pink and stood up, collecting the plates, still full of steaming food. She said, 'And what happens when you get killed?'

Leon went upstairs when they began raising their voices and their movements made the glasses in the cabinet clink, and immediately regretted it – he should have gone out of the back door, but now he was trapped. His heart beat a new beat. They both seemed to think the other one was stupid and selfish and awful. There was a shout, a slap, a loud one and then another, and they echoed through the house. He lay on his bed, thinking about who had got hit and who had done the hitting. He wondered if he should get up, say something, but he didn't know what. He decided it was none of his business. After the slaps the house was quiet and he thought about sneaking out, but he felt drained and pressed the heels of his hands into his eyes to try to get them to close. He woke itchy, still wearing his clothes, just as a breath of light was coming into the sky. There was a noise like a dog snuffling in the street and he looked out of his window, but there was nothing to see. When he lay back down there was a whine, a scritch-scratch at the front door and something about it made him climb under his sheets and pull them up to his nose. The noise carried on until he heard someone downstairs open the front door. His father must have slept on

35

the sofa. After the door had opened and closed there was just silence, and Leon slept.

In the morning, things were soft. His mother's eyes were swollen and there was a red mark on the side of her face. She smiled at Leon and her top lip was puffy. He thought he might be sick. 'It's okay, chicken. We were angry. I hit him right back.'

And when his father came down there was a mark on his face too, but he put an arm round her waist, and smelt her hair and kissed her neck. Leon went to school, a feeling in his guts that something had changed in the night.

The day Leon's father left, his army greens taut over his chest and his hat folded on one side like a listening ear, his mother became stiff. There was something wooden in the way she moved, her hair was coiled in a tight bun.

Tea was still at six, and there was still meat and there were still pressure-cooked potatoes. The same dances carried on through from the shop to the house, recipes were still performed to the letter. The same questions were asked of school, of home-work, but they were shrunken, boiled down to the bare bones. He could see the oddness of that empty chair, like a ghost at the head of the table. In the kitchen the smell of burnt sugar was paler, like the way his mother burnt sugar was a less rich version. The angel-hair crowns she made sat gummily on top of tarts and he watched her frown, shaking her head and picking the mess off and dropping it in the bin. A missing ingredient. When his father telephoned Leon tried not to listen to the taut noises she made. She called for him to come and talk but he pretended not to be in and slipped out the back. When the first letter arrived, his mother read it aloud with her hand over her mouth like something might try to jump out of there.

36

Darlings,

There are exciting things that I would like to tell you, but I will keep it quick, as I want to be sure this reaches you in the next post. Training has been hard but I am confident that we will flatten these buggers just as soon as we get to them. I am well, I have some new friends, a man, North, and a younger boy called Mayhew. He is a keen lad, reminds me of you, son. I tell them all about you, Mayhew is too young to have a family yet, but North is missing his misses too. He has a baby girl, and it makes me happy and proud that I have you at home to look after your mother.

Shortly we will be going into the jungle, but we expect it will be a pretty easy ride. Exciting to be entering a new terrain.

I miss three things – the both of you, and caramel sauce on ice cream. Be sure to have it waiting for my return.

Son, kiss your mother for me, because I cannot for now.

Love to you both

When his mother took her hand away she was smiling toothily. She breathed in and out like she'd been holding it and her eyes were glassy. She kissed Leon on the head and he felt her face wet in his hair. The letters arrived, two a month, cheery, upbeat, full of longing for treacle tart or sugar banana flummery. Complaining about the tapioca they were given, the leeches, the mosquitoes. Leon's mother took long hot baths that steamed up the whole of the top floor.

At school the teacher said, 'Hold up your hand whoever's dad is out in Korea now.'

Leon felt sorry for the kids who looked quietly at their desks, as if they were thinking about something else and didn't care anyway. He held up his hand so high his shoulder clicked. The teacher showed them a book with photographs of the kind of things you got in Korea. You got muskrats and brown bears and tigers. His dad liked animals, he'd be excited to see a tiger. Leon imagined him lying on his front very still among the ferns and watching a tiger roll with its babies in the long grasses.

At home, he practised sugar dolls. At first they had a look of his mother about them, some long-suffering frown in the eyebrows. Sometimes they had their eyes cast up, their cheeks pale pink and their hair neat to their shoulders. Then he did Amy Blackwell, her weight resting on one hip. You could tell that underneath that dress there was a sock, puddled round her ankle, showing a scratched brown calf. Mrs Kanan from the flat above the butcher's had wide arms, but as a bride she was lovely, with a half-smile. He found a piece of wood to use as an armrest so that his hand was steady as he went when he painted them.

Christmas snuck up like it'd been watching from the bushes. They put together a window display, strings of wine gums so that when the sun shone through the window in the morning they lit up like fairy lights. There was the set of Banksia men, each one painted to be a different member of the nativity. Father Christmas next to the baby Jesus with his many mouths and eyes, and his hairy sack of toys. Outside it was too hot to be in the city and people sat in their yards with as much of themselves in water as possible. Sometimes just their feet in a bucket, but he had seen a few back-yards with swimming pools and the wet noises coming from them spread a breeze over your face.

His mother whisked egg whites so that the muscle on her right arm stood out like a stick of butter. He piped snow icing round the edge of angel cakes and the light tick-tick-tick of her whisk was the only noise in the shop. She slammed down the bowl with a shout and slapped the table with the flat of her palm, then left the kitchen. A bead of sweat tickled the inside of his nose. He picked up the whisk and got the whites close to peaking before she came back in and waved him away like he was meddling in something that didn't concern him. He made treacle toffee, which he wrapped in the purple cellophane that squeaked like a mouse at every twist.

After his mother had made the pavlova and gone for one of her long baths, Leon moved the wireless into the kitchen and chased carols around the stations. Eartha Kitt sang 'Santa Baby' and it made his hands still to hear her. He tried to make a Mrs Christmas Eartha Kitt, but the head was too big and it tended to topple over. At any rate his mother's response when she came down, her hair wet and heaped on her head, was not enthusiastic either. 'Mrs Santa Claus is a white lady. A big fat white lady.'

So instead he made a turtle dove to hang above the six-tiered pavlova, so that it seemed to be swooping in to pinch the kiwi fruit from the top. It looked okay, swinging there on its fishing line, but it was no Eartha.

Christmas day was tense, full of wide fake smiles and the smell of too many cloves in the pudding. They went to midnight Mass and prayers were said for all those husbands and sons in foreign places. That was when Leon counted in his head and found that there'd been no letter from his father that month. The red smile on his mother's lips trembled as if the muscles of her mouth were tired.

Over the holiday the shop closed, and Leon went to the bridge and watched people strolling through the harbour in their Christmas outfits. Women with legs the colour of sweet nut glaze, their dresses high and tight to their throats, the clip of their short steps. The girls with the secrets under their skirts, fingernails like preserved cherries. Something watched him from under the bridge, he could feel it, something that snuffled and scritch-scratched. It threw him looks from the coolest bit of shade. A breeze from the water raised the hem of a tutti-frutti skirt and it wavered in slow motion in front of the bridge. His ears growled at him. His mouth was dry, then flooded with spit like he might be sick. People criss-crossed in front of him but his eyes stayed only on the dark under the bridge. He wanted to look at the girls again, the warm soft-ness of them, but his eyes were too tired to move, too lazy to blink, like they had nothing to do with him. That thing threat-ened to swim out at any second and drag him under, drown him in the cold shade, scritch-scratching. When he got home that night his face and forearms were tight with sunburn. He lay awake in bed feeling his skin dry, feeling it tighten notch by notch, licking his lips to taste the sun and the heat, to keep back the cold thing that waited there, under the bridge.

'Not my husband,' he heard his mother say into the telephone later that week. 'He wouldn't just stop writing.'

Mrs Shannon came into the shop, her dark glasses off for a change. She had shaded in her eyelids a light-blue colour, with a line of black that ran outwards from the corners of her eyes. She had on red lipstick and a dark-blue type of dress that he might have seen before on a younger girl. On Mrs Shannon it fitted perfectly so that her cleavage was easy to see, and it clung to her thighs and waist in a way that looked nice.

'Hey, sweetie, you bin sun-baking?' she said, a smile of perfect straight white teeth that were a little too big for her mouth.

'What can I get you, Mrs Shannon?'

'Always so polite, kiddo. I'll have a florentine, thanks, darl.' Her voice was so deep that parts of words melted before they left her mouth.

He leant into the counter and picked up a biscuit with a piece of greaseproof paper. His eyes looked for her chest, she caught him looking and he blushed, but she smiled widely.

'Um, it's on the house.' He thought he'd die of embarrassment if she gave him money.

'Ahh. Thanks, kiddo. You're a doll. So how's things in the Bunhouse?'

'They're okay, thanks, Mrs Shannon.'

'You're looking pretty grown-up these days.'

'Yeah, well.' He smiled and blushed and puffed out his chest. He thought for a moment he might try standing on tiptoe, but he didn't.

'Guess that's what happens when the man of the house goes away, uh? The next man steps in. I only had girls, y'see, when Don went away. Not much you can do about that though, an' he's back now, so whose complainin'? Would have been good to have a nice strong man like you around the place.'

'Thanks, Mrs Shannon.'

She shrugged. 'Just an observation, kiddo.' Up close, he could make out a mark on her face, close to her eye on her cheekbone. Like something had stained her there, a tea bag or a some brown chalk. A little blueing showed through the make-up as if the flesh there was off, and he realised he was staring at it.

Mrs Shannon just smiled. 'Not to worry, chickadee. He hasn't done me in yet.' She unwrapped her florentine and took a bite. 'Sa nice bit of biscuit-making, kiddo. Yummie. See you later.'

She turned and walked slowly to the door, and he watched her bottom as she went, guiltily because he had just been looking at the bruise on her face. She turned at the door and gave him a look that might have been playful. But it wasn't quite pulled off and, framed in the doorway, she looked like someone about to wade out to sea.

He turned away from the look, heard the shop bell ring signalling that she was gone and saw that his mother was watching her go from behind the fly strips of the kitchen. For a moment he felt like he'd been caught out doing something he shouldn't, but her focus was all on the woman in blue who sashayed down the street. His mother held on to a fly strip, wound it round her finger and unwound it. Her face was pale and tight, her hair wet from the bath.

Eventually a letter came and his mother paused before reading it. Her face darkened, or perhaps a shadow passed over the sun. She leant on one hip, then the other. 'Your father misses you and he misses walnut and coffee cake with morning tea. He is looking forward to seeing how you have grown. The jungle is hot. He says sorry for not writing sooner. He has been busy. With the war.'

The words came carefully and slowly like his handwriting was difficult to read. She got up and left the room, gripping the letter in her fist. Over the next two days he watched its path, saw it read and reread, while he wiped down the counters in the kitchen, saw it folded and opened and folded again, her nails sharpening the fold in its middle. It was placed between the pages of a book, shut inside a drawer, put in the bin, taken out and put back in a different book. When she took charge at the front of the shop for half an hour he took it from between the pages of *Moby Dick* and unfolded it.

Mayhew is dead.
    They slit his throat.
    North is missing. Just upped and went into the jungle.
    If either side find him now, he's dead.
    It can't be stood this jungle. It's full of scratches.
    R

Leon put the letter back in the book and the book back on the shelf. He felt the toothache cold of a shadow at his back, heard a snuffle, but when he turned round it was only his mother standing in the doorway looking at him. She held the wooden spatula that they used to pick up the cakes at the front of the counter. It dangled like a broken arm. Her face was old, all the years she'd been alive seemed to have come on all at once, just that second. She gave him a smile, dull as watered-down milk, then walked to the front door and turned the sign to closed, locked the door. She took off her apron as she climbed the stairs to her bedroom and left it lying over the banister. He waited, his fingertips still holding the taste of the letter. Then he followed her up, found the door to her bedroom open and his mother a lump under the covers. He climbed in too and they stared at the ceiling together.

'Your father is an only child.' She smiled, ran a finger along her eyebrows. 'Like you.'

He raised his head to look at her. The bun of her hair meant that her head was tilted at an odd angle, that there was space underneath her neck. He wanted to fill the space with something soft.

'I had four brothers. Harold, David, Thomas and Charlie.' She spoke the names like they were precious things, noises that weren't often sounded. She raised her hand and put it over her face. 'Then there was my mother, my father. My aunt and uncles. My sister and her children. We weren't even proper Jews – just the children of Jews. We never really went to temple, only on the big occasions. But still.' He felt the windows darkening, closed his eyes and his skin burnt hot where it lay close to hers. The thing was at the door again, but she didn't seem to hear it. The smell of the room was different, like ashes, like hot dry sand.

'I was smuggled out early. Just me, the girl. Your father the same, except he was an only child so that was precious. We lived in the same city back home but we never met. Out here it was the one good thing, that we met. And then he goes and does a stupid bitch thing like signing up. I couldn't believe it.' The word 'bitch' in his mother's mouth sounded like the most foreign thing she had ever said. She sighed. 'He didn't see those photographs. He didn't want to look, but I did, I saw. I looked close at those photographs, I wanted to see my brothers' faces. But they all looked the same.'

There was a photograph he'd found a long time ago, hidden between the pages of an atlas, cut from the paper. At first he'd thought he was looking at a record catch of fish, a netful dumped on a wharf somewhere. But then he'd seen the wax eye sockets and empty mouths, the arms and legs smooth and white. He'd seen the nakedness and that had been the worst part, that he'd wanted to see those parts, between the legs where everything sank into darkness. They'd seen other pictures at school, but there the people were alive, wrapped in shawls, saved. No look of relief in their faces. Nothing. He stayed still and watched the skin of her throat stretch and relax as she swallowed. 'But this is a different war. Yes. This is a different thing altogether.' She looked at Leon and her eyes were black marbles.

The next week a young man stood smartly at the door. Leon watched as his mother gripped him to her, heard a noise from her throat and thought, *he's dead*. The young man stood very straight, his face red, his cap in his hand, blinking over her shoulder. He said, 'There, there, ma'm,' like a Yank. Then he left.

His mother sat holding Leon's hands in front of her, her eyes bright, and white and red. 'He's been taken. Trapped. Caught. Now, this doesn't mean anything, nothing at all,' she said, her face a stone in a creek. 'This is not like the last war – these are different people. It doesn't mean anything at all, nothing, you hear?'

44

He nodded, shook free a hand and touched her shoulder. It was awkward, it seemed like some part of her he shouldn't go near. Her eyes closed and she pulled him towards her so that they collided with their chests, and there was a hard ache in his throat. He breathed wetly into her shoulder, felt the same breath going back into his lungs, thought he'd like to shake her off and run out of the shop, tear down the street, run all the way to the bridge and find the thing in the ice-cold shadows, let it eat him whole. But instead he breathed in and out, counting the breaths, swallowing, his throat compressed against her shoulder. At least he was alive. They don't shoot you in prison, they just keep you till it's time to be let out.

In the next weeks, Leon would come across his mother staring into the open refrigerator, hanging there as though something unexpected had been put inside, the eggs replaced with light bulbs. Sometimes her lips moved soundlessly. He wondered what she saw then – whether she was talking to his father. Was it him in there? She still called Leon chicken and worried about the stiffness of his collar when he went out, fussed at the edge of his mouth with a wet hanky as if there were some grub there. But when she was in the bath or at night when she closed the door to her bedroom things became very quiet, like she had sat down just inside the room and stayed still until morning. Sometimes he looked through the keyhole to check she was actually there and she would be lying in bed, the covers up to her throat, with hardly a crease in them. She lay bone straight, her chest barely rising and falling, her eyes wide open. She stared at the ceiling like she was stopping it from falling on her. Once she sat in a chair, rigid, a wax creature with a tin frame. The chair was turned into the corner of the room, right up against the wall, so that her toes must have touched the skirting board. The back of her neck tense, still as the hot air.

*   *   *

45

At school things caught at his hair and plucked at the back of his trousers. His pen moved slowly across the page, ink swelled into the paper. He felt himself trapped between the bone and flesh of his face, and he couldn't move. Everyone else's hands moved at impossible speed over their work, the noises of the classroom were high-pitched and speeded up, made no sense. He felt his own body, a sluggish weight, pale and thick, a rock with a wooden shell. With effort he stood up, ignored the squealed noises of the teacher, the weird electric sound of laughter, saw only that Amy Blackwell's blue eyes watched him as he walked out of the classroom, away from the school, heavy enough that he might sink into the ground and suffocate, or else fall on the pavement and shatter into splinters.

At home his mother was sitting on the kitchen floor, the fridge door open, flour sprayed all over, eggs smashed and warming up on the linoleum.

He squatted down by her, moved a damp curl of hair that tangled in her eyelashes. 'I don't reckon I'll go back to school, Ma,' he said slowly and she looked up at him, as if seeing him for the first time.

She put her hands over his ears, bent her neck so that their foreheads were touching. 'If you're sure, sweet chicken. If you're sure.'

3

The foreman of the marina, Pokey, was a pirate from a picture book, a scratchy beard and a cap that made his sun-cankered ears stick out like rudders. When Bob introduced the two of them there was a papery handshake and Pokey's eyes focused on something over Frank's shoulder. 'The new fella, Fred or something,' he announced to the rest of the men before turning his back and walking squatly into the cargo shed and shutting the door.

Bob cleared his throat and smiled, punching Frank softly on the arm, 'Frank here lives down on the Mulaburry flats. Out past my place.'

'Just moved there,' agreed Frank. He shifted his feet.

Bob pointed to an aboriginal-looking man who as far as Frank could see was too old to work on a dockyard, but who had shoulders like an ox and a waistline like a berry. 'This one's Linus,' said Bob. Linus winked at Frank like they'd met before and it was a secret. Next to Linus was another darker man. 'Then we've got young Charlie. He's sometimes crew, sometimes with us on the marina.' Charlie was long and thin, with hair curled midway between his ears and his shoulders. The skin of his face shone in the heat, and he smiled widely and quickly at Frank, then looked away at the sun.

'Stuart,' said Bob, nodding at a white man, freckled-faced with straw hairs poking from his cap. His eyes were red in the whites from salt and there was a small swelling on his lip where something had been burnt or cut away recently.

'You a fishing man?' Stuart asked Frank, gripping his hand fiercely.

'Don't know too much about it.' He held up his fingers as if they might show polished nails. 'City slicker up till recently.'

Stuart seemed happy about this.

'And these two' – Bob nodded to the last two men – 'are what we call the twins, Sean and Alex.' They stood flat-footed in yellow worn thongs, their toes spread, grabbing on to the ground. They had the same thin lips coated in white zinc like cricketers, and they said nothing.

'They're boat crew,' said Bob behind his hand but loudly, 'they don't make friends easily.' Frank wasn't sure of the joke, but he laughed anyway. The twins did not.

For a working marina the place had a good feel about it. There was a dark rainbow to the surface of the water, and the familiar smell of diesel overhung the sea and warmed his chest. Boats moored about the place, white yachts with fancy names *Rosalind*, *Pengerrith*, *Serendipity*, painted in navy on their sides. The slipways were white and someone had gone to the trouble of stencilling a small anchor on to every fifth plank. From the spot where they loaded he could see a sailing-club-style café that opened out on to the water, where a few couples lunched in knee-length shorts and deck shoes.

Stuart clapped him on the shoulder with a burst of laughter. 'Didn't you know you was in Florida, mate!'

The cargo was coolant and oranges, and Frank was put on the ship with the twins to be shown the ropes. You had to push the pallets as they were lowered by the derrick, had to make them swing into just the right place, bring it down straight so no space was wasted. The twins worked in silence apart from a few well-placed yups. It was satisfying work and it didn't seem odd that no one talked. Bob came and swapped places with him so he could get to know the wharf, and the twins raised their hands to him, nodded. On the wharf he directed Linus on the forklift, which was a bit more hairy. Linus liked to pretend every so often he was going to run you through with the fork prongs. Frank smiled each time and the old bloke let it up.

He found himself falling into the rhythms of working again, enjoying the loud engines and shouting hoarsely over them. The heavy-set men and their zinc-white noses dancing in time with each other, hand signals, bending at the knees, twisting to take the hook and thread the rope round it, slapping the crates so they echoed and the crane took them up, the huge boxes twisting on the rope, bulking into the hull of the ship. The pallets held row on row of the same shape, the same colour. A hive of oranges, an army of freezer coolant.

Back in Canberra, there'd been the sauerkraut factory. For nine months he'd screwed the lids on jars of pickled cabbage. There, when he was bad, it had been a terrible thing to see all the lids of all those jars, piling up on the conveyor belt, relentless, rolling against each other. There had been something awful in knowing that every one of those jars would end up in someone's cupboard, would sit smugly on the dinner table, in the picnic hamper, coldly in the fridge of someone's home.

The heat was flat but the edge was taken off it by the water, even if it was oiled. The sun burnt red strips on to the tops of his arms where sunscreen and T-shirt did not meet, but he was outside, and there was no stink of vinegar and farts, no pruned fingers from leaky jars, none of the bad breath of the other people on the line, no watery eyes following jars down a conveyor belt.

At the marina, the day passed with rope burns, the light clink of the white moored boats above the engine noise of forks and the continual flushing out of work boats. His hands tingled with baby calluses and he felt the skin of his palms creak as he spread out his fingers. Charlie stood in the full glare of the sun smoking a cigarette and Frank wondered how he could stand it, the blast of that heat and on top of that the cigarette drying him out on the inside. The smoke came blue out of his mouth.

'Don't get many of those boys in the city, eh?' Stuart was at his elbow and he felt an extra heat rise in his face.

'Suppose not.' He bent down to collect the chains he'd been untangling.

At the pub after work he bought a round and made a point of sitting next to Linus. He didn't look in Stuart's direction. Charlie and a couple of others had sailed with the ship to unload at the other end. The rest of the men were watching a women's weightlifting comp on a small black and white screen.

'Bob Haydon mentioned you might have been around at the same time as my grandparents – lived down at the bay in that little shack?'

Linus nodded at the beer, took a mouthful and fixed Frank with a powerful eye. 'Did he just?' Linus looked across the table at Bob, who glanced briefly at him and then went back to the television. 'Course my tribe'd never be too friendly with your lot.'

'Oh?' Frank swallowed a large mouthful of beer and it burnt on its way down.

'Course – your little shack's built on midden land. Sacred aboriginal meeting place. Blood spilt over that land.'

'Right. I didn't know that.' He felt a sweat break out.

Linus smiled. 'Shittingya, mate! By cripes that had ya! Nah – maybe it was, maybe it wasn't, I couldn't give the shit's tinkle.' Linus cackled hard and whacked him across the shoulder with a hand that felt like a plank of wood.

When everyone had left, Frank had one more drink alone, just to be sure. A girl with sunburnt calves leant against the bar and talked to the barman, who squeaked a rag inside a glass. They looked an easy couple, with a history. They both laughed at something, and the barman put down the glass and leant both hands on the bar top. The girl glanced around the room, seeing if anyone was watching. She was surprisingly young. She leant forward so her shorts rode up the backs of her thighs and said something into the barman's ear that made him put his tongue into the side of his mouth and look at her like he was thinking something over. The smile was big on his chops. She was young to be having sex. The thought surprised Frank as he was pretty sure he couldn't have cared less.

What had he been – fourteen, fifteen? They'd had their first girls together, him and Bo, in the back room of the pie shop, two older girls who thought they were a funny pair. 'Couple of homo boys, I reckon,' his one, Eliza, had said, a smile round her orange lips.

'One way to find out,' her friend, Beth, had joined in, lifting her hair on to the top of her head, showing off yellowish stains under the arms and bumping Bo with her hip. Eliza had been a reedy sort, but she had a curve to her back and bottom that he'd replayed for weeks to come in his head; the way it'd tightened and relaxed as they'd rutted on the floor with the flour and the dead cockies at eye level. The lino that squeaked under his arse. Bo'd lit a cigarette afterwards, like in the films, and Frank had felt ashamed of him in front of the girls. The pair of them all rags and flesh and both on the nose, but they laughed and Beth drank milk from the fridge and it spilled down her arm. It wasn't long after that he and Bo had headed out to the shack for the first time, thumbing up to Crescent and walking in the peeling sun, cans of gasoline and chicken biscuits in a plastic bag. Frank'd had the keys away with no trouble and the route they took was remembered from the funeral, in the car with the urn, his father silent and sober. It was the only time Bo ever mentioned his old man, and all he said as they sat in the back of a Ute that was driving them past the town, with the wind back-combing their hair and sunset starting to happen behind them, all he'd said was, 'Dad would'a liked this,' and Frank had wondered what sort of a man would make a person such as Bo. They'd made Mulaburry by nightfall, getting lost and inhaling the gas on the way, spending time on beaches where it looked as if nobody ever went, drinking warm beer that Bo had bought and seeing the night sky as it was for the first time. The sex and the girls didn't seem important then, they'd messed about like ten-year-olds, telling scare stories about sharks and men with axes.

As they were falling asleep Bo said, 'There's no crocodiles around here, is there?' and he'd answered, 'Dunno, might be,' even though he knew they were too far south for salties.

They slept in the sand, and woke up freezing and sore like they'd been dropped on bitumen, but the sea was something else, and neither of them talked as they watched it turn from white and peach to blue as the sky righted itself.

They stripped naked and crashed around in the waves, dared each other out beyond the breakers, cried shark a hundred times and pretended they were being yanked at from below. They had a lunch of chicken crimpies and hot beer, and Frank felt his eyes swell up with the heat and the sand and the fun of it. They let the gasoline alone because they couldn't have stood it, the tops of Bo's jubberly boobs went red and Frank felt it cut about his face. To escape the wide-open burn of the sky they barrelled into the bush, their hair dried to a salt crisp. About the time Frank started to feel sick from thirst they found a shallow creek, shaded by the tall ghost gums and the two of them lay down in it like dogs, their mouth open, the cold water crawling all over, the sand in their underpants rinsing out and their bellies swelling up with the drink.

'Shit! Look,' said Bo, 'yabbies.'

They made it to the shack and found fishing rods leant up against the window, and before Bo could draw breath to whine about being tired, Frank had them out of the door and headed back to the creek for bait. Bo was the first to get a fish, a big silver job, neither of them knew what sort it might have been. It wasn't until the poor bastard was flapping on the rocks in front of the two of them that they realised they didn't have a knife.

'I got my door key,' said Bo.

In the end, rather than bash it with a shoe or stamp on it, they stood back and let it die, each nervously glancing at the other, trying not to flinch every time it flapped like an eppo having a turn.

The shack was neat and clean, and they lit a fire outside and cooked the fish on a grate from the stove. Its skin stuck to the metal and made a good smell. The sun had barely gone down when they turned in, a heaviness in the marrow of their bones. There were two beds, but in the night he'd woken up to find Bo in with him.

''S cold,' Bo said, and Frank turned his back on him and waited tensely, ready to strike out if any part of Bo wound its way round him. Outside it was thick and dark, and inside they slept like they'd been thrown down a well. If it weren't for the sick look on Bo's face in the morning, and the girls, they might have stayed for ever.

'Gotta get back and check in on the old lady,' he said, trying to sound casual, as if his mother couldn't cope without him, like he was doing her a favour. Frank wondered if his dad had noticed he was gone. More than likely the shop was still unopened, but it didn't matter too much anyway as no one bought much from them any more. The place was too dirty, sometimes the bread was stale, sometimes undercooked. His old man seemed to take a certain amount of pride in getting it wrong. He couldn't understand why he owned a bread shop in the first place if he couldn't bake.

The barman flicked the lights on and off, and it was time to go home. The girl had disappeared, but the barman still looked pretty happy. Maybe they'd meet later. Maybe they really liked each other. Frank drove home from the pub half cut, feeling after all he was still fifteen. It would have been good to have the company of someone. Even Bo, the open-mouth breather, the fug who couldn't resist eating his own snots, even when Beth and Eliza were there.

The shack had its own morning alarm system – when the sun started to heat up the roof, the galvanised steel would creak, threatening to fall in. There was a smell, too, that came with it – engine air and dry wood, and all of it exactly the same as when he'd been small. With his eyes closed in the first moments of waking he could have been ten again and waking up with a ten-year-old's plan of crab-trap baiting and finding good sticks. But when he rolled over he felt the bulk of his body as it sagged the bed, the hairs chafing against each other on his shins, the dull morning erection and the ache in the back of his neck from drinking more than he had intended. His face was dry and he could feel a beard there. Best shave it off soon or he'd end up looking like his dad, always licking his lips like a lizard through that curly-wurly hair.

His dad's lips were white as he poured his mother's ashes into the bream hole, and Frank'd asked about God. 'Dunno about heaven, mate. She's in the sea.'

A local family had turned up and the mother had crossed herself and he'd wondered what it was, wondered if he should do it too, but there had seemed to be so little to gain by asking. His father had been the same grey as the sea. 'Everybody dies, mate,' he'd said.

54

Those thin days afterwards and their thick silence. How would she come back if all her parts had drifted out to sea? If fishes ate her ashes and if sharks ate the fishes. The fishes he and his father ate, brought to them by the neighbours – had he pawed through the flank of a bream that had eaten his mother? Could that hurt?

His father told him, with closed eyes, 'Go and play on the beach.' He tried to pull a stick through the sand the length of the beach, tried to jump the calf-high waves, but ended up watching the sea, trying to keep his eyes on one spot so the water didn't escape him, but everything changed place, and the spot that he had started watching moved on the second he saw it, disbanded and spread out, rolled over and under and became another spot of water somewhere else. A knot was tight in his stomach as the fingers of the sea spread out and closed up again and again.

After three days they packed up and went back to the shop. His dad set to work immediately, even though they arrived back late in the night. Frank had been asleep in the truck and kept his eyes closed as his dad took him up to bed, held tight against his shoulder, even though Frank suspected he was too old for that sort of carry-on. He heard him moving downstairs, heard the quiet pouring of flour and the click of the whisk in the plastic bowl that his dad used when he didn't want to make much noise. His eyes, too tired to stay open but too lazy to close the whole way, settled in between as the smell of white sponge and citrus rind leaked into his room, and he had dreamt he was sucking an orange, his feet dangling in the bream hole.

After a shave and a little fresh-water wash with a bucket, things were not too bad. There was the whole day to go and he could hear a whipbird cracking not too far off. That was good. By mid morning he was feeling fine and shimmying around the place giving it a tidy-up. When Bob's truck drove up to the shack with

55

a fridge strapped down in the back, there was a different lazy wrist hanging out of the window. The wrist belonged to a brown arm and wore green copper bangles.

'My wife, Vicky,' explained Bob, pointing as the woman pulled herself up out of the passenger seat.

'G'day.' She smiled gappily, pretty brown circles under her eyes.

With the fridge came a chicken, dead and plucked, but not gutted.

'We leave 'em guts in,' explained Bob, ''cause some fellas get cranky if we don't.' This seemed a fair explanation.

The fridge was squattish and elegantly rusted at the edges, and while Vicky looked around the place Frank and Bob walked it into the shack in the same way that Frank had walked the stove out. He had a sense of himself dancing old appliances out of the shack and dancing the new ones in. The fridge fitted neatly below the back window.

'See this?' said Bob, holding a tiny pot with a wick poking out of it up to Frank's nose. 'That's the kero and you'll wanna keep it topped up.' He took a lighter out of his back pocket and lit it, then gently, like he was holding a live fish in a cup of water, he squatted down, reached under the fridge and placed it down softly. He stood up with a crack of his knees. 'An make sure you don't shut all the windows and doors for too long, or you'll wake up dead.'

'Terrific,' said Frank. 'Drink?' He'd planned ahead for company this time, had stacked up on light beer and ice. He'd even bought nuts.

Bob looked at his watchless wrist. 'Not today, mate, got places need going to.' Making no move to leave, he leant against the fridge like it was a car.

'Any news on the missing girl?'

'Not as yet, mate. Not as yet.'

Bob looked like he was about to say something else when Vicky appeared behind him and took his fingers in hers, and Frank was winded by the ease of it. 'Nice place you've got,' she said, 'I'd love something cold if it's going, Franko.' There was a look between her and Bob that Frank turned away from to dig out a beer from his eski. 'So, how'd you come by it? Bob tells me you moved down from the city?' Vicky accepted the drink with a chime of her bracelets.

He inhaled too far, nearly choked. 'My grandparents bought it up in the fifties. No one's really lived here since then – just used it as a holiday place when I was a little kid. Haven't been up since, actually. Not for ages.'

'Really?' She had a nice way of looking interested, the tip of a canine catching on her bottom lip. 'I never knew anyone owned it. I'm afraid we've been trespassing, Frank.' She gave Bob a sideways glance and a smile. Bob blushed. He took a long drink of her beer but waved away the one Frank offered.

'So what made you decide to move down here for keeps?' she asked, taking the beer back off Bob with a small yank.

'Up here,' corrected Bob.

'Dunno – good memories I suppose – bit of a change of scene. Seems like a good place to be . . .' He felt his voice soften, but they didn't seem to notice. Vicky smiled warmly at him, but didn't help him out.

'I suppose, I just came to a point – broke up with a girlfriend and I needed a place to just get out of the city.'

'City's a bad place to be alone.' Vicky nodded.

There were a few quiet moments, then Bob punched his fist lightly into his hand and said loudly, 'Righto, we'll be off. I'll drop by some more usefuls as I come across them.' They got into the car and Bob gave him a wave. 'Laters,' he said, raising one hand as he steered with the other.

'See youse soon,' called Vicky over the engine. 'Ta for the drink.'

He watched as the truck hared away, Bob's arm held out of the window like a flag, Vicky's wrist turning slowly on its joint. He wondered what they were saying about him as they drove off, if they were laughing.

He opened up his new fridge. And closed it again. And opened and closed. It smelt of bleach and old air. He unloaded the eski. He sat down to write a shopping list. Bread. Margarine. He opened the fridge again and looked at the dead chook. Potatoes. And wondered. Carrots. How he would. Vegemite. Cook it and what it would be like to eat a whole chicken on his own. He closed the fridge and returned to his list and, just to remind himself what kind of a stupid bastard he was, he jabbed himself hard in the palm with his pen, and the pen broke in the cradle of his hand and welled up purple.

He washed up the old camp oven, unused since a trip to the river two years back. He concentrated on cooking the chicken, leaning away from thoughts that the grit in the bottom of the oven was most likely sand from the river bank they'd been to for Australia Day weekend before any of the trouble started. That any blackened dried flake of food still stuck to the side could have been the skin of an onion they had eaten together, that had sat warm in her belly and in his belly as they lay next to each other in their one-man tent. He packed the chicken into the oven with whole potatoes, roughly cut carrots and tomatoes from a sackful of over-ripes he'd picked up at a roadside stall. Most of them had black centres, but there was plenty of flesh surrounding.

He squatted over the pot with a box of white wine and let a good half-litre squirt out over the chicken. When the fire was mostly embers he made a hole and nestled the pot there. He put on the lid and shovelled hot rocks on top. He stood back, his eyes stinging, and wondered what to do with the giblets he'd wrestled out of the carcass. He picked up the board he'd spread them on and examined them in the light of the fire, the wet, woolly strings that made the bird work. He took them over to the old stove, whose door was slightly ajar, like it was peering at him. He opened the door wide and scraped the entrails inside. They glistened wetly against the matt black of the stove's gullet and he shut the door, pulling the rusted catch into place, feeling like he was forcing the jaws of a dog closed to get it to swallow a pill. He stood a moment looking at the stove and wondering why he had done that.

A light spun over the top of the cane and an engine battered somewhere nearby but passed his drive without stopping, so he went back to the fire and poured himself a mug of box wine. The Creeping Jesus made a noise in the dark, like things did – an open-mouthed shriek – and he raised his mug of box wine towards it, toasting the shriek and whatever the thing was shrieking for.

When the chicken was cooked, he sat the whole carcass on a tin plate in his lap, with the camp oven in reach for the vegetables and juices that were in it. He pushed a newspaper under the plate to stop it burning his bare thighs and pulled at a leg. The skin slid off the meat and clung to the carcass. The flesh came off the bone with a small persuasion from his tongue. The bird was tough but it was tasty and he cleaned the drumstick cartoon-like – the whole leg went into his mouth and came out clean. He pushed his fingers into the breast and tore off white meat, it came away like bark from a tree. With a mouthful of breast meat, he felt the air come hot and fast out of his nose. He was burning his mouth, but it didn't matter because he was enjoying himself. The juice ran down his chin and throat, and maybe some of it collected in his belly button for all he cared;

59

it was good. He drained his mug of wine and filled it with the stock from the camp oven. He hadn't skimmed it and the fat was heavy on the surface, giving him the feeling he was oiling the engine of his body. He swallowed down large hunks of tomato and onion without chewing. The carrots tasted warm and heavy, and he chewed them and swilled them around his mouth to remember the taste for a long time.

When the breastbone of the chook shone like a fin in the moonlight, he leant back in his deckchair and smiled broadly, felt his wide thick teeth glowing in the dark, felt his feet rooted to the ground. I did the right thing, he thought. I did the right flaming thing after all. The small wound in his palm throbbed with chicken juice and it made him laugh out loud, a great crack. Silly old bastard.

Creeping Jesus in the cane mawed again, but this time it gurgled, something between a purr and a grunt that was swallowed by the deep dark of the night. He put the lid on the camp oven and took himself off to bed, dirty and smelling of dinner.

There was work in the morning, which he was happy about. How long had it been since he'd showed up somewhere to the slow wave of a hand, the nod of 'How are ya?' It was what he'd imagined when he'd first gone to Canberra, that he'd slot in and be one of those men who weren't afraid of a bit of hard work, who drank a cup of coffee out of a tin cup and got on with it. But when he'd got to Canberra the contact he had was nowhere to be seen and he was stranded, no place to stay, no hard hat or boots, and he'd had to sleep in a bus shelter the first four nights. He'd found work as a cleaner, doing the post office headquarters where the toilets were filled anew with the runs every morning at four. It had been hard smelling that and still smile at the miserable-mouthed bastards in the canteen, as they wolfed down their eggs and beans and fried bread only to shit it out again later into the freshly scrubbed toilets. He'd got himself a bed at the YMCA with a bunch of other hopeless cases and looked longingly at the men who lunched together at the side of the road in their hard hats and reflective gear.

Charlie stood by the derrick in the flaying heat, wearing a yellow sou'wester. His legs were bare and it looked from the right angle like he wore nothing else underneath. He had the hood up to shade his eyes from the sun and dark lines of sweat ran from his hairline. His cheeks were wet and shiny as polished stones. He was chatting with a plimsole-wearing girl from the marina café, whose apron was longer than her skirt. Frank could hear the sound of their conversation, and it was all smiles and they both giggled at each other. Charlie took the lemon lite from the girl's hand and had a drink of it before passing it back, and Stuart gave a snort, tried to catch Frank's eye, but he kept his face turned away.

Instead, Stuart turned to Linus. 'Don't like your mate, Linus.' Linus looked up with total lack of interest. 'What's his trouble?'

Linus laughed and went off down the pontoon holding a heavy iron hook in both hands like an injured bird.

Stuart stared darkly at Charlie. 'Fuckin' boon,' he said.

Frank bit the inside of his mouth, feeling the word echo round the marina.

'Don't be a prick, Stuart.' Bob walked past, yanking on his work gloves. 'She doesn't like you anyway.'

'It'll be his fault Ian's not working,' Stuart muttered to the floor, but loudly.

'Hey!' Bob said sharply, climbing into the fork cabin. 'I said, don't be a prick.' Stuart picked at something, maybe a splinter in the palm of his hand, as Pokey walked by eating a large pink apple. He eyeballed Stuart, but didn't speak, just crunched on his apple, drips of juice hanging in his beard. Frank tried to keep his eyes elsewhere on the edge of the wharf as Bob backed towards it in the fork, but Stuart was wound up. Now everyone else was safely deafened by the motor, he carried on as they hooked pallets.

'I'm all for Linus, he's me mate an' all, but, fuckin', in general – you don't want to get in with them – that's what I was saying it is with Ian Mackelly's kid.' Frank gave the thumbs up to Sean who was operating the derrick and the pallet swung slowly into the air, turning slowly, cellophane glinting in the sun. Frank wanted to look like he wasn't interested, but it couldn't have been that convincing because Stuart carried on, 'She used to hang out with the blacks at school. Sooner or later these white girls hang around with the abos – they all get into trouble.'

'I think you'd better drop it, mate.'

'Don't get me wrong, Frank, like I said, Linus's me mate – an' most've them are fine on their own – it's just in a pack they're trouble – look at the old bastard now.' He nodded to Linus who was laughing with Charlie, the girl gone back to the marina café. 'All thick with that bug-eyed fella. Joyce Mackelly'll show up a week from now, but she'll be messed up. All's I'm saying is if you're a girl and you hang around with that sort, sooner or later you are going to get yourself beat up.'

Stuart wiped a greased hand across his chin and made off towards the boat.

With the drop toilet out of use, Frank had taken to going in the sea. It took some getting used to, the waves made it difficult to balance and he worried about having everything wash back on to him. After a few goes, swimming quickly away, he found it was easiest to perch on the top of a half-submerged rock, hang his bum over the edge and face out to sea. The rock was pretty comfortable and he could spend a good half-hour there, depending on the tide, perched with a lap full of cool water making him feel weightless from the torso down. The problem of the backwash was resolved, as what came out would be sucked down behind the rock and washed out to sea to be dealt with by whatever fish were ripping the water open; he could see their grey fins and white bellies from the easy chair. He could watch the weather, the shape of the sea, the difference in the horizon and the height of the white horses. A sacred type of crapping, he decided.

Memories came to him then, old ones he thought he'd finished with. He remembered when Eliza had turned up without Beth and she had a small bag of resin and a bottle of rum. 'It's lolly day,' she'd said as she held them up in plain view of a woman walking past the shop. The woman had tutted and Eliza looked after her, laughing loudly so that the woman quickened her pace. They went out to the jacaranda and ate the resin sandwiched between pieces of chocolate. It was sweet and awful tasting, and nothing happened so they set about the rum, taking quick swallows and clearing the backs of their throats with it to get rid of the musk of the mull. And then, soon after they'd got a quarter-way through the rum, things started to happen. Eliza snorted rum out of her nose when a duck took off nearby and laughed about it, tears rolling, balls of her hands shucked into her eye sockets. Frank had only been able to smile with his top lip.

'You look like a pervert!' Eliza managed to squeak out between hysterics. And then it went quiet and they did some sitting still and Frank was worried that he might piss himself, even though he was sure he didn't need to go. Eliza's face was multi-sided. She had a new hair wrap that he hadn't noticed before, purple and black thread wound around in stripes just above her ear. Like a bandicoot tail. He'd never seen a bandicoot.

'Bandicoot,' he said out loud and Eliza looked at him as if she didn't know who he was. But she did. He reached out and touched the side of her boob, which he could see was next to her armpit where it belonged. She shrugged him off. Maybe they didn't know each other. He sweated. Had he just touched a stranger's boob? Would he go to jail? Her bandicoot tail twitched.

'My mum's had it off with your dad. Did you know that? That kinda makes us brother and sister.'

Frank waded back into the shore holding his fists tightly at his sides, that ache in his jaw from clenching. There were headaches some mornings and he'd tried going to sleep with a piece of bread in his mouth to stop the grinding, but had woken up choking. To shake off the feeling he ran the length of the bay, then turned and ran back. He kept on up and down until sunspots clouded over and he felt weak and steaming, then he slopped himself in the shallows like a hot dog.

4

On his sixteenth birthday Leon was confronted by a heart-shaped cake that his mother had baked. 'We can have a party, chicken, if you'd like,' she said in a way that made his toes grip the insides of his shoes. 'You can invite your friends, we can have maybe some sherry and cake.' To look at it, so bright and red, made him uncomfortable.

'Thanks, Ma, but I'd rather not, ta.'

'Why, sausage? Are you embarrassed?'

He cleared his throat. 'No, a few friends – man friends – want to take me out somewhere, is all. I'm just busy, and . . .' He let the 'and' fill the room.

'Oh? And who is taking you out?'

'Oh, you know, the usual crowd.' He tried hard to think of who that might be. 'Darren, Sid, Johnny. Des. Mark.' He said boys' names as they came to him.

'Darren Farrow? That boy who hit you?'

'That's a long time ago, Mum. It's fine.'

The last time he'd seen him, Darren had been leaning solidly against a girl behind the Four Square at night. He'd seen Leon looking and given him the finger, which he trailed down the girl's front and hooked under her shirt, all the while meeting Leon's eyes. His fat had turned hard and he was thought of as a dangerous kind of a bloke now. It was a pity that he'd never got around to running off to Korea. Leon imagined them having a drink together and it almost made him smile.

65

His mother shook her head, but cut the cake for him anyway, and he ate a piece in front of her. It had too much colouring in it and it was dense and far too sweet; it made his teeth sing. She smiled and cut herself a piece and left immediately to have her bath, leaving her slice dead on the table, and he went to chop the date slabs that had cooled on the shop counter.

A moment later a girl put her head round the door of the shop. 'Got some black pears for youse.'

She smiled as she bumped her way through the door, ricocheting it off her hip so that the bell rang several times before she got through. It took him a minute to recognise Amy Blackwell. She took up her space differently, as if she'd been taken apart and put back together in another way somehow. Her hair was piled on top of her head out of her face, her cheeks were pink from hefting the box of pears. She wore a pair of brown work overalls that were filthy, streaked with dirt and a pinch too small for her. She chewed gum and he could smell it on her breath. He looked at her chest in amazement. They'd just grown, like potatoes do.

'Thought you could make a tart out of them,' she said.

'Thanks,' he said, frowning hard at the pears – it seemed important to look interested in the fruit. Amy blinked and shifted her weight under the box. The chewing gum cracked in her mouth.

A woman came in wearing a hat and gloves, and frowned deeply when she saw Amy in her overalls. She averted her eyes and said, 'Four rock cakes and a white loaf, please.' And her eyes flickered across to Amy again, the corners of her mouth turned down. Leon put her bread in a bag and counted out her change. He could see Amy smiling with her box of pears, she was standing tall and straight, and she didn't move when the woman tried to make out that she was in her way. She just smiled wider and the woman stared back at him like she wanted him to say something. Leon looked away. She marched out of the shop, her handbag hung in the crook of her arm. Amy rolled her eyes and he smiled.

'Um, you think I could put this down somewhere?' He fumbled from behind the counter and tried to take the box from her. Putting his hands underneath it, he trapped her finger under his, and remembered the day at school with Briony Caldwell and the secret up yours. Amy Blackwell looked him in the eye and he shifted again and had the box, but all that was in his head was the smell of her, earth, gum, sweat and old pears. The coldness of her finger clamped under his.

She brushed a hair off her forehead. 'Ta,' she said. 'Haven't seen you around school in a while.'

'Stopped going. I pretty much run this place now.'

'How's that?'

''Sgood, thanks.'

'Great.'

'Yep.' Leon shifted his weight under the box.

'Well . . . see youse later then . . .'

He stood clutching the pears, feeling like a handicapped. He should have given her a piece of cake. He should have offered her a drink, she looked hot and tired. He should have called the woman that gave her a dirty look an old cow and he should have looked happier about the pears and he should have got her to stay longer, asked her out for his imaginary birthday drinks. But the smell, the fug of pear and dirt and spearmint, made a change in the room. Something like light, like white fresh icing. Amy's spearmint gum cleared all the tubes and passages inside him, and the cold dark something had gone from the door, he'd felt it leave. He blinked a few times as the feeling faded. The warm smell of bread and cake seemed stronger, like he hadn't realised it before. It was a lovely smell.

On a piece of newspaper he squeezed sugar roses and thought

about what he would say the next time she came into the shop. He paid more attention to his work, he perfected his cherry slices, took minute care about the placement, the overlap of strawberries on the gateau, the thickness of the gelatin glaze. He thought about how he would present them to her if she ever came in again with her light like sun in a copper pan.

His mother fitted her hair bun back in place, always wet from a bath. She bothered Leon now and again about going back to school. 'There's more to life than just cakes and sweets,' she'd say, but then would trail off as if something else had caught her attention. She'd rub her eyes and blink, then smile at him and walk into the back room where he would hear her looking through the bookshelves, flipping through the books one by one, picking things up and putting them down again, finding herself extra housework before the next bath time.

At the malt bar the kids dressed up like Yanks with spit in their hair and the girls had tits like paper hats. On his day off Leon passed the place by and went into the pub where, if he sat with a cherry soda for long enough, the barman would serve him a glass of beer. 'Cos I can see you're a drinker,' he said as he put it down. 'But anyone asks and you're pinching dregs.'

The men at the bar were dangerous-looking sorts, some missing a limb or two, one who only had a thumb and little finger left on his right hand, and he would press the thumb up to his nose and point at people.

That slow thick feeling crept up on him often, but it was all right in the pub. It didn't seem out of place that his mouth moved ten times slower than everyone else's when he talked, and after a drink the feeling just melted into the alcohol and no one could tell the difference anyway, because they were concentrating on getting the grog inside them before the pub closed. When he

68

swayed to the toilets, carefully placing one foot in front of the other, no one looked at him funny. When he returned, the man with the lobster claw slapped him on the back and handed him another drink, without ever turning to look at him or stopping his conversation with his friend.

'Thank you,' said Leon clearly and he slowed himself back to his seat.

Amy Blackwell did come again and this time she brought plums. He had been making the curd for a lemon tart, grating in the rind of a green lemon stroke by stroke and tasting in between. When the bell rang he barely broke his rhythm. 'Beauty,' he said, as he took the box of plums from her.

'How's it goin'?' she asked.

'Good,' he said, this time really looking at the plums, knocking one of them on to its back, feeling it give. They were the dark purple type and he thought of upside-down caramel plum tarts.

He got her some water and, with one hand leaning on the counter, she drained the glass and put it down heavily on the side, wiping her mouth on the back of her hand.

'How's school going?' he asked, as she put down the glass.

'It's dumb and nuts,' she answered, smiling, chewing her spearmint. 'They reckon they want us to learn how to iron.'

He moved back to the bowl. 'You've come in the nick of time,' he said. The room was rousing itself into a glow, he felt it at the back of his head, the lightness, the clearing. It made him stand straight, breathe deeply. He picked up a twist of pastry to dip it into the curd and absently wiped a finger round the outside edge of the bowl, collecting a stray thread of yellow that had trailed over the side. He offered her the pastry and the glow off her was sun off water. She leant forward but passed the pastry twist and took the other hand, holding it in both of hers. She put his lemon-covered finger in her mouth, standing on tiptoe over the counter.

69

His breath stayed in his chest and a breeze came into the shop, and he could smell the lemon and the plums and the scent of the skin of her throat.

She looked at him the way she had when he'd caught her finger under the crate of pears. That finger raised behind the sheet of paper at school. She drew her lips to the tip of his finger, letting them make a pop sound at the end. ''S pretty nice,' she said, dropping back on to her heels and wiping her mouth with the inside of her wrist. The shop bell rang and she left him, finger still held in mid-air, eyes round and big, the room a white flash in her wake.

Later that week he took a plum crumble and two spoons round to Blackwell's Grocers. They ate it in the dark of the storeroom, among the potato mud and the huntsman spiders, where even her breath smelt of wet earth. He could see the silhouette of her like a halo, and he put out a hand to touch the light on her hair and heard the unzipping of her overalls. The top of his nose prickled when she touched his skin, the warmth of her belly on his. She was hot inside so that he thought it might burn him but the white light that burst was cool and clearing like a swim in the sea. She laughed between deep breaths. They chewed gum afterwards, and there was the simple fact of it popping and cracking in the darkness, the white gum in their dark mouths.

'I like it here with you,' he said.

She rolled herself on to him so that her chin rested just below his chest. Her chin was sharp and it hurt, but he let it alone, because it would be nice to have a bruise to remember the moment.

'Well,' she said. 'That's pretty lucky.' She smiled and her chin dug at him.

'You make me feel less . . . hounded.'

'Explain,' she said without pausing. He didn't know what would come out if he tried to. The sound of something scritch-scratching on its claws up behind him, that slunk into the bath with his mother and that crept from bed to bed at night, curling up against the napes of their necks, making the house creak with its footsteps; the thing that licked at his fingers when he slept so that in the morning they were cold and damp.

'Like there's something trying to sneak up all the time – some kind of thing watching, like it might like to tear everything to pieces.'

'Huh,' said Amy. 'Like God, you mean?'

He snorted. 'No. Not like that.' There was a pause.

He felt the bruise her chin was making getting deeper and was about to roll her off when she said, 'Like something's watching?'

'Sort of. Yes.'

Amy nodded digging her chin deeper into him. 'I could understand that,' she said and he breathed out of his mouth.

'It's like it has these teeth and claws, and it wants to dig them into me, rip something out.'

'I know.' She lifted her chin and moved up his body. She lay so that her soft cheek was on his chest, which was more comfortable. He wondered what she meant.

She raised her head and hair covered one of her eyes. 'I know,' she repeated and he found that it was all he could ever have wanted.

When his father arrived one afternoon at the front door, his mother let out a shriek and clung on to him, and he held her tightly too, but stared over her shoulder at Leon. He was a small man all of a sudden, his eyes big as though the skin of his face had retreated. His shirt front ballooned with air when he bent too low and held his arms round Leon like he expected him to be shorter. Leon thought he might laugh, bit the inside of his cheek to stop himself and hunched down over his father and, not knowing what else to

71

do with his hands, held his father's skull against him and was scared it might crack.

That night all three of them ate together again and his mother cooked a chicken to celebrate. She wore a dress that puffed out in the skirt and made a crumpling noise when she moved. Her hair was dry and long down her back, and it occurred to him that she hadn't cut it since his father had left. When it was time to carve, his father nodded at him to cut, handing him the carving things. It was strange to hold the long knife in front of his parents, to feel the heat rise to his face in case he did it wrong. Chook carving had always been his father's job because he complained so much if Leon's mother did it. You had to get every slither of meat from the bones, had to turn the carcass over and scoop out the dark fatty meat of the chicken's back. The bones had to be clean, sucked white by the knife. He managed to separate the leg and wing from the left side, but found the right side troublesome. He could hear that he was splintering the bone.

'Turn it round, my darling,' said his father softly. He made a circle in the air with one finger and sure enough, when it had been turned he cut through the joint without difficulty. But the word 'darling' hung in the air, and it made Leon shrug into his shirt and look round the room as if there were something he needed to be doing that he couldn't remember. His father drank deeply from his wine glass and refilled it. The meal was quiet, but that was natural. They hadn't seen each other in a long time. The easy conversations about work, eyes half on a paper, half on the plate, were what he was used to with just his mother. Now her bright questions made the place quieter.

'Did you see many animals in the jungle?' was the first one that clattered awkwardly against the walls of the back room.

'Yes,' replied his father, swallowing a mouthful of potato,

'there were a fair few monkeys about. A jaguar as well, but I didn't see it.'

Both his parents smiled in the silence afterwards, then both looked at Leon and Leon smiled back. All three took a mouthful from their forks and all three chewed drily at the same time. Monkeys and a jaguar.

The meal was short and he felt guiltily relieved. His father said goodnight, that he was tired and his mother went after him, leaving the dishes on the table. All the vegetables from his father's plate were eaten, but the small amount of chicken he had taken from the dish lay untouched, nudged to the very edge of the plate.

In the morning his mother's hair still hung down her back. There was a glow on her, her shoulders were loose, her eyes full.

His father didn't come down for breakfast, or even later in the day.

'He's exhausted,' said his mother, her palms up like she was feeling for rain.

During that week news travelled up and down the main street that his father was back, and people asked after him at the counter.

'He's resting,' he told the butcher's wife who stood on tiptoe and tried to see past him into the empty kitchen. By the end of the week his mother looked worried. He saw her watching the ceiling, listening for movement up in the bedroom, but there was none.

'I think what we should do is throw a little party,' she said, 'just for his friends on the street.'

Leon made anzacs and a three-layered cake with pale-green icing. One of the sponge layers was pink, the other two soft white with coffee-coloured cream in between each one. He made a sugar doll of his father to go on top in his army greens, his hat folded up on one side, his fingers soldered to his forehead in a salute. He stood duck-footed and straight, tiny stripes on his shoulders, broad in the chest as he had looked the day he left. The model went in the centre of the cake and behind him Leon planted the Australian flag on a toothpick.

'That's pretty, chicken,' said his mother and he let it go, because her eyes were soppy.

As people arrived, they cooed over the cake, then hovered around the easy chair where his father sat, holding cups of coffee or small glasses of sherry. Leon kept his back to most of them, trying to look busy at the table, rearranging biscuits and filling glasses. He felt itchy in his smart clothes, which were now too small for him. He looked away from the kind type of smiles that everyone seemed to want to give, just before they glanced at their watches. He overheard the butcher complaining to his wife, 'It's more like a flamin' wake than a party,' and saw his wife stick a meaty elbow in his gut. There was a low rumble of talk in the room, enough people so that no one felt too awkward about the man who sat silent, drinking wine in his easy chair, half the size that they remembered him.

Amy Blackwell arrived with her mother and they stood together, her mother chatting loudly to the barber. Amy looked silly, her hair in strange sausage-looking ringlets, an ugly little purse that was attached to her wrist and a yellow smock that looked like a pillowcase. She shot him a low look, her eye, underneath her pointed eyebrow, was like the finger she'd given Briony. It was an easy joke, it laughed at the fancy dress her mother had put her in, it asked about his smoothed and parted hairdo, and the tight, itchy jumper he was wearing. He pressed his lips together and smelt the earth of the storeroom, and turned back to the table, spilling a few dots of orange cordial on the cloth. He smiled. Mrs Shannon sat quietly in the corner, her legs crossed. She watched Amy too from behind her small glass of sherry, and there was a look on her face that he couldn't figure out.

Soon after the cake was cut the butcher, who had taken charge of the sherry bottle, started singing 'Waltzing Matilda' and everyone joined in to hide how embarrassed they were.

Leon was clearing plates when the barber touched him on the shoulder. 'Let's take that old man of yours upstairs, son, whatd' ya say?' and Leon looked over at his father whose face was wet and pale from tears, whose mouth hung open and whose eyes were shut tight. The singers were turned away from him, all attending to the conducting butcher and his sherry bottle.

They got either side of him and no one turned round as they hefted him from the room. He was led easily up the stairs and Leon's heart beat fast in his throat, and the tears ran out of his father like a squeezed lemon but he made no sound. They laid him on the bed and Leon's mother appeared in the doorway. The barber took Leon's father's shoes off while they both stood there watching. He placed the shoes under the bed and pulled a cover up to his neck, then quickly put his hand to his father's cheek. As he left the room he smiled at Leon's mother and nodded.

'It's all a little bit much for him. Overwhelming,' said his mother. 'He's just a bit *overwhelmed.*'

Leon met Amy at Central Station and they took the slow train to Waterfall, and from there they hitched a ride to the beach. Her dress was loose round her shoulders and he saw the man who'd picked them up watching her neck as she looked out of the window. Leon stroked the neck with the backs of his fingers and it was cool. Amy smiled and rested her hand on his leg. The man averted his eyes and Leon sat a little straighter.

They walked along the shoreline with their naked feet white and sock-marked on the dark yellow sand. Leon rolled up his trousers and felt the wind comb through his hair. The air smelt sweet. A man fishing on the rocks in his underpants waved. This was where, from a little way off, they could have looked like a regular married couple out for a stroll under no obligations from their parents, nothing to worry about but themselves and the business of pushing back the dark, pushing into each other and pushing forward the bright feeling, the warmth and the round salty taste of each other. They tucked themselves under a hustle of Banksia trees next to a creek that ran dark lines into the sand. They rested their feet on the polished stones of the creek bed and lay back, drinking from bottles of beer that Leon had bought from the pub.

'How about a swim?' said Amy, already standing and pulling him up with her.

'Haven't got anything to swim in.' In truth, he could barely swim in a pool, let alone the white froth and glassy-looking waves that sprayed out at the land when they tumbled. The noise of a drum roll. She was a big red smile, laughing at him as he tried to pull her back, slipping out of his hands and racing down to the water, while he was suddenly slow, unable to talk. She went in dress and all, and she dived into a wave and was gone, and he knew that he would never see her again, that some dark moving animal from underneath had taken her and that there was nothing to do. He stood in the shallows, stricken, not breathing, that coldness was back, it lurked underwater as well. And then she was up, bursting up like a snakebird, shaking her hair that ran down on all sides of her. Leon lifted his arms at her, and she laughed again and let herself fall backwards into the foam of a large wave, gone again, a shadow under the surface. When she came out, her dress sticking and showing her brown thighs, and how the tendons at the back stood out, she was still laughing at him.

'You shoulda come in, Collard, it's sweet in there!' She draped wet arms round his neck and when they kissed her face was cold and salt water streamed down her. They drew apart and she said, 'You gotta swim if you come to the beach. It's the rules.' And she bowled him over, hooking her ankles behind his knees so that they fell together in the shallows, and the coldness was gone and they laughed, rolling around with the sand in the creases of their clothes scratching quietly against their skin, and the man fishing on the rocks looked over and Leon could see, even from far away, that he was laughing too.

The picnic was sugar bananas, peaches and treacle tart. A peach warmed by the sun ran juice down their chins and the treacle tart sweated, making the syrup thin so it slid off the knife, got in the webs of their fingers and underneath the ridges of their lips. They ate everything, slowly dipping their hands into the food bag, lazily peeling the skin from a soft peach with their teeth. They talked about things he'd never realised he wanted to know. She told him how she broke her collarbone jumping out of a tree and he showed her the burn mark on the inside of his wrist that he'd got as a kid from 'messing with cakes that didn't concern him'. He wished he had a bigger injury to show her, especially when she offered him her clavicle, got him to run a finger along the bone, feel the small ridge where it had healed.

'I'd like to open a tart shop with you,' he said, skating his fingers across her throat. 'You with the fruit, me with the pastry.' He'd meant it to be lightly said, a joke, but he could see it all of a sudden, like it had already happened. He opened his mouth to test a shop name, Amy's Fruit Pies, could see it in yellow lettering on black, could hear the sound of their own shop bell, but she stood up with her still damp hair in a pile on her head. She looked feral, like she'd just stepped out of the bush, her canines stood out against her bottom lip.

'Anyway,' she said, brushing dirt from the seat of her dress. 'I'd get fat from all those cakes.' He held his hand where it was, pretending she was still next to him. With uncharacteristic deli- cacy she found a bit of wrapper in her pocket and neatly stuck her chewing gum into it, where she folded it over on itself. She looked at him and smiled brightly.

'I don't think you're the type to get fat,' he said and she laughed loudly, but she turned away from him, looking for somewhere to put her gum.

'I'm going away soon,' she said, tucking her dress underneath her and sitting down again. He felt something dangerous creeping behind him.

'How soon? Where?' He kept his voice quiet.

'Dad reckons I need a finishing school. I'm off up to Brisbane. To get finished.'

'How long will that take?'

She lay back again with her eyes closed, her arms all over the place about her head, her drying hair spread like syrup. 'It takes as long as it takes.'

He saw that he was not allowed to ask anything else, so instead he touched her hair at the ends where it was cold and soft. She opened one eye and smiled at him, a big wide smile that was sticky at its edges. She rolled over and pushed him down into the bark-smelling grass of the creek bank.

His father decided one day to reclaim the kitchen and Leon bit his lower lip watching him move things about, making things different. He was drunk and his hands trembled when he poured the flour, he banged thickly into the sideboard with his hip. Leon's mother looked like she'd been holding her breath. They made a very basic bread, working in silence, but not long after they'd started someone came in needing a wedding cake, and needing it quickly. The dog had got into the first one. His father set to baking straight away without making notes, or asking for any particulars. Leon didn't ask why, he just followed instructions, which were quiet and few. His father didn't sift the flour, or weigh anything. Leon saw half an eggshell crushed heavily into the lumpen batter. Where normally his father would have divided the mixture between four or even five round tins to stack up on each other, he scraped the lot into one large square loaf tin, usually reserved only for Heavy Date Tractor Cake, and put it straight into a cold oven without checking the time or weighing it.

After an hour he took it out again and dropped it on the side with a bang. There would be no decorations. 'It's enough that we have flour,' he said, when Leon asked. His father went to the pub, leaving the cake steaming on the counter. Feeling like a traitor Leon pushed a skewer carefully into the guts of the cake. It came out yellow with unmixed eggs.

His mother stood in front of the cake and wrung her hands, patted down her hair.

Leon started from scratch. He made an orange and poppy-seed cake, five tiers tall. He painted the whole thing in peach jam before applying a thin royal icing finish. On to the clean sheet of white, he painted stalked clementines and ivy. He made two pairs of figurines and chose the best, the most dignified beautiful couple. The spare couple lost because the bride shifted a little to one side, one hip higher than the other. There was something sarcastic about her smile and, if he was honest, he liked her too much to give her away. Perhaps, objectively, her breasts were a hair too large, her bottom too high and round. Perhaps there was something of Amy Blackwell about her. When the cake was collected, without his father having seen it, no one spotted the difference. His mother put a hand on Leon's shoulder but said nothing.

He had come to the fruit shop with a list of reasons she could give to her parents, but when he started talking she popped her chewing gum, sucked of all flavour but holding the warmth of the inside of her mouth, into his and it shocked him into silence.

An elderly woman stared at the two of them, and Amy smiled and stared back until the woman looked away.

'There's no point,' she whispered, 'it's paid for now anyway. Besides, it means I get away from them.' She touched his cheek and the old woman cleared her throat. 'Oh, for God's sake,' said Amy loudly, standing up tall behind the counter, and the old woman left the shop in a flurry of shopping bags and disgust. Amy rolled her eyes. 'Well, I'll be hearing about that later.' She smiled at Leon, who could only think that she was leaving.

And soon after, she was gone as simply as she had arrived in the classroom, her finger held up against the sheet of paper. A brown-paper bag holding two peaches that were just on the turn, with the smudged and stained note.

See you when I'm finished x

He felt a wind at his back and turned in time to see nothing at all. Something dragged at his insides, low in his chest, and he took the train to Waterfall and thumbed down to the beach. The weather was filth and no one fished from the rocks. The dark lines made by the creek on the sand looked scummy, it could have been sewage, and a wind picked up loose sand and hurled it at the backs of his legs. There was a weight of disgust on his chest.

After the wedding-cake episode his father stayed mainly in his room, ducking out to the pub regularly for another bottle.

His mother's hair was back in its bun. 'Going to town,' she announced one morning. 'Get a hairdo, have a bit of mummy fun. You'll be alright, chicken?'

He nodded and smiled, wondering what exactly she meant, seeing as he ran the shop alone as it was. Her face was pale and so he tried not to look annoyed. The bell rang with her departure.

Not long afterwards his father came down the stairs and made for the door. 'There's some things I need to get done today,' he said, wrapping half a loaf of breakfast bread in a tea towel and putting it in a paper bag.

'I made some croissants, if you'd like one,' Leon offered.

'Bread is good enough. Thank you. Must get going now. Have a good day.'

'You too.'

He waited until his father had gone out of the door and disappeared round the corner, before jumping the counter and turning the shop sign to closed. He locked up and ran down the street after him, his feet slapping hard on the bitumen. He followed at a distance and was led all over the suburbs. They circled every block of Parramatta, leaving no road uncrossed. They went down every alleyway and under every tunnel, over every bridge. A few times his father went into cul-de-sacs and Leon had to wait anxiously behind a bush for him to come out again, always with his head down, so that he could have stood right in front of him and he wouldn't have noticed. Finally, with the sun way over west, they came to the train station, which was, on a straight walk, only ten minutes from the shop.

For the first time his father raised his head. He sat on a bench on the platform. Trains entered and left the station but his father's only movement was to take a hip flask out of his pocket and bring it again and again to his mouth. People were met and seen off, they crowded the platform, then left it and crowded it again. The loudspeaker announced trains to Waterfall, Green Point, Central. People were met and kissed, were waved off, left with luggage, left with nothing. People waited and ate chips, smoked cigarettes, drank milk drinks and left all the smells behind when they went.

In the middle of it all sat his father on a red bench, looking straight ahead, bread tucked safely into the crook of his arm, fingers pressed white on his flask. Leon left him there and walked home. All the way he felt something following, but each time he turned there was nothing to see.

He wondered what to say to his mother. When his father came in, he sat at the kitchen table with a newspaper that looked fished out of a bin. He unfolded it in front of him and did not turn the pages, but stared hard at it, drinking his way steadily through a bottle of sweet sherry. Leon kneaded dough for the next morning's bread and didn't know what it meant. His mother came home and she had a new hairdo, shorter with a wave over one eye. She wore lipstick and a camel wool dress, even in the heat.

'You look pretty, Maureen,' his father said, looking up for the first time from his paper. His mother glowed like she'd won the thirty-dollar lotto.

In the mornings, with the sun bright in the kitchen, the place looked dark, but he knew it was not. It was like he'd been in the sun too long and burnt his eyes. His chest throbbed and his stomach felt tight; something sat on his ribs, peering down and breathing foully in his face.

He kissed a girl behind the boat shed at the harbour and he felt it die a small bit. But she was not Amy, and she took his hands from her breasts and straightened her handbag and her hair with one hand. He walked home alone, feeling the terrible thing rolling over and dragging itself after him in the dark.

That night he woke to his mother pulling on his sleeve. She put a finger to her lips and motioned for them to get under the bed. She's gone mad, thought Leon, but he did it anyway because she looked scared.

'What are we doing?' he whispered close to her ear.

'It's not good to wake them up when they sleepwalk,' she said and on the landing the floor creaked. The whites of her eyes shone in the dark and Leon saw the naked feet of his father pace slowly round the room. The air under the bed was thick and sweet. The feet moved close to the bed and Leon wondered if they were found, and then he saw that on his father's right foot the two smallest toes were missing. What was left was ugly grey skin. The feet receded and left the room, and they slept there under the bed. In the morning his mother made pancakes and his father sat silently at the breakfast table.

'At least he's getting out of the house, chicken,' his mother said to him as they watched his father lope down the street, away from them, his towelled bread held tightly to his body. He would go out until lunchtime and then come back, so that his mother could run her fingers through his hair, straighten his collar and sit him down to a sandwich or a piece of cake. After lunch he would go out again, mumbling something about looking for work, but the work was never found, and with Leon running the place they had no need of extra money anyway. When his father returned he'd be wobbly and thick-mouthed, looking at his tea as though it were dangerous, picking and sorting through the food rather than eating it. Then the routine became worn and thin in the middle so that he returned later and later for lunch, glassy-eyed and drunk, and then not at all, only for supper, when he would be anxiously and darkly stared at by his wife, and he'd look at the floor, his eyes as wide as they could open, his breath hard in the back of his throat. Those nights he had to be herded to bed by Leon's mother and she said quietly, 'hup, hup,' as they climbed the stairs. Leon watched out of the corner of his eye as his mother touched his father's face, only to have him flinch away; then her sad look made him pat her hand, but quickly like she would burn him.

Leon bought a used Holden off a mechanic in town and parked it proudly outside the shop. His mother frowned at it. 'It's ugly in brown, chicken,' she said, but she took it to visit a friend in Dorrigo whom she had never visited before, or mentioned. She left with a larger suitcase than she needed and she kissed them both more than was necessary, her eyes frantic and sad. The bad thing hunkered down in Leon's guts and the shop seemed so dark that at times he had to find his way around the kitchen by touch.

His father stopped coming home for supper. His mother came back from her break in Dorrigo and she seemed to have made up her mind to fill up the silence in the house.

'Mrs Shannon's pregnant again.'

'How about a walk just the two of us?'

'How about a sandwich?'

'Glass of tea?'

But the quiet answers from his father stopped. His mother tried cooking exotic meals; curried fish, pork in aspic. Anything with meat in it was not eaten and anything that was eaten had no effect on his father's expression. He started to drink beer alongside his wine. She showed him photographs that she thought might interest him, cut-out from the newspaper – Marilyn Monroe, an elephant swimming, a huge shark washed up on the northern beaches – but he would not look. He stopped lifting his head when she came into the room. He would not look at Leon's mother, but sometimes Leon would catch him staring at him, as if they had never met before, and he would have to leave the room, get into the kitchen and lose himself in a cake.

Leon followed his father again and this time his route to the train station had extended. It took them until dark to get there, going through West Parramatta, every street, into Rydalmere and through the subway, always with the same heavy steady stride, with no breaks, apart from once when his father disappeared into a public convenience, but Leon couldn't be sure if he had used it or just walked in and out of each cubicle. It seemed his father was taking a giant run-up at something, like he might try to jump over the harbour.

One day he did not come back from the train station. He was not back that night and he didn't turn up in the morning. Leon's mother sat around in her housecoat and slippers. She drank sweet tea and stared at the ceiling as if her eyes were full of liquid and she had to keep them tilted upwards so as not to spill any.

Leon sold bread in the usual way. He watched his mother out of the corner of his eye. He tried putting his arms round her but she waved him off, then pulled him back and pushed him away again. It wasn't till the end of the week that he saw that the sugar figurines of his parents were gone. His mother saw him looking at the space and smiled feebly. 'He's always been a fragile man, even before the war. We propped each other up.' She held her face in her hands and was silent a long while. 'I'm sorry, my chicken,' she said. 'I've missed him so much and he wasn't even gone.'

He didn't know where to put the look she gave him.

5

Frank liked the idea of living off the land, and he pictured himself pickling beetroot and biting into sweet capsicum and sun-warmed tomatoes. He'd have an area for experimentation, for exotics – prickly pears, artichokes, watermelons.

He paced out a vegetable garden, planting four sticks as markers in the corners and later in the day browsed the seeds in the camping shop. He took tomatoes, lettuce, leeks, curly beans, spiny cucumber and marrow. He bought a tin watering can and a set of different-sized forks and trowels. The woman did nothing but nod and smile this time, for which he was grateful.

On the drive home, he stopped short of the cane, turned off the engine and walked into the shade of the blue gums, to get a breath of their coolness and have a look around at what was his. Hot sheets of eucalyptus rose from the ground, and he thought of the creek where he and Bo had found the fat pale yabbies, Bo boasting about how he could put his hand underwater and come up with five clinging, one on each finger. If he had wanted to.

The evening he'd left Eliza by the jacaranda tree with the half-empty bottle of rum and crying because he'd shouted, because he'd *gone all aggressive*, Bo turned up with a bleeding ear and a ropy sleeping bag. 'I gotta go away, Franko,' he said. They'd walked out of the suburbs without speaking, Bo's ear still bleeding down his big neck, Frank with a sleeping bag, two stale loaves and a bagful of the dark syrup stout his old man had taken to drinking, and the gasoline tins that banged against the back of his knee as he walked. They drank steadily and thumbed a lift in the back of a truck with an old cattle dog, which was on the nose, but friendly. The dog put its head in his lap and he played with its cold ears. His old man had been face down at the kitchen table as he left, breathing wetly.

They'd walked the last few miles to Mulaburry, stopping now and again to huff on a gasoline-wet tea towel, then ambling on, blinking in silence, their eyes on the sky, which was black and gold in places. Road trains blasted by them in the dark and Frank could feel the wind from them parting his hair. At Mulaburry beach they put their sleeping sacks on the sand and built a fire to keep off the biting things. Neither of them wanted the feel of a roof over his head.

Bo looked at him in a way that Frank could see he'd already got old on the inside. 'Can't hear nothing from me ear,' he said. 'Reckon she's bust it for good.'

Frank opened a fresh bottle and handed it to him. Things beyond the gold ring of the fire moved in and out like black sea anemones.

'Reckon you should get someone to look at that?' He hoped not – he didn't know where they would find a doctor and he didn't want to be thinking about it. Not now.

'Nah. The other one's still going.' Bo made a honk that might have been a laugh. The waves rumbled on. 'I hit her back.' Bo took a dramatic swig of the bottle.

'Cripes, mate,' was all Frank could think to say. 'Well, cripes. It had to happen one day.'

Bo looked at his knuckles. He smoothed them over his lips and closed his eyes.

The air underneath the trees was hot and sweet. Even in the relative cool of the bush, Frank could feel the sun up there crackling in the gum leaves. His feet remembered the sponge of the gum-leaf floor; his back remembered sleeping on it. His wrists remembered the mosquitoes, and his mouth the creek and its crawling cold water.

He rested a hand on the bark of a tree and felt it warm and smooth in the centre of his palm. He felt his skin growing back to cover old bones that had ripped out. Then he felt eyes on him and his skin prickled, and the hair on his arms and his neck stood out. 'Get out of it, Creepin' Jesus,' he said out loud but that only made the feeling worse and he walked quickly to his truck.

Back at the shack he saw that the stove door had swung open again. Not a crack this time: it was wide open like someone had had to manoeuvre a pie dish in there. He stood in front of it. It must have been a tick the stove had, the metal expanding in the heat of the sun. Either way, something had made a meal of the guts, the inside of the oven was licked clean.

When Bob turned up with a chicken-shaped gift wrapped in newspaper and leaking bloodily from one end, Frank realised it must be close to Christmas.

'Frank!' called Bob, pitching the parcel at him like a football. He caught it, letting it swing a little behind his body, taking it deep. 'An invitation for you. From the wife. She sends you this chook to sweeten the deal – hasn't been plucked. If you'd rather spend Christmas with a plucked and gutted bird you'd better give that back an' come an' stay with us the holiday.'

The package was still warm and he had the feeling the chook had been killed just before Bob left home as an afterthought for a good joke. He looked down at the bundle, black and white and red all over.

'Well?' demanded Bob.

'Love to.' Christmas had not occurred to him. 'Thanks.'

'Right,' said Bob, turning towards the car. 'You'd better chuck ol' Jozé back to me then.' He put his arms out ready to catch. Frank threw bleeding Jozé back high and tall, and the chook landed in Bob's arms. He clambered back inside the cab, putting the newspaper bird on the passenger seat, ignoring the blood that already stained the seat cover.

'I'm telling you this for your own good – I got a kid who's seven and won't put up with visitors without presents.' He started the engine.

As he began to back away Frank called, 'What time should I come round?'

'Come round early – we open presents after breakfast.'

When the van kicked up dust and noise, and Bob's arm lazed out of the window, his usual long still wave, Frank shouted after him, 'Hey! Hey! What day is it?' but Bob didn't hear.

Down at Crazy Jack's Toy Basement he was faced with a wall of stuffed animals, a wall of dolls and a wall of things in khaki, an army made of plastic. Inspecting the firing mechanism on a civil-war cannon, he put his hand up to his face and said loudly, 'Buggeration.' When he took his hand away a small girl was watching, and he smiled and looked around hoping her mother hadn't heard. The kid picked up a stuffed dragon and backed away from him like she was dealing with a hostage situation. He smiled wider to show that he was friendly, and the girl turned on her heel and ran away down the next aisle.

He'd forgotten to ask if the Haydons' kid was a boy or girl. What kind of an arsehole was he anyway? Choosing was hard enough – and there didn't seem to be much in the way of a neutral toy. He stepped back from the dolls with bendable legs and breathed through his fingers.

A shop assistant with pink lip gloss to match her pink pinafore came over. 'Can I help?'

89

'I have to buy something for a seven-year-old.'

'Boy or girl?'

'Not sure yet.'

She looked at him strangely, but smiled. 'Well, why don't you pick a boy's toy *and* a girl's toy, so when you make up your mind which one the kid is you can give it the appropriate gift.'

He liked her use of the word appropriate and saw that her hair was thick and a strand curled at her throat. 'That's a good idea – you think you could help me pick out something for the girl – I like this cannon if it's a boy.'

She eyed the cannon in his hand. 'That's kind of crappy, don't you think?'

He looked down at the toy. 'I suppose it is.'

'How about this?' She took down some sort of disc that shot out of a bow-type attachment. 'It whistles as it flies.'

'Does it?'

'Sure.'

'Well, I'd better have it then.'

The badge on the girl's rounded front read 'My Name Is Leonie', with a happy face at the end of it. My Name Is Leonie saw him looking at her badge and puffed out her chest. Softening her voice and picking up a pornographic-looking Barbie doll she said, 'And this is the kind of thing that little girls like.' She handed it to Frank with a glossy smile and walked saucily back down the aisle to the till.

He parked by the bay with the idea that he might read the paper in some cool spot, perhaps with the rocks as shade. There was no breath off the water as he ankled about in the shallows, absently scanning the paper. No chance of rain for Christmas Day.

LOCAL SWIMMER STILL MISSING

Come home for Christmas, pleads missing girl's father. Local girl and Home Counties swimmer Joyce Mackelly has been missing since Tuesday, 19 November. Joyce, fifteen, left her weekend job at the Blue Wren coffee shop in Mclean at 5.30 and was last seen hitch-hiking between Camel Bay and Rayners Island.

Poor bastard.

He turned the page and as he did a leaf slipped out and fell into the water. A grained photograph turned black in a wave and he scooped it up and put the pulp back between the pages of the newspaper, which he balled up. He hadn't really wanted to know anyway.

There had been nothing that he could even think of buying Bob and Vicky in town. Drink was the get-out clause; he could take them champagne or a crate of beer. It was stale, going to spend Christmas with this family who had taken him on like an old friend even with him acting mad as a coot. He should probably take some as well as a present. As he tumbled these thoughts over, he waded further out, so that the water seeped into his shorts and even though it was not particularly cool, it was better than nothing, and he sat down in the sea, the newspaper a wet rock in his fist. The waves were small and water swilled round his neck. Something surfaced a little way away, a lazy flop in the water. Mullet probably, this close to the river mouth. He kept his eyes on the spot and saw it surface again over to the right this time. A flash of belly. A biggish fish. It splashed again and at the same time something bumped his calf, and he nearly shot out of the water. Making the sound of a kicked dog, he saw that it was not a shark – he was sitting in a shoal and a blunt-headed mullet was nosing at the back of his knee. The tameness of the fish, the water thick with them and their oil-slicked backs and tin-can bellies chopped the waves. A flock of gulls appeared from behind the rocks and dived again and again, noisy white streamers into the torn-up water.

Must be a school of prawns going around kicking up mud, he thought, hands on hips, watching the spectacle. Next time he was in town he would pick up a net. The shoal moved to his left in front of the bream hole, where he saw the shells of untouched oysters, hundreds of them. He felt the sun cutting off the water and hitting his cheeks, and he waded over, feeling for his knife in his back pocket. Nothing said Christmas like a hatful of wet shells.

'Ta, Mum,' he said out loud as he gouged at the rocks.

It was too hot to sleep the night before Christmas and Frank lay on top of his sheet listening to a frogmouth bark and hiss in the banana tree. My Name Is Leonie and a smiley face. My Name Is Leonie's tongue wetted her bottom lip, which was glitter-pink and thick with plastic colour. She was something between a doll and a person; and less and less a person, the buttons on her pinafore stretched over her breasts. She had a long neck and the sound of her rucking up her pinafore rustled in the cane and came right into the room. She went on for miles, the gingham sliding over her acres of white thigh. She put a finger in her mouth. She put a finger in her knickers. She didn't wear knickers – no, she did, and she took them off slowly, again and again, her dress un-buttoned from the top and showed her pineapple-sized breasts. She held her vulva open and licked her pink lips. She sucked on a toy cannon as if it were a lolly stick.

The frogmouth barked.

She slipped the cannon inside and moaned in time with the banana tree. Her tits her snatch her lips.

He lay still in the still night and thought for a second he could smell gasoline. The frogmouth barked. A wind blew and he put the heels of his hands over his eyes and pressed until they ached.

The Haydons had a big house, lifted high up on flood stilts. A veranda ran the whole way round it, with faded hammocks and pot plants dotted about the place. Wind chimes hung silent in the heat. Vicky wore a fancy red Christmas dress that she swelled from, thick in the arms and thighs with a narrow waist, the kind you thought you could get your hands round. She wore the remainder of red lipstick and when she smiled there was a speck on her tooth. She smiled at Frank and held her arms high. 'Frank! Happy Christmas!' She moved forward to put the raised arms round him and planted a kiss, hard, on each cheek.

'Good to see you, Vicky. Happy Christmas to you too and thanks for having me over.'

Vicky waved her hand in front of her face like there was a smell, and from behind the shield of her legs a dark-haired child peered, clutching a large unpeeled carrot. The kid watched him from underneath a heavy brow. It was impossible to tell what sex it was.

'Mum's drunk,' said the kid, who was swatted on the head.

'It's Christmas, Sal, your mum's allowed a drink at Christmas – this is Sal – the youngest. Now, what'll it be, Frank? A Bucks Fizz? Bob's just mixing up a batch.'

His stomach turned – youngest? Bob'd only mentioned the one kid – what if they were both boys? He couldn't give a Barbie doll to a boy. And what the hell sex was this first kid anyway?

'That'd be great, thanks, Vicky.' He worried he was overusing her name. He supposed Sal must be a girl, because Sal was short for Sally, though you wouldn't know to look at her. She was a Stig of the Dump.

Walking up the steps of the veranda, he tried to catch Sal's eye, tried to make some kind of tongue rolling or friendly wink, but the kid was having none of it and frowned deeper still at his efforts, holding up the carrot as if using it as some kind of protective talisman.

Bob was squeezing oranges, or rather a robot was doing it for him. 'Vick's present to me,' he said proudly, placing a whole orange in the shoot and following its progress down the perspex tube; watching it get pulped and ground into liquid.

'That's very impressive, Bob,' said Frank, 'my gift is a bit less useful.' He handed the plastic bag to Vicky, who nosed into it hungrily.

'Aw, Frank, youse shouldn' have! Look, Bob, oysters!'

He wasn't sure if she was being overly polite, or was drunk, or really liked oysters, but it seemed a pretty good reaction regardless.

'Goodonya, mate,' said Bob, not taking his eyes off the journey of the oranges. 'Oysters make me sick,' said Sal.

It became clear pretty soon that there was no other child – or if there was, it had moved out and wasn't interested in spending Christmas with its parents. Either way, Frank gave Sal the doll and relaxed. The kid seemed quite taken with it, he thought. She disappeared, holding it with a look of having a great many important things to get done.

The three of them set about shucking oysters and Bob told a long story about his brother that ended cheerfully with, 'An' you could see right through the hole in his hand!'

They sat and ate and gabbled like a troop of magpies. It wasn't two o'clock before they were all drunk and red in the face.

'For you,' Vicky said, wobbling over to him and grasping his hand. She pulled him over to the window, yanking him like he was an unwilling child. He glanced at Bob to see what he thought of his wife grabbing hold of someone she hardly knew, but Bob sat in his easy chair, a red paper crown square on his head, beaming at the two of them. Vicky pointed outside at the yard full of chickens. Two young chicks were cordoned off. 'Kirk and Mary,' she explained. 'Only runty ones, I'm afraid, but they should come good.'

Frank looked at the chickens, a bubble of panic growing in his chest at the idea of caring for the birds.

'Jesus, Frank! Don't look so pale!' crowed Vicky, pleased by his shock. 'It's a piece of piss – feed 'em and stop the foxes eating 'em, and you'll be in eggs up to your balls.'

Frank blinked. 'Far out, that is a generous gift. I . . . thank you.'

'Can't live on farmland without chooks. Who'd wake youse up in the morning?'

'Why Mary and Kirk?'

Bob swilled his Bucks Fizz from cheek to cheek, then swallowed hard. 'Sal names 'em. See all those chooks?' He pointed to the yard where about a hundred chickens shucked and scratched and ruffled. 'Sal names each an' every one. This arvo, we'll be sitting down to Simon.'

Sal appeared in the doorway and looked darkly at her father. She held her carrot close to her chest; it wore the pink jumpsuit that Barbie had worn earlier. Barbie the doll did not reappear for the rest of the day, but Barbie the carrot got by very well, with a seat to herself at the dinner table.

'Who's yer friend?' Frank asked when they had all sat down and Simon had been quartered. She fixed him with one large black eye and said nothing. Vicky rolled on her hips to face him, poking her tongue in her cheek to dislodge some food stuck there. 'That,' said Vicky, 'that is a carrot.' She looked at Sal and Sal looked at her plate, kicking her legs under the table. 'Ain't it, sweetie-pie?'

'Vick,' Bob said quietly.

Vicky looked down at her plate. 'Sorry, Sally, love,' Vicky said, and she reached out across Frank and squeezed her daughter's fist as it gripped its knife. Vicky tutted a little and leant back in her chair.

Frank surprised himself by standing up and on standing realised he had become pleb-head drunk. He held up his glass. 'Thank you for having me,' he said like a schoolboy, 'and Happy Christmas!' which made everyone apart from Sal cheer, although she sat a little straighter in her chair and watched, the hugeness gone from her eyes.

'Happy fuckin' Christmas!' roared Vicky and they all snorted with laughter, even Sal, who couldn't resist the word.

Vicky was telling a story and Frank couldn't recall where it had started or what it was about, all he could see was the three of them, the small family feeding together, heads low to their plates, they all held their forks with a cocked little finger. A fogged memory crept in of a time at the shack when his mum had still been alive. The way he remembered it, when they were all three inside, the shack had taken on their smells and noises, soaked it up: the big hooked fish, the endless hand-washing and table-wiping, the filleting, oyster shells, clams in milk and school prawns, until the floor and the ceiling had smelt of burnt seawater.

In the early dark evening his mother started a game of bloody beetle and the three of them kicked back, inhaling the fug of themselves, eating shellfish with hammers and pokers. In bed, he'd found a dry fish scale stuck to his face, a mother-of-pearl toenail, and he'd put it under his tongue for safe keeping, for luck.

From nowhere the words came out of him, 'Still no word on the Mackelly girl?'

'Nah.' Bob pushed the paper crown on his head back with his fork. 'Poor Ian. Cripes I'd hate to be in his shoes.'

Vicky refilled her glass and drank from it deeply.

Stupid thing to say at Christmas. He felt his food go dry in his mouth. 'Probably just gone walkabout, don'tcha think? Teenage girl, small-town-type thing?'

'Probably,' said Bob unconvincingly. 'Still, that's not much use to her parents on Christmas Day.'

'Guess not.' There was more quiet. 'I made a break for it when I was a grommet. Headed for China.' It was a lie, he realised once he'd said it.

'China eh? What's so good about China?'

Vicky laughed. 'I'd run away to China just for those little deep-fried mussel parcels they do down at China Jack's,' she said, taking her nose out of her glass and focusing on the ceiling.

The skin of her throat looked soft.

'Be easier, don'tcha think, just to pop down to China Jack's?' Bob said.

'Well,' said Vicky, standing and clearing the plates. 'If my cheap-as-chips husband would take me out there once in a while I wouldn't have to run off with the bugger.'

She winked at Frank.

'Oh, I see!' boomed Bob. 'It's not just his China food you're after? It's Jack's sprats as well!' Bob roared at his own joke, thumping the table with his fist and Frank smiled, watching Vicky box the crown right off her husband's head.

In the early hours of the next day, long after Sal had gone to bed of her own accord, Frank made to leave. He patted Bob's shoulder; Bob was slumped in an armchair, a beer warmed in his hand, and the black stub of a joint rested blunt and dead between his fingers. His eyelids drooped. Vicky showed Frank to the door and put her hands under his armpits in a strange close hug.

He knew what was going to happen, because he could feel her breath on his neck. He had the feeling that anything that happened that night wouldn't be counted and what was the harm in kissing a woman on Christmas night, with her husband and child in the next rooms?

But he made sure his eyes were fixed well over her head when they untangled, and even though some of her hair caught in his mouth he didn't look down to her face. He may have kissed her forehead lightly and he may have wanted to kiss her mouth but instead he slurred, 'Nice Christmas, Vick, ta for the chooks,' and he wobbled to his Ute in no fit state to drive, and over-gently put his charges, Kirk and Mary, clucking and sleepy, on the passenger seat while Vicky watched from the open lit doorway, so that he could see the dark shapes of her thighs through her dress. As he backed clumsily out of the drive, he saw the naked body of Barbie, folded in half and stuck through a hole in the incinerator.

6

Mrs Shannon had her hair cut like Jackie Kennedy. The baby Leon's mother had predicted never showed up and nothing was said. He always gave her something free and he wondered if it wasn't for the free treat that she kept returning, but for the chance to be given something. She was beautiful, even though the skin of her chest was dark and stretched from the sun, and sometimes underneath her sunglasses you could see flesh swollen so that it nearly touched the glass of the lens. It didn't stop her from wearing a green gauze ball gown just to walk down to the shops. She turned up one time with her arm in a sling, home-sewed stitches in her lip.

'How's the cake trade, kiddo?'

'Just fine, thanks, Mrs Shannon.'

'I'll have a lamington, please, darl.' And she held the money in her hand, fragile wrist pointing up, an insistence in the jiggle of her fingers. 'Go on, take the money. I'll be bleeding you dry.'

'What's the use living opposite a bakery if you can't have a biscuit for free?' and he gave her a florentine, not a lamington, because he knew that was what she really liked. He wondered what he would do if Mr Shannon ever came into the shop, but he'd never seen him. He'd never even seen the man walk out of his house.

The rest of the year was wet. The cake shop steamed up on the inside. His mother spent time running errands that involved being out of the shop and he wondered if she was retracing the steps his father had taken all around the city. He didn't follow her to find out, just waited for something to happen. When she came home, she was pale and thin, and she looked like she would be thrown down in a breeze. She started having the long baths again, but this time there was no steam that filled up the top rooms. He felt the water once as it drained away after she had got out and it was cold.

After the rain came an envelope with his father's handwriting on it. He watched from the back room while she stood at the counter and opened it gently, unsticking the paper flap, not tearing, looking frightened of what might be inside. She looked at the letter, her face blank, then the door chimed and she was gone down the street, melting between the parked cars. She left the letter on the table, thin blue paper folded once. There was a dot at the top of the page, like he'd been about to write but couldn't think of what to say. And then there was his signature and beneath that, in place of where there might have been a cross for a kiss, another dot, this one bigger than the first, the ink blooming from the pen nib and staining through to the other side. The postmark read something northern and when his mother returned a few hours later she took that, not the letter, to tuck into the book she kept by her bed.

The next morning Leon put a preserved cherry on top of a cake and smiled. When he looked up, he saw Mrs Shannon walk by, a scarf round her face, pulled low over her eyes. She walked like she was only wearing one shoe and then she was gone. His mother appeared in the doorway, her hat pinned to her head, a grey suitcase in her hand, and even though it was warm out she wore her long wool coat. She put a gloved hand in his hair and there was her wet face again, her nose like a beak. She dropped her arm. 'And suddenly you're a grown-up man,' she said. 'I have to go away, chicken,' and even though he'd been expecting something like this, he thought she'd insist on him going with her, thought he might have to put his foot down and explain that someone had to keep the shop running. That maybe he could help her look on a Sunday, call up a few lodging houses and give a description of his father. She took a tissue out of her pocket and rubbed her nose with it. 'I'll write, of course, when I find him, and then we'll see.' Leon felt the smile that was fixed on his face. It hurt his teeth. 'You understand, chicken?' He nodded and really he did understand, he could see it in the lines on her face, that to her it was more important to find a man who'd been missing even when he was sitting beside her in his easy chair.

In bed, Leon lay awake in the empty house. There was the tick of the bedside clock, the beat of his heart and the terrible sound of something coming for him, hoof and claw and tooth grinding in the dirt. Scritch-scratch, snuffle.

Weeks went by and sleeping was still strange and restless, but his ears didn't strain to hear anything that might be going on in another room; he didn't anticipate the arrival of his thin-voiced mother, didn't leave his spare pillow under the bed any more. There was no one to watch him close up early for a date or to watch him bring a girl back. He did it a few times, but he couldn't sleep with the girl in his bed. He found himself sitting watching her as she slept, willing her to wake up and leave because looking at her lying there he felt nothing at all. Even when they were beautiful there was nothing, hard though he looked for it. So he stopped bringing them back and sometimes he closed up the shop a little early to spend more time in the Parramatta Hotel with the men who looked darkly into their drinks as they laughed over old stories. The man with the claw hand came over and sat with him one afternoon. 'You're Collard's son,' he said and even if Leon had not been he wouldn't have been able to say no.

101

'He's gone off,' Leon said, not sure what the man wanted.

'I know. Best thing for it. If a man doesn't want company he wants to be on his own.'

'Suppose. Mum's gone to find him.'

'Seen a lot, that man. Cousin of mine was in the same camp.'

'Is he here?' He wanted to see what other people looked like – how they handled it.

'Nah, mate. He's not.' Leon took a long drink from his glass and hoped the man would change the subject. 'Bit of advice, son,' he said, waving his claw over his drink. 'Try and forget about it. No one wants to hear about it, no one wants to talk about it, no one wants to remember it. Let them alone to thrash it out. It's a healing thing. Think about other things, there's plenty to go round, plenty of other things need a good bit of thought put into. What about this new lot of oriental types and their Ho-Chee-Man? Just round the corner, mate. Worry about that while you drink ya beer.'

'Right,' said Leon, and the man winked and got up to return to his friends. As six o'clock approached and the drinking speeded up, Leon watched the claw man laughing and talking with his friends, and he thought it was good to be away from the hopeful eyes of girls. He wondered what would happen to his parents if they found each other again.

A postcard arrived. The picture on the front showed a drawing of a child in a red and white striped swimsuit and armbands up round his shoulders. He had his hands on his hips, his trunks thrust forward, standing in front of a photograph of a beach somewhere. The child's eyes were blue and his irises reflected a smiling sunshine. His cheeks were red and humped in front of his eyes.

Chicken, my son,

I've found your father. He is better than he was, and so am I to see him. He sleeps now, and I watch him, the quiet is good for both of us. He drinks less. We are staying in a little wooden house with a tin roof near the sea and there are gum trees all around, and so it smells good too. Once he feels better, in a little bit of time, perhaps I will try to bring him back and we will all three get going again. Until then I like to let him sleep and he likes to be away from the people.

He sends his love and of course so do I,

Mother and Father

xxx

It made sense to send a postcard if you didn't have much to say. Perhaps she had thought the picture of the overexcited colourful child would make him think she was just having a holiday. He tucked it in between the pages of a book along with all the other important correspondence that was lost in their small bookshelf, pressed and captured. He washed his face in the bathroom and afterwards looked long and still into the mirror. It was like someone had drawn over his face with another, the face he recognised swam in and out, a dark impression of something else shaded over the top. He found his father's Leica and felt the weight of it in his palm, and its heavy mechanic comfort. He held it at arm's length and took a picture of himself as proof.

When the pictures were developed a few weeks later, there was his face, normal and his own, and it was good to see it.

The paper's shouty headlines were all about the new war, but Leon liked to turn to the quieter stories inside, the local heroes, the record barramundi, a new nail factory to be opened by some stiff-haired boy evangelist preacher. He shaped a figure as he read, using the warmth of his hands from his coffee mug because the marzipan had passed its time.

Mrs Matsue Matsuo, mother of Commander Matsuo, one of the Japanese midget submarine men who was killed when he attacked Sydney Harbour in 1942, came today to place a wreath on Sydney cenotaph in remembrance of her son.

Mrs Matsuo wept as she was handed the charm belt that her son had been wearing when he died. The vessel, containing Commander Matsuo and Tsuzuku, was sunk with depth charges. When recovered four days later they were found to have shot themselves. The ceremony only serves to heighten negative feeling about Australia's involvement in the war in Vietnam.

The figurine in Leon's hands grew a kimono, the hair, long to the middle of the back, straight. The arms disappeared up the draping sleeves and the head was lightly bowed. When he painted the face the eyes would be closed.

Someone knocked at the door and he looked up to see one of the older Shannon kids. She stood like a straw doll, straight up and down, a conspicuous bump in her middle, she supported herself with one hand on her lower back. He opened the door with a jangle, 'Sorry – bit late opening this morning.'

'Kay.'

He put himself back behind the counter. 'What can I get you?'

'Four buns, please.'

'Sultana? Or apple?'

'Apple, thanks.'

She looked skinny in the arm and face. The more he looked at her the more she looked like a sea horse, with that balloon bump. Her hands looked large and red compared to the rest of her. He put six buns in a bag. She saw but pretended not to. It wasn't like with her mother – he felt that if he offered them for free she wouldn't accept, and worse than that she would be embarrassed. She handed over the money and he gave her 20 cents too much change and again she kept her eyes above it. He closed the till and the girl still stood there.

She looked at the paper open on the counter. She saw the figurine too, but glanced away before she could have understood it. 'They gave her back his belt, y'know.' Her words were sudden and sharp as if she hadn't really meant for them to come out.

'I heard that,' said Leon, not really sure how he should respond. He tried to gauge how old she was, but with her pregnancy and her young face he couldn't tell. She stood with the paper bag of apple buns in one hand, change clutched in the other. It seemed she would say something else. He smiled encouragingly, but felt the flush of embarrassment on his face. She had caught him off-guard. Nothing would come in response to, 'They gave her back his belt, y'know.' She gave a small nod, turned and walked out of the shop. Her dress was too small for her and rode up on her legs so that he could see bruises the size of navel oranges on the backs of her knees.

She almost collided with the postman who, for the first time ever, shuffled into the shop. He didn't look at Leon or speak, but slapped four letters down on the counter.

'G'day,' said Leon, surprised. Still the postie didn't look up, but he gave the letters one last pat, sighed and headed off again.

The brown envelope was creaky with officialdom. A roar started up in Leon's head. He stood still at the counter. It slunk in the door. Everything will be changed.

The radio sang:

Through the years my love will grow,
Like a river it will flow.
It can't die
Because I'm so
Devoted
To you.

He turned the envelope over in his hands, looked at where it had been sealed by some unknown tongue. He heard a small hiss, a growl. Maybe it was just the shop sign creaking in the breeze. He would have liked to put the letter aside and carry on with his day. He would have liked to head out right that minute, find a date and screw her up against a tree in the park with the fruitbats hanging all around, put the bastard thing back in its place, get just a little purchase on the good quiet feeling, even if it didn't last. But it was early and there were lamingtons to dip; and the letter couldn't stay unopened, it demanded him. He opened it carefully, leaving a clean rip in the top. The paper inside was thin and the black type showed through to the other side. He read it, then closed his eyes for the longest time.

He opened them when the bell to the shop rang and a short man he had never seen before walked in. The man stood in the middle of the shop floor blinking from the brightness outside. He was neat, his hair was combed and flat to his scalp, the cuffs of his shirt were spotless. 'How's the day treating you, son?' he asked, smiling, and there was a slight whiff of something old, like he'd put his immaculate clothes on over a dirty body.

'I've been conscripted.'

The man's smile stuck and Leon noticed that the rims of his

106

eyes were scarlet. 'Sorry to hear that.' The man walked closer to the counter and Leon could smell beer on him.

'What can I get you?'

'Just a loaf.'

'Big one?'

'Small.'

'Yes.'

The man stayed silent until his bread was wrapped, the money exchanged. 'It does something to a man,' he said, not looking Leon in the eye, as if he didn't want to say it, but someone was making him. 'They get you to murder people out there, son. There's no reason for it. You can't fix those people.'

He could think of nothing to say. The man left, after a second's eye contact. The bell rang and he was gone. Leon watched him cross the street and push open the door of the Shannon house before disappearing inside. So Donald Shannon was a small man after all.

That night he dreamt he was a kid, the Russian spaceship passing by overhead. Nothing exciting, just a slow-moving star. Standing outside the shop in the dark with the taste of sweet date slab in his throat and his father's hand on the back of his neck, the warmth, the easy touch. The smell of his mother nearby – apricots. The tick-tock of the whole street turning their lights on and off, the black the green the black the green. Cheers started houses away, rippling down the street until they became one voice that cried out, shrieked, 'Hello!' as it trundled by, waited for some return message, but of course there was none. He walked a few steps into the street, hoping it might do something. At the time he'd held it against the Russians. They could have done a loop de loop, but all it'd done was pass slowly by ignoring the flashing lights of Parramatta, and the candlelit vigil on the bridge that wonkily spelt out 'SYDNEY' in weak flame. In among the hallooing, in among the songs about Australia, the flashing house lights, was the doorway of the shop, dark and silent where he could make out the lines of his parents watching the sky and he pretended not to see.

7

Frank's bowels seemed to twang the tripwire of his stomach whenever the tide was high. He felt the full pinch of his gut at a later time every day, until it became too dark and he would chicken at the shoreline, squatting on the sand, then kneeling in the shallows to wash, feeling the familiar shame of being human again.

Early one morning before the sun had taken the pale edge off the place, his guts woke him, and he balanced on his rock like a limpet and yawned at the sky. There was some half-remembered dream still on him, Joyce Mackelly climbing into the top branches of a tree and watching everyone look for her with her smudged newsprint face. The water was still and unusually glassy. Behind him a butcher-bird whistled, and now and then a fat Christmas beetle flew nearby, burring like a motor. A smallish lemon shark came to inspect his toilet. It tilted itself and looked up at him, dog-eyed. He drew up his feet, pulled his bum out of the water and watched as the fish swam around the rock, then around again and then, satisfied with what it had seen, glided back out to sea.

He walked back to the shack feeling lightly drawn against the day. Sleep hadn't finished with him yet. Back inside, he lay face down on his bed and slept.

Not long later – it seemed, though the sun had moved so it shone right in his eyes – he was woken by a noise, like something with a beak was having a go at his front door, with a regular one-two-three, one-two-three, one-two-three.

Trying not to squeak the floorboards, he moved across to the door and opened it slowly, in case the bird was perched on it. There was no bird. There was Sal holding what looked like the same carrot, matured in its pink jumpsuit. 'I bin knocking for ages.'

'Jesus, Sal. You scared the living shit out of me.' Amazing that Bob and Vick just let the kid wander off like that. Maybe they'd sent her to check up on him.

She turned one of her feet so she was leaning on the side of it and it must have been calculated because it made him feel bad. She held up a coin. 'I was knocking with this dollar, so it didn't hurt my hand.'

'What do you want?' He ran a palm over his face, squeezed his eyes shut and opened them. It was the hangover. Not her fault. He breathed in deeply. 'What are you doing here?' he said in the friendliest voice he could manage right then.

Evidently it was enough. 'Came to see you. Do you have any Coke?' She pushed past his legs.

'No – you want a drink of water?'

She was silent, so he filled a tin from the tap and offered it. She ignored it and walked around the room looking at things – particularly, it seemed, the cobwebs and the unwashed dishes in the sink.

'Do your parents know you're here, Sal?'

'Oh, sure!' She was clearly lying.

He wedged the door open, feeling he might have to flee at any minute. 'Well – what can I do you for?'

'I've come to work on your farm.'

'Farm? Mate, I don't have a farm.'

'What's that, then?' She pointed to the paced-out vegetable patch, conspicuously bare, marrow seedlings gingerly sown, weeds creeping up bamboo poles.

'That's a veggie patch.'

'You got chooks, too. You could get a goat and a pig and a dog. Then it'd be better.'

'Goats stink,' said Frank.

'Do not.'

He nearly said 'do too', but Sal, fringe black in her eyes, silenced him. She took a package out of her back pocket, carefully wrapped in kitchen towel. She pulled off the paper and held out another large rudely shaped carrot, patted with mud, freshly dug.

'What's this?'

'Carrot.'

'What's it for?'

'You eat 'em.'

He let out a sigh, but she was smiling. 'Payment for working your farm.'

'You want to pay me to work on my farm?'

'Trial run,' she said, face like thunder again.

Frank took the carrot.

'It's a deal,' she said.

Handling it appeared to be in lieu of a contract. It was a good carrot, it smelt strongly of earth.

'You grow this yourself, mate?'

'Yep.'

''S a good carrot.'

'Yep.'

'Well.' He put on his best foreman's voice – the first sting of the hangover was less than he had thought. 'What'll I pay *you* to work on the farm?'

'Room and board.'

'Five dollars and tea twice a week.'

'Hokay.'

He wondered if she knew what room and board meant. 'The

111

condition is you let your ma know the deal. If it's okay with her it's okay with me.'

She nodded and padded down the steps where she picked up her bike, orange with rust, and put her carrot in its jumpsuit gently in the basket. She peddled off down the drive without another word. Kirk ran in a circle in the bike's wake, chasing the dust.

And that's the end of that, he thought, relieved. Either Vicky would tell her not to bother him, or Sal'd get sick of the idea.

He rinsed and ate the carrot, and it was good. There was a gentle headache getting at him, right where the bridge of his nose joined his eyes. He pinched at it as he sat on the steps drinking water. He'd ploughed halfway through a box of red wine the night before. But Boxing Day was always a bit like that. When he'd woken up in his bed there'd been the long morning that he lay there for, wondering how the Haydons spent Boxing Day. Maybe they went to the beach. He should have invited them to his for a barbecue or something. A pippie fire. But maybe they spent it as a family, maybe they'd had enough of him – he had been pretty drunk.

Frank wondered if he'd been out of line with Vicky. But nothing happened, did it, so there wasn't a problem. Unless she didn't like him and told Bob she thought he was a sleaze. If he had a phone he could ring them up and say thanks, gauge the atmosphere. He could drive round there, but they probably didn't want disturbing. They were a family doing family things. They would have invited him had they wanted him to be there. It wasn't enough, he realised, because even if you spent Christmas with people, even if you weren't alone then, the next day was empty, even more empty for following a day with those people and their good looks. Their easy laughs and bare legs. Frank pressed his wrists into the edge of the step he sat on, so that he could feel something through the small hangover and so that his heart could stop beating so loudly.

When Sal returned an hour later, she had her own trowel and, without a word to Frank or even a glance in his direction, she knelt down and began to dig out his newly planted marrow seedlings. He trotted over, his hands flapping girlishly. 'Mate, I just planted those.' It came out louder than he'd meant and he saw the back of her neck tense. A sweat started on his face and he tried to pull his voice back, make it lighter, friendly. 'Maybe we could have a chat about what needs doing here – you want to feed the chooks?'

She sat back, heels supporting her bottom, and regarded him with a blank stare. 'Marrows won't grow in this soil.'

So – a smart-arse. 'Well, how do you *know* they won't grow unless you try them out, mate?'

She blinked at him.

There was a silence and then Sal started to laugh.

8

The latest postcard had a cartoon pelican on it, wearing a straw hat and cat-eye sunglasses. It peered over the glasses, showing off its long lashes, and gave the kind of wink that made you wonder if it was American. Behind her was another beach, this one filled with small brown bodies and striped umbrellas. Leon turned it over.

> Sometimes I don't know what we do here. We have bought this little place, it was not expensive, this little wooden house in the forest. There's a young man I see sometimes who delivers groceries for us so that we don't have to go into town (your father cannot bear to see the people there). This man is a native – I never met one before – fancy that. We talk sometimes. I tell him about you, how grown up you are, your beautiful cakes.
>
> Your poor father still wakes sometimes and sometimes there are things he does that he does not remember in the morning.

'Love, Mum' was crushed into the corner of the card and there were two kisses, barely visible. The postal stamp was Mulaburry. Leon bit his cheek. He held the camera at arm's length, looked into the lens and clicked the shutter open. He wouldn't have time to develop this one before he went north for training, but at least he knew it was there. He wondered if Don Shannon remembered in the morning.

*　　*　　*

On the day he left the shop, closed up and with a notice on the door that had taken him three goes to figure out – Closed for the Time Being – Mrs Shannon stroked his arm and squeezed it. She didn't say much more than 'You'll be right, kiddo', but it was strangely draining and he was glad to hand over the keys to her and hop on to his bus. He wondered if Amy was done with being finished yet and where she might be. He would have liked to have sent a message to her but the Blackwells had shut up and moved away not long after she left, and there was nowhere to write to.

At the training compound up in Taroom, a bum-numbing twenty-two hours on a silver bus, they were asked if anyone had any useful experience. Construction workers were needed to renovate the R and R camp in Saigon, cooks and bakers would be especially useful there too. He didn't know why he didn't put his name forward and his palms sweated.

The uniform was good, it was a sound thing to see everyone dressed the same. You had a space that you had to keep clean and neat, and a gun that you were taught how to take apart, how to feel for the pieces of it that slotted into each other. It weighed the same as the paddle he used to get bread out of the ovens. A kid called Rod, who looked younger than he said he was, bunked above him. He'd hang his head over his bunk and watch Leon clean his gun, telling him all about his family back home, his sisters and how his father was a big deal in the city. Leon smiled and nodded back, tried on occasion to return a story, which he made up somewhat. It was strange to be so close to other people, all the time. The early mornings and the exercise meant that at night he slept like a stone, and when he woke it was good to see all those neat men with their neat boots and neat hair. After a few weeks, the flesh of his stomach shrank back and he could feel his muscles reaching out underneath his skin. His uniform didn't feel

115

tight around the middle. He hadn't realised until he lost it that he'd had a paunch.

When they trained on the automatics the sergeant slapped Leon on the back and said, 'That's the kinda shoot we want, Collard. Good one,' and he felt his chest expand and looked around to see who else had heard.

He borrowed some paper off Rod, who wrote to his parents twice a week, letting them know about all the swell stuff they were up to, how he was bunking with this real character of a guy, how he'd been singled out specifically for his navigational skills.

He leant the paper on his knees and felt oddly formal as he wrote 'Dear Mother and Father'. He couldn't remember suddenly if he'd called them something else – Mum and Dad? Had he ever talked to them like this? He might just have said, 'Hey, you,' or not spoken to them at all. He felt bad about the next line, 'I hope this finds you both well' – was it terrible to ignore that neither one of them sounded well in his mother's postcards? 'I have been called to service in Vietnam and am at my training now.' He would not give the address of the training centre. He wouldn't like another one of those cards with the cartoon character all Smiley-Dan on the front and a looney message on the back, where anyone could read it. 'I leave for Saigon in three weeks.' There was an odd rush when he wrote that. Just writing the word Saigon was like speaking a different language. 'Mrs Shannon has the keys to the shop and I will of course reopen it on my return.' He felt carried away with the formality of his voice, but he liked it. 'Your loving son', and here he realised he was angry at them both and didn't sign his name. They'd work it out.

He addressed it to the Mulaburry post office, wherever that was, and sealed the envelope.

*   *   *

When the last three weeks were up, he took a photograph of himself in the toilet mirror, feeling like a wind-up toy. The shape of his face was different, he looked reedy and older. His uniform was crisp against his skin and he held his hat in his hand, squeezed the shape out of it. On the hot bitumen with the planes huge against the sky, he had his photograph taken with Rod.

'It's time,' Rod said then, and they climbed the tin-sounding steps to the Qantas.

The lead-weight feeling of flying was not what he'd expected. He'd imagined a lightness, a small leap in the pit of his stomach, then the feeling a trapeze artist might get. But it was like being underwater, something pushed at his ears, tried to get to his brain. He couldn't concentrate on any one thing. There was the view out of the window, the upside of the clouds, which he hadn't considered before. They rolled and moved like live things, they reflected a white light into his eyes.

They levelled above the clouds, and the air and the boom of the engine leant in on his ears, and the freshly shaved skin underneath his nose dried out. He took a photograph out of the cabin window.

There was a fug about the place that was how the air felt around Christmas when you had to make bread and you couldn't open a window and let in the flies. The first deep breath, coming off the plane in Saigon, he thought he'd swallowed a mouthful of heated air from the engine, but all the air was like that and you had to plough through it. In the back of the truck on the way to the base, they'd passed through all those Vietnamese getting on with their stuff, carrying baskets and cycling, just like you saw in the cartoons about China. They even wore those sun hats, the ones you couldn't fit through a doorway in. So many people squatted by the road in a way he couldn't imagine his own ankles allowing, and the smell of fumes was unholy and it tickled the back of his nose like no smell he'd known existed. They stopped in traffic by a roadside vendor where old men perched on their haunches, eating something that looked meaty and sticky.

'Dirty so-and-sos,' someone said and everyone laughed. Leon recognised rice. Suddenly there was a school of young women on pushbikes catching up to the truck, each one of them pristine in a white outfit, their hair long and black down their backs. The men shouted and stamped their feet as the girls, without so much as a glance in their direction, overtook the truck like a shoal of fish and carried on their way.

For a week they stayed at the compound to get used to the place. Rod woke up spewing one night and when he went to the medic tent they laughed at him. 'They just said, that's life, and told me to drink as much water as I could. But then they said it was the water making me spew.' He looked at Leon for some sort of support. Leon shrugged and Rod held up his canteen of water as a question.

Sleeping was not so easy in the compound. There was a bird that carried on all through the night, uk-hew uk-hew uk-hew, and after each call he waited in the silence, thinking maybe that was the last one. It seemed to be nested in the tree by the cookhouse, but you could never see it, even though you heard it as though it were right in front of your face. On a night when it was particularly loud, and Rod couldn't stay still for wanting to spew, they sat watching as a few men tried throwing stones into the tree to scare it off, but the thing was stoic and cried back just as loudly UK-HEW.

'An' fuck you too you fucking fuck!' one man shouted, which seemed to give the bird pause for thought.

'You got much of a family back home?' asked Rod.

'Not much of one. But somewhere around I got some parents.'
Funny to say that. But Rod wasn't really listening. He was drawing
with a stick in the dirt. 'What they think of you coming out here?'

'Dunno. Guess they're not that happy about it.'

'But you knew you wanted to go, right, and you knew it was
important?'

'I was conscripted.'

'Oh.' He looked crestfallen.

'You signed up?'

'Yeah – but you've got to get permission – you've got to get
your parents to sign something. Like going on a fucking school
trip.'

'How old are you?'

'Nineteen. Soon.'

'Crikey.'

'They didn't want to sign. There were all kinds of tears about
it. They didn't come and say goodbye. Dad was too upset.' The
dirt drawing took on an egg shape and he drilled round and round
it with his stick.

'That's hard.'

'Yup. But he signed up, he was in Greece. I'd have thought
he'd understand, y'know? All's I'm asking for is a bit of support.'

Leon nodded. But it seemed like a lot to ask for.

Uk-hew, went the fuck-you bird.

By the end of the week Rod was feeling better, though still liable
to vomit without much warning. As the chopper set down to
take them to their new patrol, a man came running out of the
cookhouse, a brown lizard hacked through with a shovel swinging
from his hands. 'I found the bastard! Found the fuck-you bird!
An' he's a lizard!' The man threw the lizard down in the dust
in front of the men's feet, proudly, like he'd made it himself.

It still moved slowly, but there wasn't much left in it. 'Bastard bit me!' he said, looking pleased all the same. They watched the lizard become still.

The helicopter made him feel too light, like he might get sucked out of the open door at any minute. Rod was sick into his hand and tried to throw it out, but it caught in the wind and flew back at him. He looked dismayed. The other men just shook their heads, their faces dark and tired. It was hard to tell where the camouflage ended and their eyes began. Rod stared at the floor, and Leon did the same, deciding not to look too closely at the other men.

In the jungle you couldn't tell if the air was getting to your lungs, like a wet sock had been stuffed down there. The other men in his unit wore the same expression as the men in the helicopter.

Pete was in charge and he seemed like an all right kind of a bloke, although when he saw it was just Rod and Leon getting off to join them, he threw his hat on the floor and shouted 'Bastard shit!' before he asked to see their papers and got a bit more friendly. 'Sorry, fellas, we're a bit short. Was expecting at least another three. Anyways.' He turned to four men who looked tired and as if they might carry lice. 'Here, we've got not one, but two men to come and give us a hand. Leon here's a good shooter, and Rodney here.'

'Rod,' said Rod.

'Rod here is good on the nav. And by the look of you, Rod, you'd fit down a rabbit hole okay too.'

Rod tried to smile.

Pete pointed to the four men. 'Daniel, Cray, Flood and Clive.' They all nodded. 'Cray's forward scout, Flood gunner, then there's the rest of us behind.'

Cray nodded again, Flood did not. Instead he said, not quietly, to Daniel who was standing next to him, 'Perfect, a dago and a grommet.'

Daniel looked uncomfortable and turned away.

'Fuck off, Flood,' Clive and Cray said in unison, and everyone laughed, including Leon and Rod, although Leon was sure Rod was laughing the same as him, out of a need not to throw up.

Days passed and it was just walking with the sweat pouring through his eyebrows, which mixed with the cammo and stung his eyes. Sometimes there was the sound of far-off fighting and they'd all stop and listen. It was important not to think about breath, to breathe automatically and not panic; let the time pass without comment. When he could, he got out his camera and took pictures of fat leaves and brightly coloured spiders, of the section at rest, and Rod posing with his gun, giving the thumbs up. Looking through the lens you saw it more clearly than usual. Each of them was a rusty brown outside the jungle, but inside their skin glowed white like they'd been rolled in caster sugar, and even colouring in their faces with the thick cammo didn't help much. The whites of their eyes were luminous. He wondered at Cray at the front, how he stood it, glowing like that, his face a target. Leon pulled his hat down low over his face, but then the back of his neck was exposed. Perhaps in that other jungle his father had had the same problem. He thought of his mother's hair tight in its bun, the smell of the shop after one of her long hot baths. His knuckles looked like claws on his gun.

They took little steps, staring hard at the ground, in the trees, looking for something that might not be normal, but everything was extraordinary. The beep of a bird was enough to send rifles swinging in all directions, the echo of a tree shedding its bark made the section stop and hold its breath for twenty minutes. Behind Cray, Flood carried the machine gun and twitched like crazy every time Cray's pace slowed. Leon carried the ammunition for Flood, and he felt the strings of bullets pressing against his chest, each one a finger, tap-tapping, making that scritch-scratching against his shirt. Rod counted their steps with a clicker and Leon counted his own, just to see how they tallied up. There were so many things to step across and around, and to fall over, things to disrupt the accuracy of counting footsteps. If they hit dense bamboo, there was nothing for it but to walk round it, even though the map said straight, even though the map said three hundred steps and they took well over a thousand.

They stopped for a meal break and his skin felt like it might start to peel from the heat and the damp. He found that he'd gone almost twice as many steps as Rod and decided not to count any more. He wondered at Rod, carefully moving stones from one pocket to another, counting under his breath in case the clicker got reset, as if their lives depended on it, which they did.

They opened up their packets of food and there was a low level of talk, some smokes. Flood held up his tin. 'What kind of an army marches on lima beans?' When no one responded, he answered himself: 'A pretty crook one, that's what kind.'

The beans were like soft stones on Leon's tongue. The heat glazed him, if anything happened he might just sit there and watch it all come. Now and then he thought he could smell eucalyptus in among the rubber trees, where birds drilled and carried on like there was nothing the matter. Cray ate his meal a little distance from the others, always watching.

Leon's feet were swollen in his boots; he could feel a hot liquid between his toes. The back of Flood's neck was livid orange and muddled with mosquito bites, and he could feel them at him too, piercing through his hat and collar, drinking through the repellant, different from the ones back home, something deeper in their whine. Some of the men shook out their clothes, unbuttoned their shirts looking for leeches. One man bit his lips into a thin line

122

and tried to look only annoyed by the thick slug that had blown up bloodily on his chest. He poked at it with a lit cigarette and the thing fell off, a pat in the dust. They must be on me too, thought Leon. He checked down the cuffs of his sleeves, rolled up both trouser legs, but couldn't find any. He decided not to look too much closer; the man, having stripped to his underwear, was now looking palely into his pants.

'This is the fucking life, eh?' said Cray, catching Leon's eye.

'My oath,' said Leon and they both laughed, and it felt good.

Mail arrived in a chopper with a restock of lima beans. Flood shouted 'Fuck!' into an opened tin. Cray had a letter that made him stroke the stubble on his chin hard with his hand and walk away, looking up into the tops of the trees. There was a letter for Leon, another postcard that had been sealed in an envelope. The address on the back was the shop and there was a thin bit of tracing paper inside from Mrs Shannon: 'All good here. Take care.' The postcard was not of a beach and there was no smarmy cartoon character on the front. It was a black and white photograph, old – maybe forty years old – so that it was faded and difficult to tell what it was of. The most he could make out was that it was a picture of some gum trees, receding into darkness where the bush got thick.

> One day you will come here and you will know how the fish swim at the surface of the water, so you can see them all the time, and how the big white cockatoos bunch in one tree and shriek the mornings in. These are the things that we see now, my love my love my love.

Leon folded the little picture in two.

'You got some mail?' asked Rod in a hopeful sort of a way.

123

He hadn't been able to keep the disappointment off his face when there'd been nothing for him. But Leon couldn't help that.

'Not really, mate. Just a bill.' Rod nodded in a way that Leon could see he was hurt, so he took a picture of him and that made the kid smile again.

9

The bugger of it was that he didn't even like the ugly things. Frank'd brushed past the little table that held the sugar figures to get at a hornet that had billowed in and he'd misjudged it so that his hip had cracked against the corner of the table. The bell jar leant over and fell on the floor, where it smashed.

'Cunt!' he'd bellowed at the hornet, who drifted out through the door in a leisurely fashion. The dim glints of glass splinters were everywhere. The figurine of his grandfather lay on its side, split from the hand of his bride. His grandmother still held on to the hand, which had broken below the cuff of his wedding jacket. Rubbing the ache in his hip, Frank tried to stand his grandfather up again, but the base of his feet had flaked away and there was no balance left. The sugar was grey on the cut. Where the colouring had faded he could make out thumbprints, which made him stand still for a moment. He picked up the models of his parents and saw the thumbprints there too. Now that he'd seen them he couldn't throw them away, and he laid all four of them down on their backs. After a second's thought he gingerly high-stepped over to the sink and found a dry J-cloth, which he covered them over with, before putting on his boots and sweeping up the glass with a newspaper.

On the way to work Frank drove past the Blue Wren coffee shop. There was a fat, egg-like woman sweeping out the front. He imagined Joyce Mackelly in black and white, her thumb stuck out to the small traffic. Imagined her picture swept away by the breeze of his truck's wheels as he passed by, knocking up a dust.

They spent the day loading disposable lighters and telegraph poles, and Frank's palms became dry and calloused from pushing at the poles and landing them in the right place. The thick gloves he wore made his hands sweat like buggery. It was a long job, because half of the usual ship's crew were off and the stand-in hatch man just said 'whateveryareckon' when anyone asked for his help.

Afterwards they arranged themselves in the pub, dried out and leathered from the sun, and Stuart talked loudly about trapping foxes, while everyone nodded gravely. Frank felt a fug behind his eyes that would turn into a headache. Pokey sat at the bar alone, his eyes on the television showing a documentary about female jockeys. Frank watched out of the corner of his eye until there was only a thumb's depth left in the glass, before getting up and ordering one for both of them. Pokey nodded once in his direction, slid his empty across to him and took hold of the new glass. His attention went straight back to the television. Frank cleared his throat and smiled, but Pokey didn't look at him and Frank went back to his seat. 'He's heaps,' he said to Bob and Bob rocked back in his chair.

'Yeah, he's a real funny man. Gruff as two bulldogs fucking.' He leant forward again, talking quietly. 'That's how come we plan to murder the bastard.'

'Huh,' said Frank, not sure where this was going.

Stuart rubbed his hands together and produced a notepad. 'Righto,' he said. 'It's that time again, folks.' He put on a crappy American accent that set Frank's teeth on edge. 'It's Pokey Lotto time, come on down.'

'What's this?' asked Frank, looking behind him at Pokey, who was easily in hearing distance. He watched him take a long slurp of his drink then set it down quietly, the skin of his face glowing blue from the television screen.

'This is a long-kept tradition, Franko,' said Stuart, a smile that Frank did not like hardening up his face. 'See, why do you think we call Pokey Pokey?'

Frank shrugged. 'His second name's Poke?'

'Because he keeps a bar-room fruit machine in his kitchen. That's right. He uses it like a giant money box – keeps a jar of dollars in the fridge and puts 'em in, all his wages pretty much, they're all in there.'

Linus joined in. 'Few blokes tried to take that machine one night. Pokey got at 'em with a harpoon – right in the arse!'

Whether or not this was true, it seemed to tickle Linus so much that his laughter turned into a coughing fit and he grinned, tears of choke reddening his eyes.

'So,' Stuart continued, 'what Pokey Lotto is, is a kind of syndicate. Each bloke thinks up a bit of a plot, right? A sort of robbery, murder-type scenario, about how to get to the money.'

'Except,' Bob came in, 'the idea of the money seems to have flown out the window.' He raised his eyebrows at Frank. 'Now, we just plot the best way to murder the bugger!' They all laughed including Frank, who felt his jaw ache from the strain of it.

'I resent that, Bob,' said Stuart.

'An' I do too,' said Linus. 'Now. Screwdriver in the eye – fastest way to the brain – won't know what fucker's on him.' Linus passed five dollars to Stuart who folded it carefully and put it in the envelope before writing down on his pad, 'Linus – Screwdriver in eye.'

'Make it an accident,' said Bob, 'late one night at the marina – tap him between the shoulder blades with a forklift. Drop a cargo on top.'

Each competitor handed over five dollars.

127

'The end of the month we all vote, an' the winner gets the envelope,' explained Stuart. 'Got any ideas on you, Frank?'

He felt all eyes on him. He looked at the suggestions on Stuart's notepad that included past games. The last winner, circled in red said, 'Alex – contamination of water tank with crapping.'

'Snake in the coin jar. Death adder.'

Stuart grimaced, impressed.

It would have been good to be at home with no one else there.

'That's nice, Frank – good to get back to the original form once in a while.'

A tall aboriginal man walked to the bar and everyone looked up. It was time to go, but Frank's body felt sluggish, like it might not have anything to do with him any more. The man put an arm round Pokey's shoulder and they shook hands. Stuart banged his glass on the table. It reverberated in Frank's head, made his teeth clench.

'Just what we don't fuckin' need,' growled Stuart. Everyone ignored him apart from Linus, who laughed loudly, like he'd been told a joke. The man at the bar looked over, the white of one eye was bright red. He chewed something slowly and watched as Stuart stood up, holding his hands in fists by his sides. They looked at each other for a few long seconds but then Stuart sat down again and took a gulp from his beer. A hardness was getting into Frank's back, had wound its way up behind his ears, and his arms twitched of their own accord. He wished Stuart would piss off. Frank drained his drink. He wanted another but if he stood up something bad would happen. The rest of the bar was looking and it made his face itch. The aboriginal went back to talking with Pokey. They both laughed and glanced at Stuart.

'The good old days you wouldn't get buggers like him in here,' growled Stuart.

'Go fuck yer'self, mate,' said Linus.

'Enough, fellas,' said Bob, not loudly.

'Well,' said Stuart, shrugging his shoulders and offering his palms up like a man put in an impossible position. No one responded and he downed his drink. 'Pretty soon this place'll be more black than white – 'specially if bastards like him keep on mixing it up.' He nodded towards Pokey. 'You know that, Frank?'

Frank felt sweat beading up his face. He should go. He thought of Joyce Mackelly's face, rubbed grey by a wet thumb, up in the tree branches. He could feel people looking at him, wondering.

Stuart carried on, 'Fucker was bedded up with one of them. A full-blood as well, not even a bitch he could fuck white.' There was a feeling like the place had been struck with a tuning fork, a ringing silence, then Linus made a low fast move towards Stuart, but before he reached him Frank had thrown his drink in Stuart's face and slapped him across the cheek. Stuart fell off his chair and people all over the bar stood up. There was a low roar and Stuart came for Frank, his glass still in his hand. Frank's fingers tingled from the contact with Stuart's face, everything slowed down like a playback on the TV.

I'm going to get it in the face, he thought, just standing there, *and I'll welcome it*. Then Pokey was behind Stuart and had him round the throat, and Stuart's eyes bulged and his face was the purple of plums, green veins on his neck. He dropped the glass and Pokey dragged him to the wall with bear strength, held him up there with his forearm against his throat and shouted, 'Now just you calm the fuck down!' Pokey's face was so close to Stuart's that they could have kissed. 'If I hear another squeak out of you that I don't like that's it. For good.'

He took his arm away and Stuart bent over, hacking, a hand up to his throat. Bob slapped Frank on the shoulder and spoke in a voice that was pointedly cheery, 'Not to worry, mate, you're not the first and you won't be the last.' Stuart limped out of the door, doubled over. 'He'll be embarrassed enough about this to pretend it never happened.'

Pokey and his friend sat back at the bar as if everything were normal; the man raised a glass at Frank and Frank looked away. He'd just wanted to hit someone.

It was late in the day and the chickens were keeping an eye on him. He went inside and grabbed up the peelings and apple cores from the sink, took them out and flung them to the chooks. They pelted to it like it was roast beef. It was a worry feeding them. He'd bought a bag of chook grit and thrown great fistfuls of the stuff out, but was that enough? He'd shown them where the water was, had set them out a couple of dishes, picked up each hen and wet its beak from the dish, but they just quailed against his shirt and kicked, so he let them go. He found himself hoping he would wake up and they would both be gone, their clipped wings healed, flown away. It was lonely being the person responsible for their well-being. The way they looked at him as he moved about the veranda sometimes made him afraid, how they waited until the last moment to get out of the way of car wheels and seldom looked up at any noise apart from the feed bag. He walked past them, on his way picking up the old brown machete Bob had brought round. He shook it at Mary, said 'Ar-har' like a pirate. Mary looked back beadily and made a noise like an old door opening.

Bob had given him the machete along with a rake and a rusted incinerator. 'To be honest, mate, I pinched it from here a while back,' he'd said, planting it in a friendly way in the dirt by his feet. The thing was old and had ugly carvings on the handle, like something you might get on a cheap greetings card, birds and beetles dancing in and out of vine leaves.

He chopped down an armful of cane, just to get the feel of it. He tore off the thrash, while Kirk and Mary bothered about his

130

feet, picking up bits of leaf and spitting them out again. With a pocket knife he split a stalk down the middle and a line of juice ran out. On that last holiday, with his mum still there, he had sat out by the cane in a tin hip bath of cold water, wearing his undies and his dad's straw hat. A stem of sugar cane dipped in the water had made a cool sweet cud that he'd filtered through his teeth and spat out, into the water and on to himself. That thick smell of filter mud from nearby farms, richer than molasses, crappy and sweet at the same time. His parents – his dad with his summer-time moustache, his mum wearing lemons on her dress – had sat on the steps drinking beer and peeling prawns.

With a stalk protruding out of his mouth, he took his machete inside to oil up and clean off some of the rust. He'd set it aside on a piece of newspaper when he heard a motor and, looking out of the window, he saw it was Linus with an old brown kelpie panting in the back tray of his truck.

'How's it going?' Frank asked.

The old man smiled. 'Thought I might as well drop by for a drink.'

Did you, now, thought Frank. 'Beer suit ya?'

'She'll do.'

Frank fetched a couple and took them out to where Linus had sat himself in the sun on the steps. He didn't say thank you when Frank handed him the beer, but nodded as if to say well done.

'Just wanted to drop by and make as well you were feeling good about Stuart.'

'Yeah, sorry for causing a scene there,' said Frank, reddening.

Linus shrugged. 'Caused less of a scene than I was about to. Sometimes you wanna stab the idiot in the guts. He's not such a bad bloke, though, not really. We go back a bit.' Linus settled himself back on his elbows, face to the sun. 'Wife left him a couple of years back – left him with the two kids. Snot-nosed little buggers

131

they've turned out to be – not surprising, though. He was only a kid himself. Anyway, he likes to get het up – you could swap Stephanie for every bugger's name he gets mad at. She's had no contact with those kids, Stuart neither.'

'Jeeze, I'm sorry, I shoulda left it alone.'

'Don't be sorry. Like I said, you say those things one too many times in the wrong place, someone'll put your eyes out – worse. He needs telling now an' again. Stop that violence before it gets out of his mouth.' The old dog started to bark. Frank could see its hackles were up and one of its eyes – the one that wasn't already clouded over – showed the white.

'Eleanor! Shuddup!' belted Linus in a voice that made the dog sit down and then stand up again.

Keen to change the subject Frank said, 'Been thinking I might get a pup. Be glad of the company.'

'What? These bastards not enough for you, eh?' he said, pointing his bottle at Mary who looked stonily back. Frank laughed.

'Nah, mate,' said Linus, 'can't have a dog out here – won't work. Too much snakes or somethin'. Have a look at Eleanor there – she doesn't like the place. Won't get down outta that tray. She won't drink the water here, won't take the meat. You ask Haydon about it – he'll tell ya. He went through three pups before they called it a day. One old dog too. They just keep going off. Might be there's something in that cane or that bush. If there is, he sure likes a dog now and again.' Eleanor whined, but with a sharp look from Linus she was quiet again.

'Well, what about those two?' asked Frank, pointing at the chickens who were now looking at Eleanor.

Linus drained his beer. 'Chooks are fine. They get up in the trees. Goats are good too – I've seen people around here keep a goat or two. They've got horns, I suppose. Mad bastards anyways, with their yellow eyes, give me the willies.' He banged down his bottle. 'Anyway, hoot hoot, off I go.' And he hefted himself up with the help of the post that held up the veranda. For a moment it felt like the place might collapse but in the end it was okay and Frank waved Linus off. He found himself alone again and tried not to look at the sugar cane.

10

'Hell, it's only natural,' Flood said. 'You hunt the beast, you kill it, you take the horns.'

There was a pause while he pulled a small piece of food from the back of his mouth and sucked his finger clean of it. He was evidently happy with the food at the compound, the bully beef and potatoes.

'I heard one guy takes the heads – bleaches them out. Prob'ly be worth something when this is all over.'

'He wouldn't be able to lug around a sackful of heads,' said Cray, who was propped against a tree, with a pad of paper and a pencil stub.

'Bullshit.' Flood spat and it landed heavily in the bracken. 'Anyway, I'm starting a little collection of my own.' He tried to catch Leon's eye but Leon looked away and pretended he was listening to something else. 'I'm gonna to take the trigger fingers.'

'You're full of shit, Flood.' Cray shifted so that he was turned away from him.

Flood chuckled, then drew hard on his cigarette, the orange tip glowed bright enough to light up the sticky little mouth it poked from. As he exhaled he let out a few more humps and giggles, then looked away.

Leon busied himself with picking out the heavy green mud from the grooves of his boot with a twig. He started shaping mud round twigs, using it like modelling clay. It wouldn't hold together that well when it was dry, so he kept it small. His father had made a sugar model of him when he was born, made it the right size so that it fitted with the wedding figures from their cake. When he'd been about five, his father had taken the baby down out of the bell jar to show him. It was in a cradle that rocked when you nudged at it. A blue striped blanket came up to his chin and his pink fingers clutched at the edge of it, minute dots of white for fingernails. The cradle fitted right in the middle of his palm, the size of a sugared almond. When the shop bell rang and his father went to serve a customer, Leon had simply popped it into his mouth, without even really thinking about it. The sugar had been old, but it was still sweet, and when he took it out of his mouth again the colours had all run and the thing looked a mess. His mother walked in just in time to see the baby go back into his mouth and her scream brought his father running.

'What in hell?'

Leon kept his mouth closed over the baby.

His mother had tears in her eyes and a hand over her mouth. 'He's eating his baby self,' she whispered. They stared at him in silence. He blinked.

His father's face went red, then he laughed loudly so the place echoed. 'Well, then, I suppose that's fine,' he said. 'Taste good, does he?'

Leon nodded, his mother stared and his father went back to the front of the shop, still giggling, saying over and over, 'My word. My word, my word. There's sugar in the blood for you.'

The mud baby that Leon made, sitting in the damp shade of a rubber tree, was in swaddling, no arms or legs, just a little blackish-greenish grub, with two seeds from a split pod of some kind for eyes. With a grass stalk he put in details – eyelashes, a smile, a triangle nose and circles for cheeks. He put it in a strong patch of sunlight on the root of the tree and left it to bake.

135

Cray was oiling the handle of a machete. He held it up to show Leon and passed it to him, so that he could see that on the wooden handle were all kinds of carvings, birds and leaves of minute detail.

'For the wife,' Cray explained, 'she wanted something'd be good in the garden – we got this fireweed and bramble problem. Got this old promise to sort it out when I get back.'

Leon felt the weight of it in his hands. ''Sa keen handle – where'd you find it?'

'Took it off a Cong. Shot him in the throat and took his knife.'

He held Leon's gaze for a moment before pulling hard on his cigarette and looking down at the ground. 'Carved those things meself.'

Leon nodded. 'She's a beaut.' Some sort of bird laughed loudly. 'Really nice. You work on wood back home?'

Cray looked up again, squinting and nodded. 'Mainly I make rocking chairs.'

Leon carried on nodding and handed back the blade. 'Funny place, this.'

'That is the fucking truth, mate.'

When it was time to move on, he checked on the mud baby and found it had dried a shade lighter. Stupid to want to take it. But he wrapped it carefully in a fat leaf anyway. It'd fall to pieces. He put it into a zippered pocket and shifted his pack on to his back, careful not to knock it. He shook his head at himself and made off after Cray.

In the night, along with the things that loped in the undergrowth, the tide of mosquitoes and biting beetles that hissed and whined around Leon's ears, there was the sound of heaving. Someone was sick and in between the cries of the man Leon could hear a neighing, a rucking up of earth with claws like something rejoicing in the sound. He pulled his soft cap over his ears and curled in a tight ball, the butt of his gun poking at him like the cold nose of an animal.

When the sun came up, it was Flood who lay chalkily under his netting, an orange crust round his mouth, to be lifted out with his malaria. Leon breathed shallowly. Of all the bastards to get sick.

'That means you get the gun, old matey,' said Pete, planting the thing at his feet. 'Clive's your second.' He passed over the extra rounds and felt the machine gun heavy in his hands. It was like he'd never held one, never trained with the rest of them. To kill a man. To kill thirty men. All at once. There was a moan from Flood and he felt anger rising in him. Couldn't the bastard just live with it? It wasn't beyond the realms of possibility that the arsehole was faking it. Better to pretend to be sick than shoot yourself in the foot. But he saw a greenness in Flood's skin where the jungle had crept into his blood and was pushing out of his pores. He stood with his new gun, his back to the section, not looking at anyone, trying not to think.

They waited for the sound of blades in the air.

'By the time we set out, it might all've been over,' Leon said to Cray, who had slid himself down the trunk of a tree and was unwrapping a barley sugar. He offered one to Leon, and when he refused Cray insisted, tapping the thing on Leon's boot.

'Yep, but. If we set out now, we might all be dead in five hours' time.'

'How do you reckon we're any less likely all to be dead if we wait?'

'Nup – it's lore. It's like – I can picture myself saying to my son in a few years – however long it takes till a kid'll understand these things – I can see it – I'm sat there with my wife round a feed of whiting and there's a beer in my hand. Lena's wearing

137

this flower print dress she's got – couldn't fit into it last time I saw her – too big with bub. And I'm telling the boy about it. Telling him how to survive something like that.'

Cray tapped his helmet with another barley sugar. 'Got to just think yourself safe, then no fucker'll touch you.'

'Right,' Leon said, the sweet hard against his cheek. 'S'pose it's easier if you've got a girl in a nice dress to think about.'

Cray reached into his thigh pouch and brought out a wallet. He snaffled through it. 'Tell you what, old matey,' he said. 'Just for today, youse can borrow my wife. Just till you get used to holding on to that gun.' He handed over a folded photograph. It was colour, the woman was small-nosed with prominent canine teeth. Her dress was dark with an orange spidery flower print. Her hair was long down the sides of her face. She held her hand to her forehead in a salute. The beginnings of a pregnancy showed around the front of the dress.

'Just before training started.'

Leon handed the picture back, nodding. 'She's a lovely-looking woman.'

'Careful.'

'I mean she looks lovely.'

Cray looked at the photograph and smiled, his chest rose. 'Haven't seen the boy yet. S'posed to be a picture coming, but what with the post . . .'

Leon nodded. 'How old would that make him?'

'Seventeen days.'

Leon bit the barley sugar in half and blinked away an image he didn't want to know about. Cray sprayed with bullets against dark green, blood leaking from his mouth. He looked away and breathed through his nose. Something coursed through the leaves to one side of them, but Cray didn't seem to hear it.

The sound of the Hewie caught in the wind. When he was

hoisted up, they all waved but Flood was still, a crust of a man, his mouth a hole.

'Pretty crook way for a soldier to go, I reckon,' said Pete but Leon wasn't sure he agreed. He thought about the clean sheets Flood would be tucked into, about the quiet at night, the soft touches of nurses.

11

'Life is a cabaret, old chum. Come to the cabaret. Life is a cabaret, old chum. Come to the cabaret,' sang Sal to no tune, so that Frank stopped blocking up the mouse holes behind the bed and watched her pushing canes into the ground for tomatoes to grow up. The vegetable patch looked good, nothing fruiting, but green tips were popping up and the soil was black and freshly turned of weeds. She was setting up an arrangement of chicken wire so that the new shoots would be safe. She moved about like a black beetle, feeling through the soil with her fingertips, scrabbling at loose stones and roots as she came across them. On days when she was over, he found himself busying around, doing little jobs he felt she might approve of: like sanding down a large tree stump for an outdoors table, clearing the guttering and setting a barrel at the edge of the house to catch rainwater for the garden.

At the mosquito-biting time of day she appeared in the doorway dragging the machete behind her like a big fish. 'What do you use this for?' she asked.

Controlling a bark, he took the knife off her and lobbed it into a stump by the side of the shack. 'That's to scare the chooks with. Remind them to keep laying eggs.'

She nodded gravely.

Once they were sitting down at the new table, Frank served up lunch. 'Hope you like omelettes!' he said as he slid the mess on to her plate. She did not reply.

It was strange to eat at a table. Normally, he'd wander around shovelling the food in and not taking much notice.

'Do you know how to kill a chook?' she asked, forking the food around her plate.

'Whose chook do you want to kill?'

She shrugged. 'Any chook. Just wondered if you knew how.'

'Your mother never showed you how?'

'She takes them mostly into the shed and I'm not supposed to watch.'

'How come you want to know?'

She shrugged again.

'Well, you can wring their necks, or you can chop their heads off.'

'With an axe?'

'With an axe.'

She looked through the open doorway at Kirk and Mary, scratching in the dust.

Frank felt tense. 'What d'ya need to know that sort of thing for?'

'Just like to know. What else do you know?'

'I know how to fish.'

'I already know that.'

'Light a fire?'

'I know that too.'

'Well, okay. Tell me what *you* know, then.'

Sal sighed. 'How to fish, how to make a fire, how to build a bivouac, how to hold a crocodile, how to change a tyre, how to get water in the desert, how to dress a crab, how to peel a prawn, how to peel a prickly pear, how to skin a pineapple.' She took a deep breath. 'How to get a stamp off a letter, how to make damper, how to spell SOS with flags, how to get a fish hook out of a lip, who Ned Kelly was and how to kill a chook.' She sat back, her

141

plate now empty, and arranged her knife and fork neatly in the centre.

Frank's eyebrows were far up his forehead. He could feel them there. 'Tell you what, kiddo, I'd ask for a bit of help with that last one.'

Sal looked again at Mary and Kirk.

'I'll show you how to gut a fish next time I knock a few on the head, eh?'

Sal studied his eyes. 'Hokay,' she said as she slid from her chair. At the door she turned back. 'I like omelettes with capsicum in.'

'That one didn't have capsicum in it.'

'No.'

She took off down the steps, hopped on her bike and hared off down the track to home, leaving a line of red dust in her wake.

'Hokay,' he said and to fill up the still space she'd left he wandered outside with a beer to talk at the chooks.

Sea mist ghosted through the yellowed evening, painting the blue gums and wetting his face. A sea eagle coasted just above him, eyeing where the water's surface ripped up, white and hairy, probably a feeding school of bream. He cast to that spot and sensed the wobble of fish sucking his bait. He felt expectant and a little bit drunk, his feet wide apart, the tips of his fingers resting on the drag. He'd been fishing with Lucy on a few occasions – once, before he'd got bad, they'd taken a long weekend and camped next to a river, a little inland, and there were a few windless days when the place seemed to be there entirely for their benefit. They'd caught fish from the river when they were hungry. A jabiru stalked them as they sat by the bank, taking off and flying close enough for them to feel the wind move on their faces. There were no other people at the spot and it was easy to imagine, when the sun started to go down and deer and echidna and paddymelon melted

142

out of the bush, that they shared some secret with the land, that they and they alone lived in a way that set the precedent for all future campers. The two most perfect people on the planet. They made love in the open on a quilt that he wrapped round her afterwards, keeping the fading rays of the sun from touching her shoulders. He stayed awake, feeling the trees and dirt and water and breathing in the gloaming air. Even the mosquitoes gave them room, barely wingeing, just a whisper by his ear that made him put his hand over hers in case the noise woke her.

When the sun was fully down he carried her to the tent and laid her on the mattress, where she opened her eyes. She'd smiled, and locked her arms round his neck and grabbed at the hair there. 'Beautiful boy,' she'd said and he'd kissed the sand from her belly.

By the time he saw what was going to happen it was too late. A regular tugging at his line that he had taken for the ambling of his bait over rocks became the urgent yank of a caught fish. The fish had swum up to the surface and the eagle was swooping for it, as he stood there, gormless, his mouth working around words his brain hadn't instructed him to say yet. Just too late, he let out as much line as he could, hoping the fish would take it and swim back down, but the eagle was keen and it easily grabbed hold of the fish in both claws, not missing a beat with its huge black-tipped wings. The drag screamed and he watched in amazement as his line began to go, his rod bouncing like old buggery and he yelled at the bird, 'Let go, you idiot!' but the eagle only angled its head at him, giving him no more of a look of understanding than it would have a rival bird.

Frank floundered, holding the rod firmly in one hand, searching for a knife with the other, thinking in horror of how it would feel to reach the end of the drag, to have the bird pull and then plummet down into the water, tangled in line. With one hand he found the knife handle and held the blade to the line, and there was an elastic snap as the line was cut. The eagle kept on flying as if nothing had happened, the long string of line trailing from its claws, the fish still weaving in its grasp, shining silver where the sun caught it. The eagle flew out of sight round the bend that was the mouth of the river and Frank knelt down, his hands on his knees, breathing hard, a lump in his throat.

That night he lay awake, hearing the noise that echoed over the tops of the cane. Sometimes it sounded like a dog or a fox and other times it had the lightest touch of man or woman about it, like it was trying to shape a word it couldn't finish. He couldn't sleep for a memory of Lucy sitting at the end of their bed. He'd lain there watching her through half-slitted eyes, just lain there when he could have touched her or spoken to her, heard her voice directed at him. She'd brushed her hair without ever getting any of the tangle out of it, just pulling the teeth through, ripping, the noise of it like tearing cabbage leaves. She wore too many beads, so that they caught in everything: her clothes, her hair, the curtains. Her lips were raw like she'd been in the cold. She looked in the mirror and ran a finger round the side of her mouth. There. Better. She turned to look at him and he closed his eyes. 'I know you're watching.'

He said nothing. Let his eyes close fully.

'I know you're awake, Franko.' There was a laugh in her voice, and he thought he might laugh too, but he stayed still, slack-faced, gummy-eyed. He felt their old soft mattress sink at the foot, felt her clambering towards him, up his body, saying softly, 'Frank. Franko. Woohoo, is anybody in there?'

And her voice was soft and she was warm on top of him, and he felt the pulse of his penis under the covers, a separate heart-beat. And from nowhere he could place, anger. She had the backs of her fingers on his throat, she was stroking him, he could feel her smile next to his face and he shoved her, hard. 'Will you just let me sleep?' he bellowed and he saw that she nearly laughed, even as she had the wind knocked out of her. Her face a pale half-moon in the dim light, took the shock slowly as she understood he was not joking, and he turned his back to her.

The silence thickened, so that the room felt soupy. There was one sniff from the foot of the bed and nothing more. He kept his eyes closed, his heart beating strong in his chest, the anger remaining all the while the silence did. The sound of her gathering her things about her, the snuffle of old tissues, the heavy greatcoat with the grub holes in it shifted over her back, he heard it swamp her. She zipped something up and left the room. Out in the hall, he heard her find her keys; the scented silver jangle of her key chain. The front door opened. Closed. Her feet clacked down the street. He opened his eyes and the room was soaked in red light, the morning sun coming through the rag-rug curtains. He let the breath run out of him, the anger evaporated like it had gone out of the door with her, like he had simply given it to her.

He rolled over and reached for the phone, but her mobile rang on her side of the bed. The anger rose again in his throat. There would be no getting hold of her then, no chance of getting in there quick and making things better. What did she expect? That he would chase her out into the street naked? He threw his phone at the floor and again the anger went, and he just felt sore and sorry and lonely. That was the beginning of when he'd got bad, that was the first time.

In his camp bed, Frank plucked at the frayed edge of his blanket. There wasn't much space, but there was space enough for another body next to him, a length of mattress that was cool and vacant, an open hand waiting to receive something. The teeth in his head ached and he sat up to pour himself a drink to get him to sleep while the night dripped slowly by. Jesus was in the cane again,

145

and that didn't help matters, cooing and growling at the heavy air. It didn't seem right to drink beer, so he unearthed a bottle of brandy he'd bought to cook with and it smelt like Christmas. Something, Jesus or maybe a frogmouth, barked not too far away and Frank raised his cup to the window, 'An' you sleep tight too, sweetheart.' After a pause he added, 'Don't let anything bite.'

12

It had started as a tight feeling under his ribs, like a drawstring
for his lungs, but then in the thickest part of the night, Leon
found himself sweating and gulping like a drowning fish, clamped
to the open-air dunny. After the bouts of scorching liquid that
shot from his bowels came a moment of wonderful cold. He sat,
shitting by starlight, sweat coming off his face while his teeth chattered against the after-frost, and frog song echoed up around him,
drowning out the sound of what was going on in the toilet shute.
The meaty thick air around the dunny and an ache in his tail bone
made him feel worse, but there was no getting off the seat, and
he looked up at the cool space of the night sky and wanted that
air to come down closer to him. Over by the cookhouse someone
smoked, the orange glow of it lighting up a shine on his rifle.
Cripes, he thought, *if there was trouble now I'd just sit here and
let it come. No one'd come near me anyway with the smell of it.
They'd have to grenade me.*

There was the hollow-wood sound of an owl, beyond that the
chirrup and hiss of the night-time things. The moon looked damp
nearly hidden by banana leaves. As another cramp struck him in
the guts so that he bent forward and a creak escaped his lips, he
saw a star move. He panted with his tongue out and watched as
the satellite drew, smooth and slow as melting ice, right through
the centre of his patch of sky, happy as a larrikin.

At breakfast Pete clapped him on the shoulder. 'You look crook,
mate.'

'Not feeling great.'

'They call that acclimatisation. You've got the acclimatising shits.'

'Beaudy.'

Pete turned to face everyone and held up a couple of letters. 'Post for Clive,' he said. 'Won't be much more of this for a while.' He wasn't able to hide a greedy look at the sealed envelopes as he handed them out. 'Posties are on strike. Hopefully it'll get sorted out soon, but.' There was a long silence.

'Fuck's sake,' said Cray and he spat, then held the back of his head with both hands, his elbows far out to the side like he was limbering up for a fight. He stood on the balls of his feet and took his hat off, slamming it down on his thigh. The others swore and shook their heads, stubbed their toes into the dirt and looked at the floor. 'Who in the fuck do they think they are?' Cray walked away, his hat still held at his side; drawing his thumb over and over his forehead, he disappeared behind the cookhouse.

'All a bloke fuckin' needs,' said Pete. 'Our own cunting country. Fuck 'em.' Leon dug in the dirt with his heel. There was nothing he'd expect in the post except maybe another crazy-faced post-card from his mother. But he thought of their own postie, the miserable bastard who'd delivered the conscription notice, with his low unfriendly looks and the way he'd never say hello. He'd get a kick out of it for sure. There was a loud clang from behind the cookhouse where Cray was kicking something hard enough to dent it, but nobody took any notice, because Clive was crying. He was holding the opened letter up to his head with both hands, his eyes closed, his lips drawn back over his teeth and his body rocking in time with the quiet sobs that came out of him. They all moved close, and Pete went and took the letter from Clive's fist and swept his eyes over it. He nodded, patted Clive on the back and walked over to the noticeboard. He ripped off a flyer that warned about drinking still water, and used the tack to pin

148

up the letter. He took the pen that hung on a string from the board and wrote SELFISH FUCKING BITCH along the side. Clive was still holding his face, and Leon reached out and touched his shoulder, patted it awkwardly, felt the prominent bone that wouldn't have been there a month ago.

Pete looked at his watch. 'Right. Let's get some grog inside this man.' They all moved, with Clive in among the middle of them, prodded and patted and trundled him on, sat him down on a bench and put a small bottle of whisky in his hand. He drank long and deep from it, his nose ran and he hiccuped.

Later, when Clive was drunk, Leon stood in front of the board and read the letter. Someone had drawn a stick lady with enormous tits that had been turned into targets and a badly drawn weeping dick was pointing towards them. Written underneath it said GET THIS OFF YOUR CHEST, BITCH! In several different hands were the words FUCK HER! and WHAT A WHORE! The letter was written on paper with a drawing of a light pink bow at the top.

Dear Clive,

It's really not fair to keep on pretending, I know you'd want me to be straight with you. You remember Mike? You met him at the Summer ball at work? He's an objector, Clive, and I have to say I admire his strength. I just feel like he's the kind of person I need in my life, and I'm sorry if this hurts you, I just wish there was a nicer way of putting this.

I've been to see your mother and she knows how it is, so there's no need to worry about telling her. I'm sorry if this is all a shock, but I just had to get it off of my chest.

Yours regretfully

Sally

PS Take care.

Leon picked up the pen on the string. Amy Blackwell, what did she think about the war and everything? He imagined her turning up at the shop, all finished up, and seeing it closed. He thought about Mrs Shannon bumping into her, whether she would tell her where he was, what he was doing. Maybe she'd write him a letter. Not like Clive's letter, perhaps she'd write and say she always thought of him and how terrible it was that he was at war. And how brave she thought he was. Or maybe she objected and he'd get a letter telling him how it was better to tell them to stick it, that he was a murderer. But either way there was no mail any more, so it wasn't such a problem. He left the pen on the string dangling, the token words he'd written, FUCK YOU, meaning nothing to him and directed at nobody in particular.

He woke to the smack of a gunshot. Sick rose in his throat and someone to the left of him swore and rolled off his bunk to the floor.

'What the fuck's happening?' someone else yelled, but there were no more shots. Outside there was shouting, the tramp of boots, a thud. The first waves of light had lifted the night sky and peering low out of the barracks with the rest of the men he saw the scuffle on the ground, three men by the noticeboard. Clive was underneath Pete and Cray was crouching next to them. Pete gave Clive a heavy smack across the mouth and Clive lay still. Pete shook his head and looked up at the rest of the men holding on to their rifles uncertainly.

'Stupid bloody idiot shot the noticeboard.' The shot was a good one, Leon saw in the morning, a hole right through the pink bow at the top of the letter.

13

In Bi-Lo, Frank could not decide what he should eat, what he should wash with, what he needed and what he should have. He did one full lap of the supermarket and at the end all he had was a loaf of sliced white and a tin of Milo, and he thought, *When have I ever drunk Milo?* He put the malt powder back in the wrong place, next to microwaveable sausages.

Back at the beginning again he started with the grapefruits and oranges, gawking at apples, trying to figure out which ones. When he felt sure that all the people who arrived at roughly the same time as him were at home unpacking, he made it to the checkout, a few bags of grey-looking greens, some potatoes, milk, bread, beer, nuts and a new toothbrush. The toothbrush had glitter in it, which he noticed when he was already queuing and couldn't be bothered to change. He'd pretend it was for his daughter if anyone looked funny at him.

The shopping of the lady in front of him was curious. White envelopes and chicken livers. He imagined her at home, sitting at her kitchen table, scribbling addresses on the envelopes, stamping them and placing a chicken liver in each one, licking the seal shut; a pile of bleeding mail growing next to her, ready for the post.

A small boy stood by a pyramid of chocolate rabbits, alone, a deep crease appearing on the bridge of his nose. He turned his head before any other part of his body, top heavy and wobbly. Frank looked around him for a parent, but there was no one by the tills who looked the slightest bit concerned. When just looking didn't solve the problem, the child's eyes widened and he started to run, standing as tall as he could to try to see over shelves and through walls and round corners. He appeared at the end of an aisle, adrift and abandoned, looking for someone to ask but without the words, quite. His chin wobbled, his face reddened.

Frank felt heat in his stomach. The kid's mother was probably at the meat counter, distracted, and would yell the kid's name any minute. The boy murmured for his mother, not loud enough for her to hear but loud enough that Frank could, then he disappeared again and the calling got louder, and now it was angry, so that the kid was yelling in the voice of an older child, deep and furious.

Frank was nudged by the lady behind him and realised his shopping had collected past the checkout girl and she was waiting for him to pay. 'Sorry.' He said, digging around in his wallet for a note, trying simultaneously to throw his shopping into a bag. The checkout lady smiled at him, handing him his sparkle toothbrush and his change.

He was backing out of the car park before he thought about the kid again and he wished he'd stuck around to see him find his mother.

Back home, time passed strangely. He spent twenty minutes putting his food away and thirty just sitting inside, watching a black beetle as it moved across the room following the sun stripes. It seemed like a good life, following the yellow strip of heat, basking for a few moments, then following where it took you. The beetle wouldn't be worried about what happened when it got to the end of the room. Perhaps this beetle had sticky feet and could walk up the wall. But then eventually the heat would go and what would it do then? How long did a beetle live? Guessing from its size, not very long. Perhaps it would only live as long as it took to reach the corner of the room. When it finally bumped its nose on the wall, he went over to it and thought for a while about treading on it. But once he'd thought it he knew he wouldn't – the beetle was watching him and hoping he'd leave it alone. He prodded it with his index finger, trying to make it walk on to his hand, but the beetle pulled in its legs and he had to sweep it upside-down and into his palm. He threw it high in the air outside, but apparently the beetle wasn't expecting this, or else it didn't have wings. Either way, Kirk rushed forward and swallowed it in a second.

'Sorry, mate,' Frank called.

'What does the bunyip look like?'

Part of the deal, it seemed, of Sal's good work in the vegetable garden was this asking of questions. He'd hoped she'd ask something more survival-based, because he'd thought they could go down and hunt for pippies in the sand and bake them in their shells over a fire.

'The bunyip? Well, it doesn't look like anything.'

'What?'

'Doesn't exist. Bunyip's just like Father Christmas, mate.'

'You mean adults pretend to be him?'

'No. Not that I'm aware of. I mean he's just a story to scare kids.'

'Father Christmas doesn't scare kids.'

'Okay, well, forget Father Christmas. Think ghosts. Bogeyman.'

'Ghosts exist.'

'Well, that's a matter of opinion.'

'It is my opinion that ghosts exist.'

'And good for you.'

She took a long slow drink out of the tin cup he'd given her, eyes fixed stonily on his. 'You still haven't answered my question.'

He pretended to think hard. 'Sort of roundish with legs.'

'You are making that up.'

Frank sighed. 'Okay; you've got a kangaroo's tail – the size of an emu.' He thought a bit – some children's book from when he was a kid. 'Sort of a beak, I think, and these funny bobbles on his head. Feathers – but no wings. Scales. And maybe fins. Big sharp teeth.'

'Is it always a man?'

'What?'

'Is there only one bunyip and is it a he?'

'I don't know. I suppose there might be more than one. And maybe he has a girlfriend.'

Sal was unimpressed and turned her face away. 'You're making it up. You don't know anything about it.'

'Well, be fair. I've never met one.'

'Ha! So it does exist!'

'I didn't say that. Eat your sandwich.'

She picked up a prawn and galloped it round the plate. 'Anyway. I know he exists,' she said, teeth clenched together.

'And how's that?'

'Bunyip got my sister.'

The sheets bunched damply under his ribs, and his eyelids were light and wouldn't close. It was hot, the air in the shack hadn't moved since the sun had breathed into the room that morning. He thought about trying to sleep on the veranda, but Jesus roamed the cane and it made him less inclined to move from his sagging bed. He remembered wading through that cane, leaving Bo by the fire. He had been fogged up to the neck with gasoline and the leaves of the cane threatened to cut open his eyes. He'd sat in the firelight the night Bo's ear was bleeding all over the place, and they'd passed the gas and rag back and forth between them.

Bo'd talked to billy-o. 'I dunno, man,' he'd been saying, 'we should shoot through, move up north, there's jobs for people like us up there, there's fruit picking and farm work, and we could pick up a new couple of chicks just like that. Or the girls could come with us. Could hitch up there, or even if it's just the two of us, I dunno which is best. Man, we could get fish outta the sea and we could get us a tent or maybe we'll get a VW and we can sleep in that, self-contained like.' And he went on and on like that, and to Frank it seemed like there was something evil in the fat-mouthed idiot all of a sudden. Sat there with blood crusted round his earhole, his fat neck creasing at the back, he looked like someone you'd see molesting dogs in the park. He thought of his dad's nose, the nostrils black with dried blood, a busted blood vessel in his eye, after the pub.

Something heavy was on Frank's chest. 'I'm going to go,' he interrupted Bo, who was still talking about how their sleeping quarters would look, how they could get one of those chemical toilets or they could do their craps in paper bags and throw them out the window.

Bo blinked. 'Going where? How d'you mean?' He cocked his head to look up at Frank, shielded the bad side of his face with his hand against the fire. 'Jeeze, you look like your old man tonight.'

Frank took a heave on the gasoline rag and ink spilled out of the dark that twitched and churned at the edge of the fire. It looked like things beetled all around them, and when he turned his head they flowed from Bo's mouth and attached themselves to his eye sockets then disappeared back in again. And there was one big one that chewed at Bo's ear, drooled and snotted and rapped his skull with its fingernails, which split and then multi-plied and its eyes were the eyes of a cooked fish, white and blind and popping out of their sockets. And Bo was fat and content to let it lick at his face, let it eat from inside his mouth, pull on his tongue, this terrible fat lump with a bloody ear.

Frank stood up and walked slowly round Bo, looking him over, and Bo looked back dully, thickly. Frank kicked some sand at the fire and Bo flinched. He kicked sand at Bo and Bo shielded his face. 'Fuckoff.'

But Frank kicked some more and Bo roared, but it wasn't anger, he was just scared and then he was even more repulsive, and Frank kicked him in the fat gut to see what would happen, and Bo rolled on to his side and lowed like a cow, his face wet, and he kicked him again and then went running into the thick black, and the sounds of the bush got louder and something far away crowed a victory.

The thing that really scared him was the pit toilet. He could smell it, he could imagine the thick-backed beetles that lived down there, the little ticking crabs and the bandy-legged rats. How far down was it? It was far, it was far enough that there'd be no getting out, and the sides were slime shit and you'd be up to your waist in it, if you were lucky. And all there'd be would be that crescent moon of the toilet hole all the way up there, where the lid peeped open. It felt like his next step would be into that hole and for a time he stood still on the spot, sweating, too scared to put his foot out into the dark. Then he got a hold on himself. It was the gasoline he could smell, still all up in his nose, and he could aim himself towards the bush through the cane and that way he wouldn't even come close to the dunny. He listened to the cicadas and went towards them, then when the cane started flicking past his ears and across his eyes he ran full tilt at the sound, the rib-rib-rib, and he felt the air, wet around him. He heard the strange crow again and headed for it, deep into the deep black.

He'd slept a night, or perhaps a night and a day, on the dry leaf ground. Ants had tickled at his neck, mosquitoes had made his eyes pinholes. Watched by a million different things that didn't expect him to stay so long. The sound of something hopping through the dry leaves like a thing on a spring, of a nightbird mooing like a calf. The swish of a snake in the dark. And past all that he'd been listening for something else.

He woke in an apple-pie bed at a hospital and his old man was there, pale and red but sober. He'd touched Frank's foot through the blankets. Frank wanted to speak, wanted to know what had happened, but he couldn't, a kind of lockjaw. Before he fell back to sleep his father said, 'We'll have to chain youse to the bloody radiator, mate,' and inside Frank had felt a sarcastic laugh at his dad who kept a photo album of dead men under his bed, a grubby little cache of death porn to look at on nights he wasn't screwing some drunk woman who made the whole house smell.

It could only have been his imagination, but in the dark he felt things moving. Things too lumpy and heavy to be held up by their thin legs, things with brown spines and slits for eyes, cat-sized rodents with teeth that grew as long as their bodies, things that reached out for his face with their blind hands with claws like knitting needles. He felt air move close to his face and shut his eyes, waiting between the howls of Jesus in the bush, waited for the claws to close in on his cheek, to poke up a nostril and push into his mouth. At points he thought he heard it get closer and once he heard a scraping at the door, a snuffling, a scritch-scratch, and all that he could do was close himself up, his eyes, his palms and his ears, and hide in bed like a child. *If it thinks I'm asleep it'll leave me alone, as long as I don't move it will drag itself past my bed.*

14

Leon's feet felt wet in his boots even though he'd just towelled them, even though he'd wiped out the insides and let them dry overnight. When he'd banged them against the ground in the morning, a red centipede as thick as his thumb rizzled out, its stalk antennae up and pointing like two warning fingers. Rod cleaned his feet with his towel, which he'd managed to keep fairly free of dirt, considering. Delicately, he threaded the stubby end of it between each of his toes and then round the nails, wincing at the little toe, which looked pretty red. Leon smoked a cigarette – the ritual was too much to pass up – a cup of bad coffee, a mouthful of biscuit and a smoke. It dried you out so that your insides felt drier than your outsides. With half an inch of cold coffee left in his tin, he dipped his fingers in and rubbed it into his chin and cheeks for a bit of a shave. His razor was not sharp and it tugged at his hairs, but it was another good thing, he decided. The noise was like stripping wallpaper, but it was good to imagine yourself in a bathroom, foamed up to the gills and rinsing your razor in warm water, not old coffee, and as long as there was no mirror, well, that was okay. He finished it off with a wipe from his towel, which had been everywhere, foot and bum and face, and he felt pampered as all get-out.

Pete issued the order that they were moving out, and gave Leon a nod and a wink. 'Very nice,' he said. 'Fancy.'

*   *   *

The clouds gathered above the dark tips of the rubber trees and it could have been night. When the first fat drops hit, the jungle crackled and a thick sweet smell rose up out of the dirt. The rain bounced off Leon's face, small pebbles that went up his nose and shot into his eyes. It drowned out the sound of their footsteps and when it hit the mud it was like gunfire. They came to a creek and it could be seen to rise, its belly expanding, its surface was the cross-hatching of elephant skin. Leon waded in after Cray, the water a warm suck on his legs. The mud coated his trousers hotly and stuck like burnt chocolate to his boots. Before the rain had run the mud off him, he saw the back of Cray's neck tense like a stork that'd seen the fry. Leon held up his arm and felt all movement behind him stop. The rain drummed on the brim of his hat, the trees were still, still, still, there were just the white lines of rain falling steadily down. It got into his clothes, ran down the crack of his arse, licked the backs of his knees. He breathed through his mouth, strained his ears to listen, strained his eyes to see what the signal would be.

Thumb down. A baddie.

Five fingers spread open, then four. Nine baddies.

Cray made a pushing motion at him. A finger to the eyebrow. Wait. Wait till you see the whites of their eyes. Cray sank down and so did he, and everyone behind them was already hidden. He unfolded his tripod, careful not to jog the leaves around him, and attached the gun. No noise broke from it, no unoiled squeak that would grate above the crinkle-pat of rainfall. Even his heart was quiet, although he felt it fast against the bones in his chest. The rain on fat leaves and the drill of it on the brim of his hat. Drips hung off the end of his nose. He waited. He looked behind him to Clive, and Clive was wide-eyed and gave one nod to say 'Ready'.

And then a sound above the rain. The break of a stick. A shudder of fern. Beads of water rolled off leaves and fell on the dark ground gone to mud. A black streak of movement and, out of the green, four men's shadows picking over the ground weightlessly. Even the sound of the rain stopped, even the sound of his own blood was covered over with a pillow. The first fellow carried a rifle over his shoulder. He had womanly lips and his skin was smooth like unset caramel. He must have been younger than Leon. His black eyes darted from side to side but he didn't see Leon, not for the longest time. And when he did, all he did was stop and there were three beats of a fast heart while their eyes met, then Leon shot him and it went into his chest, just between the top and the second buttons, and he fell over backwards.

Leon moved the gun back to the next man before he had a chance to know which way to duck; the tracer bullets moved like jewels against the dark and the noise was like being between two revving motors. He knocked men off as they appeared, four, maybe five men, one after the other. Some shot back, but they could not get through his mess of bullets. He surrounded himself in a force field and by the time he ran out of ammunition there was no need for more, but he loaded up anyway, automatically, his hands steady in spite of the thump of his heart.

'Nice work, old matey,' said Cray, once they'd searched the bodies and were ready to set off again. 'First go, eh?'

Leon nodded. Smiled. Shrugged. He walked up to the boy with the smooth skin and took out his camera. There was blood on the boy's lips. He set the frame, held the box steady and took a photograph. There had been a look on the kid's face that said, 'If I pretend I didn't see you will you do the same?'

They moved out and he found himself wishing he'd got someone to take a picture of him with the dead boy. And then he wondered where that had come from.

15

Frank felt supremely efficient. He rose early with a light hangover and shook himself clean like a sheet with a swim. He ate a breakfast of eggs and billy-brewed coffee, while Kirk and Mary pecked out the leftovers from the pan. He went through the tomatoes, degrubbing and cutting back leaves, doing a job he was sure Sal would be pleased with. He went back down to the beach and fished from a spot he'd been wanting to try since he arrived. He caught a rock cod and a good-sized black fish in the first hour. The rest of the day he made small adjustments to the shack. He rigged up a pulley and a bucket so that he could have a proper freshwater wash standing up, something he'd gone too long without, and he even put up a few duckboards for a bit of privacy. A satisfying warmth spread from his chest and he would have liked to have shown his handiwork to someone. Bob had said he might swing by for a drink some time, so that would be good; he'd be able to inspect it, ask all the questions, be impressed.

In the afternoon the sun mellowed and Frank set a beer on the stump table outside. It shone a little yellow light out of it, the colour of a much later sun, and it reminded him of the comfort of being in a beer garden in the city. The smoke and sun on bitumen, the eucalyptus still hanging through the smell of spilt drinks. He had a large packet of chips and he could drink the cold beer and eat chips while he watched the sun settle and the flying foxes go out for the night. He could start reading a book, the one that was dog-eared from where he'd held it open too often and stared into space. Then, after dark, he would light the fire and set a fish on. He was still whole, there were still things that one man alone was worth. The beer hissed open as it always did and he felt a small joy at the luxury of it, the land, the beer, even the Creeping Jesus in the cane. He shut his eyes and let the sun weigh down his eyelids like coins. The butcher-bird gargled and so did its mate.

'I want you to make me pregnant,' she'd said one morning.

The sheets were hot and had been pulled down past their hips, just covering their legs. She was on her side then, looking at him, one hand stroking her belly, a look on her face that she'd been away and had just a second before got home. He smiled at her, blinked sleepily. Light from a gap in the curtain made her face pale and wondrous, the inside of an oyster shell. He teetered for a moment on the edge of sleep, but her hand slid from her belly and smoothed its way over his thigh and between his legs, making the hairs lie straight. He'd rolled her on to him like they were both great fat seals, light in the water. The sheets made the sound of the sea drawing back off a pebble beach. Her knees and arms were cool, but the sun had warmed her head and she smelt of hot hair. Her tongue moved in his mouth.

She'd never mentioned the baby again. It wasn't long after that morning that he'd started to get bad. Perhaps she could feel the change in the air. If he'd stayed inside her she could have got pregnant right then, in that warm moment.

He opened his eyes to find that the day had turned beautiful on him: the sky a dark pink, while the sun was giving out a last burst of light. A flock of spoonbills were passing over, their shadows zipping like mice over the ground. He stood to watch them go, took off his hat and waved it, holding on to the post of the veranda, leaning out like he was on the prow of a boat, his mouth open to catch the change in the air, to taste the white birds as they coloured everything.

He was drunk by the time Bob arrived, but he held himself straight in his chair.

'You right?' asked Bob, smiling.

'I'm well,' he said loudly. He got Bob a drink and settled back.

'Chinarillo,' said Bob, raising his bottle.

He nodded. ''Rillo.'

An ibis flew overhead, white wings soft and her proboscis beak an ink line against the sky, but she was nothing like the spoonbills. The two men sat and drank to the first quarter mark of their beers and the silence was not uncomfortable but not natural either. Kirk and Mary fluffed around to the front veranda.

'Girls,' Bob greeted them and raised his drink. Kirk and Mary did not look but scrubbed in the dirt at a line of ants. The low sun bumped off the red track and turned the whole distance cherry. A rosella landed on the veranda, saw them and squeaked in surprise before flying off again.

'How are your girls?' asked Frank.

'Same as ever. Sal reckons we need a goat. So that's what's new with her.'

'You going to get one?'

'Nah. Nice animals but. Take a heap of looking after. If you want rid of a chook you wring its neck. If we decided we'd had enough of chickens tomorrow it'd take – I dunno – around half a day to get through the lot of them. If we were really on it. But a goat, you've got to bleed her. And they've got all that personality in them.'

Frank laughed. 'You look at everything like that? How easy it is to kill?'

'Means you can move on easier. We like knowing we can just fold up and piss off as the mood takes us.'

163

Frank leant back in his chair and felt the solidness of the veranda under him. He thought of that last night in Canberra when it hadn't seemed possible that he was leaving, when he'd sprayed lavender-scented toilet spray to convince himself it wasn't home any more. He tilted back further in his chair, felt himself go past the point of balance and wobbled forward with a bump to knock the thoughts out of him. A small breeze brought on it the smell of a fresh open custard apple. He looked at his hands. It was quiet. There was the sound of the bottle clipping against Bob's teeth, of his deep swallow. Bob was looking out at the darkening cane and in the dim light he looked older, like an old-fashioned explorer, like he wasn't made for Australia at all, but the lonely white tundra of the North Pole or the South Pole or any pole just so long as it was lonely.

'Must be hard to just fold up and move on when you've got a kid.'

'We've done it before. Helps Vick to know she's mobile, I think.'

The chink again, glass on tooth.

'How'd you mean?'

Bob turned his head to face Frank. 'She's got things on her mind, you know – more than most. She doesn't sleep – sits up late sometimes. And sometimes she drinks.' Bob laughed loudly and suddenly, and his bark echoed. 'Nothing wrong with sitting up and getting off yer face, eh, Frank?' He raised his bottle again. Frank nodded, smiled and Bob settled back deep in his chair. There was quiet again and this time Frank tried hard to think of something to fill the quiet with, but he couldn't settle on anything, kept being distracted by the sound of crickets skiffing in the cane, a big moth caught in a web scrabbling against the roof.

'She's a strong one, but. She gets on with things for the most part. The daytime. It's just the nights get at her, you know?' He took another swallow. 'I wish I could stay awake. Be some kind of company. But I wake up and I hear her downstairs. An' I think, *Go down, bring her back, talk to her, join her, hell, get shit-faced at six in the morning with her if it helps.* But I can't help the need to sleep, can I? An' the bed's warm. An' before I've made up my mind what to do, I'm asleep again. There's good places to be in sleep.'

Bob was still, apart from his eyelids that fluttered like the moth's wings.

In the distance a road train rumbled by, the black of its back end just visible.

Frank laid a hand on Bob's shoulder as he passed behind him for more beer, but he didn't seem to notice. 'We met out west, you know,' he said as if this explained a lot. 'She's younger than she looks. She was working with the Tourist Board down on Rottenest.'

'Funny place.'

'Yeah – she lived on army barracks when I met her. It was winter – lonely sort of a place in winter. Just you an' the quokkas it feels like. I'd been travelling about with this mob of kids, left them in Perth. You know how it is – there was all the grog, the pills, sharing a sleeping bag in the back of a car with a bloke who smells like piss and mustard. You get to the point you want your privacy.' Bob laughed.

Frank thought of that night sharing a bed with Bo when he'd been ready to swing for him at the slightest breath on the back of his neck.

'We got to Perth and I just had enough, they were heading up to Broome to sleep on the beaches, and the weather was filthy. I just split, told them I'd meet them up there. Knew I wouldn't see them again. That's a good feeling – like you're shedding skin. Took the ferry over, crook as a chook all the way. Salt, wind, rain.

165

White sky for as far as you could see, and this black little dot of an island. Funny now – feels like she was waiting there for me, like I was going there just to find her.'

A paddymelon appeared at the edge of the cane and watched them. It grazed a little.

Bob went on. 'She was pregnant within a month. Funny, but it didn't worry us. Probably should've. We felt so easy then, like we could go wherever, do whatever felt good. That's where the first chooks come from. Rottenest hens. That's all we took with us. It's how it's supposed to work, you know? We got this chicken empire now. We live off the land we own. We eat out of the sea, dig in our own dirt. We want a holiday we hop in the truck; an hour down the road you could be on a desert island. It's just all so perfect.' Bob had his eyes closed and smiled.

'So, what happened?'

Bob opened his eyes 'The kid died.'

'Holy.'

'Leukaemia. A couple of years back.'

'Mate.'

'Yep.'

The silence was back and this time it stayed. Frank felt the foam of too much drink clearing, as he took it in. He felt his bum muscles tighten as he tried to think of something to say. In the end he let it go and the two of them worked through to the last of their beer, and Frank went back to the fridge softly, not letting the screen door close too sharply. Bob rolled a cigarette, appearing to put all his concentration into it, pulling away tobacco fibres, wetting his fingers and tightening the roll. The sound of bottles gasping open.

'Somethin' about this place. I dunno if it's something rubbed off from my old man – he was a hippy joker. Long hair 'n' everything – caravan, the whole fucking Kulu. Anyways, this place's been good to us – let us live on after.' Bob looked up at Frank, caught his eye. 'It was a bad death, y'see. Real bad.'

Frank plucked at the neck of his T-shirt. 'I'm sorry to hear it, mate. Really sorry.'

'She was this funny colour, that was the bit that got to me. She kept spewing up all this stuff, lime-grey – same colour as her skin by that time. An' of course all the hair goes.' He closed his eyes and let his head fall back. A moth landed in Frank's hair but he didn't move to get rid of it.

'The worst thing is you see this little budling of a creature turn into something it makes you sick to look at. You want to cuddle her up, yeah, but you can't bear the smell. You sweat at the touch of her, and you're all she's got, and she makes you feel sick. An' in the end you're prayin' for it, in the end you're standing over the bed at night holding a pillow thinking about it. An' the worst is that you don't do it, because you sort of think while she's alive there's a chance, so you don't and you watch her rip away thread by thread, one pluck at a time. An' then it's just the eyes looking at you and you're supposed to do something but you don't know what that is.'

'This is terrible,' said Frank.

Bob shrugged, took another drink, ran a hand through his hair. Frank didn't know what in the world to say. Bob went on, 'This place, it's got its fair share of ghosts around it, but it doesn't get to us. I've seen hell, mate, I've already bin there. Ha! Sounds right out of *Jaws*.' Frank noticed Bob's hand was holding his beer bottle hard enough to make the tips of his fingers green. 'Seriously. I wouldn't move from here. It's a special place, got enough violence in the dirt to strike a cow dead, but I like it here.'

The man looked exhausted suddenly in the dark.

Bob said, 'There's two hens, the first two Sal named, right after Emmy died. She calls them Mum and Dad.' He rubbed at his eye so that it looked red. He sucked on a cigarette, keeping the smoke in his mouth, tasting it. 'Vick's got this thing about them – won't let any of their eggs get eaten. All the ones that hatch out are left as layers. That winter she died, Dad must've laid ten eggs, and I came home and Vick was sat in front of a fire, her hair all wet, a towel round her middle and an egg under each armpit.' He looked at Frank and Frank smiled. Bob had creases of laughter round his eyes, but he made no sound. 'Said she was trying to hatch 'em out herself. First time we'd laughed in a while.' He closed his eyes like he was feeling the sun on his face, but the sun was out of the sky. Frank shifted, picturing Vicky, the wet hair, the nut brown of her arms and the pale eggs.

'I think that that was the sexiest moment of my whole life. The skin, the smoothness.' Bob made a line in the air with his cigarette. 'Everything. A woman and her eggs. Just seemed like the start of something else, like a sign that the whole lot of everything was going to be all right. All perfect. Like an egg.' Bob looked at Frank and Frank smiled.

'Did they hatch out?'

'Nah. Turned out they were all unfertilised, that lot. Funny to care about eggs so much.'

'There are worse things to worry about.'

'That's true. Was one of those moments you're grateful to the place for putting up with you.' On cue some bird made a sound like applause in the tops of the trees. 'What about you?'

'What about me, what?'

'Your best woman.'

Frank smiled. 'I dunno, Bob. Probably bit more obvious than eggs.'

The morning after they'd first made it into a bed together and he'd woken up with an aching hard-on, he watched the swell of her breath in her breasts, the tight skin round her ribs, the finger-point bruises there; the tips of her hair, cold on the inside of his wrist, the smell of whisky in the room, the toasty taste of their drunken sex the night before, the hope, big in his chest, that when she woke up they would do it again. Then she had rolled over on to her side and backed herself on to him, all apparently without waking, just doing it like it was the natural thing to do, like they'd been doing it for years, like it was the morning ritual. When she came she had stretched out against him, slow and quiet like a cat in the sun, and he'd come straight after, barely able to hold on. And they'd slept like that, face in her hair, eventually shrinking out of her, keeping the heat of her close to him.

Bob laughed. 'Carn. You've loved a woman haven't you?'

'Yep.'

'Well, you're pretty quiet about it.'

Frank squinted at Bob. He looked fiercely earnest. 'Well. Some things are better off that way.'

Bob looked down at his drink and back up at Frank. 'I think you're wrong there, mate.'

'Oh?'

'Things I've kept quiet about, things Vick's kept quiet about.' Bob shook his head. 'Leads to people wandering around in the middle of the night. Leads to all sorts of things. I say the best thing for it is just to say it out loud.' He paused, looking in the direction of his home, but there was only cane to see. 'I only just decided that this minute, though. I might be wrong.' He laughed, a tinkle, staring at the high wall of cane. From far away came an echo of a car horn. Frank's stomach knotted and he felt a grip of loyalty for the bloke sitting next to him. When he spoke he didn't listen to his own words, like it wasn't himself who was speaking but some character in a film. 'I loved a woman. Was terrible to her. Knocked her about a couple of times and then she left.' Bob looked up, his expression flat. Frank wanted to say more, to fill

169

the air with noise. But he let it hang there. Why not? He had done it. Let the silence weigh down the words.

When Bob spoke his voice was careful, measured. 'Well, I don't know about that. I've never felt that. But I mean. You stopped, right? Hell, you just told me about it. You must feel bad.'

'It was only a couple of times.' Bile rose in his throat as he said it. 'I don't mean that as to lessen the significance of the thing.' The thing. 'She left me before it got worse.'

Bob nodded.

There was the noise of the Creeping Jesus again in the cane, quiet but humping along, stalking like a heavy cat. Bob cleared his throat. 'What I said before. I wouldn't want to make you feel like you had to talk about it. I mean. Look. I feel like I've tricked you into this.'

But Frank carried on, strange to say it aloud. Strange to feel his skin recoil at the thought of himself.

Jesus purred a low, sexy gargle like he was having his belly rubbed.

'You ever take a look at yourself and you're surprised by the person you've become?'

He didn't have to talk about the real fights when it felt like his old man was a part of the relationship, waiting in the wings in Sydney until such time as he would be called on to join them. Until Lucy had 'fixed' the 'situation' and they had Thursday night dinners in front of the TV the three of them all together.

'I guess a bloke could understand that.' But Bob's face did not understand.

'First time, we'd had a row and she'd gone out and stayed the night at a friend's, left me to think about things.' All that night, the way he'd counted stripes in the curtains and his anger had built grain by grain like an egg timer. His chest had felt swollen. He'd broken wine glasses into the sink. 'I think she thought I'd cool off, thought I'd see it her way. But when she came in the next morning I slapped her in the face. I did it twice, once on each cheek.' Again there was a pause and he wondered what he was doing telling Bob, who was his friend. 'I suppose that's the difference. If it'd been in the heat of a fight, and I'd done it once and then stopped. But I did it twice, one, two. Like she was a kid. And I was still angry, God, I was so angry. She just stood there looking at me.'

Bob was watching the floor. Frank put his tongue on his bottom lip and left it here a long time. He shrugged and Bob looked up.

'Don't know what you're supposed to do. Apologise for it? Am I meant to talk about it? Get someone to tell me what a rotten shit I am? I don't know.'

'Well,' said Bob evenly, 'the main thing, I suppose, is that you don't do it any more.'

'Because she left me, mate. Not straight off. We tried. I got better but then sometimes I got worse. I don't think she believed it. I think that's how come she stayed so long.'

Oh, sure they'd tried. He'd skinned himself with trying, but she was so persistent, even more after that first time. She wanted it bad. He remembered her standing at the sink making tea, something tight about her shoulders, neat in a grey V-neck, her hair drawn back out of her face in an unusually sober ponytail. Her hands moved deliberately, like they were the part of her that had business to discuss.

'So I was thinking we could head over to Sydney for the weekend. There's the winter fair in Centennial Park, and I was thinking maybe we could hire a stall and get rid of some of the junk in the spare room.' She put half a teaspoon of her special soup-smelling loose tea in a mug and a normal black tea bag in a cup for him. She put down the spoon.

'Sydney?' Frank felt his toes grip the floor, his heart took a flutter.

She looked at him, lips closed but eyebrows moving up, like it was a casual thing all over. 'Yup, Sydney.' They regarded each other a moment longer, then she turned to pour the water. The noise of it was a pause.

'Is this about him?'

Her shoulders squared, her back moved as she breathed in. She unscrewed the milk and poured some over his tea bag. 'Doesn't have to be. I mean, it couldn't hurt just to go and take a look.' She put the milk down. There she was, standing there, not under-standing. 'I'd like to see where you grew up. I'd like to meet him. It couldn't hurt.'

'I've told you, you don't know what you're talking about.'

She stirred her cup, wiped the spoon on a tea towel and stirred his. Her voice shook. 'I think you are being unfair.'

He didn't reply. The silence was better than what he was thinking, that she could fuck off out of his business and that not having a family of your own didn't entitle you to glitch in on everyone else's. She took his tea bag out with the spoon, squashed it against the side of the mug, stepped on the bin pedal and dropped it in. It made a dull pat in the empty bin bag. She squatted to find the sugar in the cupboard, all in silence, all with her back to him. He knew this quiet, it was when her eyes were filling up and she was steeling herself against speaking. It was the thing she did that was not fair because he hadn't done anything wrong and she was threatening him with tears anyway.

She inhaled loudly through her nose. 'Why can't we go?' Still he stayed quiet. One sugar, two and three, and she stirred the cup and a small brown dot of tea spattered on to the sideboard. Her hand trembled and she set down the spoon with a bang. She breathed in again. 'You don't know what it's like. You have this link and you just want to ignore it. You know what it means to me. You know.' Her voice almost cracked, but she was not crying, she was angry. 'I mean, what could he have done? Did he kill someone? Did he molest you?'

'No.'

'Did he beat you?'

'No.'

'Then for Chrissakes what else is there that is so unforgivable?'

She rested her hands on the sideboard, hunching her shoulders. He picked at the wax tablecloth. She turned with both mugs in her hands, planted his down in front of him and made to leave the room with hers. 'Well, you can stay here and be silent all you like. I'm going to Sydney on Friday.' Frank stood and the chair squeaked on the lino. He looked at her, glowered over her, felt his heart beat in his throat and she avoided his look and walked away. He sat down, put his hand to his forehead, waited until the heartbeat slowed. He pressed his fingernails into his scalp. He looked at his tea, the small bubbles in it and the black specks that had escaped the bag.

She came running back into the room. 'Wait!' she shouted. Her eyes were red.

'What for?'

'I forgot to boil the water.'

She hadn't gone to Sydney that time and it had blown over.

A few months later he'd held her face and squeezed it hard, and she was crying. He'd seen the light go out, he'd seen that that was it, his last chance and it was gone.

'Creeeeeee!' went the Creeping Jesus. 'Creeeee craaaaa!'

'I don't really believe it. You don't seem like the sort of bloke that's capable of that kind of a thing, mate.'

'Well. You never know.'

173

'You try and find her?'

Frank shook his head. 'We're better off not knowing each other. New starts.'

'You miss her?'

'I try not to think about her.'

'And what about now?'

'How d'you mean?'

'Now you're telling me this stuff – now you're thinking about her. What's that like?'

He paused like he was thinking, but inside he was blank. 'Sometimes I'm worried that if I found her it'd start again. Like I said, we tried before and some of the time it was fine. But it's always there. I miss her but.'

The night around them went quiet, even the cicadas turned away, as if the land held its breath to listen.

Bob stayed until the last of the beer was gone. They should both have been stupid with booze, but it went down like water and made no difference to Frank. Bob did not slur his words and when he got up to leave his walk was straight and casual. He shook Frank's hand and they shared a smile. *You've done it now, you silly arsehole*, he thought as Bob's tail-lights disappeared round the corner of the sugar cane. *If you hadn't already done it before.*

She'd talked to him about growing up in the home early on, it poured out of her with the tip of a prod from him. She was one of those doorstep kids, too young to talk when she was left there. She didn't remember her mum, didn't remember being taken in. Did remember her first foster family, her foster-dad who insisted she call him daddy and hold his dick for him while he grunted into her hands. She remembered getting sent away from them, back to the home, the interviews as she got older, sets of people coming to see if they liked her, deciding no, they did not, and leaving. And Frank remembered that first time he'd blown

174

up at her and the look on her face, and the thought, *Oh God, I've made her life worse, not better.*

That last holiday with his mum and dad they'd had a small fire by the shack just as the end of the light went from the sky, and his dad had opened beers, one for himself and one for his mother. Clams hissed and squeaked in a wide billy, letting off the smell of burnt bacon. They sat, the three of them, on legless beach chairs, leaning back and digging out pippie flesh with cake forks. His dad told stories about when he used to be a dag, living out the back with a mob of stupid boys. He told the one about the bloke who went to test the sharpness of his knife on his leg and cut an inch down, through his jeans, and sliced open his thigh.

When his mother went back inside for more beer from the cold box something shrieked in the cane, but his father didn't seem to hear it. He looked up at the sky. Frank swapped his mother's half-full beer bottle for one that was nearly empty and drank from it in the dark. He held the beer in his mouth, an unsure taste like he'd accidentally put diesel or earwax in his mouth.

'It's a funny place, this place.' His father spoke quietly, still with his head turned to the sky. He saw that his eyes were closed. 'There are some things you can't get away from, Franko. And that's the pity.'

Again the thing in the cane. Frank's mother appeared in the lit doorway with shining bottles of beer.

16

The first night of R and R the air smelt of sesame oil and spilt beer. Leon and Cray watched the other men cruising around with the little Viet girls, who smiled happily at the drunk, hysterical men in their big new Hawaiian shirts. They'd drunk rice wine themselves and got drunk quicker than he had expected. They watched a couple, a girl in a long, green, shiny-looking dress who laughed at everything her soldier was saying. His arm was round her neck and she somehow supported him on her tiny shoulders. He was in another place, his eyes rolled forward and back in his head, he pointed at the air like he was pointing at a bird's nest. There was wet on the man's face, sweat or wine or tears and spit, Leon couldn't say. But the little girl laughed and the man liked it, and he nuzzled his head awkwardly against her neck. They weaved away and out of the room, half dancing to the music, which was something hokey and old, a waltz.

Cray pointed the bottle at them as they went. 'You could be getting that sort of game on, mate. Nothing to stop you.'

'Yeah,' said Leon. 'Maybe later on. Maybe tomorrow.'

'Christ, mate. You've come on leave too early – if I could I'd be all over it like the itches. I'm having trouble even looking at these women. You're not nancy or anything, are you? I've always suspected.'

'I wouldn't worry, mate,' said Leon. 'You're enough woman for the both of us.'

Cray put down his drink and clutched at imaginary breasts on his chest. He made to push them up and let his tongue loll out of his mouth, reaching towards his imaginary lady nipples. Leon took a photograph. They laughed and left it alone.

In the morning the swimming pool was a solid block of blue like it had a lid to it. Leon watched his feet change colour as they went in. Things looked dead under pool water. He tried to imagine his parents sitting out on a beach somewhere, enjoying the sea spray, but he couldn't. In his imagination they were like cardboard cut-outs, smiles drawn on. He'd have to get to them when he got back, that was clear. He shouldn't have let her go alone, but truthfully he couldn't quite bear the thought of the state of his mother. It had been like something was confirmed for her and she gave up in those few strange months; decided it was best to go and live with a man who stalked her in his sleep. She hadn't mentioned anything in her postcards about Leon going off to Vietnam, but he could see it now, the wobble-eyed look he'd get, the tears and the fights. Like Rod's mum, who couldn't bear to acknowledge he still existed in case he stopped. He imagined what her face would look like if she had watched him kill that boy. If she had seen him slapped on the back and known that he was proud of it, and that something at the time had felt right about it.

No one was up. Cray had caught the dawn plane back home to see the bub and lovely Lena, who maybe fitted back into her flower-print dress by now. Something tickled the back of his neck and he slapped it hard, but his palm came away clean.

A woman dressed in white wheeled a trolley that rattled with glasses and knives and forks. The smell of breakfast from the kitchens was thick and rich and foreign. A strange bird flew overhead, a cross between a magpie and a parrot, with long red legs that trailed behind it and a thick orange beak. It should have been in the jungle. He missed the covering of the jungle canopy and the heavy understanding of his gun.

Later on, when people were lolling around thinking about their first drink of the day, Leon took himself off to explore. He walked along the beach where men slept in the sun or smoked, and he wet his feet in the sea, which was shallow and hot. He smoked a cigarette, something he had started to do more and more, whenever his hands felt useless, whenever they remembered the hard weight of his gun. It gave you time as well; if someone asked you a question, you could draw out the answer by lighting up or inhaling deeply and letting the smoke float out of you slowly. The bars on the seafront were open, and the roadside stalls were filling up with people getting bowlfuls of noodles and soup, and roasted meat. Some guy back at the compound had insisted he'd eaten the tail off a dog at one of these places, but the smell was good and it made Leon's mouth water. The money he'd been given felt fat in his pocket, but he didn't want to spend it on food or drink. He could drink until beer came out of the pores on his face, but he fancied having something he could hold in his hand and consider.

He could go to bed with one of those girls with the black hair all the way down to her tailbone, the tiny-waisted women who seemed to find all the dirty, tired men endlessly funny, and who seemed to want nothing more than to look you right in the face and listen, smiling and nodding, and then take you away somewhere where no one else could see. But Leon imagined the wide-awake night while she slept next to him. The too light impression she would leave in the bed. So he found himself in a stall that sold and engraved silver lighters, the ones you flicked open with a jerk of your hand. On the side of the stall were examples of what you could have: Australian flags, American flags, rude little stick figures fucking, slogans that read 'Kill Them All, Let God

178

Sort Them Out', '36 Days Without a Solid Shat', and then lighters that were just tallies with the name of provinces.

The shopkeeper smiled widely at Leon. 'Zippo, Zippo!' he said and Leon nodded, smiled back. 'We can draw any kind sexy lady for you, we can do swearing, we can do skull and cross bones, any-bloody-thing for you!'

'Thank you,' said Leon and felt that actually he did want one. But he couldn't think of what inscription he'd have, so he pointed to one from the wall that had writing all the way round it, 'After the Earthquake, a Fire', and paid for it and put it in his pocket, then went into a bar to get a drink.

17

Frank was feeling for eggs in the nest Mary had made, cunningly hidden in a large old flowerpot under the house, when he saw Bob's car approaching. He had time to wash his hands and lift two beers from the fridge, relieved to see him after their last conversation, before he'd pulled up and unfolded out of his car. He drew breath to greet Bob, but stalled on the exhale when he saw his face. There was a brown-paper bruise under his eye and his nose was dark in the nostrils with old blood.

'You right?' Bob shook his head a little, stepped up and took the beer from Frank. Neither spoke as they opened their bottles. Bob drank deeply, breathing out through his open mouth afterwards. The hand holding the bottle shook and Bob lowered the arm to his side. A plume of smoke appeared on the horizon from the sugar factory and dispersed greyly into the sky.

'They found Ian's girl.'

'She's all right?'

'Nup.'

He drank again.

'Oh.'

A currawong flew blackly across the clearing. The sound of sheets snapping in the wind.

'Jawbone. Up at Redcliff.'

'Fuck's sake.' Frank pressed his fingers into his hairline. 'Fuck's sake.'

Bob nodded. 'Just a jawbone. The teeth in there as well. They counted her fillings.'

He closed his eyes. When he opened them again, Bob pointed to his eye. 'It's Vick. If you were wondering. She went a cock-a-hoop.' He touched his face, which peeled open in a smile and a forced laugh that looked dry and painful.

'She okay?'

'Nah. But that's just the fuckin' way sometimes. Sometimes people aren't all right and that's just how it is.' Bob squinted into the sun, avoiding his eyes.

A long silence.

The Mackelly girl. Her jawbone.

'Any ideas?'

'Dud hitchhiker most likely. Probably just passing through. Usual.'

Frank let his head nod, squinted up at the sun with Bob. There was more silence, then more beer. They drank and when their bottles were empty they got more, and when it was all gone they just sat and waited for the end of the day.

He'd dreamt he was back in Canberra. It was dull. In the dream he woke up, got dressed, ate breakfast and left the flat for work. He walked along the street and it was hot. He thought about the things he had to do when he got in to work. He looked both ways before crossing the road. Then a bird singing shrilly in the night woke him, so that he jolted out of deep sleep and felt the air shooting hotly out of his nose.

The bird queried once more and was quiet.

Eucalyptus blanketed the room. He had the feeling that the trees were peering in through the windows, that they had uprooted and crept over to take a peek. The leaves of the banana tree on the roof were a gentle *tap tap tap let me in.*

181

The wind in the cane sounded as if grasses and roots were growing, cradling the shack like a bird's nest, hugging the soft old wood of the place, creaking and splintering the walls. He thought about the feel of loose dirt on his shoulder blades, of the lick of breezes that could reach right up under the backs of his ears. He stretched out his feet and thought he could feel them take root, thought he could feel his toenails' growth speed up; the hair on his head tangling and moving as it grew, lifting tiny bits of scalp and taking them with it.

When the sky lightened he tested his limbs to see if they could move and swung himself out of bed. He pissed long and hard out through the door, his eyes fixed on the scribble gums that looked calmly back.

Juice ran down his chin when he bit into a tomato. Wiping his face, he was surprised by the amount of beard hair he was carrying around. He put a can of tea on to steep and sat on the steps reading the day. A yellow cloud in the north signalled work at the sugar plant had begun. A dog barked distantly and Kirk gobbled as Mary took a bath in the dust. There was nothing for it but to go fishing. He wet his lips with tea, pulled on some dirty shorts and an oil-stained T-shirt with the words DETTOL CLEANS across the back. He threw the remains of last night's meal to the chickens and slotted his reel into the holder on the nose of the truck. He took a pack of frozen green prawns from the cold box and put them in an ice-cream tub of cold water. 'Prawn net,' he said out loud. 'Prawn net prawn net prawn net.'

On the way out to the point, the air was thick with dust. He passed a big white cockatoo standing at the side of the road, looking as if it was waiting for a bus. The creases of its wings were lined with red dust. It watched him pass, feathers ruffled by the breeze, but not in the least bit worried about the truck. In the rear-view mirror the bird shook its head and continued looking up the road in the direction he'd come from. It could be hurt; he'd try to remember to check on it on his way home.

There was no one out at the point and the sea looked soupy. Maybe underneath its surface a dust blew too. He baited up and cast out into the waveless water, the bait plopping like a stone, taking itself down to the bottom with a thud he could feel through the line. There he felt through the pads of his fingers as the prawn rolled in the sand, as it lumbered across small rocks and seaweed. He imagined the sexy-mouthed fish watching it, shaking their heads, rolling their eyes. But he fished on, determined that one of the wrangled tugs on his line would be a fish, not a snag, and that the next cast would be the one. When the sun had melted through the yellow zinc on the tops of his ears he gave himself five more throws.

One, the bait fell off mid-air, slung out on a too hard cast, and he was sure as it hit the water he saw a belly flash, something gobble it as soon as it hit the surface. The next prawn was tightly weaved, aimed at the spot the fish had flashed itself, and the cast was executed, he thought, with minute accuracy. But nothing so much as nosed it. The third throw, when the sun was really hurting his ears and starting on the lower lids of his eyes, was more exciting: a sudden rip of life on the other end of the line, but then nothing, it took just the bait not the hook. Four, nothing at all and he found his interest waning. Normally there was the possibility, endless as the water in the sea, the millions upon millions of chances – what else happened to a dead prawn in the water other than it was eaten by fish? But now he wanted someone to talk to. He wondered if Sal was as keen a fisherwoman as she was a gardener. The backs of his hands burnt on his final throw and he decided just to drag her in, see if something would chase, but when, not far from the shore, he felt a bite, he didn't do anything other than give it a sharp tug, then whatever had bitten was gone.

He unhooked the sucked bait and threw it out – something inhaled it, breaking the surface of the water with silver. Sod it, they were playing silly buggers with him anyway.

In the shade of the bait shop he was blind for the first few minutes. He stared hard at a wall of jelly lures, waiting for the sunspots to go from his eyes. The place smelt like rubber and glue, and it was a good smell, like diesel or chalk dust, the kind you could smell too much. He squeezed the red gummy body of a squid lure and heard the man at the counter behind him shift with annoyance. He gave himself another few seconds to straighten out his sight and turned to him. 'Got any prawn nets in?'

Without looking, the man, who was younger than Frank had first imagined and who wore sunglasses inside, pointed above his head. 'Got yer basic, yer midi and yer reinforced.'

'Reinforced?'

'Get 'em done meself – weave in a bit of leather round the edge. Keep her going for good.'

'Sweet. I'll take one,' said Frank, knowing he had to buy the reinforced net or risk a long uncomfortable stare from behind those glasses.

The man softened a little and he allowed a small smile. 'What you after?'

'Uh, prawns.'

'Know a good place, do ya?'

'I've seen a few up round the sands at Mulaburry.'

'Ah. 'S good fishing place. Easiest bet on catching a few bream just off the rocks there – real girl fishing hole, but she's good if it's a feed you're after and not so much the sport. Know the place I mean?'

Frank nodded.

Back in the sun of the main street he sat himself outside the bakery at one of the aluminium tables. He ordered a black coffee

184

and a currant bun, and when the bun came it was the size of his face. He watched the street, not sure what he was looking for – something recognisable in the few people walking by, or someone who might stop and talk. He wished he'd leant up against the counter in the bait shop, quizzed the guy on where to find a jewfish, asked about sharking, as if he knew something on the subject himself. He could have told the guy how he lived on that land, could even have explained that his mother was in that bream hole, could have got the upper hand on the conversation, maybe enough that leaning on the counter could have turned into a few drinks later on, a pub quiz, a joint on the beach. It felt strange to be wishing these things on himself, of someone who didn't seem the sort of person he would have liked anyway.

He looked at his watch – nearly time for the kids to get out of school. He could give Sal a lift home, think of some things she might be interested in knowing about. Did she know how to wrap dough round a thick stick and bake it in an open fire, then fill it with golden syrup and let it drip all down you, in your hair and eyelashes? Probably. But maybe she'd appreciate the gesture. Perhaps she'd want to have a go at prawning with him, though he wasn't sure she'd be tall enough.

He paid his bill and walked to the truck, surprised at how much he was looking forward to chewing the fat with a seven-year-old. He parked up a little way from the school gates, thinking maybe it would look better if he pretended to have been passing. A bell rang somewhere inside and for a moment there was absolute stillness. Then the doors opened and a wave of kids wearing light-blue caps with flaps at the back spilled out, and he was glad he wasn't waiting at the gate. A few parents and older kids pounced, but on the whole the tide of children dispersed on their own, in tight little groups, yapping like seagulls and dropping skinny wrappings and juice cartons not too near the bins.

He nearly missed Sal, whose black fringe was hidden under her cap. He only spotted her at all because she was alone, her head down. Unlike the other kids, who wore their school backpacks slung casually over one shoulder, she wore hers tight to her back, a serious walker. She moved at a determined pace, not late but precisely on time, as if any deviation from her step would throw the whole day off track. He opened the door and realised he'd have to get out, because she wasn't looking his way. He called her name as she turned the corner. He jogged through the kids, trying not to jostle them, trying hard not to look like a Dangerous Stranger. Rounding the corner, he stopped at the sight of Sal, arms stuck out rigid at her side, being hugged chokingly round the shoulders by Vicky.

He walked backwards round the corner, thumping into a small redheaded girl who blew a spit bubble at him. 'Sorry,' he said and waded against the tide of kids back to his truck. He slid inside and rested his head on the steering wheel. He pushed his tongue into his bottom lip and made the noise 'eughn' like one of the kids might. He tried to feel silly but he just felt disappointed. Of course, after what had happened to the Mackelly kid . . . of course she'd get picked up by her parents. She was only seven. He breathed a sigh of relief, imagining what would have happened if she had seen him, if she'd thought he was collecting her and not her mother.

He didn't feel like going back to the shack, but he drove there all the same, trying to shake off the feeling that the day had been a waste. He'd bought a reinforced prawn net anyway.

The cockatoo was gone from the side of the road, just a few white feathers lifted in the breeze as he drove by. When he pulled up, Linus was there. He'd helped himself to a beer and sat on the steps wearing his old green hat far back on his head, leaning into the last of the yellow sun. His belly had snuck out of the bottom of his T-shirt and rested like a cat on his thighs. 'How's life, ol' matey?' he asked.

'Good, good,' Frank exaggerated. 'What can I help you with?'

'I already helped meself.' The grizzled old bugger raised his bottle at Frank, the white of his stubble shone against his black skin.

'Right.' There was nothing for it but to get a drink and sit with the hoary coot.

'Just wondered how the place was treating you. Getting on okay? Need any hocus-pocus doing?'

Frank laughed a loud ha! and opened his own beer.

A yellow light hit the tallest of the box trees at the edge of the bush. Frank waited, but for a long time the only noise was the far-off applause of crickets and cicadas.

When Linus finally spoke it was to say, 'Terrible business, Ian's girl.' He looked out over the cane, no eye contact.

'Bad as it gets.'

'I 'member her being born. Well, it was only fourteen years ago, so I suppose I would. Makes you think you could go back an' do something 'bout it. Gonna be some sort of memorial thing at the enda the week. I'm sure Stuart'll have told you – she had a lot of aboriginal friends. They're going to do some sorta ceremony for her. Not really sure how Ian'll see that, but.' He snorted. 'Don't get me wrong, Ian hasn't really got a problem. 'S more he'd just like to crush someone I think. Grind 'em into the ground. An' who can blame him? Heard he went ape-shit when they found out her boyfriend was a black fella. But he wouldn't have minded, not really – he just didn't know about it.'

The sun was lower down on the box trees now, a lick of yellow on their trunks. Flycatchers settled on the tips of their branches. There was a sudden brightening of everything, the sun took one final deep breath, then the light mellowed and started to fade.

Frank'd never been so aware of night falling. 'You live alone, Linus?'

'I do. I prefer to live in the town, though. Me and Eleanor. Left her at home. Not like you, not one of those "flash your bum at nature and sleep on the grass" types.'

'Oh?'

'Tell the truth, mate, gives me the willies, a man staying out here all on his own.'

He looked at the old man, but Linus stayed looking dead ahead. He sipped from his beer. Frank shrugged, tried to look nonchalant. 'Sometimes I hear a thing or two I can't put a name to. But then most of the time it's just bandicoots and dreams.' There was a silence and Frank started to form a long complicated question in his head; then, surprising himself, he said, 'What do you know about the bunyip?'

Linus frowned, looked down at his drink. 'He's that fella on TV with the orange face, isn't he? The one that's rude t' everyone? Swears a lot – a puppet.'

'No – that's a wombat – and I mean the actual bunyip.'

'The *actual* bunyip, y'say? Where did you grow up? Fuckin' out the back of beyond?'

'All I know about the bunyip is stuff from kids' books. He hangs around swamps or something.'

Linus drank from his bottle and Frank could hear it going down, heard it snake through his gullet, drop into his belly. Linus's stomach made a noise like something being extinguished. 'Firstly, it's not *the* bunyip – it's bunyip. That's the bugger's name. Secondly, what makes you think it's a he?'

'Right.'

'And third – which makes me think it *is* a he – bunyip likes eatin' women. An' not in a good way either.'

Frank shifted in his seat.

Linus's eyes shone at him from under his derelict hat. 'Fourthly, mate, I know you're a bit beyond the black stump, but if you're going to start believing in bunyip we might as well paint a gecko on your arse and give you a firestick to shake.'

Frank smiled. 'I was talking to Bob Haydon's kid about it.'

'Right. Well, she'd know a thing or two about the matter.'

The faraway rumble of a road train.

'You know,' said Linus, 'there's this old saying: "There is no way to get into an orange after your mother is dead." I don't know who said it. Some Chinese fellah. Pretty smart, though.' He smiled up at the sky.

A whistler circled high above them, called and landed in the box trees, which shed leaves and flycatchers like a shoal of black fish. Frank gave up the fight to understand what Linus was on about and sucked on his beer. It was beautiful again. Just breeze enough to blow away the mosquitoes. Clouds blended orange on a blue horizon. Frogs barked under the veranda.

'I talked with your grandfather once.'

Frank turned to look at him.

'I'd a job with the grocers – 'fore all this Bi-Lo racket. He had this standing order, before your grandmummy came out, it was a monthly deal – not much, really, just big box of matches, some kero. Few cans. Not what you'd want to live on. Anyways, I'd worked as a delivery boy maybe three months 'fore I ever saw the bloke. He'd jus' leave money on the table an' I'd leave the box for him. But one time he was around an I said g'day, an' he was a friendly enough bloke. We had a chat.'

'About what?'

'Nothin' much. Just got the sense he was lonely that day. Asked him about himself, but he didn't tell me much. Asked how old I was. I'm guessing I was about the same age as your old man was then. Asked if I'd had to go to war. I told him too young, and

189

he nodded and shook my hand. Asked me if I had a wife, an' when I said no he said, "Best way." He said, "Best way, might be another war yet." An' he told me he hoped I'd have a plenty good life. An' that was it. I told him I'd see him around but I never did. I think he'd just popped up that day because he was lonely.'

'You remember it pretty well. Long time ago.'

Linus smiled again out into the blue air. He inhaled and took a long swallow of beer, pulled his lips over his teeth and looked at the bottle in his hand. 'Made a bit of an impression I'd say. Never did get married. There was another war. And I see his point. I see his point well.'

'He didn't mention my father? Or my grandmother?'

'Nup. When she turned up was first we knew of that.'

There was something soft about the old man suddenly. Something in the way his teeth worried his bottom lip. 'Beaudy lady. We used to talk.'

His lips were wet and Frank imagined him as a young man. He would have been good-looking, the bones of him dark with heavy shadows.

Linus stifled a burp, which seemed to knock him out of his thoughts. 'She was all interested in where I come from. Not something I was used to, people wanting to know about that. I suppose she bin told to go suck by her country too. Don't think it suited her that well, being out here all on her own just with him. She said was like something had a hold on your poppy. Guess he went through it in the war or something.' He bit his bottom lip with his white teeth, squinted his eyes. 'Your grandmummy she loved him, but. She had to stay with him. Loved 'im.' Frank wanted to say something, but he couldn't think for the image of young Linus and his grandmother, the sugar figure in the wedding dress.

'When your olds turned up after they'd disappeared, I showed them around the place a bit. Nice bloke, your old man was, terrified about your mummy being pregnant. That woulda bin you, I suppose?'

Frank got up. His legs were heavy. He stood at the fridge a moment letting his breath settle. He wanted to ask questions but he was scared his voice would wobble with the beat of his heart. He brought another beer for them both and when he sat down again Linus continued, 'Plenty of people I knew had gone off to war, plenty. Plenty didn't come back. Fuckin' *I* bin in a war, I done that, I seen some bad things, we all did.' Linus shrugged. 'That's war tho', mate. Isn'it?'

Frank nodded.

'Maybe it's somethin' to do with you Europeans, you haven't seen much colour before an' so when you seen the blood, it's a shock? I dunno. But.' Linus's words hung in the air. Strange to be thought of as European.

'Either way. One day, telegram man arrived, found no one in. No one in the next day or the next. Car in front of the house. Cold box cleaned out, shoes under the bed. There was a bunch of clothes on the beach and no more Mr and Mrs.'

'They died in a car accident out at the turn-off. A road train.'

Linus looked at Frank, his eyes bright in the dark. 'Nah, mate. Nah, they didn't. You should talk to your old man about that. He'd know the story.'

'He's dead,' said Frank without thinking. Dead was easier. A closed case.

Linus looked at him. 'Well, I'm sorry to hear that.' A mosquito landed under Linus's eye and he pressed his finger to it, rolled it against his cheekbone.

'What did you talk about with my grandmother?'

'Tole her about me. She wanted to know. We talked about the old people. Important to do that. You gotta know what you can 'bout 'em. See my dad's mum was sent to the hospital islands.

191

They reckoned she was a sick one, so what they did is they sent her there to die. 'Parently she might have been pregnant. Never come back any more.' His voice changed, it sounded old. 'Dad 'members she was taken off in chains, long string of black fellas all with bracelets round their necks. For their own good, y'understand. I don't know if you know much about it over there. Anyways. You went, you didn't come back any more.'

'I'm sorry.'

'Wasn't you.' Linus laughed. 'Was it? 'N'way, my mum she was a white lady – that's how come I wasn't taken away. Got me reading and writing early on too. Helps a black fella, that.' Frank nodded.

'I member you too, you know. I remember the funeral.'

Frank moved his chair a little forward, then back again. 'Funeral?'

'Your mother's. Sat up on those rocks and watched it.' He pointed towards where the sea was, like they could both see it.

'That's weird, Linus. That makes me feel weird.'

'It probably would.'

Frank squeezed his beer bottle.

'Sad business,' Linus carried on. 'There's a sad business in men being left alone.' He inhaled to say more, but held it. A butcher-bird yodelled and Linus let the breath out. 'Your mum seemed a lot like your grandmummy.'

'My grandmother was my father's mother. They weren't blood relations.'

'But they were both married to the same blood.'

'Suppose. You reckon that makes a difference?'

Linus didn't answer for a long time. The air had changed a little, it was thinner or cooler or something. More drink.

Linus spoke, with a voice from a long time ago, and the words sounded rehearsed, like he'd heard them or said them over and over way back. 'Some fellas, they make the women lonely. Maybe it doesn't apply to you, mate, but maybe that's why you're here all on your tod?'

It would be nice if Linus were gone, it occurred to Frank. The soles of his feet felt hot and uncomfortable on the wood of the veranda, as though he'd walked a long way barefoot. 'How old were you when my grandparents came here?'

'Old enough.'

There was a long pause, one which didn't seem to have any effect on Linus, who stood and smoked and squinted as if the sun were still in the sky.

'So what am I supposed to do with that?' Frank asked finally.

'Do?' Linus turned round to look at him like he'd forgotten he was there. 'I dunno, mate, you do what you want. Like I said, I'm no spiritualist. I'm just an' old bloke, an I thought you might like a chew of advice. Give this place a bit of acknowledgement, mate. Just a bit of respect or understanding or something – that's all you need. If you're waking up at night with the ground coming alive and trying to eat you or whatever.'

Frank felt the breath coming in cold, going out hot. Felt like he'd been hit with a thick stick.

'This place has been through a lot since I've been alive, an' it went through a lot before I was alive an' it'll go through a lot after I am dead and you are dead and your kids are dead. So understand that and it won't get at you so much.' He crushed out his cigarette under his boot, bent down, picked it up and put it in his shirt pocket. 'An' careful of them bushfires too, son, they'll get right up your arse.' He chuckled and sashayed over to his truck. 'Anyway, haroo, ta for the beer. I might see you at the dead girl's thing,' he said before turning on the engine. A cassette belted out 'Addicted to Love' at full volume and Linus's tail-lights showed the dust settling in the night air.

Frank stayed and watched until there was nothing left to see.

18

'Just about the size of a good cantaloupe,' said Cray, holding his hands so they made a boxy shape.

Leon nodded. 'Sounds like a good-sized kid.'

'Yep.'

'Good with the wife?'

'Better than good, mate. Tears at your guts to come back here, though.'

As they walked into the village people looked at them, but no one ran. Maybe they were scared to run, could be they didn't know if they should be scared or not. Leon didn't know if they should be scared or not. His palms sweated on the gun. A few children followed the section at a distance, others disappeared inside their houses and came out with members of their families.

'We need you all to leave,' Pete said loudly. 'We need to clear the village, please.' He said it in French and in Vietnamese, reading from a piece of laminated cardboard, sounding each time like a bloke who lived on a sheep farm in Victoria. Nobody moved. Pete read the French phrase again. 'Vamoose,' he said. 'Scram.'

He fired a few times into the air. Leon saw the face of a young man open in shock, his eyes showed white round their black centres. People started to run, then, to grab at each other and flee towards the cover of the forest.

'That's the way,' said Pete quietly.

Clive fell over, just fell over, and everyone stood a moment and looked at him, wondering what the bugger was doing tripping up

194

when they were all trying to look serious. Then the fire started and Leon felt the blood inside him thump as he dropped behind an incinerator and made his gun ready. He heard Pete shouting into his radio for medics, 'Three-one, three-one, contact. Do you acknowledge, over. Dustoff needed urgently, repeat, dustoff for one cas, looking bad, not moving.'

He heard Daniel shout 'They're in the trees!' and aimed round the side of the incinerator bin and saw a group of blokes running like buggery towards the trees. He fired and a few bodies in black fell at the edge of the village; others, not in black, died with their arms flung out as they swam the air. His tracers drew a line across the forest and black birds rose from the trees as smoke. He'd thought that when he finished firing there would be nothing, only the squall sound of birds, but when he stopped the fire really began. Hidden by the trees, the noise started up thick and it was clear there was more than one machine gunner in there. He took more ammunition, shook to reload, shook the gun because it had jammed, shook it more, then thought everyone would kill him. The bastard thing was jammed like it'd never known a thing about shooting. He leant behind an outbuilding and shook it, twisted it, rattled it, prayed for it to open up, give forth fire. Tears on his face, he felt the teeth of a terrible thing on the back of his neck, breathing through its nose on him, in, out, hot, pant. The single rounds of the rifles barely made it through the sound of the automatics firing from the trees. He gave it a hard smash on the ground and the thing went off between his legs, digging a burrow in the dirt next to his ankle. He brought a hand up to his eyes and gave himself a couple of seconds to breathe, before turning and firing that force field up into the trees again. Cray looked at him and closed his eyes. The air was shredded.

When it finally fell quiet they heard the beats of the dustoff helicopter, but Clive was dead. The medics carried him on a stretcher, his face covered over. 'Would've been dead straight off,' one of them said, 'went through the head pretty bad.'

No one else had anything the matter with them and as the heli-copter took off, spraying dirt beneath it, they were left with a black patch of ground that Clive had bled into. Pete shucked fresh dirt over it, a look of disgust on his face, his bottom lip poked out like a sulky child and he turned away from the rest of them with his hands on his hips. 'And then there were five,' he said and gave a little snort.

The dead Cong they lined up neatly and searched, patting down the warm bodies, dipping into pockets and down sleeves. Leon gave the machine gun to Rod for the while, his hands raw from gripping it, he couldn't look at the bastard thing.

'Oi, oi, someone's over there,' Daniel called, pointing his gun towards a dark-stained wooden house.

There was a face in the window, a boy, his mouth a black O. They had their guns ready and aimed at the door and Pete called, 'C'mon out.' There was no noise from inside, so he shouted 'Out!' his voice busting from him hoarse and angry. The front door opened slowly and an old man stepped out, a woman and a young boy right behind him. The woman held a baby. Cray looked at the floor.

'Why haven't you gone already?' asked Pete, not to the family particularly. He sounded tired. 'Better have a bit of a look in there, I reckon.'

Leon took Clive's rifle and went inside with Cray. He felt like a dry river, like all the commotion was gone and nothing could happen now. He wasn't ready for it, he didn't want it. Inside it was dark; there was a smell of incense and dust and cooking, a strange smell of life, nutty and sharp. The wooden roof creaked. Cray nodded at a trapdoor in the floor of the kitchen.

Down through the trapdoor was stone silent, like all noise had been sucked out with a straw. Three chairs were turned over and a bag of rice was spilled across the table. There was a bad smell, a meal left to rot. Bowls were laid out on the table with spoons, they must've been getting ready to eat: so close to having a sit-down dinner, to sharing a normal talk, having a drink, maybe, and laughing. Eating out of a bowl, not out of a packet or your hands.

The silence was split by a high whine and Leon heard himself clench. There was a low door he'd assumed was a cupboard, the only place to hide in the cellar. It was the kind of noise kids made, playing hide and seek, excited and needing a pee, trying to hold in the urge to shout, 'Here I am! You fuckin' didn't see me but here I am!' Cray moved towards the door, stepping gently like a ballet dancer. From the look on his face the smell was worse the closer he moved to the door.

Leon's lips felt like fish scales. 'He'll be armed,' he whispered and Cray nodded. An inward count of three, and Leon trained on the door, then Cray raised his boot and kicked it open, firing into the space. A body twitched with the impact of bullets, a gun in his hand fell to the floor unfired, and Cray put his wrist up to his face and yelled. Leon thought for a terrible moment that he'd been shot in the face, but he carried on yelling and the smell hit him too.

'Fucking hell!' shouted Cray. 'Fucking fucking crappy hell!' He spat and turned away from the open door, his eyes streaming. The dead man had lost his foot and the flesh off his leg, but the bone remained. His torso teemed with small things that ate at him.

'What is it?' came a yell from above ground.

'It's all right – one dead Cong,' Cray called back up.

'Close the door,' said Leon quietly, but it stayed open.

'We should check in there,' Cray said, breathing into his elbow.

'I'll go,' said Leon, because Cray had a son at home. Cray stepped aside uncomplaining as he pushed the door with the tips of his fingers. Maggots made the man's chest move up and down. It's just meat, it's the same as rotten road kill, nothing unnatural about it, he thought and tried to keep his eyes above the level of the man's heaving chest. It was a wonder he'd been alive, still been able to hold a gun, even if he couldn't fire it. A chain held him by his good ankle to an eyelet in the wall. The room was bare, a small table held a cup of water and propped against it a photograph of a woman and a child. The heads had been ripped off them, their identity kept a secret, but still they stood on the man's table, like any bedside table in the world, a glass of water and a picture of your wife and child. All that was missing was a bedside lamp and a dog-eared novel. Empty boxes dotted the floor, a pair of pyjamas hung on the back of the door. That was it. He turned to leave, but even headless, he felt the horror of the man's family as they looked down on him, maggoty and dead. He picked up the photograph and slid it into his pocket. 'Clear,' he said as he closed the door.

Outside a few men smoked while the family huddled softly nearby, looking uncertain, the old man muttering low to the child, the woman holding the back of her baby's head.

'The guy was chained to the wall,' he told Cray. 'Must have done something.'

'Old matey down there would have been too hurt to go with them. They get chained so they have to fight to the death.'

He looked at the family. The man's knuckles gripped white on the boy's shoulders.

'You need to leave,' said Pete, turning to face the man. He pointed at the jungle with his gun. 'Go on. Get.' The man said something back, something angry, but the boy looked up at him, the face of a soft moon, and held on to the man's finger tightly. The man shook his head and the woman made to go back into the house.

'Nup,' said Pete, pointing to the forest. 'Go-On-Get-Going. Fuck off out of it!' The woman made a pleading gesture. Pete shook his head. She waved her arm, pointing at the baby, and Pete shouted, 'Get Away!'

Leon pointed his gun at the woman. She looked stunned and the old man gently held her shoulder and turned them towards the jungle. He muttered something to her and she relented. The old man looked at him and he felt a jab in his guts like he'd swallowed a pen. *I would never have shot*, he thought, *I would not ever have shot, it was just to move you along*, but the cold maw of the thing told him he was not so sure.

19

A southerly blew at the marina and brought with it the sweet smell of tarry old fish. A few blokes had long sleeves on, and Bob had a scarf that he wound round his head so that it covered his nose and lips. 'Can't take the smell of that fuckin' wind,' he said with his palms on his temples.

'Pretty changeable up here, eh?' said Frank, wishing he'd brought something warm. The sun-white hairs on his arms stood up like cactus spines and he felt girly rubbing them down.

'Yeah – we catch all the dud weather as it goes past.'

Frank nodded as if this were well-known scientific fact.

'You hear about Pokey?' Bob looked at him with one eye, protecting the other from the wind with his hand.

'Nup.' Frank pulled on his gloves.

'Some joker got him last night. Hurt him pretty bad if you want to know the truth. He ain't talking, though.' An engine started up, guttering and loud, and they had to shout over it.

'Christ. He's all right?'

'Yeah, he's around – probably shouldn't be, but what you gonna do?'

'Do we know who did it?'

'Nup. He's giving out that he's gonna find who did it himself. Find 'em with a hook.' Bob picked up his bag from the floor and pulled the scarf from his mouth. 'You ask me though, mate, he's just a scared old man. I wouldn't mind finding the culprit meself with a shovel on my side.'

Stuart passed by with an armful of thick orange rope. 'Bastard of a thing, eh?' he shouted, straining like he was carrying bricks not rope. Bob nodded, put his scarf back up and headed down the gangway. Stuart caught Frank's eye and came close to him. 'Be those black fellas again, I wouldn't be surprised,' he said, low and soft. There was a smile in his voice and he gave Frank a wink as he walked away.

At morning tea, Pokey came out of the foreman's hut. The left side of his face was the deep swollen dark of black wine gums. Stripes of red showed the imprint of a fist on his cheekbone. His left eye was closed, but you could make out the blood-red line that was his eyeball. He walked with a limp, his good eye searching out the faces of his workers, daring anyone to say anything. Most people looked up and then got on with what they were doing, but the silence was heavy. Charlie watched Stuart with an empty look on his face and Stuart giggled.

The ceremony was out in the long grasses by Redcliff. There were five or six cars all by the side of the road and smoke came up from the point, made the air thick and smell of burnt seawater and cloves. It had already started by the time he got down to the small assembly of people, and he was alarmed to see that at first glance they were all aboriginal and mostly young. They turned to look at him, then turned back to themselves, thin scarves round their foreheads. A young girl with hoop earrings and red paint in her eyebrows fanned a small fire, fed it with grasses and the smoke blew low over the lot of them. Two boys sang a song that could have been joyful, if their faces weren't stretched in the way that they were, if their eyes didn't stare, full and black. He stood a little way from them, feeling the marsh wet his boots, the sponge earth seeping. He spotted Linus sitting with his shirt off, white lines down the length of his nose. He smiled at Frank and Frank nodded.

201

Through the smoke he saw a white face, Vicky, her hair tied at the nape of her neck, covering her ears and trailing round her throat. In the heat of the gully she wore an oversize oilskin coat. Frank caught her eye and she slipped through the smoke round the edge of the gathering. They stood next to each other, and he could feel the heat of her and smell the wax of her coat. She stretched out her little finger and all at once she was holding his hand, and it was hot and wet, and she squeezed so that the bones of his fingers ached.

'Where's everybody else?' he whispered.

'Who?' she said, not whispering, but no one looked up.

'I thought there'd be others.' It felt silly his being there – he hadn't even known the girl, hadn't met her father. 'What about Bob?' She shook her head but didn't offer anything else. He stayed quiet, feeling the strange hand in his and wondering what it was supposed to mean. A girl sang a song from a movie. Celine Dion. A kid, about seventeen, his thick hair shaped into a short fin, gold chains round his neck, sat alone cross-legged close to where the smoke blew thickest.

'That's Johno, Joyce's boyfriend,' Vicky said in his ear. The boy's jaw was hard set and he blinked a lot in the smoke. His fingers pressed at each other. A dark orange scarf shone against the matt skin of his face. The boy stared at the two of them and there was something bad about the way he did it. Then he got up and made off into the long grass, and Frank wanted to leave too. Linus gave him a look and he wondered what he was thinking about the two of them holding hands. Crickets cracked all around them. The ground seeped under Frank's weight, the water stained brown from the tea trees. He tugged on Vicky's arm and she looked at him as if she'd forgotten he was there. She didn't resist when he steered her back towards the path, when he took them down the route to the beach, razor grass slicing at their shins.

'Where's everyone else?' he asked again, once they were out of earshot, just the occasional high voice and the smell of smoke on the breeze.

'Who else would you expect to come? Those are just her friends.'

'Did you know her?'

Vicky looked at him but didn't answer. She turned her head to look up the beach. The sky was pinking. She sat down in the dry sand close to the grass. He sat down too and took his boots off. She buried her feet, letting the loose white sand run through her fingers and watched as she did the same to his feet. He felt a sort of sickness about what could happen next – her strong legs, the width of her hips.

'That poor boy,' Vicky said, 'they had him in for questioning. God only knows what they did to him.'

'The boyfriend – they think he did it?'

'He didn't do it. The one that did is most likely a million miles away by now.' The sea pulled at the sand and spat it out again.

'But do they think Johno did it?'

'They?' Her voice was faraway and flat, like the questions didn't mean that much to her.

'I suppose he wouldn't be around if they thought he'd done it.' Vicky didn't answer, not even a shrug. They sat in the quiet until the sun was setting and a large, smooth, black piece of petrified driftwood that had long ago washed up and planted itself on the sand cast its shadow long and dark up the beach.

'Couple of days ago Ian Mackelly went to have a talk to Johno. Took along some of the marina boys. Bob went.'

'What happened?'

'They went to his house – place he lives with his parents and his grandfather. Little kids there too. They didn't take along anything but they rolled up their sleeves. Bob said they really just

203

wanted to talk.' Vicky smiled and shook her head like she couldn't even believe the fact.

'Well, maybe that *is* all they wanted to do.'

Vicky looked at him. 'You don't have kids.' She pushed the balls of her hands into her eyes and there was a small wet noise from them.

'They asked for Johno to come out and he didn't, so they stayed there all night. Four of them, big men, waiting with their flaming shirtsleeves rolled up.'

'I can't believe they would've hurt him, Vick. Bob wouldn't let it happen.'

'It's like I said. You don't have kids.'

The waves were quiet, the birds didn't sing, and ghost crabs scattered on the surface and disappeared into their holes. The wind must have shifted because smoke came down and threaded slowly out to sea. It blew in through their hair and Vicky sniffed. 'No spirit sticking to me,' she said.

He saw the difficult lines of her face, the hair that hooked in her eyelashes, smelt the oilskin coat.

'Bob told you about Emmy?'

Frank nodded. He wondered if he should mention those bruises on Bob's face, but it wasn't for him to stick his beak in. 'Think maybe we should go home?' he said, even though it would have been nice to feel her hot and sinking into the sand underneath him.

She held out her hand, laid it palm up on the sand. He put his over hers, not to hold it, just to cover. 'Why are *you* here, Frank?' she asked and he found that, really, he didn't know.

The next day the southerly still blew at work and it dried him out, leaving the skin of his hands tight and old-looking. He couldn't stop touching his right eye, which became blood-lined and weepy, and he could feel some bit of grit in it, like his eyeballs were drying out and sand was getting in. When work was over he went into the pub toilet and rinsed his eye, soaped up his papery hands and washed them until they looked pink. The men had gathered round a set of tables by the front window of the pub, so you could look out and watch surfers on main beach. There was hardly any swell, but still the water was speckled with them, some lying flat, some sitting upright, dangling their legs in the water and looking out to the horizon, willing a wave to come and knock them off.

'You look pretty ropy mate,' offered Bob, as he sat down. He pushed a drink across the table.

'Ta for the beer,' Frank said. 'Got some grub in my eye.'

'Listen, Vick told me about yesterday.' Frank bit his tongue. What had she said? 'Thanks, mate. Should've gone meself, just couldn't face it.'

Frank nodded and took a long drink simultaneously so he wouldn't have to talk.

Linus cleared his throat. 'How's the bass, Stuart?'

Stuart leant forward and set himself more comfortably in his chair. There was no sign that he was put out by the previous week. 'Yeah, she's pretty good, thanks, Linus mate. She's getting pretty tame.'

'Stuart keeps a bass in his pool,' said Linus, looking at Frank. There was the suggestion of laughter round his mouth.

'Really? It's okay with the chlorine?'

'Aw, mainly rainwater, mate, more of a pond right now than a pool.'

'A mosquito pot,' Linus said. 'An' a stinking one at that.'

'You're just jealous, mate.'

Linus no longer looked like he was taking a rise. The old man's eyes narrowed as if he was seeing something different from the rest of them.

205

'Sure thing, she's a pretty bass.' There was a general quiet reverence while apparently everyone pictured the fish.

'You teach her any tricks?' asked Bob.

Frank was on the verge of laughing out loud.

'Aw, she's coming on. Last weekend got one of the kids to take some footage of me feeding her. She'll come right up and take it out of my hand.'

Everyone nodded, impressed.

'Aw, and then – it was unreal!' Stuart sat up tall, smiling, leaning back on his stool. 'The kids caught a skink and threw him in, and Bassy came up and hit it – took the bloke in one go!' He used his hands to show how the fish went. 'I was spewing we weren't filming. She was too full to take any more – gonna give it another shot this weekend. Been thinking about throwing a mouse in there too.'

'Sweet as,' said Bob.

Everyone drank.

'So,' asked Frank. 'What's your plan, is she a pet or are you going to let her go?'

Stuart eyed him suspiciously, then seemed to decide it was a genuine question. 'Well, I catch her about once every two weeks – jus' using a lure – an' then at some point I'll go an' release her.'

'Righto – where at?' It had seemed to him to be a perfectly normal question, but the atmosphere at the table changed. Everyone sat up a little straighter, Linus moved his beer in concentric circles, Bob snorted and cleared his throat.

'That', said Stuart, 'is for me to know.'

Later in the evening the drink seemed to sort out the creakiness of Frank's body. His joints felt lubricated, his head light and he felt unusually spry as he kept his eye on a girl at the bar, thinking perhaps he should buy her a drink. When it came to his round, he sidled up to her. 'Anything for you?' he asked.

She looked at him like she might laugh and for a second his

good feeling died in his boots, but she smiled. 'Sure – rum and lemonade, please.'

He put in the order and leant against the bar. 'You work around here, then?' he asked.

'Not exactly – what about you, been down at the marina?'

'Yeah, been packing nails today.' It wasn't the keenest line he'd ever used.

'Nice one.' She said.

'Ta.'

'So . . . ?'

'Yeah.'

And as easily as that it was over and she had on one of those looks again like she might laugh.

'Guess I haven't been up to much lately.'

'Guess not. Well, ta for the drink anyways.' She sipped through her straw and gave him a smile that was nice, and he cheered up.

With his hands full of drink, Stuart slapped him on the back. 'Nice one, Franko,' he said, the tops of the beers running down Frank's fingers. 'You just bought the foreman's fourteen-year-old niece a drink. He'll thank you for that, I'm sure of it!' The table erupted and Frank felt his face go hot. He glanced over to where the girl sat down opposite a battered Pokey and sucked wetly on the red straw.

At midnight he found himself in the driver's seat of his truck, too tired and too drunk to go anywhere. 'Lucy Lucy Lucy Lou Lou Lou,' he said quietly to himself and then he was crying. He fell asleep strapped into his seat belt and didn't wake until it was just starting dawn. There was a red drinking straw in his shirt pocket that he couldn't place and he dropped it out of the window, preferring not to think too much about where it had come from. He felt like his guts had collapsed on each other and breathing out too far made him feel sick. He started the engine and pulled out into the empty street, glad it was too early to have to try to avoid crashing into other vehicles.

It was a soft, damp morning and things were paler than usual on the road that led home. The bark of the gums blanched at him as he drove down the track. A heavy mist hung low in the air, so that once he'd come to a stop outside the shack there was nothing to see past the cane.

Both chickens were sleeping, their white eyes closed like small barnacles, their bodies fluffed and frowsy. When he closed the truck door it sounded too loud and made his heart beat like a footstep. A rosella took off from the veranda and a large white cockatoo, which perched in the banana tree, turned its back on Frank at the same time as crapping into the open air.

His boots made a din on the floorboards. He was usually bare-footed and he trod lightly for fear of waking someone. He sat down on the side of his bed and undid his laces carefully, softly placing the boots next to each other underneath the bed. A swim was the only real cure for overcooking yourself. He tried whistling to break the ice of quiet as he floundered for his towel, but the bare windows glared at him. The banana tree swept against the roof, shhhhhhh.

He cleared his throat.

He took off his clothes and slung the towel over his shoulder, pulling at fistfuls of his hair to try to clear his head, and making it stick straight up as he walked out of the shack and down the path to the bay.

The sea was pasty, the rip a little high. Scum yellowed the tide-mark. The water was warm and his dick hardly shrank as he floated until he lost the feel of his body. He watched from the corner of his eye as he passed the bream hole and thought of his mother standing there holding a live prawn in her fingers and hesitating to thread it on to the hook. Past that, further out, was the point

208

where they'd used to set the crab trap. A memory surprised him: his father waking him at dawn before everything, when his mum was sleeping in that creaky double bed of theirs. 'Come and we'll see what the crab pot's sucked up,' his dad had whispered.

'What about Mum?'

'Man's work.'

'Hokay.'

He'd felt an odd gravity to the situation as they tiptoed out of the shack, not closing the door in case the noise woke her up. They wore just the pants they'd slept in and he'd felt yesterday's sunburn wince on his back.

When they got down to the water, his dad disposed of even his pants and flung them at the dry sand up the beach. He did the same, and went and stood by his dad as he dragged the surf ski down to the waves.

'C'mon then, Franko, in you get.' His dad held the surf ski steady in the shallow white water.

'We going in the nud?'

'Nud as a grub.'

He hesitated.

'You worried a crab's gonna have it off or something? C'mon, who'll see?'

He stepped in, cautiously viewing the funny pigskin hanging from his dad.

''S the thing I've learnt, Franko,' he said as he pushed them off into the gentle swell, 'there aren't that many places to be nude any more – you gotta take the chance when it comes along.'

His dad hopped in behind so that his legs, dark with thick hair, went either side of Frank. Water swilled crisply in the hull of the surf ski, turning warm with being near their bums. He wondered if he would get away with peeing, but thought he'd best hold it.

They lapped out to the point where the bottom was sandy and deep, and the polystyrene ball painted with the name COLLARD floated. He'd watched his dad stroke out with it the day before, seen the hooked skeleton of a blackfish dark against the sky, and he'd been sulky then that he hadn't taken him along too. But here he was for the good bit and heat rose in his chest at the thought of the two of them on their own, bringing in the food. The sky was fully light now, but still a pale impression of the day ahead. Even the sea was a calm version of itself. It rocked them gently in their long boat, there were no rips to steer against. The wind was a soft hooting breath.

'Righto, let's see what we've got here. If it's a shark, you knock it on the head.' He'd nodded seriously as his dad began pulling up the rope. Once the slack had been taken, his dad pulled hard on it, frowning, the tendons at his neck and the muscles round his shoulders pulsing.

'Is it stuck?' he asked, worried the ski would upturn.

'I reckon she might be, mate. Must be under a shelf rock or something. Hold on, we'll come about and try a different angle.' They let the tide move them gently in an arc, his dad pulling all the time.

'Crikey! She's a bugger,' his dad muttered under his breath. And then a little give. Then another and he began to pull, red-faced, hand over hand, straining, with his teeth set and his arms shaking.

'She's coming up, mate, bit by bit – we'll have caught on an old anchor or something.'

After what seemed like ages they saw the trap down in the water, full and black. 'What is it?' asked Frank, unable to keep the sense of dread out of his voice.

'Dunno, mate, but she's sure as hell something.'

As the trap came up at the side of the boat, his dad let it hang a little, so the seawater drained out and it became light enough to hold up and get a proper look at.

'By crikey,' whispered his father. 'Get a load of that, Franko boy.' Suspended over the side of the boat was a cage of crabs, a mess of bright blue swimming legs and the ticking noise of their breath, all of them muscling about, too many for the cage. 'That's at least sixteen, seventeen crabs in there, Franko.' He held the trap over the side, the great weight gone. They both stared at it, wondering how on earth to get it back in to dry land.

Frank floated on his back, remembering how the place had stunk the good stink of boiled crab for days and the noise the shells made when they tipped a bag of them back in the sea. He smiled at the memory and tilted his head back a little so the water could get at the lids of his eyes.

Something bumped his arm.

He raised his head and saw that he had drifted clear out of the bay and there was something in the water with him. After swallowing a mouthful, he felt for all his limbs and found them still there. A fin appeared a few feet away, not a huge fin, but still a fin and it didn't look like a reef shark. It hung in the water, oddly still, waiting for him to make the first move.

'Shit,' he said and he kept on saying it to keep himself calm. He tried to keep his legs in a steady stroke, but they kept shaking and flinching of their own accord. The main thing, regardless of the shark, was to get out of the rip that was taking him further and further out. He'd been caught in currents before and he knew to swim the horizon, not fight against it. He rounded the point of the bay and swam and swam, the sound of his breath like wind through a torn plastic bag. The shark kept with him, an arm's length away to the side, and he tried to keep it in the corner of his eye, tried not to turn his head to look at it, which slowed him down.

Then the fin went under.

With every kick he imagined plunging his foot right into its mouth, having his feet taken, the sharp white bone at the ankle, bleeding to death. He passed through a cold current and thought he was being swallowed whole. His guts moved inside him and he thought, *Don't piss. God, don't shit.* As he gained on the land, he fixed on the dunes, thinking about the solidness of it for his feet, and about running up into them and rolling naked in the dry yellow sand.

Paddling hard, he came into the shallows, but it didn't leave him alone. When he could touch the bottom with his flat foot, it darted at him, sending bow waves at his chest, coming for him and veering away at the last second, chasing him, herding. When he stood, he could see the back of it, and it made him fall over, get up again and fall over and get up. It was bigger than he'd thought, as long as he was, but worse were the dark streaks across the pale fish, the boxed head of a tiger shark. He ran in the water, falling every second step, choking on salt; his hand was speared by a sharp shell or point of coral, but it didn't put a beat in his progress. He ran out of the water and didn't stop until he was far up the beach, a hooting noise coming from his chest. Turning and flopping on to the ground, he watched the fin torpedo up the bay and out into the open sea.

'Fuck me,' he said, wiping his face over and over with his hands, standing up naked and bleeding with a sandy bottom.

'Fucking well fuck me.'

212

20

The gravelled road leading into the village was long and black and straight, and the only saving grace was that it was too dark to see to the end of it. The clouds hid the moon and there was no light from the village, nothing to see, no way of knowing if your eyes were open or closed, and Leon was alone.

They were expecting baddies. Most likely they would come up the road, not guessing that they had got there first. Unless they'd been warned. The rest of the section were dotted about the place, with orders not to smoke, though he suspected these would be ignored. He wished he had some left to pass the time, a tiny light might give some perspective to the black. Might ward off the mosquitoes, might take his mind off the thing that sat next to him in the dark. He held up his camera and took a shot into the black. It had been fine when they were all together, when you could see other people and think about other people, but here, alone, he thought about those three heartbeats, holding the gaze of that first boy he had killed. The feel of the thing crawling up inside him. The hole his gun had dug between his legs, the sick feeling when the barrel jammed. The dead.

The Vietnamese believed in ghosts. He did not, but he was in their country now and you couldn't help but feel it, alone in the black. He touched his eyes to make sure that they were open. The skin round his sockets was hot and dry, and the coolness from his fingertips was good. It would have been wonderful to lie down.

He thought about the yellow print on Lena Cray's dress, how it snagged over her belly.

In an instant something changed. He stayed deadly still, trying to locate what it was. When he realised he felt all of hell flatten him and horror tightened his throat. He had been asleep and something had woken him. He'd let the buggers in, they'd walked right past him, they were in there now slitting throats. He didn't move. He barely breathed. He was sure at that moment in the black that someone held a gun to his face. He felt breath on his cheek, he would hear the click of a barrel. Then calmness. *Go on then*, he thought, *go on then*. But nothing. The breath on his cheek was gone. Perhaps it had never been there. His eyebrows arched high, he watched for the first wash of light as it turned the sky. He saw the sun rise and wondered if it would make him cry. The grass was wet from dew and between his tripod and gun a spider had strung a web, and water caught the sun as he breathed the dawn deeply.

Tramping off towards the jungle again with no one murdered in the dark, no baddies showing up, he felt heavy and sick as though he'd been drinking hard the night before.

'Jeeze, you look crook,' Cray said, wiping repellant on to his neck. 'Didn't you get any sleep?'

Leon looked at him. 'I was watching the road all night.'

'Well, what did you watch? Was so dark out there, you wouldn't have seen the bugger come up and kiss you on the lips. We all bedded down, thought to hell with it.'

The corners of his eyes stung. He felt crook. He really did.

A few hundred yards into the trees the creek had come close in to the village. He heard it running from a way off. A couple of planks made a thin bridge and he was glad not to have to wade through – his boots were still stewy from the last crossing. Before they reached the bank, there it was again, the back of Cray's neck

214

tensed and he felt his fingers numb on his gun. But Cray's neck relaxed and he turned round to face the others. He didn't say anything, just shook his head and walked on.

There were bodies. The creek was stuffed with them. Women and men and children and babies, adrift. They'd taken on water, become soft like rotten potatoes. Their faces were dark holes pushed in soft fruit. A baby, swaddled still in its shawl, floated alone and he thought of the family he'd pointed the gun at. The moon-faced boy. He thought about the line of tracers he'd sent out over the trees after he'd undone the jam in his gun.

Daniel shook his head. 'Why would you get your family along? They always get shot.'

The section crossed the bridge and no one talked, there was just the clump of boots on the planks, one by one, until only Rod was left on the other side. They waited for him, no one told him to hurry up, they just watched him, tired, as he stood and continued to stand on the wrong side of the creek, with one hand over his eyes.

You had to breathe with your mouth open.

21

There was no sleep for Frank that night and none the next either. His ears were blocked, his sinuses pulsed. He had water on the ear, that was the problem. It was in there rolling about against his eardrum and no amount of head shaking, no amount of fingers in earholes made the slightest difference. His head ached. It looked like the cut on his palm had got infected, small seawater boils had formed round the opening and it throbbed in time with his sinuses. Everything was muffled and hot. He tried to eat some pilchards for breakfast but they turned his stomach and he left them for the hens to pick apart, making their beaks red with tomato juice. His beard itched, felt lumpy round the throat with whorls and clumps of hair, and he couldn't leave it alone, but the idea of shaving it floored him. He'd have to scissor it first, then the tearing grind of his blunt razor. There'd be blood drawn for sure.

Frank's eyes felt salty, the rims of them were tender and he could feel tingles on his lips that might be cold sores coming. He wanted to peel his face off and clean it from the inside. Instead he opened a beer. It was early morning, but what difference did the morning make to a man who hadn't slept? He stayed on his bed, the dark inside the shack was better on his eyes. The shark two days before was like a story he'd overheard. Every time he thought about it he heard the ticking noise all those crabs had made, their hairy legs scrabbling around in the bottom of the surf ski. They'd eaten blue swimmers for four days solid, then they had started to smell and the last ones had to be chucked, dead, back to the sea. He thought about Pokey's niece with the red drinking straw, and Joyce Mackelly's jawbone. He thought about Johno with his black hair and the way he'd disappeared into the long sharp grass. The smell of smoke was still on his skin and so was Vicky's coat. He thought of Bob, who smiled too often too widely, Linus who watched everything and knew something secret, Stuart and his kids and his fish. It was all sad and lost already, and on top of it sat Lucy and he knew what she would have said. The thought of having her nearby seemed like the most perfect thing. A body that was his to touch and to fit in front of his like a piece of interlocking shell.

The air in the shack smelt. Or maybe he smelt, you couldn't know these things for sure. It was the smell of lots of people pressed in all together, sweating up against each other, breathing their bad breath. Frank took a wander outside; the chickens were nowhere in sight. He couldn't hear the birds in the trees but he knew they were there, saw the leaves of the blue gums shifting around. He ploughed through the cane, made for the cover of the trees, where maybe the air was thinner, where maybe he wouldn't notice the silence so goddam much. He'd have to stock up on drink but he was too spliced to drive, even he knew that. With a rambling forward motion he was able to lurch into the coolness of the trees and there was the smell of eucalypt, strong and heavy but medicinal, like it cleaned up his throbbing hand, soothed his eyes.

He contemplated lying down by the creek and passing the rest of the day there, but the creek was low and there were green ants. Besides, he'd need more drink if he was going to avoid the hangover. Maybe he was sick, he thought, as he ambled on, untangling himself from a vine of stay-a-while and feeling genuine surprise at the rash of blood pricks it left round his ankle. An hour or maybe two or maybe ten minutes later, he came to the cane of the Haydons' boundary. The cane was thin and low, and it was more of a wade than a swim through it to their farm. Bob's car wasn't around and it occurred to Frank that maybe it was Vicky he wanted to see anyway. It was hot as buggery, the air was low and wet, and he was still deaf. He could feel sweat creeping down the skin underneath his beard. He scratched at his throat and felt the lumps there – hives, maybe, or boils, something growing under his skin, hatching out.

He stood outside the house and looked at the place. The big veranda all around hung with seashell wind chimes and pot plants that wrapped themselves round the corner posts. A small wind moved his hair, cooled the burn of his beard. Vicky appeared at the door in a loose white shirt, her bare legs flowing out of it, her chafed ankles and scarred brown knees.

She mumbled something that Frank couldn't understand. 'What?' he said. 'Can't hear you. Damn water in me ears.'

'I said,' she shouted, 'Jesus, Frank, you look like a fuckin' monster!' She jerked her head towards the indoors. 'Come in and have a sit in front of the air-con!'

She sat him by a machine that he could feel vibrating through his feet, it sounded like a tractor even through the buggered drums of his ears, and she went from the room. The air that came out of it was antiseptic, cold enough to give him an instant headache and burn the tunnels of his nose. It was a beautiful thing. When she came back, she was wearing a pair of worn men's shorts and holding a jug of water with ice and a glass.

'You look like you've done a pretty good job at dehydrating yourself!' she called at him from in front of his face. He took the water she poured for him and felt it go sharp down his neck. It was as though there was a spine in his throat, a stuck dry fishbone that he couldn't get wet. Vicky mumbled something and Frank shook his head at her, closed his eyes to feel the blast of cold on his eyelids. He felt hands on his face and opened his eyes to see she'd brought a basin of soapy water and some scissors. He blinked as she cut away at the tufts of hair round his face, twirling them loose round her fingers. He felt the disgust of himself and it made him angry that she was there to see it, but he couldn't stop her. He watched her watching where she cut, her tongue pink between her lips, her eyebrows drawn together. When she produced a razor and began to massage warm water into his beard he felt the dirt coming free, watched in amazement as she smiled and the lather grew up round his face. He heard the scraping from inside his body, felt the overpowering itches being scratched. The water in the basin was dark grey with hair and dirt and blood before she switched to a new razor.

She was talking now, softly to herself perhaps, and he could hear a mumble, but not the words. Her frown deepened as she shaved under his chin and he saw her wince at something there. She got up and went to the kitchen and when she came back she had a box of matches, tweezers, and a pin stuck on the end of a cork. Outside there was a roll of thunder and, as it passed over, Frank's ears cleared and hot seawater ran down his neck. There was a whine from his tear ducts. 'I can hear,' he said.

'It speaks,' said Vicky.

'What are you doing?'

'Ticks. You're buggered with them.' She tilted back his head and heated the pin in the flame of a match until it was black, then approached his throat with it. He felt a small warmth, a pressure and Vicky went in with the tweezers, her eyes squinting. Frank held his breath and she moved back. 'Got 'im,' she said under her breath and dropped the bud-looking bastard into the water. She heated the pin again and went back to it. With the pin to his throat she said, 'Bob told me what happened back in Canberra, you know.' Frank didn't reply. His face was hot. 'Reckon you might be making yourself a little bit crazy out there all alone?'

'What about you?' He felt angry suddenly, dangerous, the urge to grab her wrist and look her in the eye. But he didn't.

'What about me, what?'

'Bob catches it a bit off you sometimes. Can't tell me you're not driving yourself a little bit nuts.' There was a small sharp pain in his neck and he couldn't tell if she'd pricked him on purpose.

She smiled softly and there was a silence, an intake of breath. She sat back on her stool, another tick held tight between the jaws of the tweezers. 'It's not me that does that to Bob.'

'You mean it's not the real you?'

She smiled tightly. 'No. I mean he does it himself. I've had to pull the lock off the bathroom door. He goes in there and hits his face against the sink.'

Frank was silent and Vicky continued removing the ticks. He felt his mouth fill up with spit, swallowed it down.

'I imagine he told you it was me doing it? Being an hysterical woman all over the place? He sleeps so deeply it doesn't wake him up when he cries out at night. These real sobs like a kid.'

Another tick out, a plip in the dirty water.

'I can't lie there listening to it. When Emmy died there was none of that. We didn't cry, we just watched and that was all there was.' The room lit up with lightning and outside the storm started with the sky falling like sand on the roof.

Frank sat in the doorway of his shack, clean-shaven, and drank instant coffee, watching the rain pouring off the corrugated roof in needle stripes of white and feeling the spray of rain on his face as it bounced off the veranda.

In the afternoon, lightning struck a field far off to the north and he heard, above the roar, the sound of trucks speeding towards it, smoke a spear on the horizon.

One storm passed with another right behind and in between the sun shone more furiously than before, trying to clean up the mess, suck up all the extra water before the next one arrived. Mist rose on the top green leaves of the sugar cane. The chickens, fluffed and offended by the storm, ventured out to pull up fat earthworms from the battered soil.

The thunder that night had Frank, Kirk and Mary awake, wide-eyed and indoors: the sound overhead of great concrete wheels rumbling and warping over the shack; the blackness between the lightning, and the flat colour when the lightning stuck; the orange bucket by the blue Ute; the green green green of the cane and the white sky; the frozen water coming down, pale and thick. He imagined at each strike a figure before the darkness and wished there were someone he could crawl into bed with. Someone who would see the rain falling like razor blades and breathe their own breath into the shack so that the window would steam up. He held a candle by the mirror and looked at the marks the ticks had left under his chin. Nine little puncture marks. He wanted to show Lucy. She'd be fascinated. She'd touch them with her cold fingers. He looked at his face and wondered what he'd have to do.

The chooks were asleep on the veranda. He emptied out a whole bag of feed around the place – he had seen them get on to the roof with furious flapping, so he figured they'd be safe from foxes. He tippy-toed to the truck, hoping not to wake them as he left.

Early in the morning the rain stopped and the sky was a left-over ice-blue. Frank stopped at a roadside for breakfast. Over tired eggs and sleepy toast, he watched other people in the truck stop. He didn't know if they were good or bad, these lives other people had. Large men looked blankly out over the highway, a mess of yellow eggs and coffee in front of them or, for the ones whose stomachs had long forgotten the conventions of breakfast, a meat pie and cola. Their thoughts still seemed to be of the road. He tore at a napkin. It would be good to have something to concentrate on. He asked himself questions that he felt he must know the answers to. They must be somewhere inside his brain. The right thing to do. *What will I say?* was the one that went round and round, and came out of his mouth with answers that never got beyond hello, because he was stopped by the word Dad. The adverts on the radio spooked him, and he turned it off and ended up counting the white lines in the road as he drove over them, or finding a tune in the engine's revs.

The smell of Sydney came rolling at him as he reached the outskirts. The ozone, the diesel and the thick brown river. A ball bounced in his stomach. By the time he reached Parramatta he'd got as far as picturing opening the door to the shop so that he could say hello and hum the British national anthem.

The streets were black with past rain. The sun was bright now, thick yellow, and it bounded off the pavement taking steam with it. Familiar places started to show themselves. Old bus routes and short cuts to the centre of town. The smell of hot treats from the main streets. Trees lined the streets in countable rows. Smoke and electric light, the hum of aeroplanes, trains and cars, taxis and their beetling movements. It seemed to him everyone was putting on a show of living in a city; that the moment his back was turned the crowds of people, the bustle and movement would stop. The whole place would empty and sand would settle over the slick bitumen, dust clog up the wide windows of the shopping centres, the tide would swallow Bronte Beach and make its way up over the Harbour Bridge. When the Parramatta river appeared he was surprised by its brownness, by the earthiness of it, next to the steel and rust and concrete.

222

The Shannons' florists had closed up, he noted with a slug of pleasure. He'd gone to school with June Shannon, a snub-nosed girl with critical eyes who lived with her grandmother. He parked the truck out at the front, felt his heart slip down into his bowels and knocking, trying to come out the other end. He could walk round the block a couple of times first. But his legs took him straight there, the old grooves dug by walking home from school, from the jacaranda tree and the park at night. The last time he'd seen the place there'd been blood in his mouth, a backward glance over his shoulder to see if his dad was watching. He wasn't.

The shop looked different. The glass in the front window was spotless. Signs had been printed out from a computer and white-tacked neatly to the glass, advertising things he'd never imagined his father approving of – cheese twists and smoothies, chicken and mushroom pies, and milky coffees. There was a new sign with a pink halogen light behind it. His palms sweated and he thought about the truck waiting for him round the corner. The door of the shop opened and June Shannon stepped out, whip thin with that upturned nose. She held a fistful of blond child in one hand and a can of light lemon in the other. Frank looked at the ground and rubbed a spot of grease with the toe of his shoe. *Don't recognise me, June.* His face got hot. *Please don't fuckin' recognise me.*

But she had a memory for faces. 'Frank? Frank Collard?' She bobbed her head up and down to try to lift his gaze.

He nodded, collected a smile together. 'June. How are you?'

She looked thrilled to see him, but the blond child wriggled and tugged at her. 'I'm pretty good, Frank – Clay!' She shook the arm of the wriggling kid. 'Get back inside!'

The kid looked up at her from under a heavy brow, sullen and threatening a scream. 'But Ma!'

'Inside, now – we'll go later. I have to talk to the man here.'

Little Clay gave him an ugly look up and down, before turning round and stomping back into the shop. Frank's teeth bit his lip.

'Sorry 'bout that, Frank,' she said, flattening down her T-shirt. He shrugged, tried to smile. 'Well, we haven't seen you around here in a time!' She was talking like a woman from the deep south of America. 'Where've you been?'

'I've moved up north – country sort of thing.'

She nodded, eyes wide. 'So, you had a fight with your old man?'

He blinked, didn't know what to say, so he said nothing. Which didn't seem to bother her.

'So what d'ya think to the old place? Have we looked after her all right?' She chuckled and he didn't know what she was talking about. 'You want to come on in?' She squinted into the brightness at him. 'Give youse a Coon Cheese Twist on the house!' She chuckled again, stepping back and holding the door open for him. He saw a slice of inside. The counter was in a different place and behind it stood a man, fat and glazed like a doughnut. He wore a green apron.

'June – you live here?'

She looked unsure of herself for the first time, 'You didn't know? – Oh. Well,' she said a bit softer, letting the door swing closed and taking a few paces towards him. 'Your old man left some months back, Frank. Me an' Jimmy.' She nodded in the direction of the doughnut man. 'We bought it up from him with the money Gran left. Sorry, Frank – were you looking for him? Jeeze, that makes it kind of awkward, eh?'

He turned round and headed away from the shop without a word. His skin prickled. He worried that June wasn't as big a bitch as she had been when he was young and perhaps she was hurt by his abrupt departure, but he thought it just as likely that she watched him march away from the shop with a look of having sunk an enemy ship.

The Parramatta Hotel had been painted cream orange since he'd last seen it. There was an old black dog tied up outside, its water bowl boiling in the sun. He untied it before going in and it sloped off down the street looking over its shoulder at the pub. Inside the dark-blue carpet still stuck to his feet. A blackboard still read STEAK WITCH. It was dark and smoke drooped in the air. He ordered a beer. Horses ran on a black and white television at the bar, but no one watched them. He fidgeted with a beer mat as the drink went down him. Six men sat in quiet communion in the pool room drinking and avoiding each other's eyes. He felt sick. He tried to think, but all that would come was that last time, busting into his father's room, the smell of the grey sheets, the air thick and damp like breath. His dad lay underneath the bedsheet, the bare ticking spoiled round his shoulders. He hadn't sat up, hadn't moved anything but his eyes, which swivelled towards the door. A liquorish cigarette wilted at the edge of his mouth. Frank had felt the violence leave him because what would he do? Pull the sheets away? Leave his father naked and splayed on the bed like a baby? His father didn't speak, but there was the smallest twitch from his eyebrow, his lips hanging on to the cigarette.

'You don't even know what you've done, do you?' Frank had asked.

The tip of the cigarette had glowed weakly.

Frank drank and drank some more.

By the time the street lights came on outside the pub his legs were heavy with beer and the bar nuts did nothing to soak it up. He looked at the dirt under his nails and wanted to go home. Strange to call it home. A voice said movie-like in the gloom of the bar, 'Thought I might find you here.' It was June but without her exclamations.

'June.' He raised his glass, then looked away from her.

She smiled and he could hear it. 'You going to buy me a drink, Collard? Thought maybe we could swap stories.'

He took a ten-dollar note from his pocket and handed it to her. 'Get yerself somethin.' *Crikey*, he thought as she moved towards the bar. *I'm buyin' June Shannon a drink. Wonder if I'll get the change.* The thought tickled him and he was smiling when she got back with her own beer. She gave him the change. There was a silence while she started on her drink and he wondered why she'd come.

'So where's . . . Jimmy?'

She drank past the halfway mark of her beer before she answered, 'Top Pub.'

Another silence while he turned this over. 'How come you're not there?'

'This is my local. Not Jimmy's. Anyway – I thought you could do with a friendly ear.' She tucked a loose strand of hair behind her own ear. Then she trailed a finger down her throat and rested it on her collarbone. He felt angry and looked away. She finished her beer, got up wordlessly and went to the bar again. When she came back she had a new one for him too.

'Quick drinking.'

She shrugged. 'Thirsty. So!' The exclamation was back. 'You're living up north now then? What do you do there?'

'I work on a boat. Occasionally.'

'So, your woman left you?' she said, not batting an eyelid.

He felt his ears move back on his head. Same old June. 'My woman?' He tried to make it sound insignificant, something to be snorted at, but he snorted too loudly and sounded angry. 'What is it that you heard about my woman, June?'

She shrugged. 'Lucy, wasn't it?'

He pictured himself knocking out June's front teeth. He drank the rest of his old drink instead, and put the new cold beer in its place. He drew his lips back over his teeth and looked up at her. 'How did you know her name?'

'You say it like she's dead.'

'How do you know she's not?'

He'd meant to scare her but only scared himself.

'She was here. Looking for you.'

He breathed out another snort. 'She was not here,' he said under his breath like she was a child telling tales. Lucy wouldn't look for him here. She wouldn't look for him. He felt sick. She said nothing. Someone turned off the old television and it made a snapping noise.

'She left you?'

The beer burnt in his chest. 'That's nothing to talk about.' He slapped his palm on the table, spilling the first centimetre of his drink. There was a long silence but June didn't look uncomfortable. He wasn't sure if he'd imagined the whole conversation, if he wasn't just making this up in his head.

But she was still holding her shit shovel. 'It must feel weird to come back home and your old man's gone. I can't believe he didn't tell you! We paid fair price on that shop, Frank, I can tell you. I'd be on to him for a fix of it – you worked there for a time, after all.'

She glittered in the cigarette smoke. He was silent. He wanted to ask questions but then again, he did not. He didn't want the answers and he especially didn't want the answers she would give him.

'I can tell you where he's gone. I can tell you why. And I can tell you with who.'

He peeled a bar mat; drank his beer. There were pins and needles in his bum bones.

She took a swallow and ran her tongue over her teeth. 'Do you know about that, Frank? Know about the woman he went with?

An evangelist, Frank. Fucking true. She passed through here like honey on a stick and your old dad stuck to her.'

'I've never heard such a troop of bollocks. He doesn't believe in God.'

'Maybe, Frank, but I was here. Where were you? You can ask the guy at the bar if you like – he near as well lost his best customer.'

He felt hot and sick. He couldn't work out why he was having this conversation, why he didn't leave, get in his car and drive back home, even as drunk as he was. How had she known her name? He tried to picture Lucy talking to June, but it didn't fit. Lucy would have hated her.

'Look, Frank, I'm telling you this because you have a right to know. I got the evangelist woman's address in case they needed mail forwarded. And because, frankly' – she let the joke hang in the air – 'I was interested.'

She took a layer of his shredded bar mat and got the stub of a pencil out of her pocket. He recognised the pencil as one that had been kept tucked behind his father's ear at the shop. Then he thought *how ridiculous, how stupid – there must be thousands of millions of pencils the same as that one.* Even so he had to fight an urge to collect it from June's fingers and hold it gently in his palm. He must have drunk more than he realised. She wrote an address on the mat and drew a little box round it. Then she got up to go to the bar again.

'You seem pretty familiar with where he lives,' he said as she came back.

'It's an interesting place.'

'Interesting?'

'A real bunch of loonies. You've heard of Billy Graham? He founded it in the fifties. People there are either evangelist or they leave. Apart from that, the place's got beef.'

He took the piece of paper and looked at it. He didn't want to put it in his pocket in front of her. 'You must be pretty bored down here, June.'

For the first time she flinched. 'Well, fuck you then, Frank.' She looked like she might leave, but settled back down. 'You don't know how lucky you are.' She looked poisonous now in the smoke of the bar.

'Beg pardon?' he said, amused and letting her know it.

'So you've got nothing, well boohoo, Frank – what about me? Huh? What about me, I've got everything now, haven't I?'

He sat back a little on his stool, not sure where she was headed.

'I got the shop, I got the family, I got the fucking lump of a useless husband.' She held her fingers out towards Frank. 'I married that loser – can you reckon that?'

'June . . .'

'*And* on top of that I've got kids. Three. An' one on the way.'

'You're pregnant? Don't you think . . .'

She held up a hand. 'Don't you fucking say it, Frank.'

She drank, her eyes one long rectangle of dark. She put the glass down gently like it was precious. 'You have no idea . . . just. You can do what you like. There's no one. There's no one to think about. You work on a boat . . . *occasionally*? You're able to just leave the shop, your old man, Parramatta, fucking Sydney?'

'It's not about freedom, June–'

'Yes it fucking is.'

She stood up. To Frank she swayed, but he wasn't sure if she really did. 'You should know,' she said. 'She's pregnant too.'

June walked out of the bar.

He slept sitting up in the passenger seat of his truck. His mouth kept falling open and waking him, and when the sun came up he felt the floating heat of his hangover push against his chest. The night echoed grimly and he drove out of Sydney feeling the day cook him. He would have welcomed another storm, something to wash away the baked-bread smell of the inside of the Ute.

The way Frank remembered it, he'd come straight from school, where things had started to even out. Bo hadn't been there when he went back and Eliza looked away from him if he saw her on the street. The thought of glue or gasoline or even mull made his chest tight under his shirt. The shop door was unlocked, but the sign read 'Closed' and no lights were on. The only stock out were the four trays of scones he'd made before the sun was even up. That morning he had got the idea that things could be done, things could fix up. The past month or so, his dad had even got into a cobbled-together routine of laying out the food – shop-bought cakes, mainly, but still – and they'd talked the week he'd got out of hospital about how the shop used to be, about how good it could be made.

And so, when he found the woman in the kitchen wearing the dress with the oranges on it, something hot and sticky had risen at the back of his throat. The dress was not on his mother, so it bagged round the waist and the woman inside it had flesh at the edge of her armpits that sagged over the top. She was making eggs in a pan, which were burning, while she was smoking and looking through the cupboards, bare feet, hair the colour of wet lint.

'Who are you?' he'd asked, although there wasn't an answer she could give that might make the whole thing okay.

She turned to face him with a big smile that showed her teeth were cheesy. 'Whose yerself?' she asked, appraising him with one arm crossed at her waist, the other falling free at her side, wrist up holding the cigarette. There was a sort of rash or a pink burn along her forearms, some sort of dry-skin problem that went all the way up to the inside of her elbow. She pointed her fag hand

230

at him like she'd just solved a puzzle. 'Oh,' she said, her voice a mix of husk and moisture, 'you're the son.'

After a few hours of driving Frank had to stop at a service station and he bent over the toilet, heaving, until nothing more would come out. His eyes streamed. The tick bites itched. He bought a litre of Coke and drank it in the Ute.

Roedale was a mixed bag of dust and meat. Grey weary-skinned cows stood in grass that had turned brown and curled in the sun, while eddies of dust flew up round their worn ankles. Two large palm trees marked the entrance to the town, their heads strange and dark against the sky. You could drive from one end of town to the other in less than a minute and there were roundabouts at each end, so that you could boomerang back in if you were thinking of leaving, or take second thoughts if you were thinking of coming. He didn't falter, not one bit, he held the address hard between his thumb and index finger, and kept his eyes ahead on the empty road. He stopped at a sandwich bar, the God Bless Café, to ask directions.

The lady behind the counter had glasses that took up three-quarters of her face and below them she had very little chin. 'How doin', mate?' she asked.

'Good. Thanks,' he said, pretending to survey the dry sliced meats on display, nodding. He looked at his piece of beer mat. 'Was wondering if you could tell me where to find Fantail Rise?'

She looked at him, bug-eyed through the thick lenses. 'End a town; turn left, mate.'

She spoke loudly with long pauses between words, like she'd learnt to speak through a spelling computer. A screw loose or local colour, he wasn't sure. Too much meat at a young age.

'Thanks, mate,' he said, turning to leave.

'No warries, mate,' said his friend. 'God blesses you, mate!' she called as he stepped back into the sun.

231

He walked the main street. God's Own Greens sold fruit and vegetables, and advertised choko like it was a cure for cancer. The butcher's was called David and Goliath's, an op shop, I Work for Jesus!

There was no pub and he wondered how that went with his old man. A bottle shop would have been good, just to take the edge off the hangover, but nowhere looked hopeful.

CHRIST ROSE FROM THE DEAD AND IS COMING SOON!! in big fat letters as the town banner. A sign in the window of Saint Shortie's Snack Bar: ALL MEN EVERYWHERE ARE LOST AND FACE THE JUDGEMENT OF GOD!! Everything seemed to want a couple of exclamation marks after it; all signs were neon.

It didn't seem possible that a man like his father could live here. The last time Frank had seen him he'd been grey and silent in a doorway with nothing in his face to show there was any kind of thought going on inside. The colour he had been it was hard to imagine there was even blood in there.

Fantail Rise had no rise in it. The road was long and straight and flat, and the houses were sparse, with large front yards bristling with razor grass. He found the house and stood outside while a hot sweat got him. It was white weatherboard, with a porch – not a veranda, somehow. The curtains were bright and lace. It had been a bad idea to walk, it was just past midday and his face burnt; there were dark patches under his arms and on his chest. His feet twitched saltily in their boots.

As he stood in the drive, an orange Holden pulled up behind him and he was trapped. The woman who got out wore a broad smile of old-fashioned red. She was younger than his father, or perhaps she worked very hard to look younger. He wondered suddenly if she'd been shown photographs of him. Closer up the woman's eyes were blue.

'Hello, darl, can I help you?' she said in a voice laced with Perth and Texas. There was a silence. The woman put her hands on her neat hips, glanced behind him at the house.

'Does Leon Collard live here?'

'Leo?' The woman's smile wilted a little. She moved to the back of the car, opened the boot and started to take out shopping bags. 'What d'you want with Leo?' she asked turning round, laden.

'I'm a friend.'

The woman looked at him and smiled again. She shut her mouth and tilted her head to one side. 'You're awfully young to be his friend.' Her eyes were bright.

'Well, he was a friend of my father's.'

'Well, how about that, darl?' she asked him softly. He wondered if he should help her with her shopping, but then it might seem as if he wanted to get inside her house. They stood quietly, the shopping bags making a noise against the woman's leg.

'So . . . is he in?'

'No – but you'd better come in – help me with these, won't you?'

He took the bags from her, sweatily, and let himself be ushered inside her house, which was unlocked. She stood in the doorway behind him and checked up and down the street before closing the door. He stood, ballasted by the shopping.

The woman smiled large again. 'Straight through to the kitchen,' she said, dropping her car keys in a bowl and wiping her eyebrow with one finger. 'It certainly is a hot one today – did you come far? I'm Merle, by the way. Leo's wife.'

His face felt sugar-coated, stiffened. 'Frank,' he said, still holding the shopping, forgetting he was incognito.

Merle took the bags from him and smiled, her eyebrows raised in perfect ns. She placed the bags on the counter. 'Now,' she said, turning her full attention to him. 'What kind of cordial would you like?'

He sat on the edge of an over-soft sofa that threatened to fold him in two if he sank too deeply and sipped a bright-green drink in a thick glass. Merle was putting away her frozens and he waited, feeling like a grubby child. A black and white portrait of a young man hung over an electric fireplace, the man's expression seemed to say, infallibly and sternly, yes. Yes to what he wasn't sure, but definitely yes to something. The picture was backlit so that the man seemed to be coming from the light, looming out in the dark. WILLIAM FRANKLIN GRAHAM, AUGUST 1956 it read on a small gold-leaf plaque in a neat black hand beneath him.

He watched in alarm as a crumb of mud fell off one of his boots. He picked it up and put it in his pocket.

'I hope you like scotch fingers, Frank!' Merle said, appearing in the doorway. 'Your father's favourite.' He knew that they were not and thought this before realising she knew who he was. He pretended not to notice and accepted a biscuit from the elaborately decorated plate. The biscuit made a noise when he picked it up, a squeak against the china, which was, for some reason, embarrassing.

Merle switched on the large television that had a wooden statue of Jesus doing a peace sign on top. She snatched the remote control and muted an advert for turtle wax, then placed the control back on top of the television, next to Jesus and the scotch fingers. She settled in an armchair and made a sighing noise, like she had finally been made at ease. Frank saw that she had reapplied lipstick in the kitchen and despite her comfortable sigh, her mouth was firm and shut.

Merle's cordial was bright pink – cherry – he could smell it. What he really wanted was a cold beer, something to kill the awkwardness of this strange meeting.

'Thanks for that.' He gestured to the drink that he couldn't seem to swallow. She smiled, mouth still closed. Frank's eyes wandered over to the television, some huge supermarket with a couple gaily pushing their empty trolley towards it. There was a burst of fluorescent stars and then the couple emerged, surprised and jubilant, their trolley full to overflowing. The woman picked out a bottle of shampoo and held it to her cheek. The man inspected some aluminium barbecue tongs as though they were just the weapons he needed.

'So is, um, Leon at work?' It was weird to use his first name and Merle raised an eyebrow.

'We call him Leo now – like the lion? Due back around seven o'clock tonight, Frank – he's been away on a trip.'

'A trip?'

'He sells The Book.'

'The Book?' His brain caught up with him. 'The Bible Book?'

'The very same.'

There was a needlework embroidery on the wall – in fact, there were several. They said things like CHRIST IS BEYOND OUR UNDERSTANDING and GLORY IN THY NAME. The one that was the most impressive, that was decorated with hearts and flowers, roses and poppies, vines and oranges, read AFTER THE FIRE, A STILL SMALL VOICE.

Merle noticed him looking. 'Leo does those himself,' she said. Frank was unable to stop the honk of a laugh that came out of him. He immediately thought he would be sick. He imagined his father sitting there in an apron delicately sewing away, a small smile on his lips. 'Takes time and dedication and love to get those looking so good,' said Merle. She parted her lips and smiled again, a line of sunlight blanketing her tightly pressed shins. Frank thought about the time he'd opened his lunch box at school to find a tin of sardines, missing the key to open them, and a balled-up sock.

235

'It must be quite a lot to take in after all these years. I know that he didn't always believe, Frank.' A long silence followed during which Merle took a sip of her drink and blotted her lips on a napkin. Frank could not take his eyes off the embroidery. Merle rolled her tongue in to her cheek.

'So this place was actually invented by Billy Graham?'

Merle smiled. 'We prefer discovered. Or saved.'

'Right.' He wondered if he would have it in him to get up and leave, just to pretend he never came, ignore Merle as he crossed the room, leaving his scotch finger and lime cordial untouched, a trail of mud to the door.

'Billy was the biggest thing to happen in Roedale.' She shuffled forward a bit, lowered her voice like she was telling a fairy tale. 'When I was a very young girl, I didn't even know who Jesus was – thought he was something like Father Christmas, I think.' She sat back in her seat a little, eyes on Frank's. 'See, my family weren't the believing kind. At Christmas the town'd set up this chocolate wheel, and all the kids would line up and buy tickets and hope their number would be called, hope they'd be the ones eating all that sweet chocolate. Only – that chocolate wheel – all you'd ever win were cuts of meat.' Merle took another sip, blotted, looked towards the portrait. 'That was an ill-named wheel.'

Frank took his cordial to his mouth, wetted his top lip and took it away again.

'But when Billy called your number, that's when you really got chocolate.' She looked back at him and held his gaze.

'Right.' He nodded. This was a mistake.

'Do you understand, Frank? A place can't exist on meat alone.'

'But meat and Jesus works out for you, does it?' He meant it to sound rude, but she didn't flinch. Frank imagined what would happen when his father arrived home to find him there, but found he couldn't picture what his dad's face looked like. He thought

236

of the silence and looked at the silent television. A show with doctors, all in blue, masks, scalpels.

'Frank.' Merle spoke again, with a voice off *Playschool*. 'This place, this town, is made up entirely of believers.'

Believers and meat. He thought he might start to laugh. He knew that if he undid his hands from the glass they would shake. 'I think, maybe I'll be off – come back later when he's here.' He tensed his legs to stand.

But Merle carried on and somehow it kept him there. 'People who don't fit in don't stay. We are here and we are happy, and we are waiting for Jesus.' She leant forward, clasping her napkin in her hand. 'He can know that when He gets here there'll be a safe place to stay. He can know that there is a place He will feel entirely welcomed, a place He can feel at home.'

'Right.'

'Your father is out there.' She pointed with a stiff finger towards the door. 'In places with less knowledge and he's trying to help those people, Frank. He's found something good, he's trying to lead those people home. Like Billy did. He led us out into the light of knowledge. He showed us Jesus and once you have seen Jesus, Frank, once you have seen Him, you'll never go back, because it is too dark.'

Frank had left his father upstairs, lying in his own dirt, and on the way down the stairs the violence had come back to him and he bounced back into the kitchen, the skin on his face stinging, blood fast in his veins. The woman in the kitchen was still smiling, holding the remains of a Mighty White and fried-egg sandwich, which she dipped into the hot fat of the frying pan, smoke still touching the windows.

'Want some snack?' she'd asked and he went for her, tearing at the dress to get it off, looking for a fastening to rip at; and she

237

dropped her sandwich on the floor, but was laughing. She was strong for her weight and she fielded his attack, changing each scrabbling blow that landed, giggling like a schoolgirl. She hoisted the dress over her knees. 'Like father like son, eh?' she said, and Frank smelt egg and beer, and something strong like the bins in summer. She sat on the floor, now, and he stopped trying to get the dress off, stood back, sick at the look of her. She was laughing fit to split, tears running down her nose, making her weak. He saw himself kicking her square in the face, the feel of his shoe against the smash of her nose. But he didn't do it. He noticed that her lip was bloody, and she did too and wiped a long streak of orange on to the back of her hand, which only made her shriek harder with laughter. Frank's fists cramped and he struck himself hard in the face, three punches, one that crunched his nose and brought the taste of blood into his mouth. He turned to leave and saw his dad standing in the doorway, a towel that had once been white hooked round his hips, the liquorice cigarette still in his lips, but grey now, and dead. There was $140 in the till and Frank took it on his way out. The shop bell had rung as he left.

Frank drew breath but didn't speak, the silence was long and the doctors on the television stared at each other over a boardroom table.

'Now – Frank. How did you like my speech?' Merle laughed, tossed her hair, became serious again. 'I'm just trying to make you see – your father – he's not the man you knew. He is safe now.' She bunched one hand into a fist and held it against her pink drink. 'So if you're here to cast blame, know that he has been forgiven. Everything he has done has been absolved.'

'It's not quite as simple as that.'

She smiled, stonily. 'I'm afraid that it is, Frank.'

'You don't know.'

'He has told me everything. He is forgiven, Frank.'

'Wait just a minute, *I* haven't forgiven him.'

'Yes you have. Jesus has forgiven him. You *have* forgiven him. I can tell.'

'I tell you what, I have not!' Words tumbled out tunelessly. His heart beat against his bones and he wanted words that would shock this woman and make her throw him out of her house. 'My father does not believe in God,' he said and watched Merle's face. But there was nothing but a smile, so he went, didn't look to see if he'd left mud on her carpets.

Striding back to the Ute, his feet wouldn't move quickly enough. Shit, though, he was angry, his hands clenched, sweat itched his nose, dust in his face, the smell of someone's tea on the cooker made him want to shout at the elderly woman who crossed the road to get away from the stranger.

Her fucking *lime cordial*. He spat and his spit was green.

But he didn't drive straight home as he had thought he would and he didn't drive to the nearest non-lunatic town and bury himself in the pub. He found himself parking outside Merle's house, thinking maybe he was going back to say some of the things that were going round in his head – some of the excellent insults that he kept thinking of – but he just sat with his hands on the wheel, pointed his gaze at the middle of the bonnet and waited.

At a quarter to seven a blue Holden pulled up next to Merle's orange one. A cross hung from the rear-view mirror.

The man who got out of the car was skinny. He recognised his father's movements but not his face, not his shape. This man was bald apart from a few light strands carefully placed across his head. His shoulders were coathangerish. Frank wound down the window as the porch light came on, even though it wasn't dark outside. The man moved quickly to the back of the car, brisk and efficient,

239

neat, his hands touching everything after he had moved it, to make it just so. Open the boot, touch the door, take out a brief-case and set it on the hood, touch the briefcase, close the boot, touch the boot. Merle came out on to the porch, in a different blue dress that blew up in a sudden gust and exposed the lace top of a stocking. She batted it down with both hands.

Frank heard the sound of the word 'Darl!' and the reply, 'Sweetheart!'

He watched them embrace, his father on a lower step. Merle shut her eyes and tilted her head upwards with a smile on her lips like she was suckling a baby.

'You hungry, darl?' Frank heard as she lifted his head a little. 'C'mon in, it's pork chops for tea.'

They came apart and, holding hands, Merle led him up the steps, a boy for his bath. Frank was gone before the front door closed.

22

Something exploded right on top of them and Leon thought he would be buried alive. Clods of earth smashed down on him, the wind went from his lungs. The noise was hot, it burnt his eardrums. Somewhere he couldn't see, someone was screaming. With no time to set up he leant the gun against his hip and fired. A figure ran fast away from him, and he walked the tracer bullets across the man's back and he fell bucking like a sliced fish. Pete was at his side, replenishing the ammunition, missing three fingers from his left hand. His face was limestone, his mouth black. He handed Leon the bullets with his good hand and bled with his bad, holding the radio in the crook of his neck calling, 'Dustoff, dustoff!' Banana leaves shredded over them, hot green smoke, it seemed to last for hours.

When earth and dust and leaves had settled, when there seemed nothing left, he let his gun run dry. The screaming had stopped. A mosquito bothered Leon's eyelid and he let it.

The chopper landed and there were two baddies dead, their bodies eaten by bullets; the others had melted away. Pete held his claw hand, spitting dirt and blood and tooth on to the ground. The screaming man turned out to have been Rod, his legs both gone below the knee. Thick blood leaked from his mouth and his eyes were wide and dead.

Cray sat propped against a tree, a small leak of blood coming from between his fingers where he held on to his stomach. He smoked a cigarette. 'Flesh wound, I should think,' he said quietly.

'Bit of shrapnel scraped by me. Leave a pretty scar, but.' He looked up at the tops of the trees, watching his smoke mix with rising mist and get carried up. He waved Leon away. 'I'll be right after a smoke,' he said. 'I'll stay and keep Daniel company.' Daniel nodded to him, his hand on his smashed knee.

Leon and Pete carried Rod to where the green marker smoke of the helicopter waited. The medics arranged Rod on a stretcher and tucked him into it like he might have been cold. Someone bandaged up Pete's messy fingers. 'Well, that's it for you, mate,' he said, 'no more trigger finger. Time to get home.'

'I'll never play the flute again either,' said Pete and chuckled in a way that echoed and then faded out. 'Reckon you'll have to take us all back – Leon here he's the only bugger not wounded.'

The medic raised his eyebrows injecting something yellow into Pete's wrist. 'How many you got?'

'We were only five to begin with.'

'That's rough. Think you'd be better off getting out of here now, mate. We'll send someone else to pick up the rest.'

Pete nodded at Leon. 'You happy with that?' Leon nodded back, and they touched each other's shoulders and Pete handed over the radio. The chopper took off and Leon watched as Pete closed his eyes and held up his bandaged hand to cover his face from the dust.

Leon led the way for the stretcher bearers, just a couple of minutes away. Their radio buzzed and a voice said there was a chopper zero five minutes away. It was amazing, in just a couple of hours they would be in a hotel room. He'd have a drink for Rod and Clive, then he'd have a drink for himself.

They returned to find that Cray was dead, a long tube of cigarette ash next to him.

Daniel was tight-mouthed. 'He had one through the throat too,' he said. 'Don't know why the bastard didn't tell anybody.'

242

'Probably nothing to be done anyways,' said the medic, shaking his head.

Leon spat into the grass.

On the bitumen of the base airport he felt an awkward jab in his pocket. As stinking tired men poured around him, he looked at the mud baby that rested in his palm. Somehow it was still in one piece, brittle as pulled sugar. An eye had rolled out of its socket, but the baby still smiled.

23

It was dark when Frank knocked on the door of the shop. Jimmy was at the bowling club and their kids were watching TV with the sound so loud that he had to hammer on the door. June didn't ask questions, didn't invite him in, just slipped through the door, calling after herself that she was out for while. They didn't talk on the way to the pub, didn't discuss where to drink, what to drink. Inside, everyone's attention was on the television, where some other kid had gone missing in some country town. Frank didn't want to know about it. June ordered, dramatically, four whiskies but he found that he could hardly get through the first and felt sick, like his stomach wanted to crawl into his mouth.

After fifteen minutes of broken conversation June sighed and took his hand, leading him out of the pub, away from his drinks. He wondered if maybe the reason he had turned up to see her was that he didn't dislike her so much after all. They found a children's playground secluded from the road by mertyl bushes and didn't kiss, but he smelt the overripe-melon odour of her, smelt her neck and made her laugh with his sniffing.

But when she bucked against him it was like a competition to see who could fuck the hardest, and he thought that maybe he did hate her and she hated him, and he put his palm flat in the sand by her head so that it caught some of her hair. Her teeth made blood in his mouth and he could feel his chin doing damage to her cheek.

Explain that to Jimmy, he thought, but she rasped her face harder against his, like she wanted to shed her skin over him, and he was surprised to have the weaker stomach for what she wanted.

He made no sound coming and did not pull out. She made no comment, but in the first ten heartbeats afterwards he thought he might cry for her baby and he said 'Sorry', but not so that she could hear. Sand weevils moved beneath them, and mosquitoes started to bite at their ankles and move the air by their faces, but for a few more moments they clung together with claws and June said quietly, 'I did see her. But she wasn't pregnant. Not as far as I could tell.'

When the moment was up, she rolled over and wiped off her thighs with her balled-up knickers.

Tired and sick and full of driving, Frank stopped at an empty beach by the highway as the night paled. He took off his clothes and washed shallowly, squatting and rinsing off June and sand, cooling the mosquito bites on his legs. He wondered if Lucy would ever find out. He held his penis in the palm of his hand, tired and soft, looked at it, then out to sea again. What a bloody achievement. Plovers bolted at him from the shoreline. A flock of seagulls dive-bombed a hairy-looking patch of water and he imagined the feeding frenzy going on underneath. If he floated out on the marble-grey water now, something would tear him to shreds.

He watched the swell and thought that somewhere, hundreds of kilometres away, this water touched his own land. He felt the sand underneath the balls of his feet gently spilling away. He felt everything that was not him moving and when a truck drove past, giving him a blast of its horn, he put his clothes back on and drove home.

24

With mosquito bites still lumping his arms, Leon got stuck in wrist-deep to kneading dough. It was like he'd never left; people came and bought hot-cross buns and strawberry cream cakes. He waved at Mrs Shannon, who now walked with a permanent hobble, but with the freedom of a woman whose husband had left. Sometimes in the middle of it, though, he would see the long tube of ash from a burnt-out cigarette; Rod with his hand over his eyes; that matt black road. They were like dirty pictures and he needed to choose his time to look at them properly. At night he would sit on the side of his bed with a beer and just look at the pictures in his head, make it so that he understood every curve of Rod's hand, so that he could smell the ash, so that he felt an ache at the back of his eyeballs, the ache of trying to see distance in the black. He knew he ought to write another letter to his parents, let them know he was back, but for now, just for now, he told himself, he wanted to be left alone.

The album he bought was bound in orange felt. It had a pattern of large yellow flowers sewn on the front. 'Quite the thing, don't you know,' he said out loud as he set it on the table next to the photographs and glue. He didn't suppose he knew what the appropriate design might be – a black leather number perhaps, something more like death than a child's pencil case, but the orange felt had stood out to him. It was disposable, silly. No one would guess the contents from the jacket.

He glued the corners of the first photograph in the pile. He hadn't looked through them, and there wasn't any point in sifting through them and picking out the good ones, throwing out the blurs. They were all the same thing. He stuck them neatly down with a press of his fist. He saw green, fat leaves and strange flowers; an enormous spider with colours that had been bright, but in the photograph looked dull and no bigger than the huntsmen that lived in the larder. A group photograph that someone else had taken: he saw his own face smiling out from a crowd, down on one knee, his rifle at his side. There were thumbs up to the camera. He couldn't remember what they had been smiling at. One man – was it Flood? – held something that could have been a small bone to his face, imitating a moustache. Cray's face, closed and quiet – he had laughed after the picture was taken, but not during. Somebody swore, someone else pulled down their pants, showed a white arse, whipped by shrapnel. His own face freshly shaved in a toilet mirror, sweaty. Cray on his own, smoking a cigarette, shortly before he turned to Leon and asked something like 'You a gay boy or something?' Cray in a Hawaiian shirt, pouting for the camera, caressing imaginary breasts, the next, his tongue strained towards his imaginary nipple. More green. A blackened patch of grass. Red smoke. More green. A lemon-coloured snake. A dead guy. A dead guy with Leon standing over him, grinning like he'd bagged a prize antelope. A perfectly black square of night. More green. He carried on sticking and pressing, a small sweat pushing at his top lip.

There were thirty photographs, some overexposed, just dark-brown rectangles, and they all went in, then two that were not his own. The photograph, torn at the top, of the dead Cong's wife and child. Yellow and black and grey, it smelt like repellant and old books. The girl was shoeless, but the mother wore small black plimsoles that cut just below her ankle bones. Her feet were placed in a sort of ballet style, neat and balanced, heels together toes apart. The child's toes spread on the ground. Her hands were clenched at her sides. Then, Lena Cray with the baby inside her. A smooth, colour photograph, rounded edges that had turned white with dog-earing. The waratah dress, the small white points of her teeth. Sometimes – a trick of the pattern of her dress – you seemed to be able to see the baby moving. The sugar doll he made wore a waratah in her hair. He'd had to guess the silhouette of her bump, shaped it low on her belly like ripe fruit hanging. Her small hands supported her back, her toes turned inwards as if the balls of her feet were aching and hot. Her mouth was wide and open in a laugh. Of course, the baby was out of her now, but whenever he thought of Lena Cray it was with that bump that must have been warm and dense, that must've knocked the breath out of her husband when he leant to kiss her. On the dresser in the back room was Cray's machete, its wooden birds dark with lemon oil.

He closed the orange felt album, took it to the bookshelf and slid it in. Then he drank a large glass of water and it came back up, just as clean as it went down.

He didn't know if it was at all appropriate, but he thought of the kid and boxed two small passion-fruit tarts. Then he unboxed them, thinking that having two small portions might highlight the fact that there were two tarts and not three, that someone was missing and so was his pudding. He put in a full-sized treacle tart, took it out – treacle was over-friendly. He settled at last on a strawberry cheesecake, which was special enough to be a gift and strawberry seemed like a fruit that would be universally appreciated, a fruit that no one could accuse him of being over-personal with. He laid slices of strawberry round the edges, was careful not to make too much of the centre of the tart, so that it didn't seem like a celebratory cake but rather one that was meant for eating. He tied the box with a red ribbon, then cut it off and found a yellow one. The machete he wrapped in a pillowcase, then in brown paper. He put no ribbon on it – it wasn't his gift to give.

Outside the Crays' house in Paddington he tried to settle his hands so they didn't shake. He wouldn't stay, not unless she wanted him to. He was sure she wouldn't. But she might. She might want to talk about what he knew about Cray, what he had been like in those last weeks. He had prepared a speech in case she wanted to know how he'd died. He wouldn't lie, but he wouldn't tell everything, he wouldn't tell how Cray had known he was going to die, had seen it coming over the tops of the trees, had died with no one touching him, just one man with a smashed knee watching it happen from across a clearing. In any case she might just ask him to go away.

The house was pale pink with a large blooming jacaranda outside and he felt happy that he'd brought the right cake. There was a French-style balcony halfway up and on it a wooden rocking chair, still and solid. He watched it. He wondered if Lena still sat in it, if she spent the long summer evenings rocking their baby against her chest, if she listened to the flying foxes in the jacaranda tree and wondered about Cray and wondered *what next?*

He shrugged his shoulders, trying to loosen his shirt collar as he stood at the front door. He knocked and somewhere inside he heard a baby crying. He exhaled long and hard, breathed in through his nose, knocked again, hoped he didn't sound too impatient. Footsteps inside. He swallowed all he could, hoping an empty mouth would help him speak. The door opened a crack and a woman, older than he'd expected, looked out, her hair in curlers and a cigarette in her mouth.

'Mrs Cray?'

'No. What do you want?'

'Is Mrs Cray in?'

'Who are you?

'I'm a friend of her husband's.'

The woman looked him up and down, not in a friendly way, but not either in an unfriendly way, just in a way that suggested she was very tired and wished he hadn't come. The baby cried again. 'Look. I'm sorry,' she said, the howls inside distracting her. 'Lena isn't here. I'm her sister. Lena died.'

'What?'

'She put her head in the oven after Paul. I'm sorry to be the bearer – I really am, but she left a baby behind and it's crying, so if you don't mind?'

'Of course not.'

He stepped back and the woman nodded and closed the door. Leon heard her footsteps getting fainter inside. He hadn't known Cray's first name was Paul.

25

As he neared the end of his track, Frank saw that something was wrong. The stove was tipped over on to its side, its legs in the air like an upturned beetle. An empty car was parked outside the shack and the front door was wide open. As he pulled up he saw the vegetable patch had been dug out, splints snapped in half, Sal's careful chicken wire flattened.

He got out of the truck and spat on the ground. *What the fuck now? What else, possibly?*

He left the door to his truck open and moved quietly up the steps. Kirk, alone, warbled in a nearby tree.

'Thanks a bunch, mate,' he muttered.

Inside was as much of a mess as his few possessions would allow. His bed was turned on its side, the fridge door hung open, the sugar figurines were upended, arms and legs turned to dust on the floor.

His ears strained and his fists clenched at his sides. He looked around for something hefty to grab hold of, but there was nothing – the machete was missing from its stump.

A bird flew behind him and he whipped round, ready to swing.

'I need you to come with me, mate.'

All the blood in his body dropped to his feet and he breathed out long and slow. It was Linus.

'Jesus. What is it?' He wanted to be able to sleep lying down for a long time.

'I need you to come with me.'

'Where to?'

'Police, mate.'

'Why? What's happened?'

'I'll explain on the way, mate.'

'Tell me now.'

'Haydon's kid is missing.'

Frank opened his mouth but didn't speak. Something heavy held him on the spot, like he'd been eating sand.

'We'll take my car, eh?' said Linus, bouncing down the stairs and dumping himself in the driver's seat.

Frank joined him, but in slow motion like his bones were soft and not his own. 'How long has she been gone?'

'As long as you bin away.'

'What?'

Linus kept quiet. Frank searched for something else to ask. 'Did she run away?'

Linus looked at him, then back at the road. 'No one's sure of anything yet. All that's news is that we've been trying to get hold of you for as long as she's been away.'

'What do you mean by that?'

Linus held his look in the rear-view mirror. 'I don't think you did it, mate. That's why I've come down here. Soon as we get youse to the cops, soon as they can get some sort of alibi.'

'Did what? You think I've got her?' He blinked hard, tried to think. 'This is stupid,' he said softly.

'Didn't I just say I don't think you did it?' They passed by the roundabout and the boy he'd seen on that first day with the book was there at the side of the road with his back to them. 'You've got to admit, though, it is a coincidence – Ian's girl and then Sal. And you haven't been here long.'

'Do Bob and Vick think it was me?'

Linus looked back at the road. 'Bob and Vick don't know which way is up. They both want to beat the living shit out of everyone.'

252

Frank thought he might be sick.

Linus wobbled the car a little, anticipating a jump from a wallaby at the side of the road. 'Where's your machete, Frank?'

'What?' He looked at Linus, but Linus kept his eyes on the road. 'I don't know! Jesus, what are you about? Machete? Fuck.' He ground his hands into his eyes to try to make his brain work.

'Where've you bin, then?'

'I went to see my old man.'

'I thought you said he was dead.'

'No. That was a lie. I just haven't seen him in a long time.'

'Okay then.'

They drove the rest of the way in silence. He kept his eyes wide open, as if by really looking he might be able to work out what the hell was going on. Linus glanced at him from time to time, then looked away.

The police officer asked all his questions as if Frank were a naughty kid. He was a man who thought highly of his own eyebrows, he seemed to think they had a touch of the dry wit about them. He repeated everything that Frank said, which made it sound less and less plausible.

Frank wanted to smack him in the mouth. 'I went to see my father.'

'Yes, you went to see your father. His phone number?'

'I don't know it.'

'You don't know it?'

'No.'

'You don't know your own father's telephone number?'

'No.'

'No.'

'I have his address.'

'You have his address, but not his telephone number?'

'Yes.'

'Yes.'

The officer looked at the piece of bar mat June had written the address on and raised his eyebrows even further up his head. 'Roedale? That's a long way to get in three days.'

'Yes.'

'So. If I speak to your old man. In Roedale. He. Will tell me. That you were with him. Over the last three days?'

'No, look, he won't because I didn't see him.'

The eyebrows went up a notch.

'But I did see his wife.'

'His wife? Your mother.'

'Not my mother, no, his wife.'

'But you did not see your father.'

'No.'

'And you did see your father's wife – not your mother – and she will confirm that you were there for the duration?'

'No.' He put his thumbs on his temples and pushed his fingers into his forehead, his eyes closed. 'I stopped off at a friend's place on the way there and on the way back.'

'Your friend's number?'

'I don't have that either.'

'You don't have that either. Close friends, are you?'

'We're not really friends.'

The officer made no comment, merely closed his eyes a second and opened them again. He disappeared off into another room shaking his head. Frank tapped his fingernails on the vinyl wood covering of the table. There were arrangements of coffee rings over the surface, playful brown bubbles. His heart was creaky in his chest. He could sleep, he could just fuck the lot of them and put his head on the table and give himself one big deep sleep.

The policeman was gone a long time, or ten minutes, it was

254

hard to tell which. When he returned it was with his eyebrows set in a straight line. He looked at Frank's forehead, not his eyes. He said, 'Can you follow me, Mr Collard?'

Frank stood and walked quickly behind him, anxious to get things moving. Out of the interview room, Linus sat holding a paper cone of water. He nodded and Frank nodded back.

'Mr Collard, I am placing you under arrest,' the officer said.

'What?' Sand began again to be tipped into his belly. 'On what grounds?'

'For suspicion of the murder of Sal Haydon and Joyce Mackelly.'

'I haven't done anything.'

'I suspect you have, which is why I am arresting you for *suspicion* of murder, not for murder.'

'You can't arrest me for going away for three days.'

The officer sighed. 'I don't know what small-town movies you might have seen, champ, but we're not going to tie you to a barrel and piss on you.'

'Did you ring my father?'

'We did and there was no answer.'

It occurred to him that it was Sunday. 'They're at church – look, they're probably at church, they're very religious.'

He gave Frank a smile that was not friendly. 'Well, if they get back from "church" and if we get an answer and it's the answer we're looking for, you can go. For now you are under arrest.'

Linus shrugged. 'Just go with it, mate,' he said. 'You can always get unarrested later on.'

'Listen to your friend there,' said the policeman as he placed a hand gently between Frank's shoulder blades and guided him into another room.

So he sat on the bed in a cell, which turned out to be pretty much just an office with a lock on the door and a bucket to pee into.

255

Everything stopped and he was close to vomiting and made it to the piss bucket just in time. It wasn't until the smell of the booze and bile of the past few days had poisoned the air in the room that he remembered Sal, and that she was gone. That the reason he was sitting in a room, puking into a bucket, was that the general opinion was that he had done to Sal whatever it was that had been done to the Mackelly girl to make her end up as just a piece of shrapnel lying in the sand.

Sal was gone. She was small and angry and weird, and she was not there any more. He ran his hands over his face again and again. Time passed and he stayed still, trying to keep what was inside him from touching the walls of his body, trying to keep it cocooned and not thinking. But it reared again and again, Sal's fringe in her eyes, the grub of her knees. There was no way of telling the time, he had no watch, there was no clock in the cell and no window, just a greenish electric light, like the kind you'd get in a school hallway. He watched the corners of the room for shadows but there were none. He wanted Lucy's fingers in his hair, the way she did when he was upset, the way it gave him that guilty pleasure of feeling like a small boy.

The door opened. Bob came in. He held his fists at his sides as rocks. His skin was pale and green like he'd been pumped full of bad water. The rims of his eyes bled. There was an open cut at the side of his neck, which stained his shirt brown.

Frank didn't stand up. He didn't know if he could. He wondered if he might be sick again. Bob closed the door behind him. It was locked by someone outside. Bob looked at him, his head raised. Setting himself thickly against the door, he showed a surprising amount of muscle.

'They got through to someone. Someone said you were there.'

Frank stayed still, not feeling any relief somehow. 'I didn't take her, mate,' he said softly.

Bob nodded. 'Someone did.' He looked out of the window at the sun. 'They were going to let me in here even if your alibi didn't check out.' He spoke slowly, like he might have just woken up. 'I didn't come here to apologise, I came here to tear you open.' Bob looked sharply at him, the threat of violence in his bottom lip. 'We've looked for three days non-stop. It's been on the news – we had to do an interview. Vick had to. I couldn't . . . you know that parents are the first suspects. Especially if they've had one die on them before.'

'I'm sorry, mate.'

'It's like she was just picked up and taken away. It makes sense that you did something.'

'I haven't.'

'Why take your machete with you? Why leave without telling anyone, why leave in such a rush? You know, after you left we realised we don't know a thing about you – we didn't know how to find anyone who knows you. All I do know is you used to beat up your girlfriend.'

Despite everything, the words still made Frank's face go numb. 'You don't have to explain yourself, mate. It's understandable. You're upset.'

'I'm not explaining myself, Frank. I'm convincing myself that you didn't do it, so that I don't come over there and tear your throat out.' Outside someone coughed and it occurred to Frank that they might be listening in. Bob sniffed hard. 'But I do. I believe you. It doesn't help me, doesn't make the slightest difference to my situation. But I believe you.' He turned round and rested his head on the door.

'I didn't take the knife with me.' Frank's voice was sandy. 'It was right outside in the stump when I left.'

Bob lifted his head. 'I don't know what that means.'

'It means someone else has taken it.'

257

'Who?' Bob's eyes opened a fraction wider.

'Maybe Sal took it with her?'

Bob looked blank.

'There's no reason to think that something bad has happened to her. She might have just run off. She's into all this survival stuff. How to make a fire, catch food, bivouacs. It's all she talks about.'

Bob was silent; as though he hadn't heard, then he inhaled deeply again through his nose, keeping his eyes on the fluorescent light with all the shapes of dead flies in it. 'I don't know her very well.'

'Sal?'

'After Emmy died. I've just been shit.'

'Well, a bloke could understand that.'

'A seven-year-old can't. Why should she understand it? Christ, if anything's happened to her. If some bastard's touched her . . . I had this idea you'd buried her in the vegetables. I dug in there looking for her, while the police were off somewhere. Every time I hit a bloody potato I thought, Jesus, there she is.' Bob looked at him and shook his head.

'Let me help you look.'

In the car Frank was put through the trauma of having to smell Bob next to him. A mix of sweat, rum and sick, but then he didn't reckon he'd be smelling that much better. Through Bob's gaping shirt he could see dark lines on the skin of his chest, like he'd pressed himself to a large griddle pan.

'Where's Vicky?'

'She's scared Sal'll come home while we're out. She's scared she won't. She's been doing circuits round the house, then she gets scared she won't hear the phone ring an' she goes back in.'

There was nothing Frank could say, so he stayed quiet until they arrived at the shack.

'We've been all around here. Hundred times. We've trawled

the bush, the cane. We've shouted our throats bloody. Nothing. What can we do?'

'Look some more.'

Bob looked tired and Frank wished he had something better to say.

Parts of the bush were familiar, but he wasn't sure if they were real memories or if he just wanted to feel that he knew where he was going. Trees of a certain shape, their branches low and thick, made his pulse quicken. It was unthinkable that they wouldn't find her. Unthinkable.

He could see that Bob hadn't slept or sat down for days, his face was dust when it tilted up at the sun, and when he cupped a hand round his mouth and closed his eyes, Frank was surprised at the volume of his call. He looked as if he wouldn't be able to raise a whimper, but when he coo-eeed it was a howl. Birds echoed back, but there was no reply.

As it turned to evening they stood side by side, peering into the dense scrub that lay ahead of them. It was like a wall, or a net. It was the marker that said, 'No one has passed through here in a hundred years.' They stood and looked at it.

'She's not here,' said Bob in the voice Frank'd first expected him to have. Something between a wheeze and a murmur.

'Yup,' he said. That was it, then, was it? Sal was little more than a shard of bone now, waiting to be dug up or washed up, bleached in the sun and turned over by the sea. They stood a moment longer taking in the denseness.

Giving it one more go, Bob cupped his hand. 'Sal! Sal!'

Frank joined in: 'Hey, Sal! Sal!'

And they stood and shouted, startled a brahmany from its perch and carried on shouting at the brush, like it might turn round and produce her from its stomach.

259

They sat together on a fallen tree. Bob lit a cigarette, offered one and, although he didn't smoke, Frank took it. There was a long silence. Next time they moved it would have to be to head back. He could hear Bob's cigarette burning down with each suck. There was nothing to say. Bob dropped the stub, still red at the tip, on to the floor and looked at it. The ground around it smoked a bit. Frank stood up and crushed it out with his boot.

''Stoo damp anyway from the rain,' said Bob and he put his head in his hands.

'What shall we do now?'

26

On that first day Leon didn't stop the car for anything, not until his bladder ached in his back and his eyes began to close with the sting of squinting out the sun. The sky was a dome of white and the road was black and red. There were other cars, but not so many that he had to slow down, there was always space up ahead. As the first greens of evening streaked the sky, he rolled into a motel and crawled into bed without showering.

In the morning he was woken by thumping on the door. The small woman he'd paid for the room the night before stood there in her cleaning smock. She looked him up and down before speaking. 'Well, I thought you were dead. Anyhow, you've slept past twelve, so that's two night's board, and you've missed breakfast, but breakfast is included, so you can stay tonight and I'll slip you an extra egg in the morning.'

Blearily, he found his trousers and went to settle up the bill. When he handed over the money, he saw that his knuckles were sunburnt from where he'd held the steering wheel. The woman stood behind the counter and had taken off the cleaning smock. Now she wore a sort of blazer and cat-eye spectacles at the end of her nose. She counted out his money, glancing at him with every stroke, like he might try to back out of the deal. 'That's all there, then,' she said, suddenly flavoured with smiles. He headed back to his room to take a shower. On the way he saw the sign hung next to the vacancy notice, NO VETS and in smaller writing like a whispered threat, WE DON'T GIVE BEDS TO MURDERERS.

He didn't have the energy to do much, so he took the smudgy yellow towel and one of the pillows, tried to leave the room in a mess, but short of throwing the blankets on the floor there wasn't much to move about.

He drove inland, sleeping in the back of his car at night. It was just as comfortable as a room, he could pull over wherever he liked and it was free. He passed through places with names from another language, where the people nodded to him as if they knew who he was. He raced emus along the open, empty roads and stopped to sit on the roof of the car and watch the sun set. Sometimes he passed only three cars a day. He went through places where everything was canned – canned peaches, canned ham, canned milk and eggs. He visited a banana plantation where he stopped for a milkshake and the thing came in a vase as big as his head. Cold bananas were good. It made him think of the shop, about a seating arrangement inside, where people could pop in and order ice cream and coffee, a Milo Sunday, malted milk and a slice of gingerbread. He looked forward to stopping at these little places, where people looked at your car, not recognising it, where they asked him where he was headed, not where he had been. Further inland these places became rare, and he stopped at each one and filled up on water and fuel, and had an ice cream frozen on to a stick, which he had become partial to. The daytimes were always good.

He'd been on his own a month when the sleepwalking started. The first time it happened he had stretched out in the back of the car, stupefied by the stars. Patterns trailed across his eyes, and he fell asleep deeply and quickly. Then bam. He was out in the open, in the nick, loudly spoken words attached to some dream dying in his mouth. That first time he was only a few steps from the car and he chuckled himself back to sleep, shaking off the panic that had first gripped him, the feeling that he had to get back to the car, or some sand shark would swallow him up. But over the next few weeks things got more serious. One night it was his own voice that woke him up, a bark that echoed back to him three times before he was left in silence again, the car nowhere in sight.

'Jesus H Christ,' he said to cover the wild chug of his heart and to fill the empty space. Insects chirruped in the air around him. A frogmouth croaked but there were no trees to be seen. Something bounded off to his right – it could have been a wallaby. Jesus, it would have been easy to wander out into the road. The car turned out to be disguised by a shrub of pigface and with the light of the moon it wasn't too long before he was back on his safety raft. He locked the doors and lay awake the rest of the night.

Then, a few nights later, he awoke to himself speaking: 'After the wind, an earthquake . . .' and felt for a moment that he would carry on the sentence, as if he knew what he was talking about. He stayed still and opened his eyes, then tried to open them again, before he realised that there were no stars or moon, and the place was black as though he'd been buried. He stretched his fingers in the dark, was aware of no movement. He was back on the black road, a gun in his face, the thing in the space next to him, breathing wetly. The desert was silent, no croon of insects, no nightbirds, just his own breath and heart, and he stayed still for a long time, waiting for someone to shoot him. He crouched low to the ground, picked up a handful of dirt, stood up again, clutching it hotly. Something watched, he could feel it in the dark, the terrible mute animal with big eyes and long fingers. He could smell its mud breath.

I don't know what to do, he thought and a comet crash-landed on the earth, except it wasn't a comet, it was a road train, and it wasn't crashing it was passing by, and the air was filled with noise

263

and light, and in that light he saw his car, silhouetted against the brightness of the headlights, and as he turned towards it he caught sight of what was standing before him.

He drove for the rest of the night, pulled on a jumper to quell the shake of his bones and drove not fast or slow, watching for anything that might jump out into the road, looking in his rear-view mirror at the dark behind him.

It was just past nine when the fuel ran out. Already the sun was hot on Leon's knuckles gripping the steering wheel. The spare can was empty when he'd been sure it was full. The drinking water was gone as well and he could not remember doing that. He'd filled it at the drinking fountain at Cobar. The woman from the caravan park had come out, with her hair parted in the middle, and her T-shirt that read GIRLS SAY YES TO BOYS WHO SAY NO. STAY OUT OF VIETNAM and he'd imagined running her head under the tap, holding open her eyes and her mouth, making her see. But then he'd shaken his head and it was back to normal.

'Right on,' she'd said when he told her he was headed into the desert. 'Right on, baby.' And he'd started the engine and driven away.

The map showed nothing, just the long black line of a road cutting through all that desert, straight as a pin. A night's drive from where he had last stopped. Up ahead was Quilpie, but that was a full thumb's stretch north. You were supposed to wait, so he walked in circles round the car, standing tall to try to see over the desert to where someone might wave back at him. Far in the distance was low-lying scrub, a black line on the horizon. Past that all was heat wobble. Cicadas hissed in the brown grasses.

He took out his sleeping roll and laid it over the back window to block out the sun. All the doors were open as wide as they would go but the air didn't move. It cooked itself on the dashboard and became sweet and hot, and he tried passing the time by opening up one of the books he'd brought with him, but Sherlock Holmes did not stick and he let the book rest coolly on his forehead, smelling the stale moths of the bookshelf at home and trying not to get angry.

His tongue lost the feel of sandpaper and became a small brick in his mouth. Syrup from a can of peaches wetted his lips, but the sweetness got at his thirst and he chewed the peach halves, sifting them through his teeth to try to get all the juice out. When the sun was high and the inside of the car was too much, he lay underneath and wondered what bits of the engine would hold the cleanest water, recited the names of the stations, in order, of the West Central line. A couple of parrots sang out on their way somewhere cooler. Sometimes there was a thump through the ground – a kangaroo, a footfall – but it may only have been the blood in his ears. Sleep came, quick and unexpected, so that he woke suddenly with the feeling that something had changed. The sun had moved and seen to his ankles and shins on its way: they felt burnt and bloody, and they were big and red as peeled plums. With his eyes closed he waited to get used to it, to know that the pain wasn't going away. His throat was swollen like he'd swallowed an unripe peach.

The sun didn't burn any more, but sent low rays and long shadows out over the ground. The road was just as long and straight and empty as it had been before he fell asleep, the sand and grass and dirt were the same, deeper in colour from the lowering sun. He opened the bonnet of the car and studied the radiator. You could drink that. It was just water. He stood right over it and saw it shine back at him, put a finger down but his finger was not long enough to touch. There would be no getting it out anyway. He closed the bonnet.

As the sun set, he clambered on to the roof to sit and watch night approaching like a cloud bank. He tried to think of what had brought him out there. Someone would come – there were telegraph poles for Chrissake. They stretched over the red hip bone of the landscape, a measure of how big the space was. The furthest one he could see was a hairline in the distance.

Perhaps, in the dark, it would be easier to spot help. He could flash his headlights on and off a few times, see if it brought anything. But once the dark had settled he felt differently. There were no stars, nothing to see past the nose of the car, and it gave him the creeps. In the far distance a gun was fired, and the noise brought an old heat to his palms and his arms twitched, thinking of the kick of it. His heart beat, steady and loud, and he bit his lips in case he'd imagined it. In the blackness something padded softly round the car. He found his hammer in the boot and repositioned himself back on the roof, the hammer resting heavy and cold across his burnt ankles. The gun sounded again and this time he saw a spark up ahead, far away, but still there. There was something that sounded like laughter in the big space. He felt better. The thing in the dark was most likely a dingo.

It was cold, now, like some bastard was playing a joke, but he didn't get back inside the car. It was good on the sunburn. What was there to shoot at out there? Kangeroos, he supposed, dingoes, like the one that had passed by the car. When the desert had been silent for hours, something howled far away, one voice on its own, unanswered. He closed his eyes and lay flat, and waited for the cold night to pass.

In first pale lights of dawn Leon slid off the roof and carefully laced his boots, tying them tight over his sunburnt ankles to stop them from rubbing. He put a shirt over his head for shade. In another shirt he packed the remaining tins of peaches, resisting the urge to open one immediately to have the wetness of syrup in him. He looked at the keys in his hand for a moment, then locked the car and began to walk in the direction of the shooting.

Once the car became a spot in the distance, then disappeared behind a swell of heatwaves, he had the feeling that he was stuck on the same patch of desert, that there was a cunningly hidden conveyor belt that he walked against, keeping him in the same spot. His ankles were wet in his boots and he gritted his teeth against the steady shearing of his skin. By the time the sun was fully up the peaches were heavy and his lips were biscuit dry. He took a can and held it in front of him. He held it in front of him for a long time, until the fact had completely sunk in that he had forgotten to take the can opener. He could picture it sitting on the dashboard becoming red hot in the sun. He held the can a little longer, then hurled it as hard as he could along the road. It didn't go very far, and for a few moments he gathered himself by placing a hand over his eyes and blinking grittily. He picked it up again as he walked past it and noted that it was unscratched. He dropped the peaches out of his shirt and tied it round his waist without breaking stride.

27

There was something about the fifth day that Sal was missing that seemed to put a lid on everything. Five days is a working week. At five days you cannot say 'yesterday' or 'the day before last'. You have to say 'Thursday' and Thursday seemed like a long time ago. Frank awoke on the fifth day still drunk from the evening of the fourth. They'd gone back to Bob's house after looking for her and as Frank stood by his truck, trying to find something to say, Vicky had tumbled out of the house, a face like grey death. She came out screaming and it took him a moment to realise she was screaming at him. She picked up empty bottles that were stacked neatly at the front of the house and started flinging them at him, and at the truck, bellowing, 'You fucking whore! You killer, you baby-killing whore bastard . . .'

'You'd better go,' Bob advised, catching his wife round the waist as she marched towards the truck, bottle raised.

He was already driving away, watching in his rear-view, by the time Bob had squeezed the bottle out of her hand and was shouting, 'It wasn't him, Victoria, it wasn't, I promise you it wasn't him,' holding the woman against him. As Frank turned the corner he saw her go limp, saw Bob's face crumple in the grotesque smile that was a man crying.

He drove home in a vacuum, shallow breathing, and when he got to his house he sat in his truck and cried. Strings of spit and snot attached to the steering wheel, and every time he wiped his face to try to calm himself down it got worse, and waves and waves of something terrible crashed down over him, and he bawled like he was the last man on earth.

When he was finished with crying he went inside and drank himself to sleep. It was the only possible solution and he thanked it as it went down his throat, thank God, thank God. He woke in the darkest part of the night, close to pissing himself on the bed. When he stood up he realised he would be sick and made for the veranda, crashing his shoulder against the door frame as he went. He spewed with the bitter taste of banana peel, and retched and retched until no more would come out, straight out into the dark like he was leaning over the rail of a ship. Then he straightened up and pissed, not caring where. The Creeping Jesus howled. It was close, it was doing its thing and he had disturbed it. It came running towards him through the cane and he was scared, but could not move. The sound was right on top of him and then it stopped, just short of where he could see in the dark, and all the night was silent, the frogs and cicadas quiet, no noise from the highway. There was just the afterwards and then a kookaburra laughed long and loud and bubbly, shattering everything. He backed towards his door, not brave enough to look hard for what was eyeing him from the dark, but not game to turn and look away. He lay awake and shivering on top of the covers, too scared of the noise it would make to pull them from underneath him.

And then it was the fifth day, and everything became terrible and real again, and he wished it were night time, when some creature might gobble him up.

28

To hide the sound of the tread of his feet, Leon sang the cobbled-together refrains of songs he had listened to on the radio, but he sang with such sandy croaking that he stopped, and hours passed in silence while his heart beat in his ankles and he tried to remember why he was there. Answers presented themselves, but they were like answers to different questions. The butterfly hands of his mother flapping at the old man when it would have been better to do anything but flap. That thick jungle with the breath of the fresh dead right there in the mist for him to inhale. The thing mawing in the night. He threw his arms in the air, mouthed the things in his head, which helped unsettle the flies that landed on the sun blisters on his face and stayed there, comfortable as cattle.

At the point when he had started to imagine someone finding his body and peeling back the layers of cooked meat, picturing how the only wet thing about him might be his heart, floundering around in what liquid blood was left in his body, a speck appeared in the distance. A car. His breath came hot out of him and his throat burnt in anticipation of talking to someone, of drinking. What if the car was full of bastards and they didn't stop? Surely they would stop, who wouldn't? But if it was a car, it was a stationary one, it didn't get bigger or smaller as the minutes passed. When he got closer he could see that it was a rusted oil drum shot through with bullet holes. He stood in front of it and took it in. Someone had gone to the trouble of chalking the words

A CUNT on to the side of the barrel in a childish hand, beneath it a pair of chalk breasts, or they could have been wide-open eyes.

The drum gave out a long shadow and Leon was able to lie fully in it. The boots came off, sticking sickly to his torn ankles. He let the flies settle. For Chrissake, they looked crook. His eyes were pissed in and when they were closed, everything was red. Something touched his face, nosed him, but he kept his eyes closed. Whatever it was could stuff itself. A wind blew against him and he slipped down the barrel and didn't care except that he might be late back tonight and it would be a shame to make them worry. He saw himself tied by the wrists and dragged along behind a truck, in the dirt, the last of his skin left on the ground, laughing all the way. A bird sang 'Matilda'

It was the thirst again that woke him. He'd been dreaming of a man passing him a glass of water and he could see it crisp and cold. He took hold of the glass and brought it to his lips, but to do that took for ever and it never reached his mouth. He opened his eyes and the dark was thick, but it wasn't the dark of night – this was the dark of inside. His bladder ached dully and he rolled on to his side and heaved slowly to standing. His tongue was stuck to the roof of his mouth, but it was better than before. His stomach told him it'd been through a night of terrible drinking and his head wailed as he stood straight and leant against the wall. The wood of the house was dry and light, and it snagged on the skin of his palm. His eyes didn't like to focus on anything and he let the ground settle under his feet before he tried to walk. His ankles were hot and he could feel that they were bandaged tightly. A cool breeze came in through an open window, and Christ what a thirst! He moved unsteadily, the dark around him growing less intense, and he found the door and then another, and then, praise the lord, a toilet with a tap. He turned on the tap and the water came, sweet-smelling, warm but good, and he gulped fishlike under it. When he was done with that he pissed strong and happy into the loo, unable to stop a moan at the joy of it.

'Morning, Princess,' came a voice from outside.

He was given a bucket of water by the men who were sitting by the campfire in legless plastic chairs, and shown round the back of the house where he peeled off his clothes and doused himself to feel the sand melting out of his skin. There were seven of them altogether, all bearded and with the same quiet uninterested smile when he introduced himself. Someone gave him antiseptic cream for his ankles and someone else gave him a bacon sandwich, which he couldn't eat but enjoyed smelling. It was difficult to talk but no one seemed to take offence. Klyde, the one who had found him, looked old because of his wide matted beard but young in a Grateful Dead T-shirt. He had a smell about him of raw meat and engine oil. Somebody gave him some water with sugar and salt mixed in, and he sipped it as he took in the news that he'd been asleep for two days.

'Thought we was going to have to dig you a bed out there, mate,' one of them said, pointing into the dark with an odd tone to his voice that might have been regret. A chicken frilled in the dark. The rest of the night passed in a strange blur, sounds and colours were not how Leon remembered, and the men drank beer and commented on the hoot of an owl or the angle of a knife that someone was sharpening. He could feel his shins healing and the skin of his face was easily and drily peeled off, and mostly it was painless.

When he next woke it was to the sound of a car and the sun was high. Pulling on his clothes, he saw his brown Holden roll up to the front of the house.

'Got your car, mate,' said one of the men.

'Thanks,' he said, surprised at the generosity.

272

The man took something out of the back seat. 'And what is more, I found peaches all along the road!' The man smiled happily, showing him the cans. 'Looks like we eat pudding tonight.' He walked past Leon towards the kitchen before turning. 'Oh – and for the future, probably a good idea to fill up on petrol once in a blue moon before heading out into the desert.' He gave a wink and disappeared inside with his peaches. Leon blushed and felt like a priss.

A few days later Klyde took him out to show him around the old grazier's station and shoot some rabbits. 'No bugger can see us from the road,' he explained. 'Place belongs to Colin, he was supposed to be rearing cows on it. Here we are.' They'd come to a fallen tree, the only tree as far as Leon could tell, and Klyde had produced a sack of rotten oranges from his backpack. He started lining them up on the tree trunk. 'Pretty unusual to get a fella on his own out here. Were you supposed to be on your way to something?'

'Just getting a look at the country – never really seen much of it.' He wondered if he would be asked to leave.

'Working life, eh?' said Klyde agreeably, as if he himself were a keen businessman. 'Easy to forget about it out here.' He nodded to a fat pink sky. Klyde loaded and sighted his rifle, the tips of his fingers black from engine grease. He lined up, taking his time, then he looked at Leon. 'Mate, this is something close to heaven,' he said and squeezed off a bullet, which exploded an orange and its sweet smell came into the air. He passed the rifle over.

'It's a pretty unusual place you've got here,' Leon said in what he hoped was an even voice. The orange vibrated in the sights. It had been a long time. 'Can't thank you enough for helping me out.' He shot the orange and it burst, and he felt a deep well of satisfaction.

When Klyde next spoke, taking his aim carefully, the log now wet from juice, his voice was tight but his words were slow. His tongue darted out of his beard, pink and quick to wet his lips. 'This is where a man can just fuckin' be his *natural* own self.' He shot and missed. He breathed in deep through his teeth and as he exhaled he shook his head, putting the gun down at his side. 'There's some of us, yourself included I'm sure, have seen and borne witness to a number of terrible things. And as you'll know, those things haunt a man.' He handed the gun across. Leon found his arms suddenly lacked the strength to lift it.

'And at home everyone wants to act like we haven't seen those things, or done those things. But we have, an' that's not a fair thing. It's not.' Klyde was watching the oranges, so Leon looked too. 'I got a friend stepped on a mine out there. We all heard the click. He stood still, an' we all got round him with our ideas and shit. Tried holding it down with a bayonet, tried it from every angle, thought about tying a rope round his middle to pull him off, but we couldn't have gone quicker than the blast, we knew that. Thought up ways all afternoon, meanwhile he's stood there, sweating, at twenty-one years old. So in the end he says to pile up his leg with rocks so the mine'll only take off up to his calf, or maybe if he's lucky just the foot. An' anyway he's standing there crying and shouting, telling us all to get the fuck away and piss off, and we all take cover and you can just hear him there on his own crying and swearing. Then the boy does it and after the bang, after all the dirt comes down over us and there's that smell, we scramble up to him and he's white in the face and his whole leg's off and the other foot too. And he died. An' I told everyone there, went round telling them if any bastard ever talked about it again I'd fucking shoot them in the face, no trouble.' He turned and looked Leon in the eye. 'No bugger's looked after us.'

Leon lifted the gun and took aim again but now his heart bounced his arms. 'See,' Klyde went on, 'but here, we're all in

274

the same boat. I can tell you are, or else you wouldn't come rambling through the desert alone and half smoked. This is the place a bloke can let loose.' He inhaled and sucked air through his teeth again. From the corner of his eye he was aware of Klyde stretching out his arms at the sky. He pulled the trigger just to have taken his turn, but the bullet still found its mark. He looked at the place where the orange had been, surprised.

Klyde carried on loudly, 'This place is man town. There's no women, no children, it's just us.' He gestured to the blasted oranges like they were a field of daffodils. 'And we can do what we want.'

Leon handed back the gun and saw that Klyde's eyes were shining and wet.

No one asked him to stay, but no one seemed to expect him to go either and it was comfortable. He slept deep black sleeps and nothing woke him but the morning. The days were spent hunting and talking and fixing things, even if it was just a hole in a bucket or a blocked pipe, there was some satisfaction in it that he hadn't known before. Out the front of the house was a jungle of metal and scrap. You would pick up a piece, sit in the dirt with a drink and make things – a chair out of old fence and chicken wire, a bin out of insulated pipe. Sometimes useless things, a family of logs, each one with a different expression, wearing funnels and rusted colanders for hats, nails for eyes, scraps of oil-stained cloth for clothes. Leon cut a person out of a tin can, yellow with sharp fingernails, a ring pull for an empty head.

There was one called Colin, someone else was called Grub and there was definitely someone called Jarred, but still he was only ever able to recognise Klyde for certain. All of them wore wide beards and long hair, and everyone swapped clothes. They had a way of licking their lips with their hot little pink tongues that made it look as if they were smelling the air. Every so often a few of them would make off to the nearest shop. It was a day's trip away and the idea of going seemed dreadful. The thought of those naked beardless faces, of the chatter and the sidelong looks. Because the shop was a gas servo the food they came back with was of a type. A lot of chips, chocolate bars and beer. Sacks of cigarettes, coffee and a loaf of bread each to eat fresh. One evening someone turned up with a clutch of rabbits, which were gutted and skinned, and roasted on a stick over the fire. Among the scrap and cigarette butts of the yard was the sound of low talking, the crack of beers being opened and the smell of burning rabbit hair.

There was an old mirror in the toilet, with most of the reflection taken out of it. The toilet itself wasn't often used by anyone – you had to get water to pour it down and it was a waste. Someone had chalked the word LADIES on the door. Most of that sort of thing took place out behind the scrub and wattle, and it was a better set-up altogether than going into that dark and stinking room. But he went in there anyway because he remembered the mirror. He knew the beard was there, could feel it peeling its way through the skin of his face, but it was still a shock. It was long rather than wide, because he hadn't shaped it like the rest of them. It hadn't grown so long that it got in his way yet, but it was still long, and parts of it were white. He hadn't expected it and he sat on the loo seat for a moment to take in the time that had passed. His eyes were lost underneath his eyebrows, which had gone feral, his shoulders were like cow skin and lean, just the sinew showing. His lips were blood bitten and dark, and just like the rest of the men, when he licked his lips his tongue was surprisingly pink and quick.

Out in a dry field close to midnight Leon felt the pull of home like a bite on a reel. He was drunk, had spent the afternoon

drinking and shooting cans with Colin or Jarred, had even joined
in at lazily trying to pick off a chook. The chook was having none
of it, and after Leon had taken two lackadaisical shots it had simply
walked off round the back of the house and sat smugly in front
of the diesel barrel.

The plan hatched when night had fallen and the last of the damp
potato chips had been snaffled between them. The idea of rabbits
again made Klyde fart dirtily in disgust. Red meat was what was
called for. They piled into the back of a Ute and hooned off into
the desert, Klyde now and again switching off the headlights, setting
them adrift in the cold black air. Leon imagined he was near the
sea and that the bellows and grindings of the truck and its passen-
gers were the sounds of water attacking the land, and the high
yells of the men were seagulls and plovers.

When they came to a stop they had come up alongside a fence.
The headlights were switched on and he could make out the dense
square of a cow, her eyes round and green and glowing.

A quiet came over the truck, like boys looking through a window
at a girl changing, they hushed each other, nudged and crowded
around Klyde, who held the gun.

Another cow, smaller, presumably the cow's calf, came to stare
at the headlights. They wouldn't shoot a cow with its calf. Those
were hunting rules. Give the young a chance. Leon carried on
thinking this, as Klyde hopped off the Ute, levelling his gun at
the cow, thinking, *This is a joke, he's pissing about*, watching because
he was certain it would stop, watching Klyde walk towards the
animal, aiming as he went, watching the light of the cow's eye
glow, the flickering of her worried ears, her raised eyebrows, the
safety clicked off.

The cow's child gave a soft low moo and before the moo had
ended, a shot rang out and the small cow leapt, all feet off the
ground, tail straight out, and hurtled off into the darkness, calling

raggedly. The mother cow let out a honk, like the noise you would make if someone struck you in the chest with a cannon ball, and fell over sideways, her four legs splaying out as she dropped, her head still looking up and towards her murderers, and the ground shook with another shot and then another and the cow didn't look up any more, but her great belly sank into itself and her hind legs twitched.

Other cows lowed in the dark, feet trampled away from the noise, and above it all Leon could hear the husky cry of that small cow that had stood by her.

The butchering only took ten minutes. He stayed in the back of the truck as Colin or Jarred cut out enough for a steak each, and the cow still bled heavily and the hands of her butcher were black in the lamplight, and steaming. The sound of the sea rose again in the voices of the men and they whooped and some drew patterns on their faces with blood, and danced a corroboree round the carcass.

He thought about the sound of shop bells, the girls and their lips. The hack and cough of cars in the main street. Sex. The closeness of water, the heavy rain in the streets. The light of night time and the distant sound of music.

He kept his eyes closed on the drive back to the station, listening to the dark, and when they arrived at the house, and the meat was thrown on the fire, and it clenched up and shrank, toughening in the flames, and the smell was of hot grass-fed fat, he kept still so that his thoughts wouldn't touch the edges of his body. In the morning, before he was sober and before anyone was awake, he swung his sleeping roll into the back of his old brown car and drove thirty-three hours to Sydney, only stopping to refuel.

29

And on the sixth day Frank noticed a dark stump that sat on the periphery of the cane. In the yellow light, the sun shining each way to get in his eyes, he mistook it for the stove. But the stove was on the other side of the track, still resting on its side, and this dark smudge moved. Not much, but it did move, like a ripple of water over the bottom of a still pool. A wallaby, its ears pricked, listening. It wasn't a wallaby, he could see that much through the sun. He held up a hand to shield his eyes, wary of making a sudden move. Something carrying a club, it seemed to be, yowie, bunyip, Stig of the Dump. He opened his mouth to say something, something to let it know he was a big man here in his house, something to say he was unafraid of whatever looked at him from inside the thinnest part of the cane. His voice would have made the word 'Hey!' but when he recognised the creature with the club and his breath was taken away and his lungs closed for business, he ran towards the cane, his heart thick in his chest.

On his knees in front of the pale small face, he panted through his open mouth, shallow little breaths, creeping forward with his hands out, not touching, just reaching. Sal's face was only visible where blood and dirt had dried and flaked off. Her hair stuck up like fox ears and down over one eye like a hawk's beak. The other eye shone wetly, a bottom lip sucked red against black mud. What clothes she had on looked the same as her blood- and mud-caked skin. She stared beyond him, her iris overtaken almost completely by a large black pupil. She did not move and for a moment he couldn't make himself touch her in case she was a ghost. In her hand, what he'd taken for a club was an animal, dead, dried and wet, flattened like roadkill. He saw the eyes of a march hare, the snubbed snout of a dingo. Slowly he rose so that he was stooped over her and quietly, trying to steady his breath, he touched her shoulder. She did not flinch or disappear as he'd been scared she might, but she did not move either. So he gave her the tiniest of prods in the small of her back and she began to walk. She walked like her bones were sticking to each other. He tried to brush the thing she clutched out of her hand, but she shook her head and hung on, and he did not dare force it.

If there was one moment that he regretted not having a phone this was it. Feeling unable to drive, wanting a mug of whisky and a lie-down, he lifted her into the passenger seat of his truck and climbed in himself. He strapped her in, then himself, and started the motor. Before he drove he turned to her. 'Sal?' She looked at him, a good start. 'Are you all right?'

Sal looked at him a deal longer before she nodded. 'I'm okay, thank you very much,' she said.

'Where've you been, kiddo?'

'Had to get this.' She nodded to the mess of fur and bone that she clutched to her chest. He looked down at it again and really could not tell what kind of animal it had been. 'What is that?'

'Bunyip. Just a little one, but.'

He started the engine and drove slowly to Bob and Vicky's, feeling every stone under the tyres, certain all the time that he would crash the truck and kill them both.

30

The curtains that had been pulled over the shopfront were cold and full of dust that floated like flour in the sun when Leon pulled them down. He squinted in the light, saw the butcher's wife over the road look up at him and slowly raise a hand like she wasn't sure she was seeing him. There was a postcard propped on top of a large pile of unopened mail. The picture on the front was of a headland, a yellow beach running from it, a bird painted in silhouette on to the blue sky. 'Mulaburry Heads' in orange lettering, 'come swim in the sea'. When he looked closely he could see that someone had also painted in little black surfer figures, dotted on the crests of waves. The postcard, written in long, blue, generously spaced ink, read:

> To our darling son
> It's been so long. This is where we are, should you ever want or need us.
> All our love
> Your Mother and Father

The address was northern. He did not tear it up. After he shaved off his beard he took down the orange felt album, grubbied at the edges from being hidden away under the oldest of the cookbooks. He pressed the postcard between the pages of the orange album and put it back in its place. He would deal with it when he'd had time to think.

There'd been a few requests for wedding cakes since he'd been back, but he'd headed them off, saying he wasn't quite set up again yet for big orders – that his suppliers were still getting back to him, that his oven was on the blink. Things that he said without really thinking. He couldn't imagine his hands being useful again. Perhaps that was it. The few girls who had come by, the ones he had taken out for a drink or a walk, had found him clumsy. His hands shook if he tried to spoon cream into their mouths, and his fingers seemed large and ogreish when he unbuttoned a blouse. His hands were cold as if there were no blood in them. They were better suited to holding a gun. Out of habit he had arranged the tarts in pairs like boobs, and looking at them he suddenly felt ashamed.

A car backfired in the main street and he looked up. Over the road, a girl was framed in the doorway of the butcher's. She was overdressed and there was a feeling that at any minute a wind might lift up her dress and show the butcher her knickers. She wore white wrist gloves like a virgin from the fifties. Her high heels and her broad-brimmed hat in particular looked ready to turn against her, the one to twist her ankle and make her fall, the other to fly away – she held it firm between two fingers. Leon placed a cherry in the centre of a jam tart just as the bell on the door sounded and she pushed her way in. Her dress had a pattern of oranges and ivy, and her lipstick was fresh on and thicker than it ought to have been. He wanted to hold the back of her hair gently and blot her lips with a napkin; to trace the edges of her mouth with his index finger and neaten her up.

He looked at a lemon meringue pie and then, suddenly embarrassed, pushed it to one side. 'G'day,' he said.

'Good morning,' said the girl.

A small smile. His ears popped – he hadn't realised they were stuffed – his whole head worked better than it had before.

The girl struggled to take off one of her gloves. She gave away the heat of them by wiping the palms of her hands on her dress. She stood, leaning on one hip, and he saw that she had a ladder in her stocking. 'I was after a treacle tart.' And when she spoke he saw that she was Amy Blackwell, and he understood why the air in the place had changed.

31

'What are you supposed to do?' Frank asked the spider as it twitched like a sea anemone, its remaining legs relaxing and stiffening and finally folding in on themselves. He had woken to a cold day and before going outside had riffled through a box to find a jumper. The one he found was woollen and grey, and a bit too small. He'd rolled it on, popping his head through the top, the skin on his face scoured by the wool. As he pulled it over his midriff he felt a wriggle against his side, something a little bit frantic was happening. On inspection, he found three hairy-looking legs pasted to his ribs with a bit of sticky in between. They were big enough to make him yank off the jumper roughly, and catch his nose and make it bleed a little. He threw the woolly on the floor and checked in his shorts with horror.

But he found the spider lying quietly on the floor in its death throes, twitching softly with the rest of its legs. The thing was about the length of a thumb, just a huntsman, nothing poisonous. It still had big fangs though, he noted, impressed, and wondered why it hadn't bitten him. Perhaps he'd rolled it against himself too roughly for it to have had a chance, or maybe it had known that he hadn't meant it.

He picked the thing up with a newspaper and flung it hard outside. It travelled only a short distance, but either way was gobbled up by Kirk the moment it touched the ground. He watched the chicken, a leg still hanging out of its beak, Mary pecking at his face to try to get it.

'Great white fuckin' death,' he said as Kirk eyeballed him, wondering if there was more where that had come from.

He turned back inside to try to get a tidy-up done. Perhaps then he'd go for a swim, maybe take the prawn net down. Fill up his time usefully. He'd been bent over the sink for forty seconds when he heard the sound of a truck coming his way. That was what he needed, he decided with a smile. He went to the ice box and worried the beer to get to the coldest at the back. He broke off two lids, and the person outside stopped the vehicle and climbed the steps of the veranda with heavy boots. He turned to the open door, a beer in each hand.

Lucy's lips were pale and dry, and she'd let her hair grow long and yellow. The bridge of her nose and the tops of her cheeks showed an arc of sunburn, like a shadow cast from a hat. She was heavier than when he had last seen her, her arms were rounded and brown, and there was room in her face for dimples. Her belly lightly touched the front of her dress.

He did not blink and neither did she. He felt the heaviness of the beer bottles at the end of his arms. There must be something to say, hello at least, but when he opened his mouth with no clue as to what words might happen, a white cockatoo flew low past the house and shrieked his voice away.

'Frank,' she said and he felt ashamed that he had left the silence to be undone by her on her own. He nodded, gestured towards the chairs on the veranda, still gape-mouthed, still holding the two cold beers, but she stayed standing where she was in the doorway. His heart, his blood and every liquid part set up against him so that he couldn't speak. He was tired, suddenly, and he could just send her away and lie where he stood, feet out of the door, head propping the fly screen open.

'So this is where you've been.' She held her palms up to the sky.

285

'Sorry. I'm sorry.' His first words fell to splinters in the open air. His knees felt hot.

'You just left,' she said. A strand of hair caught in the corner of her mouth and how appalling it was that he would not be the one who was allowed to free it.

Red prickled round her eyes and nose, and her voice was a mixture of loud and quiet. 'I thought you would hunt me down.'

'I didn't want to hunt you. I'm sorry. I was awful.'

She put a hand to her forehead and hid her face. She opened her mouth and closed it again with a terrible silent cry. He opened his mouth to speak, but she waved a hand at him and he closed it. She put her hand over her mouth and looked at him. She shook her head and waved him away again as if he had come towards her. 'You don't even know what you've done to me, do you?'

Yes I do, he thought. *I do know, I do.*

Then she turned round slowly and walked down the steps.

You are watching her leave, he told himself. *You're watching her leave and if you ran down after her things might be different.* But she opened the door of her car and, without looking back, slid in and slammed it behind her. As the car pulled away he said under his breath, 'Go, go, go,' but he didn't know if the instruction was to Lucy or himself, so he stayed put as if she'd never been there, the only difference was that one of the cold beers had slipped from his grasp without him noticing. White froth collected round his toes.

32

On a Monday morning a man arrived wearing a grey suit and carrying a briefcase. Leon looked at him and saw that he hadn't come to buy scones.

'Mr Collard?'

He met his eyes for a second, hoped to see something a bit light in his bearing. There was nothing. 'That's me. What can I get you?'

'Are you the only son of Roman and Maureen Collard?'

'I am.'

'Mr Collard, my name is Gregory Thorpe, I was your parents' solicitor. I'm afraid, Mr Collard, it is my sad duty to inform you that your parents are now deceased. I'm so very sorry.'

Leon leant on the counter. A woman came in and asked for a plum tart, which he boxed and bagged, counting out the correct change, doing everything exactly as he would have done before.

The man in the suit stood by politely. When the woman had gone he said, 'Excuse my presumptuousness, Mr Collard, but perhaps you'd like to close the shop for the next half-hour while we talk? Give yourself some breathing space?'

He heard Amy moving around in the bathroom upstairs. 'No. It's fine. How did it happen?'

'I'm afraid, Mr Collard, I don't have that information. You'd need to talk to the head of police in Mulaburry for that kind of information.' There was a look about him, a quick smile and a shrug that said he did know, he just was not going to tell.

'What do I need to do?' He wasn't sure what kind of answer he expected.

'Mr Collard, I'm here to inform you of a property that has been left to you. By your parents,' he added needlessly.

Leon nodded. From upstairs came the loud clack of something being dropped and he tensed until he heard the sound of Amy swearing at herself.

Gregory Thorpe smiled pursedly and opened his briefcase, which now rested on the counter. 'The deeds to the property. Everything has been left just as it was since their deaths, as no one wanted to presume to know what you would want done with their belongings.'

He handed them over and Leon glanced at the papers. 'They don't live so far away from here,' he said.

Gregory Thorpe shifted uncomfortably. 'No. I suppose they didn't.' He smiled in what was possibly meant to be a sympathetic way. 'If you could just sign some things for me, Mr Collard, then I will leave you to your grief.'

He signed where Gregory Thorpe pointed and Gregory Thorpe looked happy. He snapped his briefcase shut. 'Well, it's been a pleasure to meet with you, Mr Collard. And I do hope you will accept my sincerest condolences.' He began to walk towards the door.

'Wait,' said Leon.

Gregory Thorpe turned to him, a look of undisguised impatience on his face. 'Yes?'

'Haven't you got some keys for me or something?'

Gregory Thorpe smiled. 'There's no lock on the house, Mr Collard. Just walk right in.'

The shack was a tribute to his mother's housekeeping: the surfaces wiped, a dishrag hanging neatly over the tap, bleached back to its original white so many times that it was little more than a transparent net. Amy left him to it, went for a slow walk up the beach, her belly swaying, her hands patting around the base of the bump.

What the superintendent at Mulaburry had been able to tell them had not been much. Clothes left on the beach, no sign of his parents, not for over two months, since the telegram with news of Amy's pregnancy had been returned undelivered. There was a selection of things left on the kitchen table, the lemon check table-cloth pinned at the edges for a neater finish. His mother's grey woollen gloves, a pearly seashell, a photograph of the three of them taken when he was a baby. A hard old loaf of untouched bread, baked to cement. They all seemed to have been laid out exactly and deliberately. He sat at the table and picked up the gloves. He knew what he expected himself to do. He expected to hold them to his face and smell them, smell his mother's hand cream, feel the touch of her fingers on his face. But instead he held them in his hands, lightly, as though they were made of dust. Then he put them down again. He looked into the faces of the three people in the photograph and came up with nothing. They were just pictures, one of a baby who didn't even know anything yet. The shell he put on a high shelf, resisting an urge to crush it underfoot, or to put it on his tongue and taste the sea. It was a pretty thing. A shame to ruin it.

The loaf of bread was heavy and cold. If he threw it, it would smash a good dent in the side of the shack, it would rip a gash in the dark old wood, leave some pale and exposed wound. It had the potential in it, he could feel as he weighed it in his hands, it had the potential to go far with an angry throw. He buried it shallowly behind the house, where either it would disintegrate or if any animal was strong enough to break into it, it could be eaten. The superintendent had been happy with the verdict, although it wouldn't be official for a few years. They were a quiet couple, queer. Didn't seem to know a great deal about living out there on their own. They'd been warned about the rips, didn't seem like the swimming types. A young aboriginal man had sadly shaken his hand and then Amy's, without saying much. There were a few around here, Leon had seen on the drive out.

The shoes his parents had never quite got used to being without, still black and polished, the laces unfrayed, the heels unscuffed, both pairs placed neatly by the side of the bed, waiting to be stepped into. On a high shelf were their wedding figurines, ham-fisted inside a glass box, not a speck of dust. There was no evidence of any kind of stove – they must have cooked outside or eaten cold. The bread they must have baked in a camp oven.

He took the shoes and floated them out to sea. They filled and sank, and he pictured their last walk into the water, barefoot, silent, on a calm day. Holding hands.

His mother's hair set.

From the hush sound of the tops of the trees whistling in the breezes came a cry of some kind of animal, just a cry, long and hollow, and he didn't turn to look. He watched Amy walking up the beach towards him and he thought about the calf inside that had reshaped her. He worried that it would hurt her, that it would kick when it came out. He worried that it would kill her. He worried he wouldn't love the calf enough.

They sat where a deep bite had been taken out of the rock, and the hole filled up with foamy water and emptied away again. The sky pinked and oystercatchers wheeled in the small breezes. The water washed in and out of the hole, and fish swam around their feet flashing belly white to the sun.

33

The day had been calm, no wind, no terrible heat. Frank could smell the first washes of winter on the salt air. The sugar cane didn't seem to tower as much as it had before.

He padded down to the beach with a plastic bag wrapped carefully round the figurines. It mattered that they didn't break up any more for some reason. He thought for a while about lobbing them as hard and far as he could, but that would not be very far and he would know that they were there, underwater, dissolving, heavy and sunk.

Instead, he lined them up on the incoming tidemark and sat back on his haunches to look at them: a strange army.

His grandparents were funny-faced, illogically weighted and old-fashioned. His grandmother's nose was too flat, or maybe she had looked that way. The bear she held in one hand had something of her husband about it, who stood arms flat to his body, hair done in old black that had sunk into the sugar and turned grey. One of his eyes looked slightly the wrong way. His shoulders were as broad as his bride's hips.

Next to them were the couple who had been his parents. His mother over-bosomed, pink-skinned, beautiful. His father oddly small. Not really like his father at all. More like the man he'd watched climb the stairs to his house in Roedale, someone who had stumbled into being happy, his smile red and overdone. His father's self-portrait. A comic weakling.

The seawater soaked into the brides' dresses. It took the black out of the grooms' shoes. Began to melt them.

'What are they?' It didn't startle him in the least that Sal was at his side. She appeared softly, like a ghost, and he'd got used to it. 'Just some dolls.'

'Are they yours?'

'I suppose.'

She was quiet for a while. 'Why are you drowning them?'

'I'm just letting them dissolve.'

'How come?'

'Makes things easier having less stuff. See, if I keep them I've got to find a place to put them in – probably in a box or something so they don't get broken. Then I'd have to find something to put them on – I'd probably have to have a whole shelf just for them – or their own special table that I'd have to build. And there's not too much room in my shack, and I'd probably bust my hip on it every time I walked by. And when you start to get older that sort of thing gets to be more of a problem.'

He talked nonsense freely and she didn't pick him up on it. He enjoyed the feeling of lightness that climbed over him.

'Oh,' said Sal, and after a moment's consideration knelt down next to them and planted a withered-looking carrot with a smiling face penned on to the fat end. She stood back. 'I don't suppose that will dissolve.'

'Don't worry,' said Frank, 'when the tide comes up the fish'll take care of it. It'll be like dissolving.'

She nodded and they both watched as his grandfather was the first to go, knocked over by the seventh wave.

'We should make something else instead.'

'Like what?'

'Something that you don't have to carry around and look at all the time.'

'How about a sandcastle?'

'A sand person?'

'Man or a woman?' asked Sal suspiciously.

He shrugged. 'We could make a carrot.'

She shook her head. 'I'm so over carrots.'

The two of them started pawing the tide's edge, blunting their fingernails on pipi shells, pushing up great cakes of sand with the heels of their hands. The work was engrossing and they forgot all about sculpting a man or a woman or a carrot and just concentrated on digging a long shallow trench up along the beach at the tideline. They had been at it for a good twenty minutes, talking each other through the process.

'There it is, now you go ahead of me and bring it down to reach me, and I'll go ahead of you and start on the next bit.'

''Sa bit of a china plate.'

'Careful.'

They looked back to where they had come from. The trench behind them had been washed into nothing more than a thin line by the sea and the five upright figures that marked their starting point had gone – Sal's carrot had fallen over and rolled in the surf. They left a slight dark stain on the sand.

'They've weed into the sea,' said Sal.

Frank looked at her, put his hand on her head. 'You are a strange person.'

She let her head rest against his stomach. 'So are you.' She pointed up the beach. 'Who's that?'

Frank watched the family train of the Haydons while he washed the grubs out of three small lettuces. Vicky sat on the middle step, cutting Sal's fringe, who was sitting on the bottom step. Bob, at the top, stroked the back of Vicky's neck with one finger, while the other hand took care of his beer. There was a new goat, just

293

a kid still, and it balanced on the stump table, one hoof in a bowl of chips, bleating. From round the back of the shack came the thick splash of shampoo being washed out of long hair. The Haydons chattered with each other, no one's voice commanding the conversation, just a gentle murmur of the three of them.

34

The drive home was long and stinking hot, and Leon let the air conditioning lay ice down the length of his throat. He smiled as he drove through the marker to the entrance of the town – it still made his heart muscle about inside him to see those strange palm trees stretching up high and away, and beyond them and everywhere the dust that blew over the road, no matter how often the local fusspots swept it. He was hungry, the day had been long, but he'd talked to some kids at a school-leaving event and he had the feeling, just the feeling.

Parking up outside the house he gave thanks, as he always did, that he had this place to come back to. The porch light blinked on and he imagined Merle taking a final glance in the mirror, painting that red on to her mouth, smoothing her eyebrows before coming to the door to see him. As he rose out of the car, there was the faintest smell of yeast, bread or beer. For a moment he remembered the feel of dough, sugar browning, light in a copper pan. Then he closed the door and was back home where he could hear a dog barking a few streets away. He opened the boot and took out his Bag of Bibles, as his wife liked to call it. He rested it against his knees and touched it one extra time to make sure it was there. Then he closed the boot just as his wife opened the door, looking beautiful in blue as she always would. The wind fossicked up her dress and he watched her bat it down. He touched the closed boot of the car as well, to make sure he was still there.

'Darl,' she greeted him.

He went and held her round her narrow waist, standing on the step below so that he could inhale her from the body up. 'Sweetheart,' he said, and some small whispering wind blew as a car engine started up and passed them by.

Acknowledgements

I am grateful to Laetitia Rutherford for her generous wisdom and guidance and for asking me to write in the first place. Ellah Allfrey, Nikki Christer and Diana Coglianese for their excellent direction, and their enthusiasm for this book. Darren Wall at Wallzo for his beautiful artwork. Sarah Barnes and Roz Simpson and the students of Bacon's College for keeping me employed, in the loosest possible sense, and all those friends who, perhaps unknowingly, helped along the way. Excellent teachers I have had, including Rebecca de Pelet, Lucy Sheddon, Colin Edwards and Stephen Knight and all those at Bath Spa University and on the Goldsmiths Creative Writing MA. For help writing on the Australian experience during the Vietnam War, I'd like to thank Dr Julian Stallabrass and those who make available the brilliant and accessible online material at Australians at War and the National Archives of Australia.

Very particular thanks go to Tim Strange. I could not have imagined the book at all without his willingness to talk, his openness and warmth. This is however a work of fiction, and all characters are entirely made up, any mistakes mine alone. Thank you Ben Strange for introducing me to Bassey as well as translating fishing and the marina to me. Any mistakes here are, again, all my own. Thanks to my Mum, Dad and Tom who have shown a huge amount of encouragement and support. Thanks, most especially, to Jamie for every thing.